. . . floating through our home and our lives, carefree, spontaneous, unrepentant and forever free of obligation, worry and responsibility.

When I questioned Daddy about her, he would nod his head, giving me the impression that I was right, and then he would stop and say, "You've just got to watch out for her, Olivia."

"When does she start to watch out for herself, Daddy? She's a high-school senior this year," I retorted.

"Some women never become anything more than older girls," he offered.

I thought he was just making excuses and it always put me in a fury. Why make excuses for her forever? Why not grab her by the nape of the neck one day and shake her until that silly, flirtatious smile fell off that porcelain face and shattered at her feet? Why not make her grow up? Why not force her to face the consequences of her actions? That is maturity, I declared in my imaginary speech, a speech my parents rarely heard, and when they did, paid little heed.

"I don't want to grow up," Belinda once had the audacity to confess. "It's boring and unpleasant and full of scowling and worries. I want to be a little girl for the rest of my life and have men take care of me."

"Don't you have any self-respect, not one iota?" I questioned.

She shrugged and softened those eyes and those lips that brought smiles to the faces of so many.

"I will when I need it. . . ."

V.C. Andrews® Books

Flowers in the Attic	Ruby
Petals on the Wind	Pearl in the Mist
If There Be Thorns	All That Glitters
My Sweet Audrina	Hidden Jewel
Seeds of Yesterday	Tarnished Gold
Heaven	Melody
Dark Angel	Heart Song
Garden of Shadows	Unfinished Symphony
Fallen Hearts	Music in the Night
Gates of Paradise	Butterfly
Web of Dreams	Crystal
Dawn	Brooke
Secrets of the Morning	Raven
Twilight's Child	Runaways
Midnight Whispers	Olivia
Darkest Hour	

Published by POCKET BOOKS

For orders other than by individual consumers, Pocket Books grants a discount on the purchase of **10 or more** copies of single titles for special markets or premium use. For further details, please write to the Vice-President of Special Markets, Pocket Books, 1633 Broadway, New York, NY 10019-6785, 8th Floor.

For information on how individual consumers can place orders, please write to Mail Order Department, Simon & Schuster Inc., 200 Old Tappan Road, Old Tappan, NJ 07675.

V.C. ANDREWS®

Olivia

POCKET BOOKS
New York London Toronto Sydney Tokyo Singapore

Following the death of Virginia Andrews, the Andrews family worked with a carefully selected writer to organize and complete Virginia Andrews' stories and to create additional novels, of which this is one, inspired by her storytelling genius.

This book is a work of fiction. Names, characters, places and incidents are products of the author's imagination or are used fictitiously. Any resemblance to actual events or locales or persons, living or dead, is entirely coincidental.

An *Original* Publication of POCKET BOOKS

POCKET BOOKS, a division of Simon & Schuster Inc.
1230 Avenue of the Americas, New York, NY 10020

ISBN: 0-671-00761-0

First Pocket Books paperback printing January 1999

10 9 8 7 6 5 4 3 2 1

V.C. ANDREWS and VIRGINIA ANDREWS are registered trademarks of the Vanda General Partnership.

POCKET and colophon are registered trademarks of Simon & Schuster Inc.

Tip-in illustration by Lisa Falkenstern

Printed in the U.S.A.

Olivia

Prologue
&

*S*pring on the Cape always had a way of surprising me. It was almost as if I never expected it would return. Winters could be long and dreary with days shaved down by the sharp edge of night, but I never minded the gray skies and colder winds as much as other people did, especially my younger sister Belinda. For as long as I could remember, our schoolmates believed winter suited me better anyway. I don't recall exactly when or how it started, but one day someone referred to me as Miss Cold and Belinda as Miss Hot, and those labels followed us even to this day.

When she was a little girl, Belinda loved to burst out of the house, rush into the open air, catch the wind in her hair, and spin and laugh until she grew dizzy and fell on the sand, hysterical, excited, her eyes nearly as luminous as two birthday candles. Everything she did was an explosion. She never talked slowly, but always spoke as if she had the words crushing her lungs and had to get them out before she died. No matter what she did or said, it was usually punctuated at the end with her gasping, "I just had to tell you before I die!"

By twelve she was walking with a mature woman's swing in her hips, turning and dipping her shoulders, resembling a trained courtesan. She waved her hands about her like the fans of a geisha girl, pretending to hide her flirtatious eyes and beguiling smile between her small fingers. I saw grown men turn their heads and stare until they realized how young she was and then, almost always, take a second look just to confirm it, their faces dark with disappointment.

Her laughter was contagious. Whoever was around her at the time invariably broke into a wide smile as though she touched them with a magic wand to drive away the doldrums, their sadness or depression. People, especially boys, became blubbering amnesiacs in her presence, forgetting their responsibilities, their duties, their appointments and most of all, their own reputations. They would do the silliest things at her beck and call.

"You look like a frog, Tommy Carter. Let's hear you croak. Come on," she would taunt, and Tommy Carter, two years older, nearly a high-school senior, would crouch like a toad and go "Ribbet, ribbet," to a chorus of laughter and applause. A moment later Belinda was off, driving someone else to the precarious edge of sanity and dignity.

I always knew she would get into trouble. I just never realized how deep the pool of disaster would go. I tried to correct her behavior, teach her how to be more of a lady, and most of all, how to tread around boys and men with caution. They were always giving her gifts and she always accepted them, no matter how emphatically I warned her against it.

"It creates an obligation," I said. "Give these things

back, Belinda. The most dangerous thing you can do is fill a young man's heart with false promises."

"I don't ask them to give me things," she protested. "Well, maybe I hint at it, but I don't twist their arms. So I don't owe them a thing. Unless I want to owe them," she would add with a mischievous smile.

For some reason it was left mostly to me to give Belinda the guidance she so desperately needed.

Our mother eschewed the responsibility and obligations. She hated to hear anything nasty or see anything ugly. Her vocabulary was filled with euphemisms, words to hide the dark truths in our world. People didn't die, they "went away for good." Daddy was never mean to her. He was just "out of spirits." She made it sound as if spirits were something you could get at the gas station when your tank indicated empty. Whenever any of us were sick, she treated us as if it was our own fault. We caught colds out of carelessness and got bellyaches from eating the wrong foods. It was always the result of a poor choice we had made and if we would just try, it would all go away and everyone would be happy again.

"Close your eyes real tight and wish it away. That's what I do," she would say.

For me the worst thing was the way she viewed everything Belinda did. Her failures were never anything more than "just a temporary setback." Her pranks and little acts of mischief were always due to the "youth in her having its way. She'll grow out of it soon."

"Soon will never come, Mother," I would say with the authority of a clairvoyant.

But Mother never listened. She waved the air around her ears as if my words were nothing more than annoying flies. Any time I complained, I had "just risen from the wrong side of the bed."

Blink and it would all go away: the storms, the

sickness, Belinda's bad behavior, Daddy's poor temperament, economic downswings, wars, pestilence, crime, all of it, would just go away along with anything else that was in the slightest way unpleasant.

Our mother's room was always filled with flowers. She hated dampness, musty odors. She filled her day with music-box tunes and actually wore rose-tinted glasses because she hated "the dull colors, the way things faded, the annoying dark clouds that poked their bruised faces in our way."

Belinda, I decided, was far more like her than she was like our daddy. Both of us favored Mother's petite build, and it was clear early on that neither of us was ever going to be much more than five feet one or two. Mother was five feet one in her bare feet. Belinda was even smaller than I was, and, I would have to admit, had the most perfect face. Her eyes were bluer. Mine were more gray. She had a smaller nose, and her mouth was in perfect proportion. Her lips were always set in a soft twist that put a tiny dimple in her left cheek. When she was very little, Daddy would touch it with his finger and pretend it was a button. Belinda was then supposed to dance, and dance she did, flamboyant even at ages two and three.

Daddy would beam a smile so deep it went right to his heart as she turned and did pirouettes in the living room, always with her right forefinger pressed to the top of her head. Mother laughed and clapped as did any guests we had at the time.

"Can't Olivia dance, too?" Colonel Childs, one of Daddy's close friends, once asked. I'd look up and Daddy would stare at me a moment and then shake his head slowly, his eyes intense and firm on my face.

"No, Olivia doesn't dance. Olivia thinks," he said with an approving nod. "She plans and organizes. She's my little general."

After we were older and Daddy continued to refer to me from time to time as his little general, Belinda would tease me by saluting in the hallways or at the dinner table. Then she would laugh and hug me and say, "I'm just fooling with you, Olivia. Don't look so hateful."

"Being serious about yourself and having some self-respect isn't being hateful, Belinda. You should try it."

"Oh, I can't. My face won't make those lines in my forehead. My skin just snaps in revolt," she cried, rushing away with her giggles trailing behind her like the ribbon tails on a kite.

She was so frustrating all the time. Why was it that neither my mother nor my father saw what I saw? Our daddy was rarely displeased by anything Belinda said or did, and if he was, he would get over it so quickly, it was as if it had never happened. The moment after he raised his voice to her, he would check himself and seize control of that otherwise wild and fiery temper.

Many times I had witnessed his rages, saw him unleash his fury against politicians, government officials, lawyers and other businessmen. I saw him take servants to task so harshly they left his presence with their eyes down, their heads lowered, their faces pale. He was so biting and sharp with his words, he could skin someone alive with a sentence.

However, the moment he chastised Belinda, he began his retreat. I could almost see him reach out and pull the words back to his lips. If her eyes so much as glassed over with tears, he would treat her like she'd been fatally wounded, and in the end either buy her something new or promise her something wonderful. It was as if her smiles and laughter made it possible for him to get through the day.

Sometimes, when we were all together at dinner or after dinner in the sitting room watching television or reading, I would look at Daddy and see him staring at Belinda, his face full of admiration, his eyes feasting on her delicate features the way an art collector might appreciate some rare antiquity, some masterpiece.

Why didn't he look at me that way? I wondered mournfully. I had never done anything that made him ashamed or unhappy. I knew he was proud of my accomplishments, but he behaved as if he expected no less. I realized he took me for granted, but I always delivered, whether it was an award at school, compliments from his business associates, or accomplishments at home.

When I completed finishing school with the highest possible commendation, he kissed me on the forehead and shook my hand. I almost expected him to pin a ribbon on my chest and give me a promotion. My reward was to be given a place of responsibility in the family business until that day when some fine young gentleman would approach Daddy and ask for my hand in marriage. I never understood from what well he drew these buckets of hope and expectation. Daddy simply refused to believe that times were different, that young men looked for women with qualities other than a "fine family" and didn't behave so formally anymore. It was almost as if he believed he and our family were exempt from the social and political changes that affected everyone else.

If he was ever challenged in his beliefs, he would shake his head and say, "It's simply not good business for people to behave badly. There's no profit in it. Whenever you do anything in this life, you should stop and ask yourself What's the bottom line? If you do that, you'll always make the right choices."

That was something he should have taught Belinda, I thought, but he never lectured her. In fact, he rarely gave her any advice. She was permitted to be a free spirit, floating through our home and our lives, carefree, spontaneous, unrepentant and forever free of obligation, worry and responsibility.

When I questioned Daddy about her, he would nod his head, giving me the impression that I was right, and then he would stop and say, "You've just got to watch out for her, Olivia."

"When does she start to watch out for herself, Daddy? She's a high-school senior this year," I retorted.

"Some women never become anything more than older girls," he offered.

I thought he was just making excuses and it always put me in a fury. Why make excuses for her forever? Why not grab her by the nape of the neck one day and shake her until that silly, flirtatious smile fell off that porcelain face and shattered at her feet? Why not make her grow up? Why not force her to face the consequences of her actions? That is maturity, I declared in my imaginary speech, a speech my parents rarely heard, and when they did, paid little heed.

"I don't want to grow up," Belinda once had the audacity to confess. "It's boring and unpleasant and full of scowling and worries. I want to be a little girl for the rest of my life and have men take care of me."

"Don't you have any self-respect, not one iota?" I questioned.

She shrugged and softened those eyes and those lips that brought smiles to the faces of so many.

"I will when I need it," she declared.

Sometimes, talking to her tied my stomach into a knot. I would feel the very muscles in my arms and legs contract into ropes of steel. The frustration threatened to fracture me. I wanted to reach out and slap some sense into that silly little face.

And then she would hug me and say, "You will have enough self-respect for both of us, Olivia. I just know you will. I'm so lucky to have you as my older sister."

Afterward she would rush off to meet her friends and flirt with her throng of male admirers, leaving me to tend to whatever chore or duty Daddy had set out for both of us.

I must confess that sometimes I would stand there and watch her flit about and wish I was more like her. When she put her head to the pillow at night, it was always filled with candy-cane thoughts, whereas mine became Main Street for the parade of worries and the review of obligations. Her ears were full of music and promises. Mine were stuffed with facts and appointments. I was Daddy's living diary of events. He could put the tip of his finger on Belinda's dimple and make her smile the smile that warmed his heart, but he could only point his finger at me and get me to recite the purpose of a business date.

It wasn't that he was ungrateful. I believed him when he bragged about his "little general," but something in me, the Belinda in me, wanted him to mention other things about me, too. I know he thought I was more significant and more promising when it came to success for the family, but didn't he ever think of me as being pretty, too? Couldn't I be attractive and responsible simultaneously?

Unfortunately, I concluded and feared, Daddy was like most men, weak when it came to a flirtatious smile, a flighty, silly gesture, a quick hug and kiss as if affection were any sort of substitute for responsibility and industry.

Something inside told me if I wanted men to admire me, I should imitate my sister and let bubbles float around in my head more than thoughts and ideas.

But would I be happier? Most of the men I had met in my life tried to convince me I would, but I was determined not to become some man's toy like my mother had become for my father. Belinda thinks she's happy, but she doesn't understand how little men really do think of her, how small their respect for her is, I concluded. They might crave and desire her, but when they were satisfied, when they had used her, satiated themselves and discarded her, where would she be but mired in misery, off someplace crying about her lost youth and beauty, hating the world for having such a thing as aging. She would die a little girl.

I would die a woman, and I would not be used or abused to satisfy some man. Yes, there was a part of me that wanted to be like Belinda, but that was the part men planted in me, the part I could subdue.

Call me little general. Call me Miss Cold and call Belinda Miss Hot, I thought.

But in the end, they will call me with respect, and really, in the end, what mattered more, respect or love? No one really knew what love was. How many husbands and wives had this so-called magical bond?

The choice was simple, I thought: be a dreamer or be a realist and make the day conform to what I wanted and not what I hoped.

Belinda danced and my father smiled. My mother fled from pain and darkness, and I, I stood behind them all, like some impregnable wall, keeping disaster away from our doorstep. In the end they would all appreciate me.

And what would anyone want more than that?

The tinkle of Belinda's laughter fell along the dark corridors of my own doubt, filling my mind with little sparks, keeping me from being absolutely sure.

1

Cries in the Night

At first I thought I was dreaming, for when I woke and opened my eyes, I heard nothing but the low whistle of the wind blowing up from the ocean. The stream of moonlight filtering through my sheer white curtain bathed the walls in a pale yellow glow. My window shutters banged against the clapboard and then, I heard the sound again, this time with my eyes wide. I listened, my heart tapping like a steadily growing drumbeat in anticipation of some important announcement or event. After a moment I heard it once more.

It sounded like a cat in heat, but we had no cats. Daddy hated pets, finding them more of an obligation than a pleasure. The only animals he said had any purpose was a watchdog or a seeing-eye dog, and he had no need for either. Our house was far enough away from the downtown Provincetown area and surrounded by walls ten feet high with an entrance gate Daddy had Jerome, our grounds keeper, lock every night. Daddy also kept his shotgun under the bed, "just in case." It

11

was, he said, a lot cheaper than feeding some mongrel, and that, he concluded, "was the bottom line."

This time the sound was even louder. I sat up so quickly someone would think I had springs under me, but I realized the shrill cries were not in my imagination or from nightmares. The noise was coming through the wall between my room and Belinda's. It wasn't a howl, exactly, nor was it a screech. There was something familiar about the sound and yet something starkly unusual. It was certainly not a noise Belinda would make herself, but there was no doubt it was emanating from her bedroom.

I stepped off my bed, scooped up my robe from the chair beside my bed, and shoved my arms into the sleeves as I left my room. Daddy and Mother had already come out of their bedroom. Mother was still in her nightgown and Daddy was in his pajamas. The dreadful sound continued.

"What in all hell . . ." Daddy started for Belinda's closed door. I followed, with Mother a distant third, but when Daddy opened the door and realized the horrendous scream came from Belinda, Mother charged forward.

"Winston, what's wrong?" she cried.

Daddy flicked on the light, illuminating the most amazing and alarming sight before us.

Belinda was sprawled on the floor, her nightgown bloody and crumbled up to her breasts. There, lying between her legs was a newly-born infant, the umbilical cord and afterbirth still attached.

Belinda's eyes were wild with terror. The baby's eyes were closed, and it jerked its tiny arm and then stopped moving.

"Jesus, Mary and Joseph," Daddy exclaimed under

his breath, his feet hammered to the floor by astonishment.

Mother's eyes rolled back in her head and she folded at Daddy's feet as if her spinal cord had turned to jelly.

"Leonora!"

"Take her to bed, Daddy," I said. "I'll see to Belinda."

He gazed back at the sight once more to confirm it was indeed still there and not in his imagination. Then he squatted, slipped his arms under Mother and lifted her like she was a baby herself, carrying her back to their bedroom.

I entered Belinda's room, quickly closing the door behind me. Our servants downstairs were surely awake by now as well. Belinda whimpered. Her eyes rolled as if the room were spinning. She had her arms raised, but she was afraid to touch the infant or herself.

"I couldn't stop it. It just happened, Olivia," she moaned. Her whole body shook. I stepped up to her and gazed down at the bloody sight.

"You were pregnant? All this time you've been pregnant?" I asked incredulously.

"Yes," she said, gasping.

Now everything made sense. A number of times during the past few months Daddy and I had made comments about Belinda's gaining weight. She was ravenous at every meal lately and didn't seem at all concerned about her widening hips and bloated face. I really didn't care. It was more Daddy who complained. His precious little Barbie doll was disappearing right before his eyes and in its place grew this self-indulgent creature I called my sister.

Oh, once or twice, I said things like, "Aren't you afraid you'll lose your entourage of boyfriends?"

She didn't seem concerned even though it was true

that fewer and fewer young men came around to visit her or ask her to go sailing, take walks on the beach or spend an evening in town. Now that I stared down at her squirming on the bedroom floor, her child quiet and unmoving between her thighs, I realized why she had so adamantly kept me from seeing her naked a number of times. A quick search of her closet would result in the discovery of a pair of girdles in a box. What I also understood now was her sudden and uncharacteristic interest in and desire for those baggy dresses she used to refer to as "Granny clothes" whenever I wore them.

I knelt beside her and put my hand on the infant's tiny chest. It felt cold already and it did not vibrate with any heartbeat, nor did it rise and fall with any breath.

"I don't think it's alive," I said.

She whimpered again.

"Please, Olivia, get it away. I . . . can't touch it," she said.

I didn't move quickly. I stared at the wrinkled little creature for a while, studying its facial features, its blue lips and its fingers so tiny even one of my own small fingers was the width of nearly all five of one of its hands.

"It was a boy," I said, more as a thought voiced aloud than anything she wanted to know.

Belinda closed her eyes and began to hyperventilate. I watched her suffering for a moment, still dumbfounded at how well she had kept this secret. What would our daddy think of his precious little princess now? I wondered.

"Do you have any idea, even an inkling of an idea, how terrible this is, Belinda? Didn't you consider this inevitable outcome and think about what it was going to do to our parents? Why didn't you come forward earlier so Daddy could have done something about this instead of deceiving everyone and hiding your condition?"

"I was afraid," she murmured and began to sniffle and sob. "I thought everyone would just hate me."

"Oh, and now we just love you?" I countered. She closed her eyes and held her breath a moment.

"Please, please, Olivia, help me," she begged.

"How many months were you pregnant?" I asked.

"I don't know exactly, but at least six or seven," she said quickly.

"That's why this child is so tiny. It's a premature birth. I knew you were having sex with some of your boyfriends, Belinda. I just knew it. I told you this would happen. I warned you. Now look, just look at what you've reaped with your wild, selfish behavior."

She sobbed an apology.

"Right," I muttered. "We'll all just blink and it will be gone."

"Please, Olivia . . ."

"Who is the father?" I demanded. She didn't reply. "You've got to say, Olivia. Whoever he is he bears at least half the responsibility. Daddy's going to want to know. Who is it? Arnold Miller?"

He was a boy she had been with a great deal more than the others.

"No," she said quickly. "Arnold and I never went far enough."

"Then who was it, Belinda? I'm not going to play a guessing game with you. Tell me! If you don't tell me, I'll leave you here wallowing in this . . . disaster."

"I don't know," she wailed. "Please, Olivia."

"How can you not know unless you . . . my God, Belinda, how many boys have you slept with? And so closely together that you can't pinpoint who would be the father of this . . . this child?"

At the moment I didn't know what bothered me more: that she had so many lovers or that I had had none.

She just shook her head.

"I don't know, Olivia. I don't know. I don't want to blame anyone. Please."

"You'll have to tell Daddy something, Belinda," I warned. "He won't settle for an 'I don't know.'"

She opened her eyes and gazed up at me, and for a moment, I thought she was going to reveal the father of her baby. Was it someone I knew well, too?

"Well?"

"I can't blame someone if I don't know for sure," she finally declared. "Can I?"

"They're all to blame. You might as well name all of them and let each one sweat," I said, thinking that would be a just and poetic revenge.

"I can't," she wailed. She shook her head so hard, I thought she would tear it off her neck.

"All right, suit yourself. You'll see what's going to happen now. You'll see," I predicted.

I rose and went to her bathroom to get some towels. Then I returned and rolled the dead infant onto one. I placed it and the afterbirth and umbilical cord on the bed just as Daddy opened the door and stepped back into the room. He looked around, his eyes avoiding Belinda for a moment. He gazed at the child before turning to me with a questioning look.

"He's dead, I think, Daddy," I said.

He nodded.

"Most likely," he said and approached the bed. He reached down slowly with his big hand and put the tip of his forefinger on the infant's neck. "Yes," he said. "A blessing."

Belinda began to wail.

"Stop it!" I snapped, hovering over her. "Do you want Carmelita to hear and come running up here?"

Belinda muffled her sobs and turned over on her side.

"Can you get her cleaned up and back to bed?" Daddy asked me.

"Yes, Daddy."

"Is she . . . bleeding or anything? Are we going to need a doctor?"

"I don't think so."

"Make sure. I'll be right back," he said.

"How's Mother?"

"I have her calmed down a bit, but she's still trembling badly," he said sorrowfully.

"After I get Belinda into the bathtub, I'll look in on her," I promised.

"Good." He hurried from the room.

"Get up, Belinda. I can't lift you and carry you into the bathroom. I'm going to run some water in your tub. At least cover yourself for now. You look absolutely disgusting moaning and wallowing on the floor," I said.

She whimpered her reply and started to brace herself on her elbows. There was blood on her legs, but she didn't look to be bleeding anymore. She took deep breaths again and sighed so deeply I thought she had passed out.

"Are you in any pain?"

"I don't need a doctor," she said. "I'll be all right."

"Maybe you don't need a doctor, but whether or not you'll be all right remains to be seen," I said.

I glanced again at the dead infant. I couldn't make out the color of its few strands of hair because its head was covered with sticky blood. There was no way to study it and determine who the father could be, I thought, and went to the bathroom to run Belinda's tub.

After I helped her get in, I heard Daddy return to the room. I went to the bathroom door and saw he had brought a small cardboard shoe box along. He glanced at me as he lifted the dead infant, wrapped it more tightly in the blanket, and then carefully, as if it were still alive, put it in the box.

"We've got to clean this up ourselves," he said, nodding at the floor. "I don't want the servants knowing anything, Olivia."

"I'll take care of it, Daddy."

"How is she?"

"She's all right. She'll live," I said sharply. He nodded again and lifted the box in his arms.

"What are you going to do, Daddy?"

He paused.

"I'll have to bury the poor thing," he said.

For a moment I just stood there staring at him clutching the makeshift coffin in his arms.

"Don't we have to report it to someone?" I asked.

"If we do that, Olivia, this terrible event will be headline news in every home and tavern in Provincetown. It would definitely do Belinda no good, and it would be very damaging to the family. Apparently, she did a good job of keeping all this a secret from us, but question her vigorously and make sure no one else knows about it," he added.

"Yes, Daddy."

"Don't forget. As soon as you finish with her, please look in on your mother."

"I will, Daddy."

He stared for a moment and then looked at the box in his arms.

"It has to be this way," he concluded, more for himself than for me, I thought. He turned and hurried out of the bedroom with the box cradled securely in his arms.

I returned to the tub and saw to it that Belinda washed herself. I helped her dry her body and then I brought her a new, clean nightgown. After I got her back into bed, I went downstairs to the utility room. I found I was tiptoing and slinking along in my own home, moving like a burglar to keep from waking Carmelita, our maid and cook, or Jerome. I got a pail, a mop, rags and some detergent. Then I returned to Belinda's room and filled the pail with hot water.

Fortunately, she had lowered herself from the bed onto a throw rug and the rug had absorbed most of the blood. I rolled up the rug and then washed away any traces of the horrendous event. Belinda lay there with her eyes closed, moaning softly, occasionally sobbing. As I worked, I rattled off a relentless series of complaints and chastisements.

"You've really done it this time. Mother is beside herself. Daddy looked pale enough to be a corpse, too. We'll all have nightmares forever. What did you think, it would all just go away without anyone knowing?"

I paused and looked down at her wilting little face.

"Did you think being pregnant was like having a cold or the measles? Maybe you damaged yourself forever, Belinda. Maybe now you'll never be able to have a child decently. No one will want to marry you. What were you thinking?" I ranted. How could this be happening? I wondered. How could anyone, even Belinda, do such a thing to herself and her family?

"Please, Olivia. Please, stop. Please," she begged putting her hands over her ears.

"I'll stop. I should stop and let you clean up this mess," I muttered. "Does anyone else know about your being pregnant? You didn't tell any of your bubble-headed friends at school, did you?" I followed. Most of Belinda's friends were silly, spoiled girls I called the Bubble Gum Club because I thought their brains were full of bubbles.

19

"No, no one knows anything," she swore. "I always got dressed and undressed in private when I took physical education class, and I never showered at school."

"You better be telling the truth," I warned her.

I went to the bathroom and cleaned up the tub so Carmelita wouldn't find any traces of this tragedy.

Daddy returned, his dark brown hair wild, his eyes full of torment and shock. He saw the rug and the wet rags and picked everything up.

"I'm going to bury all this too," he mumbled. "It must be as if none of this ever happened."

He looked about madly.

"You've got everything, Daddy."

"Good," he said and charged out. I had never seen our father look more crazed. It actually frightened me more than it frightened Belinda, who was lying there with her eyes closed most of the time. I imagined she was afraid to look him in the face now.

After Daddy left again, I went to see how Mother was doing. She was sitting at the edge of her bed, working up the strength to stand and see about Belinda. She still looked quite pale, her breathing labored.

"Mother, you should lie down again," I said rushing to her side.

"How is Belinda?"

"She'll be all right. I got her cleaned up and back to bed."

"And . . ."

"Daddy's taken care of all the rest."

"Taken care?"

"The baby died right away, Mother," I said. "It was premature. Daddy took the baby and buried it someplace. He said he doesn't want anyone to know."

"Buried?" she gasped and shook her head. "God forgive us," she whispered.

I thought she would fall forward to the floor, so I seized her by the elbow and tried to get her to lie back, but she shook her head.

"I have to look in on her, Olivia."

She wobbled when she stood. I put my arm around her waist and helped her to the door. She grew stronger as she walked and returned to Belinda's bedroom.

Belinda started to sob as Mother approached her.

"I'm sorry, Mommy," she whimpered. "I'm sorry."

Mother sat on the bed and held her in her arms, and as Belinda cried, Mother rocked her.

"Poor child," she said.

"Poor child? She oughta be whipped," I muttered, but I couldn't help feeling sorry for her, too, even though I didn't want to give her an iota of sympathy.

"There, there, dear. It's all right. It will be all right," Mother chanted.

Finally, Belinda sucked back her sniffles and wiped her cheeks.

"I know I should have told you, Mommy, but I just couldn't. I was too ashamed and afraid," she explained.

"That made a bad thing worse, Belinda. You can't keep such a secret from your parents, or your sister," she said, gazing at me. Belinda looked at me, too. "We all love you and would want to help you."

"I know, Mommy. I'm sorry," she said.

"How did such a thing happen?" Mother asked in a hoarse whisper, looking more at me than at Belinda now.

For as long as I could remember, Mother turned to me to learn things about Belinda. She always expected I was in charge of my younger sister, but I had been away at finishing school most of this year, and knew about Belinda's exploits only through gossip and the little I observed on holidays. This was Belinda's senior year, and I thought she had been given too much freedom, much more than I had been given. Without me at home, Mother didn't keep a good account of Belinda's whereabouts and activities. She was permitted to sleep at her friends' homes and stay out way past midnight. Daddy was always too busy to notice, I thought, and now look at what had resulted.

"She says she doesn't know who the father is," I declared. "Apparently, there are too many candidates."

"What?" Mother asked, her face twisted in disbelief. Did she think Belinda was some sort of angel just because Daddy always treated her like his little cherub? "Too many? How can there have been too many, Belinda?"

"I don't know, Mommy. Please, I don't want to think about it. Please," she begged and started to sob again.

"We should know," I insisted. "Daddy should know and go see them."

"Maybe it's better we don't," Mother concluded, succumbing to Belinda's teary grimaces and wails. "What good is it going to do anyone now?"

"People should be responsible for their actions, Mother. Daddy's going to want to know," I added firmly.

"I'm thirsty," Belinda moaned.

"All right, honey. All right. Olivia will get you some water."

"I need something colder, something with ice," she demanded.

"So go get it," I snapped.

"Olivia, please," Mother said, turning her soft eyes to me.

"We shouldn't be babying her now, Mother. She's done a terrible thing to all of us," I said, feeling abused too. Mother just held her gaze, pleading with her eyes. I turned and hurried out of the room and down the stairs.

Carmelita had finally been roused by the sound of the

footsteps on the stairway and the activity above. She was a tall, very dark skinned, half-Portuguese, half-Negro woman, what we called a Brava on the Cape, and she had been working for our family for the last ten years. She was in her mid-forties, lean, with a narrow face and eyes the color of obsidian. Carmelita was the perfect maid and cook for our family because she was strong, efficient and discreet. She seemed to have no opinions about any of us and kept to herself when she wasn't working.

Her licorice-black hair was down to her shoulders when she emerged from her quarters to greet me. She was in her nightgown and robe.

"Is someone sick?" she asked.

"Belinda," I said.

"Oh. Is there anything I can do?"

"No thank you, Carmelita," I said. "I can take care of it," I said firmly. She fixed those dark eyes on my face for a moment and, expressionless, nodded and returned to her maid's quarters at the rear of the house. I knew she didn't believe me, but even when I was just a young girl, Carmelita never challenged anything I told her.

When I was in the kitchen getting Belinda's drink, Daddy came in through the rear door off the pantry. He stood there a moment, his face streaked with sweat, his hands caked with dirt.

"It's done," he said. "How is it up there?" he asked, his eyes shifting toward the ceiling.

"Mother's with her. I'm just getting her a cold drink."

Daddy nodded and looked at his smudged wrists and hands before looking back at me.

"You understand why I'm doing it this way, don't you, Olivia? The bottom line is it's the best way to protect the family."

"I understand, Daddy."

"She told you no one else knows about this?"

23

"That's what she said," I replied, not without a smirk of skepticism that Daddy chose to ignore.

"Good," he said. "Good."

"She won't tell me who the father is, however," I added. "She claims she doesn't know."

He shook his head.

"Maybe it's better. We can't go accusing someone and stir up a nest of hornets."

"Whoever it is, he shouldn't get away with it, Daddy."

"It's done and over," he said. "Let it all be buried," he added and then left to wash up before returning to see Belinda. Once again, I thought, my spoiled sister gets away with something terrible.

When I returned to Belinda's room with her water, I found Mother had her lying back comfortably. I gave her the cold drink and she sipped it and smiled up at me.

"Thank you, Olivia. I'm sorry I put you through so much."

"Yes, you did," I said without flinching. She looked like she would burst into tears again and make Mother feel more terrible. "Just rest now, Belinda. You don't want to get seriously ill," I added mercifully. She changed her expression instantly to one of gratitude and then reached out to take my hand.

"You're my best sister," she said. I nearly laughed.

"I'm your only sister, Belinda."

"I know, but you're so good to me."

"She is good to you. She's good to all of us," Mother said smiling at me. "What we all have to do now is get some rest."

"How can anyone sleep after this?" I muttered. If Mother heard, she chose to ignore me.

Daddy came to the door and looked in at us.

"Well?" he asked.

"She's doing fine, Winston," Mother said.

"That's good. It's better we behave as if this didn't happen," he advised.

"You might as well pretend there's no ocean out there," I declared.

"Your father's right, Olivia. It won't do any good to talk about it, even amongst ourselves. Let's close our eyes and imagine it was a nightmare," she suggested.

It didn't surprise me to hear her say such a thing. It was the way Mother handled most of the unpleasantness in her life. Not even an event like this would be any different.

She leaned over to kiss Belinda who smiled at her, and then she left the room. Daddy stood there a moment gazing in at me, at the floor and then at Belinda.

"Everyone just go to sleep," he said and left.

I looked at Belinda. She offered me her small smile, but I just shook my head at her.

"I'm so tired, Olivia," she said. "I feel so weak inside, too, but I didn't want to alarm anyone. Daddy wouldn't want me to have to go to a doctor."

"You'll live," I said. "Just go to sleep."

I checked the room once more and then started out, pausing in the doorway to look back at her. She looked small, like a little girl again. In moments she was asleep.

I lay awake in my bed thinking not of Belinda, or of my parents. I thought about that dead infant whose spark of life went out so quickly and who was interred someplace on our grounds so soon afterward, he surely had no memory of ever being born into this family.

At the moment, I thought, he was the lucky one.

Belinda remained at home for the rest of the week. We told everyone she had the flu. I thought that Carmelita knew something far more serious had occurred. She brought Belinda her meals so she saw that Belinda wasn't coughing or sneezing. However, Mother pampered her and behaved as if our lies were really the truth. I heard her talking to her friends on the telephone, telling them how sick Belinda was.

"One day she was fine and the next, she was as sick as a dog," she rambled, describing the symptoms, even claiming she had phoned the doctor for instructions.

It all disgusted me. I was especially amazed at how quickly Daddy had adjusted to the façade he and Mother had created. The following morning he was up and dressed at his usual hour, already seated at the breakfast table, reading his newspaper as though the night before really had been just a bad dream. The only indication in his face was a quick but sharp look at me when Carmelita came into the dining room and inquired as to Belinda's health. That was when Mother went into her long, detailed explanation, pouring out her brook of bubbling white lies. Daddy looked pleased.

Since I had returned from finishing school, I had gone to work for him as an apprentice accountant. Daddy decided that it would be a waste to send me to some liberal arts college, "just to fill the time, until you find a decent and proper man to marry, Olivia. Any man you marry will appreciate you more for doing something practical," he added.

I wasn't excited about going to college anyway, and I had always been very good with numbers. Daddy claimed I had a good mind for business. He said he knew that even when I was just a little girl selling cranberries from our bog. I set up a stand on the street that ran by our property. Tourists thought it was sweet seeing a little girl behave so seriously about money. What impressed Daddy was that I took my money and had him put it into an interest-bearing savings account rather than spend it in the candy or toy stores.

"At least I have someone in the family to inherit my business," he declared. He had come to accept that he wouldn't have a son, but in time, I believed he no longer thought of me as an inferior substitute. He gave me too many compliments at the office for me to believe that.

Daddy was truly a self-made millionaire, a success story that illustrated the American dream: a small entrepreneur who made good business decisions and gradually but firmly built a bigger and bigger business. He was written up in many regional magazines and once in the Boston papers.

He had begun with a single fishing boat and then bought a second and a third. Before long, he had a fleet of vessels providing seafood for an ever-growing national market. He expanded into the canning of shrimp in Boston and built an impressive financial chain of related businesses, making the shrewd move to get a commanding interest in the trucking facilities so he could control his overhead. By his own admission, he was at times a ruthless businessman, smothering competition, dropping prices to drive them out of his territories. He became more and more influential in politics, picked up government contracts and continued to expand his reach and hold on his markets.

After less than six months, I knew our mother company inside and out, and Daddy even permitted me to sit in on some of his business meetings to listen and learn more. After they ended, he often turned to me to get my opinions, and a number of times, he took my advice.

Belinda, on the other hand, didn't know the first thing about our business. According to the way she behaved and thought, money came into our lives like rain. When we needed it, it was there, and there was never a drought, never a time when she ever heard the words, "We can't afford that, Belinda."

I often lectured her about being ungrateful and unappreciative.

"You take everything for granted as though it's owed to you," I accused.

She gave me that sweet smile of hers and shrugged. I could accuse her of murder and she would do the same. She rarely argued or denied anything. It was as if she believed she would be immune from responsibility and guilt, that she had been given some holy dispensation and could do whatever her little heart desired, no matter what the consequences.

It was even true now, I thought disgustedly, with our parents claiming it was better to pretend nothing happened. Belinda just had the flu. I almost believed Daddy had convinced himself he hadn't buried a premature infant.

The day after when I returned from the office, I wandered out behind our house, curious as to whether I could find the unmarked grave site. Our land behind the house ran nearly a full acre before it reached the cliff that looked out over the Atlantic Ocean. It was a sharp descent to the rocky beach below. There were some safe pathways that led down to the small private beach we had, only a clam shell's toss away. Our yard had sprawling maples and some oak trees, and a large part of it remained uncultivated. Poison ivy grew among the brambles and wild roses and more than once, Belinda had wandered too close, suffering the results for weeks after.

A large lawn was bordered by crocus clusters, Emperor tulips, jonquils and daffodils. There was a gazebo and a pond with benches around it, and I found it so restful to sit there and look out to sea.

Sometimes, I would walk out to the edge of the cliff and watch the tide, mesmerized by the rhythmic move-

ment of the waves, the breakers, the spray shooting up
from the rocks, listening to the seagulls scream as they
plummeted for clams. I would go to the very edge and
close my eyes. I could feel my body sway as if it were
tempted to fly off the cliff and crash on the rocks below.

When she was younger, Belinda was frightened by the
ocean. She was not fond of sailing, hated the danger of
man-of-wars and the smell of seaweed. She rarely, if
ever, went hunting for driftwood. The only reason she
could see for going to the beach was to have a party and
then to stay far enough away from the water so as not to
even be sprayed by the waves crashing against the shore.
Once, when I was nine and she was seven, I took her out
to the edge of the cliff with me and asked her to close her
eyes. It frightened her so much she turned and ran back
to the house. I thought about that now and wondered
what I would have done if she had fallen.

Jerome had just finished doing some weeding when I
stepped out back to find the grave. He nodded and
headed for the shed. With my arms folded across my
body, I walked as casually as I could down the slate rock
pathway, my eyes flitting from side to side, searching for
signs of dirt that had been disturbed. I walked all the way
out to the edge of the cliff without seeing anything.
Where could Daddy have put the carton and other
things? It wouldn't be just a little hole, would it?

I went around toward the maples and paused when I
thought I had found an area under one of the trees that
looked like it had been dug up. I stepped closer and when
I knelt and inspected the ground, I decided this was the
place. It put a shudder in me and I rose as if I expected
the dead infant to cry for help, even with its muted
voice.

Years later, I would come here again and find the place
overgrown, but in the midst of the crab grass and flat

emerald weeds, would be a patch of juniper swaying in the ocean wind, reminding me of that horrible night.

At the moment I was angry about it, though. I didn't like feeling creepy and morose. I didn't like burying Belinda's sins because I didn't like lies. When you lie, I thought, you make yourself vulnerable and weak. Daddy was a much weaker man in my eyes because of what he had done, though I was sure that he had his nightmares, too.

I fled from the spot, hating Belinda for putting us all in this horrible place.

Daddy should have made Belinda suffer her consequences and not leave her to be pampered upstairs all week, I thought. I believed he would never bring it up again, but he surprised me one night toward the end of that week. He was in his den going over the family accounts when I walked by and he called to me.

"Close the door, Olivia," he ordered as soon as I entered. I did so and then turned to him. He sat behind his desk stiffly. "We've got to put all this behind us, Olivia. I notice you've been different all this week, looking at me as if you expected me to say or do something more."

"I don't mean to be your conscience, Daddy," I said and he winced as though I had spit at him. "I'm sorry. It's just hard for me to pretend nothing happened."

"Listen to me, Olivia. The most important quality is loyalty. Every family is a world unto itself and every member of that little world must protect it at any cost. Only then can individual liberty, interests and talents be pursued. Build the family first, Olivia. The only rule for morality is what's good for the family is good," he said, his eyes firm. "It's the lesson my father taught me and the lesson I hope you will take to heart.

"Among ourselves, we can criticize and regret, but we

have to put it aside when it threatens the family. It's the credo I live by, Olivia. It's the only flag I salute and the only cause for which I will give my life."

I stared a moment. Daddy looked like he was about to cry now. His lips were pressed together so hard, his cheeks bulged.

"Don't condemn me for loving all of you, loving my family name and reputation so much, Olivia. Learn from it," he pleaded.

I took a deep breath. Daddy and I had had many conversations in the past, but I rarely if ever saw his eyes fill with tears. I felt bad for him, felt sorry I had made him feel any guilt.

"I understand, Daddy," I said. "I really do."

"That's good, Olivia, because you're my hope. You will have many decisions to make for our family after I'm gone, and I hope you will always remember this week and remember what I told you to use as your guiding principle."

"I will, Daddy," I promised.

He smiled and rose. Then he walked around the desk and put his arm around me.

"I'm proud of you, Olivia." He kissed me on the forehead. "Very proud," he said.

I watched him return to his desk. He looked tired, like a man carrying too many burdens. I remained a moment until he lowered his eyes to his papers, and then I left him.

His words clung to me even after I had put out the lights that night and lowered my head to the pillow. They lingered with the memory of his tear-filled eyes.

There is a terrible price to pay for being a leader, I thought, a terrible burden.

Maybe Belinda was better off than any of us, especially me.

Look at what she had done and yet tonight, like most nights, she embraced her stuffed animals, closed her eyes, and dreamed of parties, of tinkling bells, of ribbons and music and boyfriends dangling on her smiles.

Whereas my dreams were about a patch of dirt behind the house and my father, lowering the carton into the ground while through his tears he chanted, "For the family. It's all for the family."

2

It's My Party

For the first few days, Belinda was truly an invalid. She didn't eat well and what she ate, she often didn't keep down. Her usual rosy complexion evaporated and didn't return until toward the end of the week, which was just in time for what she had planned. On Saturday, three boys from her high-school class arrived at the house after lunch to visit her. They brought flowers and candy. Carmelita appeared in the doorway of the sitting room where Mother, Daddy and I were.

"There are three young men here to see Belinda," she announced with little emotion.

"Three?" Daddy asked, his eyebrows lifting.

"Yes, sir."

"Boys?"

"Yes, Mr. Gordon."

Daddy shifted his gaze to me and I frowned.

"That's very nice," Mother declared. She smiled my way even though I continued to scowl.

"Show them in," Daddy declared and stiffened up the

V. C. ANDREWS

way he usually did for a business meeting he anticipated would be difficult. He had a way of bringing up his shoulders and lowering his neck until he resembled a bird of prey. Daddy was barrel-chested, stout and very intimidating when he swelled up and put a glint of steel in his eyes.

I knew each of the boys Carmelita showed in. They had all been here to take Belinda on a date at one time or another this year. There was Arnold Miller, who had been my prime suspect only because Belinda had spent so much time with him recently. He was very tall, easily six feet four, good-looking with light brown hair and green eyes speckled with brown. From what Belinda had told me, she fancied him because he was something of a school sports hero, their star basketball player and star baseball pitcher. Most of the girls wanted him for a boyfriend. Belinda enjoyed being envied more than she enjoyed being loved.

Arnold's parents owned a lumber mill and garden equipment store, one of the biggest retail outlets in Provincetown. Arnold was the oldest of three children, all boys. I thought he was a little shy, but I couldn't be sure if that was an act he put on in front of me. Belinda only giggled when I had first asked her about him months ago.

Next to Arnold stood Quin Lothar, who kept his amber hair long, nearly to his shoulders, which was something Daddy detested in young men. Quin was also very popular because he had his own band at school, but in my opinion he wasn't anywhere as good-looking as Arnold. Quin's features were too large and he had a narrow forehead with eyebrows that hung too far over his brown eyes. The right corner of his mouth always seemed tucked into his cheek, giving him an habitual smart-aleck smirk. Now that I gazed at him, I thought he had to be the father. He looked capable of making Belinda pregnant and not caring.

He was dressed sloppily, in worn trousers and a faded pullover, and obviously didn't care about his appearance or making a good impression on my parents.

The third young man was Peter Wilkes, a short, chubby boy with a round, soft face. His father was President of the Cape Coast Savings. Belinda said he always had money to spend and the others kept him around and called him Pocketbook, even to his face. Belinda bragged that she just had to look at something and wish it was hers and he would go buy it for her.

He wore a button-down white dress shirt, slacks and laced dress shoes, but somehow, maybe because of the way his clothes hung on his obese body, he didn't look any better than the other two.

Quin was their spokesman.

"Good afternoon," he said. "We came to see how Belinda is doing. We thought we could cheer her up," he added.

Peter folded his cheeks into a smile and lifted the box of candy in his hands.

"If it's okay, I'd like to give her this," he said. "Imported chocolates."

Arnold carried the flowers. He just nodded, holding them up like the Statue of Liberty holding the torch.

Daddy said nothing. He had a way of holding his words back just a moment longer than anyone antici-pated. It was something he did to put people off rhythm, a way of testing them. The silence, as short as it was, made the three boys uncomfortable. They gazed quickly at each other, squirmed in their clothes and looked from me to my mother to the floor and then back to Daddy.

"I brought her some notes from classes she's missed, too," Peter added reaching into his pants pocket to produce some papers.

"That's very thoughtful," Mother finally said.

"Aren't you boys afraid of getting sick yourselves so close to the end of the school year?" Daddy questioned, his eyes narrowing suspiciously.

"No sir," Arnold replied quickly.

"We won't get that close to her," Quin added, digging the corner of his mouth deeper into his cheek. Peter widened his smile.

"I hope not," Daddy muttered. "Olivia," he said turning to me. I knew what that meant. He wanted me to show them to Belinda's room and remain as a chaperone.

I rose with obvious reluctance.

"Maybe she's asleep," I said.

"She knows we're coming," Quin quickly inserted. "We called earlier and told her we'd be here about now."

"She should have told us, too," I muttered, gazing at Daddy. He nodded his agreement but said nothing more. Instead, he went to his newspaper and then plucked one of his cigars out of the case on the table beside him.

"Are those Havana cigars, Mr. Gordon?" Peter asked as Daddy began to light it.

Daddy raised his eyebrows.

"What do you know about cigars?"

"Not much, but my father smokes Havanas. I can get some for you," he added, his attempt to win favor blatantly obvious.

"I'm quite capable of getting my own," Daddy replied sternly.

"Are you here to visit Belinda or jabber with my father?" I asked them.

Quin poked Peter with his elbow and the three followed me out of the study and to the stairway.

"Normally, my parents don't approve of my sister having male visitors in her room," I said as I led them up. One of them snickered, but I didn't give him the satisfaction of showing I had heard.

I paused outside Belinda's bedroom door and turned as the three gathered anxiously around me. What power did Belinda possess to cause young men to exhibit such enthusiasm and desire? I wondered. Was it simply her promiscuity or did she indeed have something extra, something I could never have, something given at birth, a quality of excitement, a promise that stirred their male hormones like witches stirred their brew.

"Just a moment," I said. They were breathing down my neck in anticipation. If they were horses, they'd be choking on their bridles and snorting, I thought. I knocked.

"Yes?" Belinda called.

"You have visitors. Are you decent?"

"Yes, Olivia. They can come in," she said and I opened the door.

Anyone looking at Belinda now would surely challenge my report of her birthing. Even I had to admit I was impressed with how radiant she looked. I knew Carmelita hadn't been up here after breakfast, so it was clear Belinda had straightened up her room and opened the curtains wide to permit the soft, bright sunshine to come pouring through, making everything look clean and fresh.

Belinda was wearing one of her sheerest nighties, the neckline of which dipped into her cleavage, revealing breasts well matured. With the blanket lowered, the contour of her breasts was all but fully revealed. She wore her well-brushed hair down to her shoulders. The strands turned up softly at the ends. Belinda always had richer looking hair than I, but she fussed with it far more than I bothered with my own. If she had her way, she would turn the walls of her room into mirrors. She never seemed to tire of looking at her own image.

"Pull up your blanket or put on your robe," I ordered. She blushed and pulled the blanket against her chest quickly.

"Now, who's come to see me?" she declared like some Southern belle.

The three boys moved timidly into her room.

"They claim they called you, so I don't know how you could wonder who it was, Belinda," I remarked. She ignored me and concentrated on them.

"I brought you these," Arnold said quickly and thrust the bouquet of red roses toward her.

"Oh, they're just beautiful, aren't they, Olivia? Can we find a vase for them?"

"We?" I asked.

She tilted her head with that childish grin.

"Well, I don't think it would be proper for me to get out of bed myself," she said, her eyelids fluttering so emphatically, I thought she might fan herself up and off the bed.

I grunted, stepped forward and took the flowers. There was a vase on the dresser. I went into the bathroom to fill it with water.

"I hope you can have candy," I heard Peter Wilkes tell her.

"Of course I can," Belinda said. "Olivia loves candy, too," she added loudly as I returned from the bathroom.

"I certainly do not," I said. I put the vase down on her nightstand and stuffed the long-stem roses into it.

Belinda giggled and began to open the box. She

plucked a chocolate and held it between her lips, closing her eyes and moaning so lustfully, the three boys widened their own eyes and shifted about as though they were in torment.

"Belinda, that's disgusting," I said. "If you're going to eat it, eat it. Don't salivate all over it first."

She laughed and sucked in the round treat, offering the boys one. Each took a candy. I shook my head vigorously when she turned the box to me.

"Can you please put it on my table, Olivia," she said.

I sighed deeply, not hiding my annoyance. How had I suddenly become her maid? I wondered, but did as she had asked.

"Tell me everything, everything I've missed and leave out nothing, no matter how small it seems to you," Belinda said clapping her hands and falling back on her large, fluffy pink pillow. Her hair fell around her face like a frame, bringing out the brightness in her eyes.

"Arnold pitched a shutout yesterday to finish the baseball season," Peter declared. "He went the full nine innings and gave up only three hits!"

"Oh, don't start talking to me about sports. All I ever hear from you boys are scores and errors and double plays. It's boring."

"Boring?" Peter said.

Quin laughed.

"Sure it is," he said. "Jock stuff is always boring." He leaned over the bed toward Belinda. "I wrote a new song for the band. We're calling it 'Take me to the Beach.'"

"You must have them play it for me," Belinda said.

"Sure. You'll come down to the garage as soon as you're well enough."

"I'll be well enough Monday, won't I, Belinda?"

"You look well enough right now," I said dryly.

"Quin got caught smoking in the boys' room yesterday. He won't be in school on Monday," Arnold revealed with a gleeful smile.

"Really! Tell me about it," Belinda said, sitting forward excitedly as though Quin had accomplished something significant in her absence.

"Frog-eyes came in just after I lit up. He must have been watching me from his doorway, just looking for the opportunity. He's been after me ever since I wore those funny glasses and imitated him, remember?"

"Of course I remember. That was so funny."

When Belinda laughed, they all laughed.

"And people wonder why I don't want to go into teaching," I muttered. They turned to me.

"You said you didn't like Mr. Garner either when you were in high school, Olivia," Belinda said.

"I said he wasn't very enthusiastic about his work, but I didn't say he was a frog."

They all laughed again as if I had meant it to be funny.

"Jerry gave Barbara a pretty expensive ring. It's the closest thing to an engagement ring," Peter continued. "He told me they intend to get married soon after graduation."

"I already know about that. Marcia Gleason told me last night on the phone," Belinda said.

"Suicide Jerry, that's what we call him," Quin said laughing.

"Don't make fun of him," Belinda moaned as if she were seconds from bursting into tears. "He and Barbara are really in love. It's wonderful when you can find someone with whom to spend your whole life, someone who will care more about you than he does about himself, someone like my father."

The three boys stopped smiling and accepted her rebuke. How she dangled them on strings, I thought, studying them each more closely. Who was the father of her dead fetus? Certainly not Peter Wilkes, unless Belinda got him to get her something expensive in a trade. She could do that, I thought.

"Anyone else come down with the flu this week?" I inquired. One of them surely knew the truth about Belinda.

Quin and Arnold looked at each other and then shook their heads.

"I don't think so," Arnold said. "Bobby Lester was out, but he twisted his ankle at the game."

"We only have a couple of weeks until finals. It's hard to miss class now," Peter said, "which reminds me, Belinda. Here are my notes from English literature class."

"Oh, thank you, Peter. That's so sweet."

"Sweeter than the candy?" I asked. Belinda laughed.

"My sister is so funny sometimes," she explained. She took the notes and put them beside her. "I'll do some studying later."

"That will be unusual," I remarked under my breath, but loud enough to be heard.

"Olivia!"

"You know you have to pass the final in English to graduate, Belinda."

"You said you'd help me study," she whined. The boys looked from her to me to her as we spoke.

"I will if you're serious about trying."

"I am."

"I'll come up and study with you this week," Peter offered quickly.

"That's very nice of you, Peter. See, someone cares about me," she cried with delight. Her eyes slid from one boy to the other, melting each one into a doting admirer as she passed her gaze like a benediction, turning them into worshipers in seconds. The sight disgusted me.

Where were the real men of today? I couldn't imagine Daddy acting like this when he was their age.

"I wish you had been at the game, Belinda. When I threw that last pitch . . ."

"There you go again, talking sports. If you don't stop, I'll close my eyes and fall asleep," she threatened.

If the conversation didn't center around her, she wasn't interested.

"I just wanted to say I was thinking of you. This one's for Belinda, I thought," Arnold told her.

"Oh." She perked up, her dimple flashing. "Well that's different. You won because of me. I want everyone to know that," she declared. Arnold nodded like a soldier taking orders to go forth and bellow the news in the streets of Provincetown.

"They asked my band to play at the graduation party on the beach," Quin blurted, attempting to win back her attention.

"That's wonderful," Belinda cried.

"Can I pick you up and take you to the party?" Arnold asked quickly.

"I can get my father's Cadillac," Peter suggested.

"I'll just come by with my motorcycle. You can watch us set up," Quin added.

Belinda considered the offers and looked at me.

"What would you do, Olivia?"

"Walk," I said dryly.

She broke into a long, loud laugh and clapped her hands.

"Walk. I love it. Yes, who will walk with me?"

"If that's what you want to do," Arnold said quickly. "I will."

Maybe he was the father after all, I thought. She had denied it too quickly.

"I'm not sure yet. I'll think about it," Belinda said

coyly. She dangled her promise of acceptance like bait and the three stood there nibbling like poor dumb fish.

I retreated to the corner of the room where I sat and watched and listened to them all go on and on about their plans for graduation night. There was an air of excitement about them that I longed to share. I hadn't attended any graduation parties when I had graduated. Daddy, Mother, Belinda and I simply went to have dinner in the Steak and Brew House. Afterward, I sat in my room and gazed out the window into the night, thinking about the bonfires on the beach, the music and the laughter I was not sharing. No one had asked me to go and I hated attending parties with my wallflower girlfriends. The worst thing was to stand around and hope some boy would show me some attention, as if I were a beggar looking for a handout of affection. I would never give any boy the satisfaction. If loneliness was the price to pay until someone right came along, than that was the price, I decided, and tried not to think about it.

But it wasn't easy going to sleep and wondering what sort of man would come knocking on my door, bringing me boxes of candy and flowers and standing around anxiously, waiting for a compliment, a look of pleasure, a promise from my lips as did these three hovering over Belinda.

"It's getting late," I finally announced. They all turned to me as if just realizing I was still there.

"Yeah, I've got to get to a rehearsal," Quin said.

"I hope you feel better," Arnold said.

"Me too," Peter followed.

Belinda sat forward, permitting the blanket to fall too low again. The three sets of eyes widened and held on the depth of her cleavage. I cleared my throat loudly and nodded at her and she pulled the blanket back up.

"I'll call you tomorrow," Arnold promised.

They all made the same promise and then started out. I followed them to the doorway and watched them descend the stairs before turning back to Belinda.

"Wasn't that nice?" she asked.

"Which one was it, Belinda?"

"Pardon?"

"You know what I mean. Who was the father?"

She shook her head.

"I told you. I don't know, Olivia. Besides, Daddy said we shouldn't talk about it anymore," she cried, turning her face to the pillow.

"Was it one of them? It was, wasn't it?"

"Please, Olivia."

"Does he know, whoever it is? Does he know what happened in this room?"

"Stop it, Olivia." She put her hands over her ears. "I won't listen to you."

I closed in on her.

"Did you call him and tell him what went on, what your father had to do? Did you?"

"No. I don't know who I would call, I told you."

"Disgusting, Belinda. It's disgusting enough to do what you did, but to not know . . ."

She started to cry.

"I'm going to get sick again and I won't be able to return to school," she threatened.

"Won't that be a great loss for the school," I muttered.

I left her sniffling and went downstairs to find Daddy. He was in his office filing some papers. It was where he kept all our personal tax documents and family papers. He turned from the cabinet when I entered.

"Don't you think that was nervy, coming here like that, Daddy? Surely, one of them . . ."

"Don't, Olivia," he said, holding up his hand. "We've put it out of mind."

"I know, Daddy. I'm just . . . so angry at her for what she's done," I said.

"Yes, I know, but you've got to look after her, Olivia. We've learned that lesson."

Why Daddy tolerated weakness in Belinda and no one else, including my mother, was a question that stuck like a bone in my throat.

"I'm depending on you to watch over her," he said. "She'll listen to you."

"She hasn't up until now, Daddy. That's been proven in a terrible way."

"I know, but I believe she will change," he insisted.

I stared at him a moment and he had to shift his eyes from mine, something he rarely did. We had an unspoken but realized connection, an understanding, Daddy and I. We knew we couldn't lie to each other.

He was lying to me right now and he knew I knew it. He didn't really believe Belinda could change.

Why was he lying?

My anger at Belinda expanded like a balloon filling with hate because she was making Daddy lie.

Someday, I vowed, she would understand and appreciate what she has done and she will beg forgiveness. In my heart, however, I believed it would be too late for me to grant it.

Remarkably, Belinda passed her finals in English, just barely and with a great deal of tutoring. I had the distinct impression, however, that she also got a little help from her teachers, maybe because of Daddy's position in the community. During the week before the graduation ceremony, Mother asked Daddy to take us to Boston to find a nice dress for Belinda. She wanted her to look special. It was as if Mother had discovered a way to compensate for the terrible thing that had occurred: to dwell on Belinda's festivities so intensely there was no time to think about or remember anything else. In one spending spree, she would wipe away the dark clouds that clung to the corners of our home. There would be no shadows, no reminders, nothing but bright and happy things. Daddy seemed more than eager to please her and follow her lead to the world of "see no evil, hear no evil."

At the last moment Mother decided to outdo even herself and have a designer come to our home and create an original dress for Belinda to wear. The cost would easily be three times as expensive as an off-the-rack dress, but once again, Daddy surrendered before any battle and to my surprise, put away his famous measurement of "What's the bottom line?" This time, there was no bottom line.

I had to admit Belinda looked beautiful graduation day. It was a perfect afternoon for an outdoor graduation ceremony, too. A gentle, warm breeze came in from the ocean, and the sky was turquoise with puffs of clouds moving imperceptibly across the horizon.

It had been decided that Belinda would attend the same finishing school I had attended, only she would go immediately and start with their summer session. Daddy thought it was wise to get her away as quickly as he could, and get her into formal training to make her more of a lady. His intentions were clear: he wanted her to be a prize for the right young man.

My graduation couldn't be held outside. It had occurred on a rainy day. The auditorium was stuffy and very uncomfortable with dozens of small children crying, flashbulbs going off everywhere, proud parents and grandparents waving and gaping like visitors at a zoo. I had felt like a caged animal, squeezed in with my classmates, waiting for the speeches to end.

Belinda's graduation was more like a grand picnic.

Streamers and balloons decorated the grounds. Sunshine made everyone look bright and alive, full of happiness. Young children could go off and play, out of the way of the adults. The "Pomp and Circumstance" march flowed melodiously through the warm air. Everyone rose and the graduates, all looking cheerful and excited, came down the aisle to take their seats on the platform.

Maybe because it wasn't my graduation, it also seemed to go a lot more smoothly. The speeches weren't as long and before we knew it, they were handing out the diplomas. Daddy surprised me with his excitement, behaving just like all the other proud fathers, rushing down the aisle to take a picture of Belinda accepting her diploma. When I graduated, he relied on the professional group photographer and never moved from his seat. Belinda took her diploma with her usual flair, practically spinning completely to beam a smile in his direction.

"Thank heavens," Mother muttered beside me. "I had my fears."

Afterward, we celebrated at the Clam and Claw, a seafood restaurant near the Point. Daddy invited some of his business associates to join us and pretty quickly into the celebration, I saw that Belinda was getting bored. She exploded with happiness as soon as Peter Wilkes appeared at the restaurant.

"Oh, good," she said as he approached. "I thought I would die of boredom."

"What's this?" Daddy said interrupting his conversation to look up at Peter.

"I guess I'm a little early," Peter said.

"That's all right. Isn't it, Daddy?" Belinda followed with exuberance.

Daddy smiled with embarrassment at his guests.

"Well . . . you haven't finished your meal yet, Belinda."

"Oh, I can't eat anymore, Daddy."

"Where are you going?" I asked when she stood.

"To the beach party, silly. Remember? Daddy said it was all right," she added.

I looked at Daddy. His eyes met mine and then slipped away quickly.

"Well, now you get home early, Belinda. Graduation or no graduation . . ."

"Oh, Winston, don't be an ogre," Mr. Collins said. He was one of Daddy's business partners. "A young girl graduates high school only once."

"Thank heavens for that," Mother said and everyone at the table but me laughed.

Belinda rushed around the table to give everyone a hug and a kiss. She even stopped to throw her arms around me.

"Thank you, big sister," she said. "I love the suitcase."

I had given her a quality piece of luggage for her trip to finishing school. It was a practical gift, one of the few she had received.

Peter gave me a weak smile and hurried along as Belinda tugged on his hand.

"Bye," he called.

I gazed at Daddy. He watched them go, looked at me, and then turned to talk to Mr. Collins.

We left the restaurant a little over an hour later. The night proved to be as beautiful as the day. It was actually balmy. I looked out toward the ocean as we drove home and thought how wonderful it must be to be at a beach party right now. A nearly cloudless sky revealed so many more stars. The Big Dipper never looked as clear or sharp.

When we arrived at home, I went directly to my room. All I wanted to do was fall asleep, fall asleep and forget, fall asleep and dream I was someone else, someplace else. It took me a long time because I tossed and turned, lying there at times with my eyes wide open. Sleep was behind a locked door and not ready to embrace me.

You have to suffer first, I thought. You have to suffer with your loneliness.

I finally fell asleep only to be woken by a gentle and then loud knock on my door. At first I thought it was part of a dream. Then I sat up and heard it again.

"Yes?"

Daddy poked his head between the door and jamb.

"I hate to bother you, Olivia, but . . . well, your mother's worried, too."

"Worried? Why?"

"It's nearly three in the morning and Belinda has not come home."

"That never worried you before," I said sharply.

He hesitated.

"Yes, well, considering what happened . . ."

"We aren't supposed to talk about it, Daddy," I snapped. I wasn't feeling very charitable.

"Please, Olivia."

"What do you want me to do, Daddy?"

"Could you go look for her?"

"At the beach?"

"Yes," he said. "We don't want her to get into any more trouble."

"I can't believe she would do anything like that, Daddy," I said. He remained in the doorway.

"I'm more worried about your mother," he said.

"All right," I said. "I'll go find her."

"Thank you, Olivia."

I rose and put on a pair of slacks and a sweater. I grabbed my light jacket on the way out and hurried down the corridor and stairs, driven mostly by anger. How could she be so insensitive and selfish? She knew what

Daddy and Mother had suffered. No matter how generous and forgiving they were, Belinda always took advantage.

I got into my car and headed for the beach road I knew they had taken. There was one area on the east end that the school kids always favored, even before my day. Sure enough, as I started down the road, I saw cars were still parked there. This was going to be an all-nighter.

I found a space and parked and then plodded over the sandy beach toward one of the bonfires. I heard laughter to my right and radio music caught in the wind. It whipped at my hair and spit some sand into my face. The ocean roared in on a line of whitecaps.

I saw couples wrapped in blankets around the fire, but none of the girls was Belinda. They gazed up at me curiously. Some even had bottles of whiskey and wine.

I continued toward the next bonfire, my anger boiling over like a pan of hot milk. Once again, I did not see Belinda, but I did recognize Marcia Gleason and Arnold Miller. Arnold nearly jumped out of his blanket when he saw me bearing down on them.

"Where's my sister?" I demanded.

"Belinda?" he said stupidly, sitting up slowly. I could see Marcia was topless under the blanket.

"No, my other ten sisters. Of course, Belinda. Where is she?"

"I'm not sure . . ."

"Someone is going to get into a lot of trouble if I don't find her within the next minute," I threatened. "Do your parents know where you are and what you're doing right now, Marcia?" I asked pointedly.

"I thought she went home," Marcia whined. "The last time I saw her she was going for a walk with Quin over the hill," she added, nodding toward the bank behind them. I glared down at her a moment.

"I hope I don't have to come back," I said and started toward the small rise in the beach. I heard Arnold chastising Marcia for telling me anything.

For a long moment after I reached the peak of the small hill, I saw nothing. Then, I caught a movement to my right and spotted two heads popping out of a sleeping bag. I drew closer. The movement within the bag was not hard to translate. It brought the blood to my face.

"Belinda!" I screamed, but my voice was carried off by the wind. I screamed it again as I approached and finally, they both stopped and hesitated. I called her again.

"Olivia?" I heard her say.

"Damn you," I cried and they scurried like rats, Quin groping for his clothing on the sand. He was pulling up his pants by the time I stepped up beside them. Belinda hadn't moved. "How can you be doing this?" I demanded.

"We were just . . . ." Quin scrambled for his sneakers.

"I know what you were just doing, Quin Lothar," I said.

"I gotta go. It's late," he said and lunged to his feet, not taking the time to put on his sneakers. In a moment he had disappeared into the darkness.

Belinda whimpered.

"You ruined my graduation night," she said through her sobs.

"I ruined . . . Do you know Mother and Daddy are beside themselves with worry and now that I've come for you and have seen what you were doing, they had every reason to worry. How could you do this after what's happened?" I asked, my voice filled with amazement. Was there no bottom to Belinda's descent?

"We were being careful," she said.

"Oh, that's a relief to know. Do you just jump into anyone's sleeping bag on the beach, Belinda?"

V. C. ANDREWS

"No. It's graduation night!" she declared as though that was a license to lose all morality.

"Just put your clothes on and come home with me immediately," I said.

"But everyone is staying out all night."

"Daddy sent me to get you," I declared to impress her. She didn't move. "Belinda, I'm not going home without you."

"This is horrible," she cried. "You were happy to come get me. You don't want me to have a good time because you never do."

"If this is what you call having a good time, you're right," I snapped back. "Just get dressed. Now!"

She got out of the sleeping bag and began to put on her clothes. I couldn't watch her. It filled me with too much disgust. Instead, I turned away and looked toward the sound of the ocean.

Was she right? Did I come here to get her because I was jealous? If I had met someone to whom I was attracted in high school and who was attracted to me, would I have been on the beach too?

Something inside me told me no, I would have been more sensible, but at the moment, that didn't make me feel better or superior. It put a rock of sadness into the bottom of my stomach.

Belinda sulked as we trekked over the beach toward the car. The music followed us along with the laughter.

"I'm not going to be around all the time to save you from yourself, Belinda," I told her when we reached the car.

"Good," she fired back.

She was fuming all the way home. After we entered the house, she marched up the stairs and slammed the door to her room. Daddy came out.

"She all right?" he asked.

"Yes," I said. I decided not to give him any of the gritty details. He didn't seem to want to hear them anyway.

"Thank you, Olivia," he said. "You're the strength, the steel spine of this family. You always will be," he added with a nod. It was as if he had declared me heir to his throne, whether I wanted it or not.

It was who I was to be.

I fell asleep dreaming about that sleeping bag we had left empty on the beach.

3

A Wolf in Sheep's Clothing

For a while I thought Belinda wouldn't attend the finishing school or that Daddy would give in to her and postpone it until the fall. A few times, he tottered on the brink of caving in to her pleas. She tried desperately to get him to do so, moaning and groaning about not having the summer free to enjoy with her friends.

When Daddy vacillated, I helped prop him up again.

"You know she needs it more than ever, Daddy. It was your good idea. Don't let her pull the wool over your eyes. She'll be more than a handful for all of us if she has nothing whatsoever to do with her time," I reminded him. He pressed his lips together and held tight, but Belinda didn't give up.

"Who goes to school in the summer? Only people who have failed classes. I didn't fail any classes," she wailed, choosing to make our dinner hour as unpleasant as she could every night until she got her way.

"It won't be like going to school, Belinda," Mother told her. "It's a special school with beautiful grounds and dormitories, isn't it, Olivia?"

54

"Yes," I said, "with the finest facilities and some of the best teachers."

"It's still a school. I still have to be in stuffy classrooms while the sun is out and my friends are sailing and having fun back here, don't I?" Belinda moaned. She pouted, refused to eat, stomped about the house, sulked and made everyone else miserable as her day of departure closed in on her.

All during the week before she left, Belinda insisted on having her boyfriends and girlfriends come to the house and bid her good-bye as though she were off to war and they all might not see her ever again. Every time someone left, she was in tears.

"No one will write me or call. They all say they will, but they won't. They'll forget me quickly," she complained through her sobs.

"If that happens, that will show you they weren't very good friends anyway," I told her.

'That's right," Mother echoed.

'Oh . . . poop!" she cried, her face red with frustration, and ran up to her room.

Actually, I enjoyed her last minute antics, enjoyed her stream of complaints, her sobbing and sulking. From my expression, she saw she could find no sympathy in me, and no matter what she said to Mother, no matter what disaster she predicted, Mother found a silver lining.

'You'll meet new people, make new friends, see interesting new things, learn so much. What an opportunity for you, Belinda, dear. I wish I was young and going off to finishing school, too."

"And I wish I was old and past all this," she fired back with the tears flying off her cheeks.

That made me laugh: Belinda wishing herself old.

"You don't know what being old is," I told her. "As

soon as you see the first wrinkle on your face, you'll threaten to commit suicide."

"I will not. You're being dreadful to me, Olivia. You'll miss me when I'm gone," she threatened, which only made me laugh harder and make her sulk more.

Finally, the day of her departure arrived. She did little to make herself ready. Carmelita had to pack everything with Mother's supervision. She wouldn't even pack her own toiletries. We were all supposed to go up with her in the limousine, but I managed to get out of the trip. Daddy was disappointed. No one could handle Belinda in our family as well as I could; however, I was determined not to sit in a car for hours and hear her whine about how cruel we were all being to her.

She put on an award performance when Daddy told her to come out and get in the car. She stood on the walkway and looked back at me, her eyes filled with tears.

"Good-bye, Olivia," she said with her hands clutched at her heart. "Good-bye house. Good-bye good times and childhood and being young and having fun. They're turning me over to ogres and teachers with whips in their eyes who will make me feel like some sort of mistake. I'll have no one to go to for help either when I'm tired or lonely." She paused and looked at me. "Stop smiling, Olivia. You know I'm not exaggerating. You were there. You know what it's like."

"Belinda, you will stop being spoiled, if that's what you mean, and for once, you might have to consider someone else's feelings before you consider your own," I said.

"You're just being mean as can be. I hate you," she spit at me and turned to the car, but before she got in, she looked back at me. "Please call me, Olivia. Call me tonight. Please," she pleaded.

"I'll call you," I promised. "Now stop being a spoiled brat and make things easier for everyone," I ordered.

She sucked in her sobs, took one deep breath like someone going under water, and got into the car. I had to smile. Maybe I would miss her, I thought, but I hoped she would change a little, grow up just a little, and do just what I said: make life easier for us all.

A deceptive period of calm did follow Belinda's departure. Daddy and I were busy with his companies. Belinda called and cried over the telephone for a few days and then gave up. It looked like we might have an uneventful summer after all.

Now that Belinda was safely and securely filed away like some embarrassing set of documents, Daddy turned more of his attention to me, and, without my realizing it, arranged for me to have a date with Clayton Keiser, the son of our accountant. There was nothing subtle about it. On the way home from our offices one day, Daddy told me the Keisers were coming to our home for dinner on Friday.

I had met Clayton before, of course. He was five years older than I, and he, too, worked for his father now that he had graduated college. I had never given him more than a passing glance, and, during the whole time I knew him and his family, I had spoken little more than a dozen words with him.

Clayton's father Harrison Keiser looked like he had been discovered by a casting director to play the role of an accountant. He was a slim, beady-eyed man obsessed with details, no matter how small or insignificant they might be to other people. His son Clayton was practically a clone. They both had small, round faces, large dull brown eyes and thin noses with the tiniest nostrils. Clayton also inherited his father's pasty complexion and soft, very feminine lips. The one gift from his mother's side was his auburn hair, rich and thick, which he kept cut close to his head, almost in military style.

I was too many classes behind him to remember him in school, but I knew he was unathletic, the quintessential bookworm with his thick glasses and meek manner. Although he was an excellent student, he wasn't class valedictorian because the school policy averaged in physical education grades. Daddy told me there was a big argument about it at the time, but the policy wasn't changed to suit Clayton. I thought teachers and administrators simply didn't want him to be the valedictorian and represent the best of the school in front of all those parents and guests.

Clayton wasn't more than two or three inches taller than I. He was still a very slim, almost fragile-looking man, quiet, but with a scrutinizing look that made me feel he was assessing my assets and liabilities on some net worth document entitled "Olivia Gordon."

I was oblivious at first to what Daddy and Harrison Keiser had plotted and didn't notice how much of the conversation at dinner that night centered around both Clayton and myself until Daddy finally said, "Maybe Clayton should ask Olivia to the opening of that new show at the Sea and Shore Art Gallery. I think they share an interest in art."

I know I turned a shade brighter than crimson. My eyes darted from Daddy to Clayton to my mother who sat smiling like a Cheshire cat.

"Not a bad thought, eh Clayton?" Harrison Keiser followed quickly.

"No, sir."

"Well then," his father coaxed, nodding in my direction.

Clayton looked up from his plate at me as if he had

just realized I was there, too. He dabbed his lips with his napkin and cleared his throat.

"Yes. How would you like to go to dinner and to the gallery opening, Olivia?" Clayton asked in front of the entire table. It might as well have been declared on the front pages of the local newspapers.

Nevertheless, for a moment I couldn't speak. It was as if my vocal cords had declared a mutiny. I saw Daddy staring at me, expectantly. Finally, I gathered enough air in my lungs to utter a response. Of course it was yes. What else could I do?

The conversation then turned to what was the best restaurant for us to go to before the opening. Clayton had no opinion and neither did I. In fact, our entire evening was planned by our parents as if we were pieces on a chess board. Clayton's father suggested he go to his men's shop to get a new suit and tie. His mother thought he should do something different with his hair. My mother talked about a dress she had just seen, a dress that she decided would be perfect for me for such an occasion.

The four of them continued their discussion of our arranged date without once turning to either Clayton or myself and asking us for an opinion or a reaction. Clayton glanced at me a few times, but for most of the dinner, he sat with his eyes directed downward, concentrating on eating as he lifted the spoon and the fork with his father's precision, blotting his lips with his napkin almost in synchronization with his father. They were so alike, it was frightening.

At the end of the evening, before the Keisers left, Clayton finally turned to me. Everyone stopped talking as though the prince was about to utter some royal edict.

"I'll come by at six-fifteen, if that's all right with you," he said. "It will take fifteen minutes to get to the

restaurant, which will leave us an hour for dinner and
then it's about twelve minutes from the restaurant to the
gallery."

I felt as if I should synchronize my watch with his. I
simply nodded. He pressed his lips together, which was
his best effort at a smile, and then turned to join his
parents at the door. Everyone said good night and they
left.

Immediately, I spun on Daddy.

"Why did you do that? I felt like I was trapped and I
had to say yes."

"He's a fine young man, distinguishing himself in his
father's firm. Such young men are not so easily found
these days, Olivia."

"I'd like to find my own young man," I said.

I could see the reply in Daddy's face: You're not
making any attempt to do so.

"I'm just trying to help you, my dear. Surely, there's
no harm in testing the waters. It will cost you nothing
but your own time," he added, strongly reminding me I
was doing nothing else with it. "And then there is this
new showing at the gallery. You like that sort of thing,
don't you? The bottom line is it's no big sacrifice."

"I know, Daddy, but . . ."

"Your father's right. You should go out more, dear,"
Mother said. "You should be seen socializing. Even if
things don't work out between you and Clayton, other
young men will see you dressed up and beautiful and
think, there's someone I'd like to know. That's how
wonderful things happen," she continued. "We'll have
such fun fitting you for a dress, finding your shoes,
getting you some new costume jewelry, going to the
hairdresser."

I realized that this was something Mother wanted to

do for herself as well as for me. With Belinda gone, there wasn't much talk about romance in the house.

"All right," I said, relenting, "but I can't imagine myself having a good time with Clayton Keiser."

"You never know about these things, dear," Mother said. "When I first went out with your father, I thought the same thing."

"You did not," Daddy remarked quickly.

"I never told you, Winston, but I was deathly afraid of you that first night."

"Really?" he said smiling as if that was something of which he could be proud.

"Everyone told me to be careful. Winston Gordon is a man who gets what he wants and he wants a great deal. He has insatiable appetites," Mother explained.

Daddy's eyes flitted from her to me and then to her for a quick smile.

"Well, maybe that was true then, but I've become somewhat more restrained in my maturity. I try to find balance, analyze everything carefully."

"Even this arranged date for me, Daddy?" I said with a bitter smile.

He thought for a moment and then nodded.

"Yes. Yes, Olivia, I think this is a sensible young man. I hope you enjoy your evening," he concluded and went off to smoke his cigar.

Mother lost herself in a flurry of activity that week, preparing me for my "perfect" date. As it turned out, the dress she thought was just right was not and she insisted we go to Boston. I tried to change her mind.

"It's not an important event for me, Mother. It's just a date. I even hate that word. It's not a date. It's a . . . scheduled event," I said.

"Nonsense. Every time a young woman goes out in

public, socializes, it's a major event, Olivia. There's no harm in your making yourself as attractive and as presentable as possible, is there?"

"I guess not," I said reluctantly. Maybe she was right, I thought. Maybe I was not putting enough emphasis on myself, my looks, my image. Maybe it was time to be more of a woman than a successful daughter. I let her lead me about, have me measured, pampered, styled and dressed until I dared to look at myself in the mirror and conclude I, too, could be attractive, pretty, and I, too, could break men's hearts. Belinda did not have a monopoly on beauty in this family. It was time I gave her some competition.

Precisely at six-fifteen on the night of the gallery opening, Clayton drove up to our house and pressed the door buzzer. I waited upstairs, my heart pounding mostly because of sheer nervousness. I was just like an actress with stage fright, unsure that my feet would move forward. I had no reason to be insecure. My hair was cut and shaped into the most fashionable style. I wore a sparkling gold and diamond necklace, and gold earrings with tiny pearls. Mother gave me two of her rings as well. My dress was made of emerald green silk, with a V-shaped neckline that plunged farther than I would have liked. Mother insisted I put makeup on my neck and breast bone with just a touch of rouge on that part of my bosom that was visible. Many times I had chastised Belinda for looking too seductive. Now, I struggled not to chastise myself.

Up until the time Clayton arrived, Mother hovered about me like a magic sylph, fluttering her tiny wings, touching a strand of hair here, brushing out a crease there, straightening my necklace and checking to be sure my perfume was not too strong and not too weak.

"Oh you're beautiful, Olivia. You really are. Belinda would be deathly jealous," she said, which brought a smile to my face.

Belinda had called in the afternoon. Mother had kept her abreast of my preparations, and Belinda moaned and whined about not being able to be here to see me.

"I'm stuck up here learning how to walk with a book on my head and sit properly and stand properly and choose the right fork and spoon, while you go out on dates! It's not fair, Olivia."

"You've gone out on many dates, Belinda. One too many," I reminded her coldly. "And besides, while I was in finishing school learning these things, you were having more good times than you should."

"Oh poop," she cried. "If you really cared about me, you'd get Daddy to have my prison sentence reduced up here. That's all this place is, Olivia, a fancy prison for snobs. I haven't been able to make a single friend. I just see lots of nostrils. They hold their noses too high."

I had to laugh at that.

"I'm absolutely, terribly miserable. Even the male teachers are . . . are like old ladies. They don't give me a second look unless it's to teach me something stupid like how to correctly address someone for the first time."

"Just think of how accomplished you'll be when you graduate," I said.

"I don't care," she said and started to catalogue a whole new set of complaints.

"I've got to go," I interrupted. "I have too much to do to waste any more time."

"Then go. Go and have a wonderful time and then think of me locked up and chained by the rules," she concluded.

I heard the door buzzer and sucked in my breath.

"That's Clayton," Mother declared. She opened my bedroom door as if she were pulling back a stage curtain. "Have a good time, Olivia."

"Thank you, Mother," I said.

Carmelita had let Clayton in. He stood in the foyer looking up as I descended. I thought he resembled a bank teller in his suit and tie, waiting to receive a deposit. I hoped he would stop being so stiff when we were alone.

Daddy came rushing out of his office.

"Well, now, looky here. Doesn't she look beautiful, Clayton?" he urged.

"Yes, sir," he said and turned to me. "You look very nice."

"Thank you."

Carmelita stood off to the side, watching without expression. When I turned to her, however, her eyebrows rose and a look of genuine surprise formed on her face. It made me feel more confident. I guess I did look beautiful. I only wished Clayton would have been more demonstrative when he spoke and looked at me.

"Well," he said gazing at his watch, "we're on schedule. Shall we go?"

"Yes. Good night, Daddy," I said.

"Have a good time. Both of you," he called.

Clayton's car was immaculate. He opened the door for me and I got in and remarked about it as soon as he got in.

"It's five years old," he said without gratitude for the compliment. It was more like he expected it. "You really have to keep a car about seven years these days to make the most of your investment," he said, and then went on to talk about depreciation schedules.

When we sat in the restaurant and were given our

menus, Clayton reviewed each entrée, explaining the cost and value to me.

"We handle a dozen restaurants," he continued, "so we know what the best values are."

"Why don't you just order for me then," I said dryly and handed the waiter my menu.

"I would be very happy to do that," Clayton said and did. Finally, his conversation turned to something other than assets and liabilities. Or, at least I thought it did when he began to ask me questions about myself, the work I did for my father, and what I did to entertain myself.

Throughout the course of the meal, he glanced at his watch and commented about how we were doing. Most of the time, he concluded we were on schedule, but when the desserts he had ordered took longer than he anticipated, he became a little agitated.

"We really don't have to be there just when it all begins, Clayton," I said. He looked at me as if being late for something was a violation of the eleventh commandment.

"People are known by their sense of responsibility, how well they keep to their schedules," he assured me. "That's why our clients feel confident about doing business with our firm."

"Oh. Well, not everything is business, Clayton."

"In the end," he insisted, "everything is business."

I didn't feel like arguing. We had our desserts and I let him rush me along. He remarked that we had arrived at the gallery two minutes later than he had anticipated, but it would be all right.

"Thank goodness," I said. "I was beginning to worry."

He nodded, missing my sarcasm.

Many of the people who attended knew both Clayton

and me. I saw the look of amusement in their eyes when they realized we were on a date. Many of them had nice things to say about my appearance.

Clayton did appear to know a great deal about art, but he managed to evaluate each piece in terms of its potential market value, deciding which would be a good investment and which wouldn't.

"Maybe some people want to buy it because they like it," I remarked, "and not for how much money it might bring them in twenty years."

"You should always consider what something's going to be worth down the line," he retorted. "No matter what you do from birth to death."

I was beginning to think Clayton Keiser had no emotions, no heart, just a calculator in his chest. However, after what he had planned to be our allotted time at the gallery, he surprised me by asking if I would like to see a piece of property he was considering purchasing.

"I think it's the perfect location for a house," he said. "Just far enough away from people to give you privacy, but not so far that you feel out of touch. And there is a view," he added, "which of course raises its potential value."

"Of course. Yes, I'd like to see it," I said. "Do we have enough time left on our schedule?" I kidded, but he didn't smile.

"I believe so, yes."

We drove about two miles out of Provincetown, south on the highway until he slowed down and made a turn up a side road. It was barely a road, with only a gravel bed, but it ended on land that rose and then sloped down toward the sea. There was a wonderful view of the night sky.

"Well?" he said.

"This is a beautiful place. You're right, Clayton."

"Thank you," he said.

"Should we get out?" I asked after a long silent moment.

"No. It might be muddy or rough out there. You can see it all from here anyway," he replied dryly, but he didn't start the engine. Again, a long silence passed.

"Clayton?" I said.

He turned quickly and before I could react, leaned forward and kissed me. It took me by such surprise I was speechless. I thought I might even laugh. It was the most awkward kiss in history, I thought. He missed my lips and kissed my cheek.

"Olivia Gordon, I do find myself attracted to you," he declared.

"What?"

"I think we could be very successful together."

"Clayton, we've just gone out for the first time and I hardly think . . ."

He lunged at me again, this time seizing my shoulders so he could pull me toward him. His lips fell on my neck. I started to struggle. He held me tightly, surprising me with the strength in his fingers, and then he practically dove at my breasts, pressing his mouth to them and shoving his tongue into my cleavage, the hot wetness nauseating me immediately. He groped at my bosom and maneuvered himself until his weight was on me, his left leg trapping my right leg.

I cried out and continued to struggle, but he pressed on, pushing his pelvis against my hip. I felt his gyrations and heard his quickened breathing and moans. As he lowered more and more of his weight on me, I began to feel like someone drowning, someone being pushed under water.

I managed to get my right hand out from between our bodies where it had been locked against his chest and my own, and I began to pound the top of his head. He didn't seem to mind or to feel it. His movements grew more frenzied until he cried out like a man in pain and collapsed against me.

For a long moment we lay there, motionless. I was afraid to turn or straighten up, afraid he would initiate some new attack on me. His breathing grew more regular.

Then, he suddenly sat up, straightened his tie and wiped back his hair.

"Thank you," he said. "That was very nice."

"Take me home immediately," I said with as much command in my voice as I could muster. I was still so surprised and frightened, I couldn't stop my heart from pounding.

"Of course," he said calmly. "It's just the right time anyway."

He started the engine. I sat as far from him as I could, my shoulder against the door. He turned the car around and drove down the gravel road, not speaking until we were on the highway.

"So," he said, "you like the property. I'm going to buy it this week. I can build us a beautiful home there."

"Not me," I said. "You can't do anything for me."

"Pardon?"

"I don't know how or where you got the idea you and I could ever . . . Just shut up, Clayton. Just take me home."

"Really? I thought . . . Oh. Well, you should give consideration to the value of that property and the potential a marriage would bring to our families and ourselves."

I said nothing until we reached my house. He started

to get out to open my door, but I jumped out of the car and slammed the door before he could come around.

"Good night, Olivia," he said. "Can I see you again?"

"See me again," I said nearly laughing. "I think you're a sick, disgusting individual. I don't want to ever see you again," I said and rushed up the steps and into the house.

Both of my parents were still up, my mother reading, my father watching the late news on television. He lowered the volume immediately after he set eyes on me. Mother put her book on her lap and smiled. A few moments after looking at me, however, that smile evaporated.

"What happened?" Daddy asked, his eyes small. I couldn't hide my emotions from him. Besides, my hair was messed and I looked like I had tumbled down a hill.

"Clayton is an oaf," I replied.

"What happened?" Mother asked, her lips trembling in anticipation.

"He was not the gentleman he pretends to be," I said. "Let's leave it like that. Okay?" I followed looking at Daddy.

"All right," he said. "No harm done, I suppose."

"Fortunately, no," I said and marched up the stairs to my room. When I looked at myself in the mirror and saw how disheveled I looked, how far I was from the pretty, put-together young woman I had been earlier in the evening, I started to cry. Then I sucked in my tears, telling myself this is just what Belinda would do.

Only, . . . Belinda probably wouldn't have put up as much of a battle.

In the days that followed, Daddy never mentioned my date nor asked any questions. Whenever I saw Harrison Keiser, I noticed that he looked away. I imagined Clayton had told a different story, blaming me for the failure of the relationship.

Mother concluded it just wasn't meant to be. Sometimes she had a fatalistic attitude, especially when it came to romance. About five days following my disastrous date, my only date in a year, she stopped at my bedroom and knocked on the opened door.

"How are you doing, Olivia?" she asked and immediately grimaced in anticipation of an unpleasant response.

"I'm all right, Mother."

"I'm sorry your date with Clayton wasn't a success."

"I'm not. I'd hate to imagine what life would be like married to such a creature."

She smiled and sat on my bed. My mother and I had never really had what other daughters called their mother-daughter talks. Most of what I knew about men and about sex I had taught myself. On a number of different occasions, Mother had tried to get into an intimate conversation with me, but neither of us was very successful at it.

"Sometimes," she began this early evening, "I feel to blame for your . . . present situation. I feel I should have done more to help you find someone, Olivia."

"That's silly, Mother."

"No, no, it's not," she insisted. "My mother did a great deal to help me. She was a very understanding, very sensitive woman, a great companion."

"I'll be just fine," I said.

"Of course you will, dear. You are too intelligent not to succeed in every way. I know you're far more intelligent than I am, even more intelligent than your father, although I would never dare tell him that."

I started to protest, but she put up her hand.

"Sometimes, however, it's better for a woman to seem less intelligent, Olivia."

"What?" I started to smile, but saw an expression on her face I hadn't seen before. She looked suddenly wiser, more perceptive.

"Sometimes, a woman can't be as headstrong or as direct as a man. Most of the time, in fact. Instead, she has to be more subtle, a bit of a conniver. You have to learn how to play a man like an instrument to get what you want or get him to do what you want."

I sat back, a bit shocked.

"What are you saying, Mother?"

"That there's a secret to forming and maintaining a good relationship with a man and that secret is simply to let the man think he's always in charge. Whenever I want something, really want something, I manage to get your father to think he wanted it first, that it was his idea. That way, he doesn't feel he's being manipulated, you see."

She leaned toward me and smiled.

"Even though he is."

I snapped back as if a rubber band held me on the seat.

"That's not true, Mother. Daddy knows exactly what he is doing all the time and he never does anything without evaluating the consequences thoroughly."

"Of course, he doesn't," she agreed. "But how he evaluates it and how he reaches a conclusion is my little secret. I think you have to relax more when you're in the company of men, Olivia. You act as if . . ."

"As if what, Mother?"

"As if you have to compete, to win something, to show them up, and men just don't appreciate that in a woman. You have to work on being more subtle."

"Be more like Belinda, is that what you're saying?"

"I suppose, in a way," she admitted, nodding.

"And get pregnant and pop out babies in my room in the middle of the night?" I shot back. She stiffened.

"Of course not, dear. You have to know when to say no, when to be firm."

"As long as you give them the impression it's their idea to stop, too, is that it?"

"Yes," she said.

"Frankly, Mother, I don't want to be that sort of a woman, that sort of a person. I want to always say exactly what I feel and be as honest as possible and if a man can't stand that, he's not the man for me."

"Oh. Pity," she said softly, more to herself than to me.

"I don't think so, Mother."

She looked at me a long moment and then sighed deeply.

"I just want you to be happy, Olivia."

"I will be happy, Mother, but on my own terms, with self-respect," I insisted.

"Very well. You're so smart, Olivia. I'm sure you'll find the right man and make the best wife and marriage."

She stood up and gazed around my room a moment.

"You might do something about brightening your room, dear. Have the walls painted, get new curtains and a new bedspread. It will be easy to get your father to agree to that," she added.

"By making it seem his idea?"

"Yes, exactly."

"I'm fine, Mother. I'm fine as I am," I said.

She nodded and then turned to leave, pausing at the doorway.

"If you ever want to talk, Olivia, I want you to know I'll always want to talk, too."

"Thank you, Mother. I won't die an old maid. I promise," I said.

She smiled as if I had uttered the magic words and then she left.

I gazed at myself in the mirror.

How can you be so certain of that, Olivia Gordon? Who is out there, waiting for a woman like you?

Surely someone, I thought, someone who won't mind that I have brains, too.

I was about to get up and prepare for dinner when I heard Daddy's heavy footsteps on the stairs. I knew he was practically running and I went to the doorway.

"Olivia," he said, "you've got to come with me."

"What is it, Daddy?"

His face was flushed.

"Embarrassment, utter embarrassment. I received a call from the finishing school's chief administrator, Rosemary Elliot, just a little while ago."

"What?"

"Your sister has been expelled for . . . immoral activities."

73

4

Always a Bridesmaid

Daddy and I left without telling Mother any details. Daddy simply said we were going to bring Belinda home. Actually, he didn't know any details either.

"All Mrs. Elliot would say," he told me after we left, "is I must come to take her off the property. She wouldn't discuss the matter over the phone, but would wait for our arrival at her office. It sounds very bad, very bad. What could Belinda have done?" he wondered aloud.

"Knowing Belinda and what she has done recently, anything imaginable," I replied dryly.

Daddy said nothing. We rode in silence for a while.

"What will you do about her now, Daddy?" I asked. "There is still a great deal of summer left and you've got to make plans for the fall. She's not registered in any other school." He sighed and shook his head.

"I don't know, Olivia. What do you suggest?"

"How about the Foreign Legion?"

He almost smiled.

"I guess we'll have to find something for her to do at the office for the remainder of the summer at least," he said.

"Why don't we wait to see what horrible things she has done at the school, Daddy? If it's as bad as they seem to suggest, you might want to put her under house arrest. I'm serious," I said when he glanced at me. "Don't permit her to socialize or go on dates, to the movies, to the beach. She has to learn sometime. You're always telling me to find something worthwhile from every situation, no matter how bad that situation is. Well, do the same here," I concluded.

He was silent again. Why couldn't he agree? Finally, why couldn't he do something about Belinda before she ruined our family?

My own memories of the finishing school returned as we approached the beautiful grounds and buildings. While I was there, I had made only one real friend, Katherine Hargrove from Boston. We studied together, revealed our thoughts about boys and the other girls at the school to each other and promised each other we would stay in touch, but shortly after we left the school, Katherine became engaged to the boy back home her parents had wanted her to marry. I received a few letters and wrote back. She invited me to her wedding, but I didn't attend. I made up some excuse about being too involved with my father's business, and I know she was offended. She wrote no other letters, not even a postcard, never called and never responded to the one letter I wrote months afterward.

How easily friends drift apart, I thought. It was almost as if we became different people once we were apart, and the people we were and whom we knew became strangers to us. I realized I should have been at her wedding, but it bothered me that she was engaged and getting married while I hadn't even struck up an acquaintance. Everyone else at the school had predicted I'd end up an old maid and I knew many of those girls would be there, smiling smugly, convinced their prophecies would prove true. I should have had the courage to face them down, I thought, for Katherine's sake as much as my own.

No, I wasn't perfect. I was capable of making mistakes, but nothing I did ever approached Belinda's errors and sins. She was so much of a problem, I was practically overlooked. Even in our younger days, I found myself neglected, found Daddy paying more attention to her because she was such a handful for our mother. How many intimate father-daughter talks had Belinda enjoyed? How many times had he done what he was doing now: running to her rescue? Yes, I told myself, I did resemble the good child in the Biblical parable of the prodigal son, wondering if being dutiful, productive and responsible wasn't the reason I was being ignored when I needed attention and affection as much Belinda.

We went directly to the administrative building and the head mistress's office. When the secretary saw us, she practically fainted, her blood draining from her face in anticipation of some ugly and unpleasant scene. What could Belinda have possibly done? I wondered, now struggling with my own imagination to think of something that would merit such a reaction.

"Mrs. Elliot will see you," she said a moment after going in and out of the office. She stepped away from the door as if touching us might contaminate her.

Mrs. Elliot, a woman of about sixty with bluish-gray hair and gray eyes, rose from her wooden desk chair. She was only about five feet five, but her demeanor, the power in her eyes, the stiffness in her shoulders and her imposing bosom rising with each deep breath made her look much taller. She had an emphatic chin and strong, masculine, pale red lips, now pressed tightly together in an effort not to frown or scowl.

"Please have a seat, Mr. Gordon," she commanded, gesturing to a chair. She looked at me, deciding whether or not to invite me to stay.

"I'd like Olivia to be here," Daddy said quickly.

"Yes, that will be fine. Olivia was one of our better students. I can understand your reliance upon her. We had expected the same high quality behavior from your younger daughter," she added dryly. "Which makes all this that much more of a disappointment," she continued with her eyes small and dark.

"What happened? Why are you expelling her?" Daddy asked, his body still tense, his hands gripping the arms of the chair so hard the veins were embossed around his knuckles.

"I'll get right to the point, Mr. Gordon, even though this is all quite unpleasant to imagine, much less to discuss. I don't want to pretend everything has always been perfect here at our school. We have had our share of problems. Our girls come from diverse backgrounds and from many places. We're bound to experience some difficulties. After all, we're educating young people, some of whom haven't had the best possible upbringing.

"Girls have had liquor in their rooms, broken curfew, violated no-smoking regulations, not kept their rooms in proper condition. Olivia knows that to be true while she was here herself," she said nodding at me. I nodded quickly. "We have, on occasion, had a male visitor remain too long, but never, never have we had a young girl bring liquor into her room, permit smoking and entertain two young men at the same time all evening," she added without pausing for a breath.

"What?" Daddy asked, as if he hadn't heard anything she'd said. "Entertain two . . ."

"Entertain, you understand, Mr. Gordon, is rather a euphemistic term for what occurred." She looked at me and then back to him. "Both young men were disrobed and in the same bed with your daughter, who was also naked," she said and swallowed as though she had just taken a tablespoon of castor oil.

Daddy stared.

"Both?" he finally said.

"I'm afraid so, Mr. Gordon. Mrs. Landford, the housemother, came upon them herself when she smelled the smoke and heard the laughter. The two young men were quite inebriated and would have been arrested if it weren't for the need to protect the reputation of the school, and, as much as possible, your own good name. However, they were brought before the local magistrate discreetly and given a sentence of probation. They are not from any area school, I might add. They are . . ." She looked at me. ". . . boys from the nearby village. Garage mechanics," she concluded with some difficulty.

"Christ," Daddy said.

"You can understand now why we are all this upset, Mr. Gordon."

Daddy nodded.

"I'd like this all to simply go away and the best method for that is for you to take your daughter home immediately. I'm sorry. This isn't the place for her. We can't do what we did for your daughter Olivia, I'm afraid," she added nodding at me again.

"Where is Belinda now?" Daddy asked. His face was

so red, I thought the top of his head might explode at any moment. I wanted to feel sorry for him, but I kept hearing a voice inside me repeat: *As ye sow, so shall ye reap.*

"She's been confined to quarters and told to pack her things. We would appreciate your taking her home with the least amount of commotion possible, Mr. Gordon. I'm afraid, as you know, there is no refund when a girl is expelled, and under the circumstances, a review board hearing would only exacerbate the situation for you, and for us. I hope you agree about that," she said, her eyebrows hoisted, poised.

"Yes, yes," Daddy said. "Olivia, could you fetch her?" he asked me. "I'll bring the car around to the dormitory."

"Yes, Daddy," I said. Mrs. Elliot smiled at me.

"How are things with you, Olivia? I thought you might attend Boston University," she said. "Are you enrolled there or some similar school?"

"I didn't go on to college, Mrs. Elliot. I decided to help Daddy with his business," I said. She turned to Daddy.

"I'm sure Olivia is a great asset to you, Mr. Gordon."

"Yes, she is," he said in a voice so broken and tired, I didn't recognize it.

"How unfortunate for us all, Mr. Gordon. You have your burden to bear, your own hard road to travel," she said. Daddy nodded and looked to me.

I rose and left the office. The secretary glanced up at me and tried to smile as I hurried past her and out the door of the administrative building. I crossed the campus as quickly as I could. The classrooms were all dark, except for the music suite where the school orchestra was holding a rehearsal. The music was carried by the breeze. It seemed to fit the occasion because it was a march.

About a dozen or so girls were reading, talking and watching television in the lounge at the dormitory. They all looked up when I entered. None knew who I was because I hadn't come here with Belinda, but Mrs. Landford knew me and came hurrying down the corridor the moment she had set eyes on me.

"Hello, Olivia," she said with a small, quick smile. "How are you?"

"Not as well as I could be," I replied. She nodded and then shook her head.

"I'm sorry for your family," she said.

"So am I. Where is she?"

"Right this way." She turned and I followed her down the corridor to the next to last room on the left. "She's all ready," she said and nodded at the side entrance. "You might just want to go out that way."

"Like thieves in the night," I remarked. She took on a pained expression in her dark brown eyes and then knocked on Belinda's door.

"Who is it?"

"It's Mrs. Landford. Your sister is here for you, Belinda," she explained. It took a moment before Belinda opened the door. Just like her to make me wait, I thought. She was in her high-school jacket, the one with all the varsity letters Arnold had given her, and a pair of slacks. Her hair was brushed back and tied and her suitcases were packed and beside the bed.

"Hi, Olivia," she sang as if nothing in the world had happened. "Where's Daddy?"

"In the car, waiting," I said angrily.

"You two take those suitcases and I'll get the two small bags," Mrs. Landford volunteered.

Belinda deliberately took her time, sauntering across the room. I saw the tiny smile on her lips, the look of satisfaction. She was getting what she had wanted all along. I had no doubt she deliberately got caught. I even suspected that she might have engineered the entire disgusting event just for this purpose. I seized the suitcase.

"Let's go," I ordered. "Now."

"Well then, fine," Belinda said taking the other suitcase in hand. "I certainly don't want to stay here a moment more than I have to," she quipped as if she were the one who had demanded to leave.

Mrs. Landford followed us out the side door. Daddy was sitting in the car, staring ahead. When he saw us coming, he jumped out quickly and opened the trunk. I handed him the first suitcase.

"Hi, Daddy," Belinda said handing him the other. He said nothing. He took it and then the bags Mrs. Landford was carrying.

"Get in the back, Belinda," he ordered and she did so, pausing before she closed the door and turning to Mrs. Landford.

"Good-bye, Mrs. Landford. I'm sorry if I caused you any embarrassment."

"If?" I said. "If?"

Belinda widened her smile and got into the car.

"Good luck, dear," Mrs. Landford told me, squeezed my hand and returned to the dormitory. I turned to Daddy, half expecting him to go into some sort of rage, but he just shook his head.

"Let's just go," he said and hurried around to get into the car.

He didn't say a word until we left the grounds and were heading for the highway.

"So, Belinda, are you satisfied?" he asked.

"I hated that place, Daddy. I told you I did. I don't care about being expelled."

"How could you . . ." He stopped himself and pressed

81

his lips together as if he had to lock the words back into his throat.

"What were you thinking, Belinda?" I asked. "Didn't you care what this would do to our family's reputation? No matter what, this is going to get out. The other girls will tell their families and friends."

"They're no better. They're all a bunch of stuffy snobs, but they all do things, too. They just don't get caught," she said in her own defense.

"Right. I'm sure they're all exactly like you," I commented dryly.

"Well, they are!"

"Never mind," Daddy finally said. "I don't want your mother knowing about this. When we get home, you'll simply tell her . . . you were unhappy there."

"That's not a lie," Belinda followed.

"Of course it's a lie," I charged. "It's not why you're being brought home."

"Well, you lie sometimes, Olivia. You're not a perfect angel," she wailed.

"The difference, Belinda, is you're comfortable with a lie." I turned and looked back at her. "I'm not. Your life is practically one big fat lie."

"I knew it. I knew you'd hate me now," she moaned. "Just stop the car and let me out on the road somewhere. I'll find a new home and a new family."

"To terrorize and destroy?" I asked.

"No. Just stop the car!"

"Let's not do this," Daddy said. "It only prolongs the agony and we've got to think about your mother, Olivia. Please."

"Sure," I said. "Let's sweep something else under the carpet and let her get away with another gross act. We're not doing her any good, Daddy," I insisted.

"I'll take care of it," he said. It was an empty promise.

I could almost hear the echo inside it. But I let him hold on to it, and I simply stared out the window most of the way home. Belinda fell asleep in the back, a tight smile of content and satisfaction on her face. Once again, she had gotten what she had wanted.

Whether Mother could see through the falsehoods or not, she went along with it. She even felt sorry for poor Belinda, who ate up the sympathy, milking the situation and taking advantage until I glared so angrily at her, she stopped and went to her room. The next day Daddy concluded that the only thing to do, at least for the time being, was to find her something to do at the office.

"At least we'll be able to keep an eye on her most of the time that way," he reasoned. I joined him in his den without Mother present.

"What can she do, Daddy?"

"Put her to work filing, Olivia."

"Filing?"

"Find work, make work, keep her occupied. Please," he pleaded. "Sending her off to another school is just going to be a waste of time and money. She's not a student."

"What do you expect from her then?" I asked.

"I expect . . . hope to find her a suitable husband as soon as possible," he replied.

Before me? I wanted to ask. You want to get her off and married in her own home before me?

"You mean pass off the responsibility to some poor, unsuspecting clod," I chimed.

"She has some qualities to recommend her, Olivia. She is an attractive young woman. Don't you think she might grow up a little now?"

"No," I said firmly. "Not as long as you insist on excusing her every act of misconduct."

He stared at me and then sighed.

"Please, please don't make this any more difficult for us than it is, Olivia," he pleaded.

Why was he like this? Where was the strong, firm man who ran a string of businesses with such authority and assurance? Maybe Mother was right, maybe Daddy was like all the other men, easy to manipulate after all. Maybe my mother was the smarter of the two.

"You're being had, Daddy," I said uncharitably. "You're a fool for believing her tears and her moans and her batting eyelashes."

He turned white before the blood rushed back into his face.

"That's not true, Olivia. It's what I've told you before, what I've tried to get you to understand above all . . . family, family is the most important thing. We've got to protect her because she is the weak link. I was hoping you would have grasped all that by now and be my true assistant in this," he said.

"All right, Daddy," I relented. "I'll try to find her something to do, try again to make her into someone respectable and responsible."

"That's more like it, Olivia. Now you're being a true Gordon," he said.

However, it took a lot more than my resigning myself to Daddy's logic to make any of this even come close to resulting in what he wanted. Belinda, of course, enthusiastically agreed to go to work at the office, but every morning, she refused to wake up in time. Every morning I had to be the one to wake her and prod her into dressing herself quickly. Most mornings Daddy had to leave without me and I had to drive myself and Belinda to the office. She was always half awake when she arrived, moaning and complaining about getting up so early.

"If we own the business, why do we have to keep such dumb hours?" she demanded.

"Precisely because we own the business, Belinda. If we don't look after it, who will? The other employees don't have our interest at heart. This is what it means to be responsible and successful," I lectured, but my lectures, just like the ones she had gotten all her life from her teachers, went in one ear, were twirled around until they were so mixed up they made no sense, and then were dumped out of the other ear.

She moped and moved through the office like a somnambulist, doing in hours what it would take any other person minutes to accomplish. Anything distracted her. She could spend an hour gazing out the window. She was on the telephone with her friends every chance she got, despite my repeated warnings and my constant chastising. Each time I reprimanded her, she would cry and go running to Daddy who would then ask me to go a little easier on her.

"Go easier?" I cried. "Even the little work she does has to be redone. She misplaces files, gets them out of alphabetical order, loses documents . . . she's doing it deliberately, Daddy. It's the same old game. She wants to be home and loose and allowed to indulge herself in entertainments and not do any work, so she does it badly and hopes you'll give up on her."

"I know," he said. "Please have a little more patience with her. Keep trying," he urged.

Once again, I wondered why. What was it about her that made Daddy so soft, so pliable and so forgiving? If I came close to asking such a question, he merely shook his head and begged me to keep hoping and believing and trying to make her a better person.

Daddy hadn't forgotten his intention to marry her off

85

as soon as possible. The attempt he had made to arrange a relationship between me and Clayton was completely forgotten, however. I was put on the perennial back burner and Belinda was moved up to the front. It wasn't something he made obvious, however. It was just like fishing. He cast his bait and hoped the right fish would be caught on the right line.

The first big attempt came when the Childs were invited to a most elegant dinner at our home, far more involved than the dinner party that had been designed to snare Clayton for me. Colonel Childs was Daddy's attorney and his son Nelson was finishing his last year of law school. No better fish swam in our waters, and I was beginning to think no better shark than Belinda swam in them as well.

Four or five times a year, Daddy would host an elaborate dinner party, usually inviting ten to fifteen guests, hiring a service staff, and having a caterer prepare an elaborate, six-course dinner. Sometimes, there was even entertainment: a pianist or violinist for after dinner. Belinda always hated these parties. They were far too formal and far too restricting for her. She had to behave properly, follow proper etiquette and keep from doing or saying silly things. She never liked the music, never liked sitting quietly and being obedient. Usually, Mother or Daddy excused her before the evening was half over and she retreated to her room to gossip on the telephone.

I realized something more than usual was intended when I discovered Daddy had only invited the Colonel and his family to dinner. I knew the Colonel well, of course. He was at our offices often for one matter or another. Daddy was involved in so many business enterprises these days, there was always some legal question or problem to be addressed. On a half dozen social occasions, I had met his wife Elizabeth, an attractive, stately woman from one of New England's finest families. They had only one child, Nelson, who took after his mother in height and his father in good looks.

Nelson Childs was one of those Adonises who glide through high school on a magic carpet, successful in studies, in sports and in social life. He always looked well put together, organized, relaxed. Teachers favored and admired him. He was polite, obedient, and yet far from being thought a teacher's pet. He commanded the respect of his peers and was elected class president, captain of his basketball and baseball teams, and the winner of the school's best male citizen award at graduation.

We were nearly five years apart, but it might just as well have been a decade. Even though his father was my father's attorney, Nelson barely recognized my existence in school or anywhere else for that matter. He probably couldn't see me over the heads of the girls who gathered around him like bridesmaids hoping to catch the bouquet of his attention and go on to be his girlfriend, his date, or merely the object of his immediate interest.

His eyes were more hazel than brown and the few times that I was close enough to see, I thought there were specks of gold in them as well. He kept his light brown hair short, but with a little pompadour to give it some shape and style. He did have an electric smile, his face brightening with a glow that warmed the target of that smile. Cupid, as far as I was concerned, rode on Nelson's shoulders, directing arrows just for his own impish amusement.

Somehow Nelson navigated these amorous waters

without smudging his good name. He never went steady and yet never made any lasting feminine enemies playing the field. It was as though all the girls he dated understood he was beyond being captured. He would never belong to just one girl; he belonged to them all.

I began to eavesdrop on the Colonel and Daddy's conversations whenever Nelson's name was mentioned. I knew that he was in his last year of law school and yet had not met anyone who had won his romantic interest. The expectation was Nelson would graduate, pass his bar exams and work in his father's firm. All that was left to plan was his family; then he would begin a perfect existence, just as his father had.

My memories of Nelson and my understandings acquired from listening in on the conversations about him made me question the wisdom and reality of Daddy's plan. What would a man like Nelson Childs want with a dizzy, frivolous, conceited young woman like my sister Belinda? Daddy was not only wasting his money on this sort of dinner for that sort of purpose, he was wasting everyone's time. Belinda, I thought, would first be intimidated by a man with as much intelligence as Nelson, and second, would never want to settle down with anyone so firm and organized in his own beliefs. Why couldn't Daddy see that?

My memories of Nelson Childs were overwhelmed by his actual appearance the evening of the dinner. For me, although I tried not to show it, it was as if a celebrity I had only seen on television, in the movies, or in magazines, suddenly set foot in my home. Time away at school had matured him. He looked like a man of substance already, a young man with stature, personable and accomplished.

Mother was charmed. Daddy beamed at the prospects

and Belinda was titillated when Nelson was introduced to her before he was introduced to me. When he did turn my way, he smiled and laughingly recalled me in junior high.

"Yes, I remember you. You were such a serious little girl," he said. Belinda enjoyed that.

"She still is," she said. "Everyone calls her Miss Cold and calls me Miss Hot."

"Really?" He stared at her a moment with interest that made me envious.

"Only Belinda's bubble-gum friends say those things," I remarked.

"Bubble gum?" he asked, turning to me.

"Bubbles for brains," I muttered and he laughed.

Our parents went into the sitting room for cocktails and hors d'oeuvres, while we were left to show Nelson our house. He lingered about Daddy's books in the library, commenting on how good a collection it was.

"I've never read one of them," Belinda bragged as though that were an accomplishment.

I grimaced in anticipation of Nelson's reaction, but he simply laughed.

"Well, if they say a little learning is a dangerous thing, then Belinda is not in any danger," he declared.

I laughed when Belinda did, thinking she doesn't understand that he's really making fun of her. Or was he? His gaze lingered on her when she laughed. Her laugh was musical and she had a way of brightening her eyes and making her face glow that caused her to stand out, no matter where we were. It was as if a candle of femininity had been placed within her silly heart and lit to burn brightly and be reflected in the eyes of every man who gazed at her with interest.

"What are your interests, Belinda?" he asked.

"Interests?"

"He means what do you do with your free time, Belinda? Which is really, most of your day now. Belinda just does some light filing at the office," I revealed, hoping to stop his curiosity at the gate and show him quickly that Belinda was someone with very limited ability.

"I hate it too," she said quickly and he laughed again. "Summers are for fun, not for work. No one our age should have to work in the summer," she declared.

"Most people are not as fortunate as we are, Belinda, and have to work to make money to live and go to school," I reminded her.

She shrugged as if I had said something so insignificant it didn't require a response.

"Well, we're fortunate. You just said so yourself, so why work?" she countered. Nelson laughed again.

"She's incorrigible," I said. He nodded.

"Yes."

"Is that bad?" Belinda asked. Nelson thought a moment.

"Maybe not," he said. "Maybe it's refreshing once in a while." He looked at me quickly. "I understand not for you and your family, however, Olivia."

Now it was my turn to shrug.

"What she does with her life now is no longer important to me," I said. "I've given up."

"She doesn't mean that. She's always saying awful things she doesn't mean," Belinda explained.

Nelson nodded as though he understood.

We were called to dinner and Nelson gallantly stepped up between us and took both our arms to escort us into the dining room. All the while I kept telling myself, a man like this would only be temporarily amused by

someone like Belinda. Surely, he wants someone substantial, someone like me.

Daddy had the table arranged so that Nelson sat
between Belinda and me. Belinda spent a good deal of
the time giggling and whispering in Nelson's ear. Mother
tried to reprimand her with stern looks now and then,
but Daddy had made the mistake of permitting her to
have two glasses of wine. It made her giddy.

The conversation at the table went from politics to
fashion. When Nelson spoke, everyone listened. He had
a charismatic air about him, a commanding presence
and an eloquence of language. I found myself agreeing
with most everything he had to say and let him know it.
He did seem to appreciate that and for a while, his
attention was on me far more than it was on Belinda,
who, as I had expected, even hoped, grew bored and
restless.

However, she surprised me when the dinner ended
and coffee was going to be served.

"I don't want to drink coffee. Why don't we take a
walk on the beach instead," she proposed.

Nelson considered.

"Not a bad idea. It is a very warm evening," he said.
He glanced at me and I saw he was going to do it.

"It would be nice," I chimed, reluctantly giving
Belinda credit for a good suggestion.

We excused ourselves. Daddy looked very pleased. I
could see he thought his plan was working. As we started
out of the dining room, he leaned over to whisper.

"What a perfect match, huh Olivia? A perfect way to
solve our little problem," he said.

I gazed at him and then, in clear, sharp tones replied,
"I thought the Colonel was your good friend, Daddy.
How could you do this to him?"

The smile left his face as if I had slapped him.

"She's not a bad catch, Olivia. She's the prettiest girl in Provincetown," he said.

I felt my heart close like a small fist had wrapped around it and squeezed so hard, it put a pain in my chest. Tears froze beneath my lids. I swallowed and nodded.

"Right," I said. "I forgot."

I turned and caught up with Belinda and Nelson just outside the door on their way to the path that led down to the beach.

It was a glorious night with so many stars the sky looked like it was filled with thousands and thousands of glass chips glittering down to the edge of the world. The air was warm and more humid than usual, too.

"Look at the stars!" Belinda declared. "Isn't that the Big Dipper?"

"Where?" Nelson stepped up beside her and she pointed, leaning against him. "No, that's the Little Dipper. Over there," he said, physically turning her, "is the Big Dipper."

"I didn't even know there was a Little Dipper, too. Did you, Olivia?"

"Of course," I said.

"Don't you just love the way the stars glitter on the water?" Belinda followed, not even taking note of my response. She seized Nelson's hand and tugged. "Come on, let's take off our shoes and run on the sand."

"What?"

"That's ridiculous, Belinda. He's wearing nice shoes and . . ."

"No, it's all right," Nelson said laughing. "I think I might enjoy it."

He sat beside her and pulled off his shoes and socks. Then he looked at me.

"Aren't you joining us, Olivia?"

"I know how cold that water is," I said.

"No, it's not," Belinda said leaping to her feet.

"Belinda used to be terrified of the ocean," I said.

"Well, I'm not anymore," she cried. "I have to step into it once in a while to cool off, remember? I'm Miss Hot."

Nelson laughed and she tugged on his hand again. I watched as the two of them went running down to the surf.

"You're going to get soaked," I shouted, but the roar of the sea drowned out my voice. Reluctantly, I slipped off my shoes and socks and drew closer to them.

Belinda squealed and continued to splash and run with Nelson clinging to her hand. His laughter trailed out to sea. Suddenly, Belinda stopped. We were a good thousand yards from the house and before us, the beach was dark, deserted.

"It's so warm and the water's not really cold, is it?" Belinda asked.

"No," Nelson said. "Surprisingly, it isn't." He looked back at me.

"It's not exactly a bathtub," I said.

"I'm going in," Belinda suddenly declared.

"What?" Nelson's face glittered in the starlight, his smile soft, gentle.

"Skinny dipping. Haven't you ever done that?"

"Belinda!" I cried. "Don't you dare."

"Oh, I don't mean right down to naked," she said. "You can't see much out here anyway. Haven't you ever gone skinny dipping, Nelson?" she challenged.

"Oh, sure, but . . ."

"Don't look unless you're coming in after me," she declared and unbuttoned her blouse.

"Belinda, stop that this instant," I ordered. She peeled off her blouse and quickly undid her skirt. A moment later, she was standing in her bra and panties.

"Here goes," she screamed and ran toward the waves. Nelson looked at me.

"What do you say?" he asked.

"Absolutely not. I'm going back to the house," I said, my heart pounding.

"It does look inviting," he said, nodded to himself and then took off his shirt.

I stared, amazed as he slipped out of his pants, not at all inhibited by my presence. Then he called to Belinda and charged at the sea. I watched the two of them splashing and frolicking in the water. She threw herself into his arms and they both sank for a moment, re-emerging and laughing like two teenagers. I was fascinated, jealous and angry all at the same time.

"If you're not coming in, maybe you can get us some towels," he called.

"Yes, Olivia. That would be nice."

Belinda stood in the water, the starlight making her bosom glimmer. Her panties had become transparent, and Nelson's shorts didn't offer much coverage either.

"All right," I shouted. "I'll be right back."

I hurried through the darkness, slipping on the sand, cursing Belinda under my breath. When I reached the house, I was careful to enter and get to the laundry room without being noticed. I gathered up some towels and rushed out, feeling like a co-conspirator. By the time I returned, they were both out of the water, sitting very close to each other.

"Hurry, we're freezing," Belinda cried.

"I don't doubt it. You'll both probably get pneumonia or something."

"We'll be fine," Nelson said. I tried not to look at him when I handed him the towel and cast one at Belinda.

"Better get out of the wet stuff," Nelson said moving off a bit. He wrapped the towel around himself and slipped his underpants off. Belinda, not as modest, took off her bra and panties. I stood between her and Nelson and handed her clothing to her as quickly as I could.

"Anyone can look at either of you and see you've been in the water," I said after they were both dressed.

"Let's go up to my room and dry our hair," Belinda suggested.

The two of them hurried toward the house, me following behind, feeling like a third wheel. Up in Belinda's room, I watched the two of them dry their hair. Belinda went into the bathroom and put on another pair of panties and a bra.

"Just keep these here for me," he told her handing her his wet underpants. "Until they're dry."

"I can put them in the dryer downstairs," I suggested.

"No problem. I'm fine," he said. He looked at Belinda. Her eyes were dazzling with excitement and laughter. "That was great," he said. "Never thought one of my parents' dinner parties would be this exciting. Thanks."

He turned to me.

"Well, I guess we'd better show our faces and pretend all is well. How do I look?"

"Fine," I said reluctantly.

"I'll be down in a moment," Belinda chimed.

Nelson and I left and started to descend the stairway. We could hear our parents talking loudly in the sitting room.

"You're sister's terrific," he said.

"You don't have to live with her," I replied. He laughed.

"Yeah, I bet she's a handful, huh?"

"A handful is an understatement," I told him.

He laughed again.

He was smart enough to see my point. I was sure. But did it matter?

Men were blind. Some, deliberately, I thought.

5

Going to the Chapel

If any of our parents had noticed Nelson and Belinda had gone swimming, they made no mention of it before the evening ended. After Belinda came downstairs, she and Nelson were hungry again, probably from their frolicking in the water, and they had dessert and coffee. I just had some coffee. Nelson and I did most of the talking, discussing politics, Cape Cod and business. There was no music after dinner, no entertainment this time, so after we were finished, Colonel Childs declared it was time for him and his family to go. Nelson had to go back to law school early in the morning.

At the door Nelson told Belinda and me he would look in on us when he returned. Daddy gazed at me with some excitement in his eyes, but I shook my head. After Mother went upstairs with Belinda, Daddy pulled me aside in his office.

"Well? How did they get along?" he asked.

I thought a moment and then flopped into the leather chair adjacent to his desk.

"Dreadfully, as I expected," I said. "She made a fool of herself as usual."

"What?" Daddy sat behind his desk. "What happened? They seemed to be getting along so well at dinner."

"She wanted to go for that walk on the beach, but she had something else up her sleeve, Daddy. She pulled off her clothes and challenged him to go swimming with her."

"Pulled off her clothes?"

"I was so embarrassed, I thought I would die."

"Oh no," Daddy said, his face losing its robust color put there from all the wine he had drunk.

"Oh yes. I kept trying to get her to behave, but it was no use. Belinda will always be Belinda, Daddy. We might as well accept it."

He nodded, sadly.

"Well, I tried. I had an idea and I tried." He looked up at me, his eyes glassy. "I'm tired. Let's get some sleep," he said.

"Don't worry, Daddy. You'll figure something out yet," I said. He smiled quickly and patted me on the shoulder.

"Right, right," he said.

"As I suspected, Nelson Childs is looking for a woman of some substance," I added as I left the office. "Belinda just isn't right for him."

"I see," Daddy muttered behind me, but he never suggested or assumed Nelson would be a good prospect for me. His attention was committed solely to Belinda as usual. "However, I'm not about to give up. I have something else up my sleeve," Daddy said.

I turned on the stairway.

"What?"

"Give me a few days to work out the details," he

replied cryptically. I thought he meant he was going to come up with some other approach to getting Belinda and Nelson Childs together, but he had an entirely different prospect lined up, and this one was, in his terms, "more sensible from a business standpoint." Also, he thought it might help if we held one of our formal family meetings and he proposed the idea to Belinda himself.

"So we can avoid any further misunderstandings and bad behavior," he explained when three days later, he announced his decision to have the meeting.

"You might as well wish for the whole world, Daddy, if you're going to wish for no further bad behavior from Belinda."

"We'll see. We'll see," he said, his eyes firm with determination.

From time to time, Daddy held these sessions to talk about our family, our business, our home and our lives. Mother even kept notes as he wished so he could look to her when he wanted to refer to something he had previously announced or asked. The journal she kept was our family history, as far as he was concerned. Mother entered all our important dates in it, birthdays, confirmations, vaccinations, childhood illnesses, graduations, and other significant events. Keeping the record of our lives was something very important to Daddy. It made us seem more like a country unto ourselves.

I finally decided I had better have a conversation with Belinda about Nelson Childs just to see if she had hopes of ever being romantically involved with him. Nelson hadn't called or returned as he had promised, but trying to figure out what Belinda was thinking at any particular time was like trying to harness the wind.

I went into her room and brought up the subject as she was getting ready for bed.

"Nelson?" she said, tossing his name as if she had known him intimately for years. "Hardly." She gazed dreamily at herself in the mirror, fluffed her hair and then, with a painful grimace, studied a pale blemish on her chin.

"Yes, Nelson Childs."

"I don't think about him much," she said with annoyance. "I don't think he would be that much fun."

"What do you mean?" I was still suspicious. She could easily have contacted him without my knowing. "You sure enjoyed yourself with him at dinner the other night, getting down to your underwear and swimming in the moonlight."

"Oh that. Big deal," she said. She turned to me. "It's not the first time I've done something like that. It seemed like fun and he wanted to do it."

"Why don't you think about him now then?"

"He's too . . . career minded. All he talked about when you left to get us our towels was his school and his plans for being a successful politician. He thinks he's going to be President of the United States someday. I thought he could be a little boring and told him so," she added. "Just like he was with you when we had chocolate cake, remember?"

I was astounded. With as much concern as she might have for throwing away an old magazine, she could cast off a catch as good as Nelson Childs. And because he was boring? Nelson Childs could never be boring, I thought. She was the one who was boring.

"Let me understand this. On the beach, after you two had gone swimming, you told him you thought he was boring?"

"Yes, I did."

"And what did he do?"

"He just laughed. He laughed at everything I said and

did. So you see, I'm sure he doesn't think all that much of me. He hasn't called me, has he? You mailed his underwear to his school and he didn't even call to thank us, did he?"

She was right about that. I was very disappointed he hadn't responded. I had taken great pains to pack the garment so no one would ask any embarrassing questions.

"Frankly, I don't care if he does call or comes around again. I don't want to think about him."

"Fine," I told her. "Don't think about him."

She turned from the mirror.

"Why are you getting so angry about it?" She stared at me a moment and then smiled. "You like him, don't you, Olivia?" she said. "You finally fell in love with someone!"

"That's not true."

"Yes, it's true. Sure, it's true. My sister is in love," she declared to her mirror image as if it proved I was just like her. "Do you dream of him, fantasize about being with him? Why don't you call him? Why don't you go visit him at his school?" she asked, still looking at herself. It was as though she were talking to herself.

"You don't chase after men like that, Belinda," I snapped. "And I didn't say I was in love with him. You did."

"You are," she said confidently and turned back to me. "So what? Why hide it? I never do whenever I fall in love. And why can't you chase after a man? What makes them so special?"

"It's not that they're special. We're special. That's why we shouldn't act so desperate. I swear, talking to you is like talking to . . . a four-year-old sometimes."

"Don't get upset with me just because I know you have a crush on Nelson Childs."

"I don't!" I screamed.

"Yes, you do. I might just tell him myself one day."

"If you do anything like that, Belinda Gordon, I'll personally rip out your tongue," I threatened.

She smiled impishly, her eyes full of glee.

"Belinda, I'm warning you."

"Okay, okay," she said, but she didn't stop teasing me for days, doing things like pretending at the office that Nelson was on the telephone, or by writing N.C. on my notepads. No matter how I swore or glared at her, she simply laughed. "The Little General's in love," she sang.

I told Daddy about her antics at the office, but he didn't chastise her. Instead, he bought her a songbird in a gilded cage. She had wanted one for some time. It seemed that no matter what she did or how she behaved, Daddy always rained gifts on her, whereas he simply gave me a substantial salary. His justification was I could buy myself whatever I wanted. Belinda couldn't, but whose fault was that if not her own?

I knew Daddy had an ulterior motive when he bought her the bird, but I predicted the bird would either starve to death or die of some other form of neglect.

"It will not," Belinda retorted. "It will be very happy living in my room, a room full of sunshine even on rainy days. Won't it, Mommy?"

"Yes, dear," Mother replied like some windup toy whose button had been pressed.

Nevertheless, Belinda had to be reminded to clean out the cage and feed the bird every day thereafter, finally complaining and asking why the maid couldn't do it as well as everything else.

The following Tuesday night, Daddy declared we would have the family meeting after dinner. There were important things to discuss.

"Oh, not another one of those dreadful meetings,"

Belinda cried at the dinner table. "I didn't do anything wrong, Daddy. Did someone say I did?" she asked, glaring my way.

"It's not about anyone doing anything wrong," he said.

"Did we spend too much on clothes again?" she asked looking to Mother.

From Daddy's expression, I could see he knew nothing about that.

"Let's just wait until after dinner, Belinda," Mother replied quickly. Whatever she had spent on Belinda, she didn't want Daddy thinking about it now. "It's better for the digestion if we don't discuss heavy matters while we eat."

"Why do we have to discuss any heavy matters at all?" she whined. "Men like to discuss heavy matters, but women shouldn't have to."

"That's a ridiculous thing to say. Women aren't any less intelligent, Belinda. In many cases they're more intelligent," I told her.

"Who wants to be more intelligent?" she muttered.

Belinda pouted and deliberately only nibbled at her food, but I was intrigued. Daddy hadn't yet told me the details of what he was going to discuss. I knew only that it had something to do with Belinda's future, another solution, perhaps, but Daddy had kept his plan to himself.

We gathered in his den-office as usual, Belinda and I seated on the red leather settee, Mother in the leather chair to Daddy's right, her notebook opened, pen in hand, waiting.

"You have today's date?" he asked her.

"Yes, Winston."

"Good. Then we'll bring the meeting to order. All of us understand that it becomes necessary from time to time to make some sacrifices, to make some efforts for the good of the family," he began.

"I hate it when he says that," Belinda muttered. "It usually means he wants us to do something hard."

"Shh, dear," Mother said. She remained poised to write down the important words.

"Just like days of old when kings and queens thought about gaining power and wealth, they would think hard about the marriages of their children and how those marriages could benefit the family, the kingdom," he continued. "Well, the most successful families today think the same way. Nothing's changed in that regard.

"Belinda," he continued, turning to her, "you know Carson McGil, Daniel McGil's son, the one who went to private school. I know you do because he's spoken to you a few times just recently, hasn't he?" he asked before she could offer a response to the first remark.

Belinda shot a glance at me and then looked at Daddy.

"I didn't do anything bad with him, Daddy. He just offered to buy me something cold to drink and then I went for a walk with him on the dock."

"Apparently he was quite taken with you. He came to my office a few days ago to speak to me about you," Daddy continued. Neither I nor Belinda had seen Carson there. I looked skeptically at Daddy, but he ignored my expression. "A fine young man, outstanding, proper. He asked me if he could ask you for your hand in marriage." Daddy added quickly.

"What?" Belinda said.

"He wants to marry you," I translated. She sat there with her mouth open.

"Carson McGil wants to marry me?" She was about to laugh, but Daddy scowled.

"Yes, and I thought it would be a fine match. He's

going to inherit his father's cannery business and we're talking about a merger with one of our enterprises."

Belinda looked at me again, this time for some support, but I just stared at her without much expression and certainly no sympathy.

"I'm not in love with Carson McGil and even if I was, I'm not ready to marry anyone," she said.

"Why not?" Daddy demanded.

"I'm just not."

"Of course you are. You're an attractive young lady with enough to satisfy any good man."

"Olivia's not even engaged," she pointed out quickly.

"Olivia's developing a career at the moment. She'll be right behind you, I'm sure," Daddy insisted. He gazed at me and then quickly shifted his eyes back to Belinda. "I'd like you to give this serious consideration, Belinda. The young man would like to court you," Daddy followed with those eyes of intimidation, his shoulders rising.

"Court me?"

"Romance you," I said with a small smile. "Get you to fall in love with him."

"That's exactly right and you'll fall in love with him, I'm sure," Daddy insisted. "How could you not? He's good-looking and very intelligent. He'll make you a devoted husband."

Belinda looked totally confused and I was enjoying every moment of it.

"It's the best thing that could happen to you, my dear, and it will help the family a great deal. Does everyone agree?" He looked at Mother.

"Yes," she said. "I think it would be fine for Belinda to get married."

"So do I," I chimed. Belinda looked like she had been struck in the head. She gazed at Mother and Daddy and then at me before looking down, a strange smile on her face.

"I don't know the first thing about being a wife," she said. "I can't cook, sew, clean, keep books and I don't have any patience for children."

"Really?" I said. "That's really too bad considering you almost had one."

There was a dead silence.

"We're not supposed to talk about that," she finally said.

"So don't," I followed. "Mother, you can put down that I agreed with Daddy. Carson McGil would make a wonderful husband for Belinda and it would help our family. I know we've been in a negotiation with his father for most of the year."

"Belinda? Will you agree to let him come court you?" Daddy asked.

Belinda looked at the ceiling and sighed.

"I suppose," she said. "But if he doesn't like me, don't blame me," she added.

"Then it's settled," Daddy said. "I'll get back to him and he'll call you. He's a fine young man, distinguishing himself in his business. Don't throw away a good opportunity for yourself," Daddy warned.

"We could have an old-fashioned sort of wedding, a ceremony behind the house, couldn't we?" Mother asked.

"I don't see why not," Daddy said. "Why don't you work up a preliminary guest list, dear, and as the time draws closer, we'll review it."

"How can you plan my wedding? I didn't fall in love yet!" Belinda exclaimed.

"To be honest, Belinda, love is something that happens after a wedding, real love that is," Daddy said.

"Just keep thinking of what you can do for the family and you'll see, it will all work out for the best." He clapped his hands and declared the meeting over.

Belinda was numbed by Daddy's announcement. A part of her wanted to be outraged and indignant that such an important aspect of her life would be dictated to her; but then there was that vain face smiling back at her from her mirrors, fanning the flames of her ego by convincing her that she was so worthwhile a catch, men would come to her father to plead for the chance to get her to fall in love with them. I realized quickly that she saw it as a form of an audition. If Carson didn't work out, there would soon be someone else knocking on the door.

"I really feel bad that Daddy expects I will marry before you do, Olivia," she told me that night. "It's almost as if my beauty is a curse, I suppose."

"That's all right," I said swallowing back my laughter. "I'll survive."

"Carson has become a very nice-looking young man. Have you seen him recently?" she asked.

"No, but I don't get out as much as you do, Belinda. If you say he's good-looking, I'm sure he is."

"Daddy's so worried about me," she muttered. She thought a moment. "I'll try and see what happens," she concluded with a sigh so deep, I thought she would deflate and collapse.

"Do that," I said.

Satisfied now that she was dating Carson because she wanted to, Belinda welcomed him warmly when he came courting. Carson was an only child, spoiled and protected from the day he was born. His parents decided he would attend private schools from kindergarten on, and so he knew few of the young people in the community. I had met him on two different occasions and found him stuffy and conceited.

He was somewhat effeminate with his long eyelashes, his very long, soft hands and his slim, six-foot one-inch frame. He had dark brown hair, greenish-brown eyes and perfectly shaped lips. I thought he had a better complexion than most girls I knew. I knew most would kill for his eyelashes.

The second time I met him, I told Mother I thought he had been brought up by a textbook. Everything he wore always matched perfectly. He always said the right things, the proper things. In short, he was nearly the diametric opposite of Belinda, which made the prospect of such a union even more amusing to me.

However, Belinda enjoyed being the center of everyone's attention now, and especially enjoyed leading Carson about on an invisible leash. She beamed when he opened doors for her and pulled out her chair for her at dinner. She was even more flamboyant than usual when she was brought to restaurants or gala affairs in his Rolls Royce. Now that she was being courted by such a gallant prospect, she insisted she needed more expensive clothing and real jewelry. Daddy put up very little opposition when Belinda and Mother went on one of Belinda's frequent shopping sprees to Boston so she could have just the right thing to wear to some event Carson was taking her to.

From what I could see, Carson was dazzled by her. Most of the girls he knew or pursued were not impressed by him, despite his perfect behavior and good looks, yet here he was winning the heart of one of the town's most beautiful, eligible young women. Belinda saw where and how she could take advantage of him and soon was treating him more like a golden retriever, sending him on

errands, having him fetch this and that, making him
jump with a look or a gesture.

And when he asked her to marry him, giving her a
diamond big enough to pop eyes, she waved it about like
a flag, never sitting without pressing her palm to her
cheek so the ring was obvious to everyone around her
and never wearing gloves.

Mother began to plan the wedding and Daddy felt like
he had succeeded in reaching the most important goal of
his life: soon, soon, Belinda would be another man's
responsibility. As for Belinda, she surprised me by her
apparent enjoyment of every aspect: the announcements
in the social columns, the invitations to the formal
dinners, the adulation and attention.

"I'm finally respectable," she told me one night. "And
you thought it would never be."

She laughed and went off to prepare to go to dinner
with Carson.

However, something gnawed at my walls of compla-
cency until suspicions began to slip out and tickle my
imagination. I watched Belinda and Carson together
more closely. Yes, he doted on her, but Belinda usually
got bored with someone like this quickly, I thought. She
was tolerating him more than I would have expected.
She was being too cooperative for Daddy. Something,
the little voice inside me warned, was amiss.

The truth was I often gazed at her and Carson and
thought to myself she could devour him in minutes. She
teased him often; she made him do silly things; she
laughed at things he said and whenever she kissed him,
or stroked him with affection, it resembled the affection
a sister might give a brother. Certainly, they had not
reached the stage of love Belinda was accustomed to
reaching in a relationship, I thought. I doubted that they
had been to bed and when I asked her about it, she

laughed and told me, "Carson believes a man and a woman should not sleep together until they're married."

"And what did you say to that?" I asked.

"I told him that's what I believe," she said.

"So he believes you're a virgin?"

"Olivia! Of course he does. Why shouldn't he?"

Why shouldn't he? I thought. I'm sure your name's on bathroom walls, dear sister. What about your old boy-friends and the one who made you pregnant? Carson didn't know any of these boys of course, and if he heard them say anything about Belinda, he wouldn't believe it anyway, I thought, and for that matter, he wouldn't frequent the places where Belinda's name could be written on the bathroom walls. He was perfect, and believed that Belinda was too. Maybe he wanted so much for her to be true, he made himself believe. Everyone, I concluded, chooses his or her own version of the truth, fits it to his or her own image of how things should be, and throws back those aspects that don't fit as easily as throwing back small fish. The only reality was the reality we accepted.

Despite this explanation for Carson's behavior, it still didn't satisfy my musings concerning Belinda. Why was she being such a good daughter and such a perfect fiancée? Daddy wanted to believe she had changed; she had come to some realizations about herself and her life and she had grown up, practically overnight. Daddy was yet another person choosing his version of reality, I thought.

The wedding was planned for the spring. Not a day went by now that Mother didn't consider, discuss or investigate some aspect of the affair. It was going to be one of the most elegant and extravagant weddings on the Cape, and Belinda would be the star. She wallowed in all of the attention, stacking catalogues of wedding dresses, samples of materials, pictures of hair styles, shoes, flower arrangements, dresses for bridesmaids, all of it in her room. Caterers, designers, arrangers, were parading in and out of the house weekly, making their presentations and answering questions. The event took over our daily lives and became the sole subject of conversation at dinner and at Daddy's family meetings. It was truly as if the world now revolved around Belinda, her happiness and her wishes. The princess was about to become a queen.

Despite all this, all the reasons why Belinda should be and apparently was very happy, I remained skeptical. Her tolerance of Carson continued to bother me. This was the longest she had been with any one man, especially one who wasn't yet a lover.

True, her social life was a whirlwind of activity. There wasn't an event, an affair that Carson didn't propose they attend, and for each, Belinda had to make special preparations. It did take over much of her life, enough to get her away from the office and fill her days. Daddy was never as happy and Mother was very relaxed as well.

"Ain't it grand?" Daddy said one day. "A year ago we thought she was going to be a lifelong disaster, going from one tragic event to another, and now . . . now she's going to be a real Cape Cod lady, huh?"

"Yes, Daddy," I said. "I hope so."

"Don't be so dark, Olivia. When things are planned as well as this was, they usually work out. Just do your homework," he instructed, "and you'll always do well."

I smiled and nodded to make him comfortable, but in my heart, I was nowhere as convinced as he was. And then, one March night, my suspicions justified themselves vividly, too vividly for me to stomach.

I was still awake when Carson brought Belinda home early from a charity affair in North Truro. Daddy and

Mother had gone to bed because Daddy had a bad cold and Mother was feeling like she was about to come down with one herself. I watched some television and then went up to read. I had only my small night lamp on. The house was quiet. I heard Carson's Rolls pull up and I heard Belinda get out and be escorted to the front door. She came in and up the stairs very quietly. I poked my head out as she was passing.

"What's wrong?" I asked.

"I have a bad stomachache," she said. "Cramps. My period's coming, and besides, they were just making speeches. I fell asleep twice! I'm so tired. I'm going to sleep."

I nodded at the typical Belinda answer and watched her go into her room. I read a little longer and then put out the light. As I drew the covers up to my chin, I heard the floor creak outside my door and then distinctly heard someone going down the stairs. Curious, I rose and peered out just in time to see the top of Belinda's head disappear below the steps. I thought she had probably gone down to get herself something for her cramps. I felt like a glass of milk myself and threw on my robe. When I got downstairs, however, she was nowhere to be found. In fact, the lights were off in the kitchen.

However, I noticed the rear door was slightly open and I went to it quickly and stepped out on the landing. At first I saw no one and then I caught sight of her moving rapidly over the beach toward our boathouse. She was practically running. Why was she going there this time of the night? I wondered.

I went back to the foyer at the front entrance and got one of my jackets out of the closet. Then I returned to the rear door and followed after Belinda. We had a larger, grander boathouse than most other people because of Daddy's original enterprises, his boats and activities. A few years previous, before Daddy turned his den into an office, he had taken a part of the boathouse and turned it into a small office furnished with some file cabinets, a desk, some tables and chairs and a sofa. The walls had cork boards covered with data about the weather, fishing and lobster traps.

The night sky was streaked with thin, veil-like clouds, but the half moon was bright enough to penetrate any obstacle and illuminate the ocean and the shore. About a dozen yards from the boathouse, I thought I heard the sound of laughter and then spotted a small light in the office window. It was coming from the oil lantern on the desk. Drawing closer, I listened harder and thought I recognized the other voice, a male voice. It turned my heart into a small parade drum. For a moment I could barely breathe. I sucked in some air and stepped up to the window.

At first, I saw nothing, no one. Then I spotted them on the floor because the glow of the small lantern made their naked bodies glitter. I pulled back, feeling as if I had been punched in the stomach. No, I thought. It can't be. How can it be? It's a dream. I'm standing out here in a nightmare of my own making. I'll close my eyes hard and then open them and be back in my own bed, snug.

Of course, I wasn't. I was there beside the window. The wind had picked up and the surf crashed on the rocks below. Slowly, I peered through a corner of the window again. He was above her, his hands on her breasts, his back arched, his face turned in my direction. She had her arms around his waist and her legs raised and wrapped around him. He opened his eyes and I was sure, by his expression, he saw me looking in the window.

I didn't wait to hear him cry out. I turned and ran all the way back to the house, coughing and sputtering when

I reached the wooden steps up to the yard. I was dry heaving. My stomach felt like it had been turned inside out.

Then I looked back because I heard the sound of a door in the boathouse being opened. I saw him standing there, silhouetted in the moonlight, looking in my direction.

"Nelson?" I heard her cry. "Come on back. Come on. There's no one there. I don't have all night."

"All right," he said, lingered a moment and then returned to the office.

I took two deep breaths, held my hand to my heart to stop it from pounding a hole in my chest, and walked back to the house. I was so soaked with my own sweat, I felt as if I had fallen into the sea. I made my way to the front, hung up my coat, and returned to my room. There, I pulled off my nightgown and went to the bathroom to shower. I put on a different nightgown and crawled back into my bed, pulling the blanket up to my chin.

My heart thumped dully under my breast. I lay there, my eyes wide open, convincing myself I had indeed been outside and I had indeed seen them in the boathouse. This was no dream, no nightmare of my own making.

In two months, I thought, she was supposed to be married to Carson McGil in a ceremony that would take place only yards from where she lay making love with the only man I loved.

I heard Belinda return to her room, but I didn't get up to confront her. Instead, I pretended I knew nothing when we both met at breakfast the next morning. She rattled on and on to Mother about how boring the event had been and why she had to come home early.

"I never heard you come in," Mother told her. "Did you hear her, Olivia?"

I looked at Belinda.

"Yes, I heard her come home," I said quickly. Belinda smiled.

"I had to take something for my cramps and fell right to sleep myself," she said. I stared at her, but she didn't notice.

"I have to get to work. We have a lot doing today," I said and left the house as quickly as I could because I felt if I remained a moment longer, I would scream out what I had really seen and who knew what that would do to Mother. I shuddered to think what would happen when Daddy found out.

As I turned down Commercial Street, I saw Nelson Childs and his father come out of The Sea Loft, a popular breakfast place. They shook hands and Nelson started toward his shiny red car. Impulsively, I turned into the space behind his car and he looked up, surprised. When he saw me, his smile of confusion faded and his face turned deathly serious. Then, he caught his thoughts in midair, flung them into the back of his mind, and smiled again, his hand up in greeting.

I rolled down my window.

"Good morning," he said stepping up to my car. "I just had some breakfast with Dad."

I could see from how nervous he was that he suspected he had seen me in the window the night before.

"I think you and I should have a little talk, Nelson."

"Talk?"

"About last night," I said firmly. His lips quivered and his eyes filled with trepidation.

"Last night?"

"Why don't you just get into my car?" I suggested. He nodded and went around quickly to get in. For a moment we both sat there silently.

"I heard Belinda leave the house after she had come

home from a date with Carson. I was curious, so I followed her to the boathouse."

"Oh," he said. He looked ahead. "I thought it was you."

"I'm disappointed in you, Nelson. You know you're having an affair with a woman who's engaged to be married soon, and a woman, I might add, who isn't very bright. She's my sister and I love her, but I recognize her failings. She's not sophisticated when it comes to male-female relationships."

He started to smile.

"I don't mean she's not a good lover. I'm sure she is . . . quite the lover, but she's been in trouble before, bad trouble. You have no idea how bad," I continued, relentless now. "My father has had more than his hands full rescuing her from one disaster after another, but this is one that threatens the very foundation of our family and I won't let it happen."

I spun on him.

"I would personally expose the both of you," I said. "You might as well pack your bags and take the next tugboat out of here, Nelson Childs. You talk about becoming an elected official, building a law practice? On what? A big scandal?"

"Olivia, please, I . . ." He looked down. "I don't even want to try to defend myself. You're right, absolutely right," he confessed. "I let my hormones take control. It would destroy both our families."

"I can expect something like this from Belinda. In fact, I was anticipating it, but to discover that you were involved . . . I never would have thought it, Nelson. I'm so disappointed," I added, nearly in tears.

He nodded.

"I'm disappointed in myself, too." He turned to me, his eyes wet, his lips firm. "You really have no reason to believe me, Olivia, but I swear to you I won't disappoint you again," he said.

I turned away and stared out the window, my heart pounding. How handsome he is, I thought. How much I wished he would embrace me, want me, risk all for me as he had for Belinda.

"Well, I want to have faith in you, Nelson," I said.

"Thank you," he replied quickly. "I have a great deal of respect for you, Olivia. It's important to me that I don't lose the respect you could have for me."

I gazed at him. Why couldn't he think of more between us than mere respect?

"People earn each other's respect," I said.

"That's right."

I held his gaze for a moment and then looked ahead.

"All right then," I said. "This will just be between us."

"Thank you, Olivia. You won't be disappointed in me," he promised.

I nodded. I was disappointed already, but I didn't know how to express why. I started my car engine.

"I've got to go back to school this afternoon," he said. "Have a good week."

"You too," I said without looking at him.

"Bye."

I watched him get out and walk to his car. He turned, smiled and waved and I pulled away, my heart heavy, its thump more like a chime in a grandfather's clock, declaring another second, another minute, and soon another hour of my life had passed and still, still I was all alone.

Two weeks later, Daddy came into my office at work to tell me that he had just heard Nelson Childs had become engaged to a young woman from a prominent Boston family.

6
&

Sour Grapes

*D*uring those weeks between the time I had confronted Nelson and when I finally heard about his engagement, I permitted myself to fantasize about us. I chastised myself afterward for being a fool, even more foolish than Belinda because she could fantasize and then forget it and just fantasize about someone else, whereas I treated my broken dreams as if they were family heirlooms, shattered beyond repair.

I had actually anticipated a phone call from Nelson. I imagined that he had left our talk in my car believing that I was someone exceptional, someone so special he wanted to know me more, see and talk to me more. I was substantial. Surely someone as intelligent and as ambitious as he was would realize the importance of having a wife who had my qualities.

I envisioned him waking up one morning, slapping himself on the side of the head and saying, "What was I thinking? Here was Olivia Gordon all this time, unattached, attractive and sensible, and I go having assignations in the dead of night with her childish sister, risking my whole career, my reputation, my family's reputation, and for what?"

Any minute that phone in the office or at home would ring and it would be Nelson asking if he and I could have dinner the night he returned from college. I would pretend to consider and then agree and we would go out and have a wonderful time, discovering we really did have similar interests and ambitions. The date would grow into another and another, and in weeks, a few months at the most, he would ask me to marry him. Belinda's wedding would be followed by announcements of my own engagement and impending nuptials. In days I would soar so high and so far past her, her head would spin. Finally, finally, I would be rewarded for being the good daughter.

Daddy's words about Nelson therefore resembled a clap of thunder in my head, a storm of No's and disbelief twirled in the angry clouds that swirled around my thoughts in a tempest of agony.

"The Colonel just called to tell me Nelson's engaged to a Louise Branagan. Her grandfather was a state supreme court judge. It will be in all the social columns next week and they're planning on an engagement party a month after Belinda's wedding."

I barely acknowledged Daddy. I simply stared up at him, my blank expression masking my crushed heart.

"I guess I was way off the mark thinking I might make a marriage between Nelson Childs and Belinda, huh?"

"Yes, Daddy," I said, and I thought, we were both well off the mark.

I was worthless for the remainder of that day and during the days that followed. I moped about the house, hid from people and especially avoided Belinda, who floated on her own laughter and smiles as if she were made of air and the rest of us were lumps of clay. She went on and on about the wonderful life she and Carson were going to have, the home she would have him build, the clothing, the cars, the trips she had planned.

"We have decided . . . actually, I have decided . . . that we should go to Bermuda for our honeymoon. We're going to stay in the most expensive hotel, too. I went to the travel agency and I told them to find me the best and not to be concerned about cost. Just charge it to Carson McGil. I'll have to get used to saying that now, won't I, Olivia?" She smiled. "Just charge it please, charge it to Carson McGil."

"When you marry someone, Belinda, you care about him. You don't set out to bankrupt him or hurt him in any way. You and he are supposed to be together, for better or for worse. You're supposed to look out for each other," I lectured.

"That's ridiculous. I shouldn't have to look out for him. He should always look out for me, protect me, provide for me, want to do everything possible to make me happy," she retorted.

"And you do nothing to make him happy?"

"If I'm happy, he'll be happy; if I'm sad, he'll be sad," she threatened. "Carson's already learned that and accepted it. He knows if he wants me, he takes me as I am, and, dear sister, he wants me, wants me very, very much."

She giggled and whispered.

"I've been promising him the greatest of honeymoon nights, pleasure beyond his wildest imagination, and you should see the way he drools. I swear his tongue dangles like a dog's sometimes. He treats every one of my kisses as if each was a jewel, so I deliberately don't kiss him very often. He thinks I'm terrified of sex."

I shook my head and she grimaced.

OLIVIA

"I won't be unhappy, Olivia," she insisted, pursing her lips. "I'm doing all this, marrying Carson because it's good for the family, but I don't have to be unhappy too, do I?"

"Perish the thought," I said. "In the beginning I actually felt sorry for you, Belinda. I thought you might be doing something you really don't want to do, but now I realize Carson's the one I should feel sorry for, not you."

"That's dreadful. What a dreadful thing to say." She smiled, her eyes twinkling in the moonlight. "I hear the ding-dong of jealousy," she sang.

"That's not true."

"Ding-dong, ding-dong."

"Stop it!"

"Well, stop trying to make me feel bad. Carson is very happy he has me. If you ask him today, he'll tell you he's the luckiest man in the world. He probably is. He's getting the woman of his dreams," she added and went off believing in her own propaganda.

She was far from the woman of his dreams. It sickened me to think all men were as gullible and blind as Carson McGil, but that's the way it looked to me now. Even Nelson Childs was beguiled by my sister.

One Saturday afternoon soon after, Carson came calling on Belinda to take her on a shopping spree in Boston. She had already bragged to me how much of his money she would spend and how she would insist he take her to one of the fanciest restaurants in the city. Then she would fall asleep in the car and leave him to drive her home like a chauffeur.

"And," she added with confidence, "he's happy to do it."

Daddy was fishing with some of his business associates

and Mother was upstairs in her room, nursing another one of her bad stomachaches. They were coming more frequently lately. She blamed it on her own nervousness concerning Belinda's impending wedding and all the preparations. I believed her.

Carmelita let Carson in and had him wait in the sitting room. I was in Daddy's den reviewing some bills he had asked me to check. I heard the doorbell, listened and then went back to my work. Moments later, however, I was surprised when Carson came to the den door and looked in on me.

"Oh, sorry if I disturbed you," he said with a weak smile. "I'm just waiting for Belinda. She's late," he added.

"As usual," I said. "It's all right, Carson. Come in, please," I said sitting back in Daddy's oversized leather chair. I'm sure I looked like Goldilocks sitting in Papa Bear's chair.

"This is a nice den and office. It has . . . personality. I can see your father here. The room fits him like a glove," he muttered, his eyes darting about, avoiding mine. Why did my presence make him so nervous? I wondered.

"Is everything all right between you and Belinda?" I asked directly.

He turned sharply and nodded.

"Oh, yes, sure. It's just an exciting time for both of us. She so much wants to do the right thing," he added.

"Finally," I muttered.

"Pardon?"

"Nothing. It's nice that you two are so happy," I said and pulled my chair up to the desk, intending to return to my work and end this silly chitter-chatter before it really had begun.

"Well, we have our little ups and downs just as any couple would, but overall . . ."

I gazed up at him. He was having some last minute stage fright, I thought. Maybe he wasn't as stupid as he appeared. Suddenly, I did feel sorry for him.

"My sister is lucky to have landed a catch like you, Carson."

"Oh no," he said modestly, his face turning a bright pink, "I'm the lucky one."

"It's generous of you to say that," I said, "considering her troubled past."

"What's that?" He smiled with question marks in his eyes. "Troubled past?"

He clutched his hat against his chest as if it were a shield to protect him from the slings and arrows I might throw his way.

I smiled with bitter sweetness.

"Well, now that you're practically a member of our family, it's not wrong for you to be aware that Belinda's had problems. She was in finishing school, you know, but it didn't work out and we had to bring her home."

"Oh that, yes," he said with a look of relief. "She told me all about it."

"Told you? Told you what?" I said sitting back again, my finger tips pressed against each other.

"How she was wrongly accused of stealing some girl's jewelry in the dorm and how the other girls, all jealous, took the other girl's side. She couldn't continue living there under those circumstances," he declared with the firmness of a protector.

"Is that the fairy tale she devised?"

"Excuse me?"

"Belinda was expelled, Carson. You might as well know the truth. You're going to discover it anyway someday."

"Expelled for stealing," he said nodding.

"No, not for stealing," I replied. He stared a moment, looked at the doorrway and then sat.

"What was it then?"

"Let's call it promiscuity," I said. His eyebrows nearly leaped off his face.

"Promiscuity?" He paused, raising the level of his courage so he could say his words. "You mean of a sexual nature?"

"I don't know any other," I said as sweetly as I could. "But she learned her lesson from that, as well as the other things," I said. "You shouldn't be concerned now."

"What other things?"

"Problems she had when she was in high school," I said as casually as I could. "All girls have some."

"Did you?"

"Nothing like the ones Belinda had, but Belinda is Belinda," I replied.

"What's that supposed to mean?"

"We're all individuals, Carson. Some of us are more liberal with our bodies than others, have greater appetites. It's what makes for horse races, right? Differences? You love her because she's who she is, don't you?"

"I . . . I thought I knew who she was."

"Well, what do you two talk about if not each other's pasts?" I asked in all innocence.

"I told her all about myself, yes, but she never mentioned any . . . promiscuity, you say? Expelled for it? What sort of promiscuity? I mean, what did she do?"

"You have to understand she was so much less mature then," I said.

"It wasn't very long ago," he replied quickly.

"The events matured her," I said. "Sometimes that happens when things are bigger than we expect."

"You mean there was something of a scandal?"

"Almost. Daddy and I stopped it before it started," I bragged.

He shook his head, his eyes glassy, numb.

"I had no idea. Who else knows this?"

"Besides the family . . . administrators at the school, some other girls, of course, and of course the boys involved," I said.

"Boys? You mean there was more than one?"

"Oh, why talk about something a girl did when she was young and immature, Carson. That's not the girl you know now, right? That's not the girl you proposed to, the girl you want to build a home for, the girl you want to have your children, if she still can have children, of course."

"What? Why couldn't she?"

"That's an entirely different matter, Carson. I don't feel right discussing it, even with Belinda's future husband. It's something that should be between you, your wife and your doctor," I added.

"I had no idea . . . about any of this," he said shaking his head. "I don't put my ear to the walls surrounding gossip, and I know so few of Belinda's contemporaries. None of her girlfriends, in point of fact."

"You're not missing anything there," I said. "Her friends are . . . mostly undesirable. You won't want to have any of them to your home, much less your wedding."

His mouth dropped open.

"I'm sorry," I said, "but I promised my father I would review and correct these documents today and . . ."

"Oh, yes." He rose.

We heard Belinda bouncing down the stairs. He looked at me with the expression of a man who was about to go to his doom.

"Carson McGil," she sang in the hallway. "Where are you hiding? I know you wouldn't dare be late for a date with me. Carson?"

He started out of the den as Belinda appeared in the doorway.

"There you are. Visiting with Olivia? How nice. We're on our way to Boston, Olivia."

"I know. You told me twice already, Belinda."

"Don't you get tired of doing men's work?" she said with her little impish smile.

"It's not men's work. It's not women's work. It's work," I said. "That's a word that has never felt at home in Belinda's vocabulary," I explained to Carson. He nodded.

"I don't want to make it comfortable in my vocabulary," she whined. "Play," she followed, "that's the word that will be the most valued guest in my house. Right, Carson, dear?"

He looked at her and then to me.

"We better be going," he announced.

"Have a nice time. Both of you," I said.

Carson nodded and started out of the room. Belinda's eyes grew small with suspicion for a moment and then, whatever thought had flashed across her movie-screen mind disappeared and was replaced with her usual fanfare.

"Thank you, Olivia. We will," she promised and spun quickly to shoot her hand under Carson's arm.

I heard them leave the house and all grew quiet again. The small tight ball at the bottom of my stomach dissipated and waves of warm glee traveled to my heart, oozing satisfaction through my veins. Watching Carson's face shatter like some thin, plastic mask felt good. Men should feel the brunt of their own stupidity. They should feel the heel of truth come down on their naked feet.

126

I had no sense of guilt. If Carson couldn't accept Belinda for what she was, that was his problem, not mine. Someday, he would come see me and thank me for being so honest, for being the only one who dared to open his eyes. Belinda would have to be honest with him, too. A marriage should have truth as part of its foundation, shouldn't it? It was wrong for Daddy to keep it all buried. How would he like to buy a boat that had weak joints in its hull? How would he like to discover the truth when he was already out to sea? Well, that's what it would be like for Carson McGil, wouldn't it? One day, months into their marriage, the truth about Belinda would reveal itself and Carson would feel like a man on a sinking vessel. It was better he went to sea knowing the dangers, the weaknesses in his little boat of love.

For a while that afternoon, I felt like someone who had performed a great act of charity. Who would criticize me for ensuring that my sister's marriage was based upon trust? Yes, I felt very good. I felt as if I had struck a blow for every decent, sensible woman in America, and if men like Nelson Childs and Carson McGil didn't appreciate that, well, too bad. Someday, they would.

After I finished Daddy's bookkeeping, I had lunch and went out to read in the gazebo. It was a gloriously sunny day with only pockets of milk-white clouds bursting here and there over the azure sky. The sea was calm; the sailboats looked dabbed by an artist's brush on the canvas of the Atlantic Ocean. There was a fresh, even delicious scent to the salt air. I really did appreciate and love our home. I could be no other place. This was where I would make my life, find my own husband and raise my own family. I felt more confident about it, more sure of myself, despite the recent events. Nature demonstrated itself all around me and taught the lesson: the strong eventually win. It's only a matter of time.

I hadn't been sitting there long when, like a small bomb exploding, Belinda burst through the back door of the house, tears streaming down her cheeks, her hands raised as if she had puppet strings tied to her wrists.

"There you are! There you are! You traitor. You jealous, horrible sister."

She charged over the lawn, her high heels catching in the grass and nearly tripping her. She pulled off her shoes and flung them angrily before continuing toward me.

"What is it, Belinda? Why are you back so soon?" I asked calmly, lowering my book to my lap.

She fumed for a moment, stammered and then took hold of the railing.

"You told Carson about my being expelled from finishing school," she accused, her right forefinger pointed at me like a knife. I could see she wanted to poke it right through my eye.

I shrugged.

"He already knew you had left finishing school abruptly," I said, still in a controlled, soft voice.

"Yes, yes, but he thought it was because I had wanted to leave, because I had been accused of stealing someone's stupid costume jewelry!"

"What? I didn't know that, Belinda. How am I supposed to keep track of all the lies you tell people? If you had a story you made up, you should have informed me so I could corroborate it when Carson asked. I thought you had told him the truth, so I just . . ."

"Just what? How could you tell him I was caught in bed with two boys?"

"I didn't tell him that," I said, now speaking with convincing assurance. After all, I hadn't. "I never said you were caught in bed with anyone."

"You didn't? But he said . . . so I just thought, and

then I told him. Oh, I told him too much too fast," she cried.

"Yes, I bet you did. You volunteered more information than you had to give him. But that's the danger in building a relationship on a floor of falsehoods, Belinda. You never know when you're going to step through it and trip yourself."

"He was so shocked and he kept asking me questions about my high-school life. I just thought some of the boys had spoken to him, told him lies, exaggerated . . ."

"Bragged about making you pregnant?" I asked.

She looked at me.

"Yes, something like that."

"You mean you told him you were pregnant?"

"Not exactly. He wanted to know about my having children. He never talked about children before, so I didn't know what he meant. He said maybe I couldn't have children and I said of course I could. He wanted to know why I was so positive. I didn't say anything, but he . . ."

"He's not as stupid as you hoped, is that it?" I asked.

She shook her head.

"I don't know. He got so angry at me he just stopped the car, whipped it around and drove me home. He said he had to go off by himself and think things over."

She pouted, her arms across her breasts.

"The nerve of him," she fumed.

"If he loves you as much as you think he does, a little misunderstanding won't matter," I said.

She considered and raised her eyes to me.

"What should I do? What should I tell him?"

"If he calls you and complains, you say take me as I am or don't take me at all. That's what I would say."

"Yes," she agreed, nodding. "I will. Imagine him

turning around and taking me back home after promising to take me shopping and to dinner. What am I supposed to do with the rest of my day now? I'm all dressed and I spent hours on my hair and makeup."

"Did you let him know that?"

"No. I should have. I will," she said. "I'm going to call him up and insist he get back here or else."

"It's a nice day," I said gazing at the sea. "If he doesn't come back, just come out here and read."

"Read? Read! I have things to buy. I wanted to get a new cape for my red velvet dress," she whined.

"I'll be here," I said, "if you don't go off to Boston."

She stared at me a moment and then, biting down on her lower lip, her eyes blazing, she spun and marched back to the house.

I looked toward the boathouse. Imagine if Carson got wind of that, I thought. He would probably drive around in circles for days. It brought a smile to my lips. I recalled a quotation I had recently read. "A man falls in love through his eyes, a woman through her ears." Carson McGil was the best example of that, I concluded. Maybe one day I'd have the quotation embroidered on a pillow and send it to him so he could sleep with the wisdom under his head. Men, I thought disdainfully.

I returned to my book, never more content with myself.

Belinda fumed for the remainder of the day because Carson wasn't home to receive her irate phone call and didn't return her call until early in the evening. We had just finished dinner, eating under the atmosphere of a wake. Belinda sulked after ranting about how poorly Carson had treated her. Daddy's face was folded into a deep scowl, his eyes dark, his forehead wrinkled as he brooded. Mother, still having stomach trouble, ate little, whimpered in pain occasionally, and sat with her lips trembling most of the time. Belinda ate even less. Only I seemed to have a robust appetite. I tried building some conversation by talking about the new book I was reading and what a beautiful a day it had been.

"Well, it wasn't beautiful for me," Belinda reminded us. "I spent most of it waiting around a telephone."

"I'm surprised at you, Belinda," I said. "You never let a man run your life like this before."

She glared at me a moment and then blinked rapidly and nodded.

"You're right."

"Oh dear, oh dear," Mother moaned.

"You're disturbing your mother," Daddy warned. It was more like a growl. Belinda returned to her sulking and I ate quietly.

As soon as dinner ended, Mother went to her room, clutching at her stomach. I thought she had a pale, pasty complexion.

"Why doesn't she see the doctor?" I asked Daddy. He looked toward the door thoughtfully.

"She will. For the moment I think it's just her nerves. This Belinda business," he added with a wave of his hand. Belinda had gone back to her room as well. "What could have happened between them?" he wondered.

"All I know is they had some conversations about her past, Daddy. Carson wasn't happy about it, and she told him more than she had to, I guess. You knew he would eventually get to know some of her indiscretions. People don't keep their gossip under lock and key in Province-town any more than they do anyplace else."

"Umm," he said. "I didn't think any of that would matter once they were on their way to the altar," he muttered.

Suddenly, we heard Belinda coming down the stairs

quickly, bouncing on the steps. She hurried to the door of the dining room to announce Carson had finally called.

"Good," Daddy said.

"And?" I asked, seeing a look of irritation in Belinda's eyes.

"He's just picking me up to talk, not to take me anywhere nice. He'll be here in ten minutes," she replied. "I hope he has earplugs because I intend to give him a piece of my mind first."

"Now don't say anything you'll regret later, Belinda," Daddy warned. "A mature person thinks before she speaks."

"I know what a mature person does, Daddy. He doesn't turn around on the way to Boston and decide he can't take me where he promised he would take me, and he doesn't fail to answer my phone calls all day, does he? I think I'm more mature."

"All I'm saying is keep in mind you two are going to be married soon. You have a life to build together and you don't want to go and spoil things now," Daddy advised.

"It's Carson who's spoiling things," she insisted.

I couldn't contain a small smile, but I pressed my lips together so Daddy wouldn't see. Belinda could be pigheaded when she let her pride and her arrogance become her lead horses. In that respect she wasn't unlike many people I knew, even Daddy.

Belinda went to the bathroom to check her makeup. A little while later, Carson was at the door; however, Belinda did not permit him to enter. She greeted him herself and went outside with him, ordering him to drive off immediately.

I went into the den to discuss the work I had done for Daddy that day. He seemed distracted and went up to check on Mother. When he returned, he told me she was asleep, but groaning.

"I don't like it," he said shaking his head. "She has no fever. It's not a stomach flu."

"Don't be the doctor, Daddy. Get her to one in the morning."

"Yes," he said. "You're right, Olivia. You're always right when it comes to doing the sensible things. I wish Belinda had one-tenth of your good sense," he said, "but I'm afraid she was born without any."

Nearly a half hour later, the front door slammed and we both looked up with surprise and anticipation. Then we heard Belinda charge up the stairs.

"What's that all about?"

"I don't know," I said. "I'll find out."

"Come right back and tell me everything she tells you," he said.

I nodded and followed Belinda up the stairs to her room. She had her door closed. I knocked softly and opened it to find her sprawled on her stomach, her head hanging over the side of the bed. She wasn't crying as much as she was fuming.

"What happened?" I asked.

She turned and I saw her face was a shade darker than pink, her lips a bit white in the corners. Her eyes were burning with rage.

"He says that he can't marry me now. He says he spent the whole day thinking about it and he had a discussion with his parents about it and they agree. That's where he was all day, talking to his mother and father instead of talking to me. He wants me to tell Daddy that he'll pay for any expenses we might have incurred up to now. I threw my engagement ring out the window of the car."

"You what?"

"I just opened the window and tossed it out as we were driving. That's where we've been most of the time. He was out there on the road with his flashlight combing the brush and dirt. He didn't find it," she said with satisfaction. "He said he'll be back there in the morning. I hope he spends the rest of his life looking.

"'How could you throw away a ring worth thousands of dollars!' he screamed. I laughed in his face. I said, 'How can you throw away a woman like me just because you heard some rumors and believe some stories?' You would have been proud of me, Olivia. I told him he was a wimpy, wet noodle, a mama's boy and that the only way he would ever get into bed with a woman was if he went to some dark neighborhood and paid a prostitute and then she might reject him anyway.

"You were right. He doesn't really love me, not if he can do this to me. I told him he still owed me a shopping spree and a dinner in Boston and I would send him that bill, too."

"So the wedding is off," I said nodding.

"Daddy's going to be mad about the business, but I couldn't help it, Olivia."

"I'll explain it to him," I said.

"Would you, please? Thank you, Olivia. I'm so lucky to have you as my big sister. You are wise. Thank you for your good advice, too," she said. "Well," she continued almost without a beat, "I guess I should call some of my friends and let them know I'm a free agent again, huh? Can't let moss grow under my feet," she said and went to the phone.

I watched her for a moment before leaving to go down to Daddy. Other women might be heartbroken and cry all night, but Belinda behaved as though she had simply lost a high-school date.

Daddy looked up from his desk as soon as I appeared in the doorway.

"Well?" he said before I had completely entered the den.

"Carson broke off their engagement. The wedding is off, Daddy."

"I was afraid of that," Daddy said after he sucked in his breath and held it a moment. "Your mother's going to be devastated."

"He told her he would gladly pay any bills you might have incurred. She threw his engagement ring out of the window," I added quickly so he wouldn't wonder if there was any chance of reconsideration.

"She did what? Threw it out the window? Did they find it?"

"No," I said.

"My God. That ring was worth twenty-five thousand dollars, Olivia. McGil was bragging about it to me just the other day."

"That's Belinda," I said and shrugged.

"She's a madwoman. We'll never find anyone for her now, not after that story gets out."

"Maybe not, Daddy," I said. "Maybe we'll have to face that fact and do the best we can."

"Yes," he said. "Perhaps so." He stared down at his desk and then he raised his tired, sad eyes at me. "Well, I guess I had better put my mind and my energy toward your well-being, Olivia. I'll have a better chance at success."

"I'll be fine, Daddy."

"I know you will. That's my consolation," he said. "But I can't neglect you because she's a failure in every way and in everything I try to arrange for her."

He rose.

"I guess I'll have to go up and break the news to your mother. I might wait until the morning if she's still asleep," he said.

"You probably should anyway, Daddy. Give her a chance to get a good night's sleep so she can recuperate from that stomach problem."

"Yes. Yes, you're right again, Olivia."

He paused in front of me and kissed me on the forehead.

"Good night, and thanks for being my little general," he said.

He was so distraught, I nearly shed some of those tears that had formed under my lids, but they stayed where they were. I watched him leave with his shoulders slumped, his head down. He was so depressed; Mother was sick upstairs, and Belinda was chatting happily on her phone, quite recovered from her dramatic breakup with Carson. In a day it would be as if he never existed.

Yes, I thought, one of these days, perhaps years from now, Carson McGil would meet me. He would nod, maybe take off his hat, and say thanks.

I was as sure of that as I was of tomorrow and the promises Daddy would make to me.

7

&

A New Beginning

Daddy waited until the morning to tell Mother of Belinda's aborted wedding. She took it very badly and in fact, was unable to come down to breakfast. It was a gray day, the cloud ceiling low and ashen with a stiff breeze blowing out toward sea. Daddy thought we were in for a nor'easter and went out with Jerome to make sure things were securely tied down. Winter had been so mild this year that we were all somewhat complacent. It seemed ages since the last real storm. However, as the day progressed, Daddy's predictions for it became more and more of a reality.

I went upstairs immediately to visit Mother when Daddy informed us she wasn't feeling well enough to come to breakfast.

"She's not hungry at all," he added. "I'll have a cup of tea brought up."

"I'll take it," I said and went into the kitchen to have it made. Belinda had already made plans to spend the day at Kimberly Hughes' home where I was sure she would be joined by her other bubble-gum girlfriends who had nothing to do but hear all about her broken love affair with Carson. I could just imagine the exaggerations and the histrionics Belinda would perform. She really enjoyed being the center of attention. In fact, she was so absorbed in her plans, she barely asked about Mother.

It nearly broke my heart to see Mother pale and teary-eyed, the redness around her eyelids so bright it looked as if some of the rose coloring had dripped off her glasses. Her lips started to tremble as soon as I approached the bed. She reached up for me with her limp, cold hand.

"Olivia, what happened? Winston's making no sense. Why is the wedding off? All the plans we've made, the guest list, the decorations and . . ."

"Please don't permit this to upset you, Mother," I said. "Drink some tea. Get something warm in your stomach."

"I will," she said, "but you must sit here and tell me all you know."

The teacup rattled against the saucer precariously when she took it from me. She brought it to her lips and barely sipped, her eyes searching my face anxiously for clues as she peered over the edge of the cup. I sat beside her on the bed.

"None of us should really be surprised by these events, Mother," I began calmly. "We've always tried to protect Belinda from herself. We've always tried to keep her sins and mistakes buried."

Mother winced at the word and I stopped, realizing the not so vague reference to the premature infant that lay under the ground in the rear of our home.

"When you keep things hidden, when you lie or leave out all or part of the truth, you always risk being exposed

138

and looking even more dreadful. That's what happened with Belinda. Carson found out about some of her past indiscretions and was upset. Belinda didn't know how to deal with it. She actually told him even more than he knew. She had been pretending to be so virginal and innocent throughout their engagement. The contrast between the illusion and reality probably frightened him away more than anything else," I said. I paused, looked down at my hands and asked, "Daddy told you about the engagement ring?"

"What about it?"

"I hate telling you these things when you're so sick."

"I'll be all right. Tell me," she pleaded.

"Sip your tea, Mother. Please."

She forced herself to do so. I saw from the way she closed her eyes and grimaced that even that bothered her. It set my heart to pounding.

"You're seeing a doctor today," I insisted, "even if I have to take you there myself."

"All right, Olivia. All right. You were saying something about that engagement ring?"

"She threw it out the car window when Carson became upset with the lies."

"What? You mean . . ." She shook her head as if to shake the words out of her ears.

"It's gone. He couldn't find it. It's like looking for a certain fish in the ocean."

"Oh dear, dear. What will people think and say? That was such an expensive ring."

"They'll get over it," I predicted, but she shook her head again, this time with slow deliberation.

"No. It will be like the Potter affair," she said.

Mother was referring to the infamous story of Helen Potter, daughter of a multimillionaire beer and wine

V. C. ANDREWS

distributor in Hyannis Port who, after she had been
engaged to the son of a wealthy Boston builder, was
discovered naked in bed with her closest girlfriend. They
claimed it was all innocent, but the damage was done
and the wedding plans ended. Helen was sent to Europe
and eventually disappeared in a myriad of stories, some
describing her changing her name and wedding a Hun-
garian baron, others talking about her becoming a flam-
ing lesbian in Paris and living on the Left Bank. The
truth really didn't matter. Her girlfriend went on to
become a doctor and live in California, but the Potters
became personae non gratae when it came to social
events and never recovered. Mr. Potter eventually had a
stroke and died with only his wife and servants at his
bedside. It had become the subject of gossip and glib
jokes, but parents keen about their social status often
used the Potter Affair as a threat to keep their sons and
daughters within the confines of good behavior.

"It's nowhere near as serious as that, Mother. Everyone who knows Belinda, knows she's impulsive and
silly."

"What will become of her?"

"In time she'll find someone else, I'm sure," I said, but
not with any real conviction. Mother just closed her eyes
and nodded. Then she handed me the cup and saucer.
"You need to drink more," I said.

"I'm tired. Let me rest, Olivia."

"I'm going downstairs and getting Daddy to arrange
for you to see a doctor or for a doctor to come here,
Mother."

"It's just my nerves," she said.

"It can't be just nerves. It's lasted too long and . . ."

"I've neglected something and I'm nervous about it,"
she suddenly confessed.

I stared, my heart pounding.

"What are you saying, Mother? Neglected what?"

"A while ago I noticed I had a small lump, so small it wasn't any bigger than a pea."

"A lump? Where?"

"Here," she said touching her left breast. "I mentioned it to Doctor Covington in passing and he advised me to come in for an exam, but I . . . I just thought it would go away."

"Mother!"

"It hasn't. It's gotten a little larger and I'm just on pins and needles thinking about it. That's why I can't eat and why I'm so tired."

"You're going to the doctor tomorrow," I ordered. "I'm going right down to tell Daddy."

She didn't put up any resistance.

"All right, but don't worry him. It might still be nothing at all."

"As long as you go to the doctor," I said.

"I will."

I rose and hurried down to tell Daddy Mother had agreed to go to the doctor, but I didn't keep my promise. I told him why she was so nervous. He turned pale and called Doctor Covington immediately.

"He says he was after her to come in. My God, she said nothing. I should have been more concerned with her failing health."

"As long as she's going now, Daddy."

"What? Oh, the doctor says it's better for us to bring her to the hospital immediately, especially after what you said about the lump growing larger. He'll check her in and give her tests there," Daddy concluded.

"I'll get her ready," I said and hurried toward the stairway just as Belinda had come down.

"We're taking Mother to the hospital," I told her. She was half out the door.

"Oh, why?"

"She has a lump on her breast. That's why she's been so nervous lately."

"A lump? Why would she have a lump? Ugh."

"Sometimes it's nothing serious, but many times it's cancer," I said.

"Cancer?" She thought a moment and then asked, "What's going to happen?"

"She has to be examined, tests have to be done."

"Oh. Well, what should I do?"

"Do what you think you should do," I retorted and went upstairs to help get Mother ready.

Belinda went to her friend's home, but left word with Daddy that she would call the hospital from there and then come over if necessary. The weather turned bad so quickly, however, we were lucky to get Mother to the hospital. The rain came down in rolling sheets and turned the sky leaden. It was still raining hard when Belinda finally did call. Daddy told her to stay where she was. That, I assured him, didn't break Belinda's heart.

But it really was raging outside. The wind had trees so far bent over, branches cracked. Traffic came to a standstill. The sky turned darker and darker until it looked like an eclipse. Then the rain continued, now falling in shelves of cold, icy drops that splattered against windows and thumped on walls and roofs. Lights blinked on and off. Everyone was scurrying about, agitated by the fierceness of the storm.

Fortunately, Doctor Covington had gotten to the hospital just five minutes before we had arrived, and was there to oversee Mother's admittance.

Doctor Covington had just turned sixty, but still had a

full head of what Mother called chameleon hair. In the daylight or bright lights, his hair looked amber, but at night or in subdued light, it looked dark brown. He had been our family doctor for as long as I could remember. A soft-spoken man of few words, he was nevertheless firm and decisive when he made a diagnosis or prescribed a treatment. I remember thinking he had the perfect temperament and disposition for a doctor: confident to the point of being arrogant, but because of that, you felt safe, felt you were in good hands. There was no room for democracy when it came to evaluating health. I told that to Belinda once when she complained about Doctor Covington being too cold.

"He's got microscopes for eyes and a thermometer in every finger," she whined. She was only about twelve at the time, and I thought she was funny. "Stop laughing. He doesn't have blood in his veins. He's got cough syrup."

"You don't have to like him, Belinda. He's not running for any popularity awards. You don't take votes. You listen and you do what he tells you to do."

"I don't like him," she insisted.

"Then don't get sick," I told her.

Doctor Covington wasn't very tall, maybe five feet eight, but I never thought of him as anything but impressive and commanding. He was married and his one child, a son, had gone on to medical school, too, and established himself at a hospital in Connecticut. Mother liked his wife Ruth, but she was a very private person and not fond of following the social circuit. They rarely accepted dinner invitations and had few affairs at their home, keeping most of their guests to his associates and his and his wife's family.

Daddy and I waited in the hospital lobby, trying to

distract ourselves and pass the time by reading magazines and occasionally talking with some of the staff. Finally, Doctor Covington appeared.

"Well, Winston," he began, "as it turns out Leonora's problem isn't so much her stomach, but as you now know something she's kept to herself so long. I'm afraid of the consequences. She was afraid too, I believe, and that's what's given her the stomach troubles. I'll run some tests on her stomach, but I'm confident we know the cause. As to her more serious problem," he continued, "unfortunately, she was in denial, refusing to believe it could be anything. I hope she was right. We're going to do a biopsy immediately. In the meantime I'll treat her stomach cramps. If that's all there is . . ."

"What do you think?" I asked directly. My heart was thumping madly, drumming out a tune of fright in the cage of my ribs, but Daddy seemed unable to talk.

"It's best not to jump to any conclusions without the laboratory work, Olivia," Doctor Covington replied.

"But there is a possibility of it being malignant?" Daddy finally asked.

"Of course there is. That's why women should never neglect symptoms," Doctor Covington said, gazing more at me.

Daddy made a small moan.

"Let's not assume the worst. Let me do what I have to do to get a firm diagnosis, Winston. We'll perform the biopsy. I've already contacted Doctor Friedman in Boston, a specialist who is a friend and a colleague. He'll confer with me as soon as we have some results."

Daddy nodded.

"The weather's not letting up any. Looks like a rough storm," Doctor Covington remarked, gazing out the front doors. "She's resting comfortably, now. I gave her something to help her sleep. You two might as well go home. Come back later, Winston."

"We'll be at the office should you need us," Daddy said.

"Good idea. Keep busy," Doctor Covington said.

"Looks like it's storming on our family, too," Daddy muttered after Doctor Covington left us.

"You heard what he said, Daddy. Let's not assume the worst."

He nodded, but not with optimism in his eyes.

We had a terrible ride to the office, passing two accidents along the way. The storm didn't let up until late in the afternoon. Most of the day, Daddy and I kept busy, but every once in a while, he would stop by my office door and look in to say he hadn't heard anything.

"I guess she's resting comfortably for now," he remarked. "We'll go there before dinner and then we can go to a restaurant afterward," he decided. "Has Belinda called?"

"Not since late this morning," I told him.

"Better she be occupied than in our hair," he said.

When she hadn't called by five, I called Kimberly's house. The phone rang so long, I thought no one was going to answer. Kimberly finally did, but had me wait almost another minute before Belinda picked up.

"I was just going to call you," she said quickly. She sounded out of breath.

"What have you been doing?"

"Nothing," she replied. "How's Mommy? Is she coming home tomorrow?"

"Hardly, Belinda. She's had a biopsy performed on her and they're treating her stomach problem." I explained everything and she was silent.

"Daddy wants the three of us there before dinner and

then we'll go to eat someplace in town," I told her. "Can you get yourself over here within the hour?"

"Oh yes. Bruce will take me."

"Bruce? Who's Bruce?"

"Bruce Lester, Kimberly's cousin. He's very cute, but he's only just a high-school senior," she said.

I didn't want to ask any more questions. I was afraid of the answers. She arrived forty-five minutes later and we all went to see Mother. The sedative the doctor had prescribed to keep her calm made her lethargic and sleepy. She dozed on and off while we were there. I saw Belinda was uncomfortable with the sight of her hooked to an I.V. Finally, Daddy decided we should leave.

Once away from the hospital, Belinda rattled on and on about her day, describing her girlfriends, many of whom she hadn't seen for a while. Neither Daddy nor I paid much attention, but she didn't seem to notice or care.

"Everyone thinks I'm better off without Carson. They all say it would have been a disastrous marriage anyway. His mother would have been interfering with everything, giving her opinions, making my life miserable. Things work out for the best sometimes," she chimed.

Daddy stared through her, barely eating his meal.

"Right, Belinda," I said. "You're not enrolled in any school. You don't have any skills to speak of. You have no other prospects at the moment. Things have worked out for the best," I said dryly.

She laughed.

"Don't worry. I'll have other prospects when I want them," she said with so much confidence, it irked me.

Daddy raised his eyebrows and then shook his head.

"Let's worry about your mother right now and nothing else," he finally declared.

It put an end to Belinda's babbling, for which I was

grateful. The moment we entered the house, however, she ran upstairs to get on the telephone and continue her banter with anyone who would listen. I felt sorry for Daddy. He looked so much older and so tired. All my life I imagined Daddy had steel in his bones. No man ever looked stronger or commanded more respect. It wasn't as painful as it was frightening to see him look weak and defeated.

He poured himself some brandy and sat in his office staring out the window at the gradually clearing sky until he was too tired to keep his eyes open.

Belinda didn't go with us to the hospital in the morning. She couldn't rise early enough and both Daddy and I thought it would be better not to have her moping about as we waited for Doctor Covington.

"I've got her stomach calmed somewhat," the doctor explained, "and she's eaten. She's resting comfortably."

"How long before you have results?" I asked.

"Another day at least," he said. "I'll be on the phone with Doctor Friedman this afternoon."

I sensed that he was expecting the worst. Why else would he want to confer with a specialist so quickly? I didn't say anything about it to Daddy. We visited with Mother who wanted to know immediately where Belinda was.

"We'll bring her around later, Mother," I said. "She couldn't get herself up early enough and neither Daddy nor I had the patience to wait for her," I explained. I saw the pain in her face.

"What will become of her?" she muttered.

"She'll be fine," I said.

"Of course she will," Daddy agreed. "A young woman who looks like that and comes from a home like ours? How can she not be fine?" he growled.

Mother nodded, but not with any confidence. Our eyes

met for a moment and she saw my true feelings. I couldn't lie, not to Mother and especially not about Belinda.

As I had anticipated, the worst happened. It was almost anticlimactic. Sometimes, you can feel tragedy settle in around you. It comes on the wind, a gray beast, heavy with skin of glue, and it sticks to your inner soul, weighing you down, settling like a parasite to suck out your hope and your happiness.

Doctor Covington called us to his office late the next day. This time Belinda came along with Daddy and me. She sat quietly, her face suddenly the face of a five-year-old, full of terror as well as innocence.

"I'm afraid the biopsy was positive, Winston," Doctor Covington began.

"Is that good?" Belinda whispered, a little too loud.

"I'm sorry," Doctor Covington said looking her way, "but no, it's not good. Doctor Friedman thinks we should perform the mastectomy to be followed by chemotherapy."

"When?" I asked before Daddy could finish sucking in his breath.

"We can schedule her this Tuesday in Boston," he replied.

Daddy nodded, his shoulders slumped.

"Then let's do it," he said firmly, but worry tormented his dark eyes.

"We'll move her to Boston later today and begin pre-op," Doctor Covington said.

"Does she know?" I asked.

"Yes," Doctor Covington said. "I don't believe in hiding a diagnosis from the one person it concerns the most," he said.

"You told her? But she'll be so sad," Belinda moaned.

148

"Actually, she took it rather well," Doctor Covington said. "Your mother looked up at me and said, 'So you'll fix it. I'll blink my eyes and it will be gone.'"

He started to smile. Tears came to my eyes. Just like Mother to be that way, I thought.

"That nor'easter the other day," Daddy said with a deep sigh as we left the doctor's office, "wasn't anything compared to the storm ahead."

We followed the ambulance that took Mother to Boston. At times I thought Belinda was more excited about us staying in a Boston hotel, eating in restaurants and having time to do some shopping than she was worried about Mother. No matter how I snapped at her, she continued talking and acting like a child on an exciting trip. Finally, at the hotel, she burst into tears after I chastised her for flirting with the bellhop.

"I'm just as frightened as you are, Olivia, and just as worried. I'm only trying not to think about it. You don't care if you think about it. Your brain is like . . . like a castle compared to the little house mine is. I don't have as much room in mine and I'm not as strong as you are, so stop yelling at me!" she pleaded, her face twisted in pain.

I stared at her a moment. She was right, I thought.

"Let's not argue now," Daddy pleaded. "We've got to look strong and cheerful for your mother."

"Well, tell her to stop picking on me then," Belinda moaned.

"I won't say another word. Do whatever you want. Make a fool of yourself all day, for all I care," I said. She was satisfied.

Eventually, Daddy gave in to some of her requests and whenever we were away from the hospital, he took her shopping or gave her money to go to department stores herself. The boxes piled up in the hotel room. Running out of ideas, she even bought things for me.

The surgeon told us that the operation went well, but results and prognosis would have to wait until after the chemotherapy. As soon as she had made a complete recovery from the operation, therapy was to begin and that could take place at a hospital closer to home.

The third day after the operation, Mother was more buoyant and alert than we had seen her for a while.

"See," she told us, "I knew the doctors would fix things."

Belinda saw this welcomed buoyancy in Mother as an opportunity to talk about all the things she had bought and all the places she had been. It did amuse Mother, and I began to wonder if Belinda being the way she was wasn't better after all. They laughed a lot and Daddy's spirits rose as well.

He hired a special duty nurse to care for Mother when she was brought home, and for a while it looked like we had come through the storm. Daddy and I returned to a regular work schedule and Belinda picked up where she had left off on her social life. Every night we had discussions about what her future might bring. Our optimism blew out of proportion, I know, because we even talked about having her enroll in one of the better universities. Daddy promised to talk to some of his influential associates and see what he could do.

Mother began her chemotherapy, which in the very beginning was quite devastating. She lost her hair rapidly and was back to being listless and exhausted most of the time. The house began to look more like a wing in the hospital with the nurse rushing about, the paraphernalia to care for Mother's needs, and the doctor's frequent visits.

I almost didn't notice the first days of spring, but Mother reminded me when she asked to be taken out to see her flowers and hear the birds. The daisies bloomed and the petunias spread. Sunlit lawns filled with crocus clusters. The tulips, jonquils and daffodils burst colorfully from the earth. Our trees were full and green, and once again the junipers swayed on the hills in rhythm with the warm breezes. Sailboats were seen more frequently on weekends now. It did look as if the world had come back to life and with it came a reason to hope and be happier, a time to give birth to romance and relationships, a time to expect something wonderful to happen.

However, I was still taken by surprise one day when a young man, Samuel Logan, the son of a man who owned a small lobster boat fleet and distribution company came to visit Daddy, but spent most of his time talking with me. He was a tall, well built man a little over six feet tall. He had devilish green eyes highlighted by his dark complexion and light brown hair. I thought he was by far the best-looking man who had ever shown any interest in me.

"I think it's very nice how you work side by side with your father," he said. "I know from just a few conversations with him that he puts a high value on your service. Most of the women I know are just window dressing. I mean," he added quickly, "there's nothing wrong with looking good. You look real fine, but it's nice to have something more in the package."

I didn't reply and he looked flustered.

"I don't mean package like some sort of merchandise. I mean to say, a more complete person. I guess I'm not the best at expressing myself," he concluded when I still sat there staring.

"I understand," I finally said. His smile flashed on, happiness brightening those green eyes even more.

"Good," he said. "So, what do you say to having some dinner with me tonight?"

"Excuse me?"

"Um . . . going to dinner. You'd choose the restaurant, of course," he added.

"You're asking me to dinner?"

"Yes, I am," he said firmly. "I would consider it an honor if you would show me about Provincetown. If you're free, of course," he added. "I don't mean to be imposing myself. I mean, if you want to think about it . . ."

"It's not the biggest decision I have to make," I said. "You want something other than seafood, I suppose," I added, sounding too much like a hotel concierge instead of a woman who had just been asked on a date.

He smiled.

"I'm never tired of that, but I do like Italian food."

"I know just the place," I said.

"I knew you would. Should I make the reservations?"

"I'll do it," I said. "Come by at seven."

"Seven it is," he said slapping his knees and then standing. "I'm looking forward to it. Well, then, I'll just say good-bye to your father and be on my way."

I watched him nearly stumble over himself to return to my father's office. He waved before he left. I sat there, shaking my head in wonder. I didn't know how long I had been waiting for someone I considered good-looking, someone I knew Belinda would consider good-looking, too, to ask me on a date. It seemed it would never happen, and here it had happened so easily and so quickly it made my head spin. I went in to tell Daddy.

"So he finally asked you, did he?" he said.

"What do you mean?" I began to grow suspicious. "You've been matchmaking again?"

"No, no," he said quickly. "He asked me about you

152

and I said you might consider going out to dinner. That's all. Honest," he replied, lifting his big right palm toward me.

"He wanted to ask me out on his own accord?"

"Yes, Olivia, he did. Stop squinting at me like that. Stop being so leery."

"Are we taking over his father's company, Daddy?" He fluttered about his paper work. "Daddy?"

"We might," he admitted, "but it has nothing to do with Samuel Logan asking you to dinner."

"Why do I wonder?"

He shrugged.

"Don't. You're a nice-looking young lady and it's time some nice-looking young man came around, Olivia."

I held him in my gaze until he had to shift his eyes away. I wanted to believe him. For a little while, I thought, I'd be more like my mother and like Belinda. I'd take a chance on my dreams and permit myself to believe in rainbows.

When I went home that night and told Mother I was going on a date, she was very happy for me. It put a little color in her wan face and she sat up in bed to review all my choices for a dress to wear. As soon as Belinda came home and saw me preparing for a date, she became excited, too. It was as if she thought my going out with a man justified everything she had done by suddenly making me more like her. She sat on my bed and watched me flutter about my room, choosing earrings, fixing my hair.

"Why don't you let me do your nails, Olivia? I'm good at it. I did Kimberly's today."

"I never polish my nails," I said.

"Well, you should. Men like a lot of color. You need a darker lipstick."

"I'm not wearing any lipstick."

"Oh," she said laughing. "Then it definitely has to be darker, and you should do your eyebrows."

"I'm not going to start being someone I'm not, Belinda, just because some man asked me to dinner."

"You don't have to change yourself, but you can make yourself more attractive. It's not a sin unless you overdo it," she declared. "You're competing with other women," she concluded.

"What?" I turned on her. "Hardly. I didn't ask him to ask me to dinner. He did of his own volition."

"His what?" She shook her head. "It doesn't matter. When you're out with a man, you want to look better than the other women he might see. What's so terrible about it? Just fix your hair differently. Don't let it hang limply, and put on some makeup. Here," she said opening her purse, "try this shade. It works for me and we have nearly the same complexion."

I gazed at it, considering.

"It won't bite you, Olivia. If you don't like how you look, wipe it off."

"All right," I said.

She smiled like some devilish beguiler who had tempted me to take the first steps toward sin.

"I'll fix your hair," she followed and went into the bathroom to get my brush.

"Wait, I didn't say . . ."

"Just sit down and let me do it, Olivia. For once, let me do something for you," she pleaded.

I stared a moment. She looked very sincere.

"Okay," I said. "What's the difference?"

"You'll see. There's a lot of difference," she promised and began.

An hour later when I looked at myself with my eyebrows thinned, a bit of rouge on each cheek, lipstick, my hair neatly brushed and styled, I dared to think I might just be as pretty as Belinda after all.

"You have nothing nice to wear," she declared. "Take one of my dresses. Choose one that's a bit tight across here," she said indicating her rib cage, "and," she whispered, "wear my new padded bra."

"I don't need that. I have a nice enough dress." I showed her the one Mother had approved, a dark blue silk dress with a delicate lace collar. Belinda grimaced.

"It's not very sexy," she said. "It looks like a dress for one of Mommy's tea parties."

"I don't want to look sexy. I want to look decent, proper."

"Boring," she sang, rushed out to her room and returned with the low-cut black evening dress she wanted me to wear. "At least try it on," she said. "With the bra." She held the garments out until I took them. I went into the bathroom to dress. It had been some time since I had been naked in front of anyone, even Belinda. I didn't want her measuring my breasts and studying my waist and hips to see if there was any fat. She had developed faster than I had at her age and her development didn't seem to want to stop, whereas mine hit a plateau and ended.

When I stepped out, she whistled.

"Is this Olivia Ann Gordon? My sister?"

"Oh stop it," I said but glanced at myself in the mirror. I did look sexier than I ever had. It put a flutter in my chest. Did I dare go out in these clothes, looking like this? "I don't know," I said.

"Do it, Olivia. You won't regret it. Show it to Mommy and Daddy, too."

"I don't know," I said again, but I did go into Mother's bedroom. Daddy was there, sitting at her bedside. They both looked up when I entered, Daddy's face full of surprise. Mother smiled.

"You look absolutely beautiful, dear," she said.

"I knew I had two beautiful daughters," Daddy said. "Any man would have to be blind not to notice you, Olivia."

"It's not too much, Mother?"

"No, I think you look fine," she said.

"See?" Belinda boasted. "I did it. I dressed her."

"Which is why I'm not sure," I said but Mother gave me an approving nod. "Okay, I'll go like this."

"Where are you going?" Daddy asked.

I felt my chin drop.

"Oh no. I forgot to make the reservation!" I cried. Mother actually laughed. I hurried out to make the call and hoped there would be no problem. I wanted us to go to Antonio's on the Point. To me it was always a special little place. Fortunately, they had no difficulty booking us for seven-fifteen. All I had to do was wait for Samuel Logan.

He was nearly fifteen minutes late and apologized, claiming he had gotten lost looking for our home.

"I went up the wrong road and got directions from some elderly man who sent me down another wrong road," he explained, his gaze continually moving from my face to Belinda, who stood behind me waiting to be introduced.

"This is my sister Belinda," I finally said. She nearly leaped at him, her hand thrust at his face as if she expected he would kiss it instead of shake it.

"Oh yes. I can see the resemblance," Samuel said.

"Olivia thinks she looks too sexy in one of my dresses," Belinda blurted.

"Belinda!"

"No, she's fine," Samuel said smiling at her. She batted her eyelashes and smiled coyly.

"That's what I told her. See, Olivia," Belinda said, her eyes fixed on Samuel.

"We're late," I said. "I don't want to lose the reservation."

"Right," Samuel said. "Pleased to meet you, Belinda."

"Likewise, I'm sure," she said. He laughed and we left the house.

"I didn't know you had a sister," Samuel said. "Your father never mentioned her." He opened the car door for me and I got in without replying. "Where are we going?" he asked after he got behind the wheel.

"Antonio's at the Point. It's a small place but the food's the best and it has a pretty view from every table," I said.

"Sounds perfect. What does your sister do? Does she work for your father, too?"

"Belinda doesn't do anything," I said sharply.

"Nothing?"

"She plays," I said.

"Oh. Nice life if you can have it," he said. "No wonder your father thinks so much of you."

"You and my father apparently talked a great deal about me," I said.

He laughed.

"Well, since we might become partners, I thought it would be a good idea to know you. You and I will eventually take control of our family enterprises. Of course, yours is far greater than mine and you might even take us over, but I can't think of a better company to consume Logan Enterprises."

"You have no brothers or sisters?"

"No. My mother died when I was young and my father never remarried."

"Sometimes, I wish I were an only child," I muttered. He heard and laughed.

We were lucky to get a table right by the window that overlooked the water and gave us a good view of the lighthouse. The blinking lights of what looked to be a luxury liner moved slowly across the horizon, and the sky had a purple glow around it.

"What a wonderful choice of a restaurant, Olivia. I see I can leave all the major decisions in my life up to you," Samuel said.

"Your life? I'm hardly in your life, just going to dinner with you, Samuel."

His smile resembled the smile of someone who knew a deep, dark secret.

"That's an oversight that I hope will soon be corrected," he remarked. His boldness was so surprising, I nearly laughed aloud. At his request, I ordered for both of us.

As usual, the food was delicious. I know I drank too much wine because I could feel the heat in my neck and my face. Samuel dominated most of the conversation, talking about himself, his education, his family and his plans.

"I've traveled somewhat, but I have yet to find any place as wonderful as the Cape. How about you?"

"I haven't traveled all that much," I said, "but I do like it here."

"Exactly. I knew from the first time I laid eyes on you that you and I had a great deal in common, and I don't mean just business interests," he said.

Even with too much wine in me, I raised my eyebrows in surprise. What did we have in common? I had yet to hear anything significant. It seemed enough for him that he believed and said it. That made it gospel.

I had to admit that he was a congenial, personable man. He seemed mature for his age, and very settled.

"Do you like sailing?" he asked.

"I do, but I'm not good at it. I'm a good passenger, though."

"Perfect," he declared. "I'm good at it and I'm a terrible passenger. I like keeping busy when I'm on a boat. I even help out our fisherman and do the nitty-gritty work. My father thought that was the best way for me to learn the business anyway, doing it, not inheriting it. Looks like you're the same way, right in there, doing it," he said.

He reached across the table and took my hand.

"I'd like to take you sailing tomorrow. Maybe we can pack a lunch. It's promising to be a perfect day."

"I don't know," I said. "My mother's not well and I might be needed."

"I'm sorry about your mother. I hope she improves, but I hope they can spare you for a few hours. I'll call you in the morning, okay?"

"Well . . . okay," I said.

"Good."

He held onto my hand and I let him until I heard a familiar voice, the voice that need only utter a single word, a single syllable to set my heart racing.

It was Nelson Childs coming down the aisle, holding the hand of a tall, elegant looking brunette with soft blue eyes and a figure that looked like it was molded by a sculptor.

"Olivia. How nice to see you," he said pausing. "I'd like you to meet my fiancée, Louise Branagan. Louise, this is Olivia Gordon, an old friend," he said. I thought he put far too much emphasis on the word "old." She extended her hand.

"Pleased to meet you," she said with a brilliant smile.

"Likewise," I said. "This is Samuel Logan."

"I know Samuel," Nelson said quickly and the two smiled at each other like co-conspirators.

"You do?"

"Aye, we've tipped a few together in our day, haven't we, Samuel?"

"At least one too many," Samuel said. "Hello, Louise. It's nice to see you again."

I looked from him to them, my surprise blooming like a rash on my face.

"I hope you'll both be at the engagement party next week. It's looking like my parents overdid it as they overdo everything," Nelson said. Then his face became more serious. "How's your mother, Olivia?"

"She's doing the best she can," I told him. I was waiting for him to dare to ask about Belinda, but he nodded sadly.

"Well, we don't mean to interrupt. Enjoy and hope to see you soon," he said.

"It was nice meeting you," Louise threw back at us as they continued on to their table.

"Aren't they a nice-looking couple?" Samuel said admiring them.

"I'm tired," I said. "It's been a long day and I have to look in on my mother."

"Oh sure. Let me get the bill," he declared and signaled for our waiter.

Samuel did all the talking on our way to my home. I was only half-listening, still having trouble getting over the sudden meeting with Nelson. He looked even more dashing and mature than ever, and it irked me that Louise Branagan did seem to be a proper fit on his arm. How could I ever have competed with such a social star?

"So I'll call you about ten A.M., if that's all right?"

OLIVIA

Samuel said as soon as we turned into my driveway. The
gate had been left open for us.

"What? Oh, yes."

"I had a wonderful time, Olivia. I really did," he said
pulling to a stop. "I hope you did, too."

"Yes, I did, Samuel. Thank you."

He leaned over and dropped a quick kiss on my cheek.

"I'm looking forward to tomorrow, to a lot of tomor-
rows."

Once again his boldness took me by surprise. I could
only nod. He got out quickly and rushed around to open
my door. He escorted me to the front door and there he
put his hands on my shoulders to turn me to him.

"Good night," he said and leaned in to kiss me on the
lips this time. "I feel like a pirate who's discovered a
buried treasure," he said and returned to his car, leaving
me speechless at the door.

Cape Cod was famous for its weather, famous for the
way a storm could sweep in and sweep out, all in the
same morning. No wonder Samuel Logan liked it here so
much, I thought, and went into the house, flushed and
overwhelmed by his energy and determination. Someone had lit a fire under him, I concluded. I only hoped it
was me.

161

8

Deathbed Confession

There were times when I believed that Samuel Logan had been advised that the way to my heart was to dominate my every free moment. Not a day passed since our first dinner date that he didn't call and propose some activity. Most of the time, I did enjoy his company. Our sailing date was pleasant and successful. He was skillful at boating, and looked to be even more comfortable at sea than he was on land.

"The sea is in my blood," he told me. "Whatever percentage that salt normally makes up in our bodies is doubled in mine. My father says that as a baby I was most content when he and my mother took me in a boat. The roll of the waves and the sound of the surf was the best lullaby. We are both children of the sea, Olivia. Our lives are so tied up in it, we can't go far from shore."

I would sit and listen to his speeches over dinner, or in the car, or just while we were walking through town and I would think that if Samuel Logan was anything, he was surely a good salesman. I had to admit to myself that I enjoyed the attention, enjoyed being taken to restaurants and the movies, having car doors opened for me, having a good-looking man escort me everywhere until people began to take note and think of us as an item. I know Mother was happy for me. Belinda, on the other hand, took all the credit.

"If I hadn't talked you into fixing yourself properly, you might never have kept his interest, Olivia."

"If he's only interested in me now because of a little lipstick and rouge, I feel sorry for him," I told her. She took it wrong, of course.

"So you've slept with him. How was it?" she asked one night while I was preparing to go out to dinner again with him. "Everything you've hoped it would be?" she added with that silly, little laugh.

"Of course I haven't slept with him," I snapped. "I don't jump into bed with the first man who comes calling. Or with every man who comes calling, like someone I know."

"Hasn't he tried?" she followed, undaunted, her eyes sparkling wickedly. "Haven't you wanted him to try?"

"Stop it," I said turning back to the mirror. "You might have this sort of a conversation with your bubble-gum friends, but not with me."

"I'm just wondering what you do then," she said with a shrug.

I spun back on her.

"You're wondering what we do? We do what mature adults do. We go to dinner. We talk. We admire the scenery. We go to art galleries or to the community theater or a film and talk about the story, the characters. We get to know each other better to see if we really belong together, and then, then, after we are comfortable with each other, we develop in other ways," I lectured.

She burst into laughter.

"What is so funny, Belinda?"

"By then you'll both have gray hair and no teeth," she declared.

"But I won't have to hide a pregnancy or be thrown out of a finishing school," I countered. Her smile flew off her face like a frightened bird and was quickly replaced by a scowl.

"I was just trying to be funny, Olivia. You don't have to get nasty."

"I'm going to be late," I said wanting to abruptly end the silly conversation. I turned away from her.

"Right." She went to my dresser drawer. "I need this tonight," she said taking back her bra.

"Where are you going?"

"Out to develop in other ways," she snapped back at me and left my room.

I felt myself blush deeply red with anger and then thought more about her and smiled. It was amusing. For the first time I could remember, Belinda was actually jealous of me. Our parents were talking about my relationship with Samuel, asking me questions about social affairs while she stood or sat by listening. Family friends made comments to her about my romantic involvement and not her own. Most important, as far as I could tell, despite her flirtatious manner, Samuel didn't pay her any particular attention. Envy dripped from Belinda's lips and she didn't know how to keep it from staining the pink clouds on which she floated. Spite and anger were her only means of defense. I thought it was purely out of simple vexation when she announced one night at dinner that she wouldn't attend the Childs' engagement party.

"You can go with Olivia and Samuel, Daddy," she told him. "None of my friends will be there anyway."

"You should be trying to make other friends, Belinda," I said.

"My friends are just fine."

"They're fine if you want to remain forever in high school," I retorted. Her eyes took on the shine of forthcoming hot tears.

"You think you know everything about men now just because you have a steady date all the time. You just can't stop being bossy about my life. I'm not you."

"That's always been fairly obvious."

"I don't want to be you!"

"Stop this bickering immediately," Daddy ordered. Fortunately, Mother was always upstairs at dinner now, and didn't have to listen to Belinda's whining.

She stuffed a piece of bread into her mouth and glared at me as if to say she was smothering her words, but not her thoughts.

"If you don't want to attend the affair, you don't have to, Belinda," Daddy consented.

I looked at him, surprised. He wouldn't want to insult his friend Colonel Childs, but then on second thought I realized he was probably happier Belinda wasn't going. He wouldn't have to worry about her behavior or silly things she might say. He was worried enough these days. Mother seemed to be growing weaker and weaker and her stomach problems had returned. He and I were afraid that her next evaluation would bring us all only dreadful news. The threat hung over our house like a tempest threatening to wash our family out to sea. Daddy wore a mask of gloom, his eyes dark and heavy with lines I hadn't seen before etched from his nose to his lips. He walked with a lumbering gait, his shoulders dipped, his strength sapped by shadows of gloom clinging to the walls of our home, cowering in corners, licking their lips in anticipation of the dread that would come knocking at our door. But something else came first.

The morning of Nelson Childs' engagement party, Samuel phoned to ask if he could see me immediately.

"Can't it wait until you come by to take me to the Childs' affair, Samuel?"

"No," he said. "I want to have a special moment with you, Olivia. Please," he pleaded.

Mother had been sleeping longer and longer every day and with the nurse there, there wasn't much for me to do. I agreed, fixed my hair, put on one of my new cotton blouses and a matching skirt and went downstairs to wait. Daddy had gone to the office to complete some work. He promised to be home early enough to dress for the party. However, he said he would go himself instead of with Samuel and me.

"No need for a third wheel on your bike," he quipped. "You can ride very well on your own these days, Olivia." He tried to be amusing, but I knew he didn't want to go without Mother. She insisted he show himself and represent her as well. Belinda, still determined not to attend, deliberately rose earlier than usual and left for Kimberly's house where she claimed she would spend the day.

"Those snobby parties are boring anyway," she said as her parting remark, "but tell Nelson good luck for me," she added with a twinkle in her eyes. "I hope he's got what he wants."

I decided to simply ignore her so she just trailed that silly, little laugh behind her and left.

I was alone when Samuel rang the doorbell. I let Carmelita greet him and show him to the sitting room where I waited.

"Well," he said gazing about nervously. He was wearing a business suit and tie, "your sister's not at home?"

"Fortunately, no," I remarked.

He looked relieved about that, too.

"Fine," he muttered still standing just inside the doorway.

"What was so important that it couldn't wait for later in the day, Samuel?" I demanded. "It's only a matter of a few more hours."

"This couldn't wait a few more minutes," he said smiling like someone who had a deep secret he wanted to reveal. "Mind if I sit?"

"Of course not. Please do," I said and he took the chair across from the settee. He fumbled his hat in his hands for a moment and then smiled again.

"Well, it's a fine day for the Childs' engagement party," he said.

"Yes, but I knew about the weather before you arrived, Samuel." He saw my patience dwindling.

Finally, he cleared his throat, straightened his shoulders and began.

"I was thinking on the way over here that you and I haven't been together all that long, but we sure have spent quality time together, and so," he continued, barely taking a breath, "it's not the length of time that matters between two people, it's the value of the time they've spent in each other's company. Do you agree with that?"

"Certainly," I said.

"Then you agree that our time together has been valuable?" he asked encouraged.

"I wouldn't spend time with you otherwise," I replied. "I'm not one to waste my time."

"Of course not. In fact, that's what convinced me I was not being too forward, not rushing things."

"Things? What things, Samuel?"

"Things between us. I came to tell you that I've enjoyed your company so much, I don't want it to end, but even more important, I don't like the interruptions."

"Interruptions?" I had to shake my head and smile with confusion. What was he talking about?

"Nights, mornings, pieces of afternoon . . . I mean all the time in between our dates," he said.

I still looked confused and shook my head.

"What are you saying, Samuel?"

"I told you I wasn't the most eloquent of speakers. It takes me a little while to get to the point." He stiffened up in the seat. "What I mean to say is I want to make a steady diet of Olivia Gordon."

"What? Steady diet?"

He reached into his pocket and plucked out a small box. His smile widened as he rose from his chair and then went on one knee before me.

"I thought you might like this done the old-fashioned way," he began and opened the box.

In it was an engagement ring that rivaled the one Carson McGil had given Belinda, only I thought this one had a more elegant gold setting with baguettes.

"I took the liberty of ordering this," Samuel continued, "in the hope that you would give an engagement between us serious consideration."

Stunned by the twinkling diamond and the proposal, I sat dumbfounded. He remained on his knee, holding out the ring in its box before me. Slowly, almost like one afraid that if she touched it, it would disappear, I plucked the ring out of the box and looked at it closely. It was breathtaking.

"Not having a mother to advise me, I had to depend on an expert jeweler," he said. "I hope you like it."

"It's a beautiful ring," I gasped. I was hypnotized by its magical twinkle.

"Try it on," he urged.

I considered it and then did so, finding it a perfect fit. I turned my hand around to look at it from different angles. The hand that I thought looked so thin and bony now looked like it belonged to a princess.

"How did you know the correct size?"

"That was a bit of conspiracy," he confessed, "between me and your father. He got me one of your present rings and I had it fitted."

I dropped my hand to my lap as if the ring had taken on the weight of a lump of lead.

"My father already knows about this?" I groaned with disappointment.

Samuel nodded.

"I didn't want to appear too forward in his eyes," he said quickly. "And I thought if he got one of your rings to me . . . well, as you see, it worked as far as fitting."

"I don't like secrets, especially when I'm the only one not in on them," I intoned as if I stood behind a pulpit.

He shook his head.

"I assure you. Nothing sneaky was done. No one else knows about this," he said. "Please," he continued, "don't get the wrong impression."

I played with the ring, tugging it as if to take it off and then turning it on my finger. He watched, his eyes widening in fear and anticipation.

"I do believe with all my heart that we can have a wonderful life together, and I hope you feel the same way," he continued, his eyes fixed on my fingers. "We share interests. We share ambitions. I hope I haven't upset you," he added when I didn't respond.

"It's so sudden. I hate being surprised. I like preparation."

"I know, but why can't good things be sudden? Bad things often are, as you know yourself. Anyway," he went on, "I decided that today, a day we're going to Nelson's engagement party, would be a great day to announce our own."

I thought about it and smiled to myself. Yes, wouldn't it though, I thought. I wondered about the expression on Nelson's face when he saw the ring on my finger, and the expressions on the faces of all those people who were satisfied in believing I would never be married. They were convinced I would end up a spinster, running my father's enterprises, while my sister, my beautiful sister, landed some rich and handsome young man. Wouldn't they be shocked?

"Don't you think it would be a good day to make such an announcement?" Samuel pursued.

I snapped out of my reverie and gazed down at him. He was looking at me as if I were about to pronounce a verdict in a court. His eyes were filled with anxiety and the dread of hearing a refusal.

"Yes," I said. "It would."

His face exploded in a smile. He kissed my hand and jumped to his feet.

"How wonderful. I'm the happiest man in the world, happier than Nelson Childs because I'm sure we'll have a better marriage," he added. My eyebrows turned up at their centers.

"Really?"

"Yes, really, really. We're perfect together, Olivia. We didn't need some social matchmaker bringing us together. The moment I saw you in that office behind that desk working like a bee, I knew you and I would be a great team. We'll own the Cape someday. I swear.

"I've had my sights on a special home for us, Olivia," he continued. "It's a large two-story house, very old and prestigious, the original portion having been built around 1780. I'm planning on gutting it and modernizing it. We can build onto it. I'll take you there tomorrow and you can begin to plan it out with our architects. I want it to be ready for us the day after our honeymoon," he said.

"It does sound like you've been planning this for some time, Samuel, longer than we possibly could have known each other," I commented with narrowed, suspicious eyes.

He stared a moment and then laughed.

"Well, I've been planning to find the perfect wife for some time and I've been planning where we would live. The house is situated on a most desirable piece of land between Provincetown and North Truro, with its own private access to the beach, just like you have here, and room for gardens and a view of the sea. You'll see you're not giving anything up in marrying me. I'll take you there in the morning, first thing," he promised. "I'll come as early as you want. What time do you want me?"

I had to laugh.

"Let me catch my breath, Samuel. You're making me dizzy spinning and jumping and making these dramatic pronouncements like some town crier."

"I want to; I want to keep you dizzy with surprises and happiness," he said. "I've got to go home to tell my father the good news, and then I'll be back in three hours to take you to Nelson Childs' engagement party. We'll steal the limelight," he promised, slapping his hands together.

He started out of the room and then turned and rushed back to plant a quick kiss on my cheek.

"Thank you," he said. "Thank you for making me the happiest man in the world."

He turned and left me sitting there, dazed, the diamond glittering under the light of the lamp beside me, my heart galloping.

What a wonderful surprise this will be for Mother, I thought as I stood up. My legs felt a bit weak under me as the realization of what had happened sunk in. I was engaged and to a very handsome man. In a sweeping moment, I was ahead of Belinda again and the proper thing would happen: the older daughter would be married first. Mother would surely be pleased and she so needed something to make her happy and bring a smile to her weak, thin face.

As I started for the stairway, I heard a voice within me ask, "But do you love him, Olivia?"

I paused.

"He didn't mention it," I muttered to myself. "He didn't even ask. It was as if he knew that love was something I believed grew between two people. Those who claimed they were struck by lightning and heard bells ringing every time they kissed were people living in a fairy tale, putting themselves into romance novels and films. In the end when reality set in, they were the most disappointed. The best marriages were ones like the one I was about to consent to: a marriage built on sensible, logical blocks, giving it a firm foundation. Love would come later, I thought. First, we had to respect each other and succeed together. Then, we would look into each other's eyes and say, "Yes, yes, there's another strong bond there, an emotional tie that is now strong enough to hold two independent people together securely. Now it's proper and right to say, 'I love you,' and have it mean something."

I climbed the stairs and went to Mother's room. She was dozing. Her nurse looked up at me.

"I'll stay with her awhile," I said.

"Very good." She rose. "I'll just go down to have some coffee," she said looking at Mother. She shook her head, her eyes dark. "Call me if you need me," she said before leaving.

I sat by the bed and studied Mother's small, burdened

breaths that made her chest look heavy. Her bald head ravished by the chemotherapy was wrapped in a silk scarf. Her skin was so pasty white, she looked like she had no blood.

After a few more moments, she whimpered and grimaced and then opened her eyes to see me sitting there.

"Oh, Olivia, dear. Have you been here long?"

"No, just a few minutes, Mother. I came to tell you something so you would be the first to know," I said, despite the fact that Daddy had been in on Samuel's plan, perhaps even before Samuel had thought of it himself.

"What, dear?" she asked trying to turn toward me. I fluffed her pillow and helped her sit up. Even though my hand moved around her face like a hummingbird, she didn't notice the ring. It was as if she had grown partially blind.

"Samuel Logan was just here, Mother."

"Really? What time is it? Is your father dressed?"

"It's early. Samuel didn't come to take me to the engagement party. He came to declare his own engagement."

"Oh, he did!" She started to shake her head. "I didn't know he . . ."

"To me," I said.

"What? To you?"

I lifted my hand to exhibit the ring. She gazed at it and then I got the smile I wanted, the smile I had hoped for, the smile my mother wore so often in her life, that bright, happy, hopeful beaming that turned her eyes back to the jewels they had once been. Color even returned to her sweet face.

"Oh Olivia, how wonderful! What a beautiful ring. You're engaged. What a wonderful piece of news to give me!"

"So you really have to get better, Mother. We have our own engagement party and wedding to plan, and I have a house to build. You'll have to help me with the architect. There's so much to do. We don't have time for this illness nonsense, Mother."

She lowered herself back to her pillow and smiled strangely at me.

"Why are you looking at me like that, Mother?" I asked, feeling a dark shadow cross over my heart.

She sighed and closed her eyes. For a moment I thought she had actually passed away. She was that still and her eyes were closed that long.

"Mother!"

She opened her eyes.

"You just sounded more like me than ever, Olivia. You were never one to ignore the hand before your eyes. All these years, whenever I refused to see hardships or pain, disappointments and defeats, you would chastise me. Stop pretending, Mother, you would say. It doesn't make it disappear if you ignore it. It's still there. Remember?"

"Yes, but . . ."

"Well, I have come to a point in my life when I have to follow your good advice, Olivia."

She turned to gaze at her rose-tinted glasses, sitting atop her bedside table.

"There's no point in putting them on now. It won't change things. Living in my own imaginary world was comfortable, but it wasn't the right thing to do. I always knew that, Olivia. The truth is I was selfish. In that respect Belinda is more like me than she is like her father. Funny," she said with a small, weak laugh, "you turned out to be more like him. It's pleased him. I know. It's made him feel better about what he did years and years ago," she said, her eyes out of focus now as she gazed at pictures inside her head.

"What do you mean, Mother? What did he do years and years ago?"

Her eyelids fluttered and she turned to gaze back at me, her face now full of resignation.

"I am dying, Olivia. Doctor Covington was here earlier and you know how brutally honest he can be. It's his philosophy to be direct and honest with his patients."

"Mother . . ."

"No, no, the results are in again and they're not good, Olivia. It's spreading, raging through me. I can almost feel it oozing through my bones," she said with another small laugh, more maddening.

"Daddy never said . . ."

"Don't pretend you didn't know I wasn't getting better, Olivia. You're not good at telling little white lies because you can't tolerate any falseness or dishonesty, no matter what the purpose. The ends never justify the means for you, my daughter. I am not silly enough to go to my Maker thinking He can tolerate any dishonesty either. This is a day I've dreamed about, a day I've dreaded, and not because it's a day when I have to face my own demise. It's a day when all my make-believe gets swept out the door, when the winds of truth come rushing through and wash out the pretend, the façades, the masks. There's nothing left now but honesty."

"Please don't do this to yourself, Mother. We'll get another doctor. We'll . . ."

She held up her hand, weakly.

"I'm not as upset about it as I thought I might be. When you live a life that's essentially built on lies, you think you are going to panic when that false foundation crumbles, but do you know what, Olivia? I feel a sense of relief. I feel . . . strangely enough, stronger because of it. You were right about facing reality and how that makes you a stronger person."

"I'm not making head nor tail of what you're saying, Mother. I'm going to have my own discussion with Doctor Covington and your other doctors and . . ."

"This doesn't concern him or them," she said. "It concerns you and me, Olivia. You and me first, and then your father," she added.

She closed her eyes again and was silent so long, I thought once more that she had passed on. Finally, she reached out for my hand and gazed at me.

"I want you to understand and believe that your father and I have grown to love each other as much as any two married people can and do. He blusters about, complains about my spending, or the way I handle the servants, you and Belinda, whatever, but after he's made his speeches and swung his arms about like a human windmill, he collapses in my arms in this bed and we hold each other before we sleep and we comfort each other and we do what we must to strengthen ourselves for the days to come. You and Belinda have never seen that part of him, but it's there. Believe me, Olivia, it's there and it's important. I do love him very much."

"I know that, Mother."

"Do you?" She smiled. "You always believed your father had his hands full with me, didn't you? You always believed he fumed and raged about this house like a man trapped. Be honest with me, Olivia. Don't pity me today because of what's coming tomorrow."

"Yes," I admitted. "There were many times I felt that, but he always seemed to deal with his dissatisfaction and go on."

She nodded, smiling.

"That's the strength that comes from our love, Olivia. I hope you will have it with Samuel. Of course, you won't have it immediately. It comes with time, with respect, with the realization that together you are one in the end."

"I know, Mother. I don't expect more," I said lowering my head.

"You deserve more," she said. "You've been an ideal daughter, both to me and your father. He's very, very proud of you, Olivia," she said, paused, and then added, "as proud as he would be were you his own daughter."

I looked up sharply.

"What?" Surely she's has lost her wits now, I thought. "I am his own daughter."

She shook her head.

"The day you were born, Winston and I made a vow. It was more his vow than mine."

"What vow?"

"Never to reveal the truth. He swore he could live with it. I hadn't fallen in love with him yet, but I don't think I ever loved him more than I did at that moment."

I shook my head.

"What are you telling me, Mother?"

"You know that your father and I were brought together by his parents and mine. Our lives were more or less planned by other people. I didn't think I could live with him, much less love him. There was someone else, someone not half as desirable in the eyes of my parents, a young man, a fisherman who worked for your grandfather and your father. Now," she said looking off, "he seems like a dream to me, nothing more."

I thought my heart had fallen into my stomach. My chest felt that empty and cold. I shook my head. The room began to spin so I closed my eyes and breathed deeply.

"Don't hate me. Don't hate anyone," Mother said, almost in a whisper now. She was getting very tired.

"I don't understand what you're saying, Mother."

"You don't want to understand, Olivia. You're acting like me again. While I was engaged to your father, I still saw this young man. We were intimate and I became pregnant right before my wedding. Your father knew. My fisherman left and Winston and I were married. My fisherman wasn't the sort who stood by his actions anyway. He was a drifter, a free soul, handsome and as harmonious as a songbird. His laugh was like a melody to me. Sometimes now, I think he wasn't real. I think maybe I did imagine him. Maybe it was all a fantasy. That's how you know me best, pretending," she said. "Well that was the old me; the new me must strip away the lies and stand naked with the truth.

"I thought about dying without telling you. I asked myself what good will it do? You might have a terrible reaction, hate me, love your father less, hate your sister, but then I kept returning to the realization that I was going to stand before the great Judge and without a clear conscience, without relieving myself of the guilt, I would not be able to raise my eyes and look into His. So, maybe I'm doing this for selfish reasons, Olivia. Forgive me and please, please don't hate me. I'm a frightened woman who is trying to get strong enough for what is to come."

I simply stared at her. So this was why my father forgave my sister so easily, why he cared more about her future than he did about mine, why he had tried to get her married and secure first. This explained the aloofness, the gap, the slight formality I always sensed between myself and him.

I went from shock to anger and rage and then to simple resignation. What could I do about any of it now? How could I be angry at my mother when she was at death's doorway? I did feel a surge of resentment for

Belinda, a jealousy I never imagined, but I had no time for it now, no time to feel sorry for myself, no time to rant and rave, no time to confront Mother and Father and berate them for living a lie and for betraying me and forcing me to live the same lie.

"Winston never loved you less, Olivia. He decided he would think of you as his own and he never faltered. I swear to you. He never once brought this up or threw it back at me. Your father, the man you respect for being coldly realistic and strong never gave up the illusion. He accepted what was and made it his reality and mine and I love him more for it. Please, please love him more, too," she pleaded. "Say something, Olivia."

I shook my head.

"It's so much to take in at once, Mother."

"I know, but I'm going to ask you to make a promise to me on my death bed, Olivia. Promise me you will never tell anyone, never tell Belinda, and never tell your father what I have told you. It's the last thing I will ever ask of you," she said. "Will you, promise? Please."

I closed my eyes. It was like swallowing down the truth and burying it inside me.

"I promise," I said.

"And you never lie," she reminded me. She smiled and with all her remaining strength, sat up to reach for me.

I hugged her and she put her arms around me as firmly as her weak arms would permit. I held her longer than I had expected, held her as if I were holding onto her for dear life. She kissed me on the cheek and closed her eyes.

I lowered her back to her pillow. She smiled again and reached up to take my hand.

"I've made myself a bit tired. I'll just rest, but wake me when your father comes home. I want to celebrate your engagement to Samuel with him," she said. Her hand softened and fell back to the bed like a small sparrow losing the power of flight.

I fixed her blanket so she was comfortable and then stood there looking down at her. She seemed to diminish right before my eyes, shrink into a little girl. I left her sleeping, her mind surely filled with lollipops and candy canes.

I didn't remember walking across the hallway to my room. It was as if I had drifted on a black cloud. Suddenly, I stood before my vanity mirror and looked at my face, laughing at myself now for the resemblances I had once imagined I had to my father. Lies and deceptions were truly brothers born from the same desperate need to survive in a world filled with entrapments, most of which we created for ourselves out of our own lusts and fantasies. What a fool you've been, Olivia Gordon. The lesson was clear. Survival was more important than honesty.

Honesty was perhaps the greatest luxury of all, and those who could afford it, who could house it and wear it and walk with it were the really blessed people in this place we called our home. They were never afraid to speak, to be heard.

The rest of us? The rest of us had nothing but muted voices.

9
&

A Turn
for the Worse

*D*addy put on an Academy Award performance when he returned and I showed him the engagement ring. Of course, I was tempted to shatter the illusion of surprise about my engagement and tell him I knew that he had already known Samuel's intention, that I knew he had been part of the planning, but with Mother dying in the room upstairs, we so needed some good news. I decided I would join him in the world of make-believe. We were a family out to sea, grasping desperately for a life raft of hope. As for the revelations Mother had told me, I was determined that for now and perhaps forever, I would keep them well hidden inside me. Daddy would never look at my face and see what I knew.

"I'm very happy for you, dear," he said. "I'm happy for all of us. It's a perfect union. You'll be happy together and we'll build something profitable. The bottom line is marriage can be a sensible partnership, too."

"I know, Daddy. I've already told Mother and she is very excited. She looks so tired and so much weaker, though. It's the cure that's killing her now."

"Yes," he said sadly, despair returning to wash the happiness out of his eyes. He shook his head. "I don't know if I should go to this party. I'm not much in the mood for people and music and laughter."

"Go for a little while," I told him. "Show your face and then leave," I said. He nodded.

"You're right. You always have the sensible suggestion, Olivia."

He kissed me on the forehead quickly and I couldn't help but think that the way he kissed me was somehow reserved, cold. Something inside him, despite his promises to Mother and despite his own desire, kept him from being fully my father.

He congratulated me again on my engagement before looking in on Mother.

I had, on my very own this time, gone and bought myself a new outfit for the Childs' engagement party. It was a two-piece navy blue wool knit suit with a silk blouse. I put on a thin pearl rope necklace and matching earrings and then indulged myself with more makeup than ever, choosing one of Belinda's brighter reds for my lipstick. I stood before the mirror and tested the length of my jacket sleeve as I moved my arm about, just to be sure my ring was always highlighted. Satisfied, I went to show Mother how I looked, but she was still asleep. Her nurse looked up from the book she was reading, looked at Mother and then turned back to me to shake her head softly, her eyes dark with concern. I nodded and backed out of the room, quietly closing the door. I'll stop in when I return, I thought and went downstairs to wait for Samuel.

Samuel was so excited and happy he nearly bounced in his seat as he talked, filling me in on his father's happy reaction to the announcement of our engagement.

"Did it make your mother happy?" he asked as we drove to the Childs' house.

"Yes, but she's not doing well, Samuel. I'm very concerned about her condition," I said. "Each day she grows weaker and smaller. It's as if she's fading away in that bed."

"I'm so sorry," he said and was silent. Dark thoughts like the tide crawled up to soak our brains in dreary images.

However, our heavy moment didn't last long. The sight of the Childs' estate, with the line of expensive cars building in the driveway, people in elegant dress milling about and music from the small orchestra wafting through the air, brought us out of our morose mood. Everyone who was anyone in Cape Cod society was present, as well as social editors with their photographers trailing right behind them snapping pictures of important couples, politicians and wealthy businessmen.

Since it was a partly cloudy, warm day with a gentle breeze coming in from the southwest, it couldn't have been more perfect for an afternoon affair. The guests were everywhere: on the porch, around the tables set up in front of the orchestra, or just wandering about the lawns and gardens. Through the line of red maples behind the house, patches of deep blue ocean were visible.

Overflowing with a thousand anxieties, I got out of Samuel's car when the valet opened my door. Samuel and I stood for a moment contemplating everything. Naturally, every new arrival drew the interest of the guests already gathered, so all eyes were on us for a moment. I saw people lean toward each other to whisper, heard laughter to my right, and then caught sight of Nelson and his fiancée talking to a half dozen couples near the outdoor bar. I thought he was looking my way as he listened and nodded to whomever was speaking.

"Let's get some champagne," Samuel suggested, took my arm and led me toward the roving waitresses. With our glasses in hand, we approached Nelson's parents and wished them the best. Nelson's mother noticed my ring immediately and asked about it.

"We thought we might as well join the happily married couples in this world," Samuel declared.

The news spread so fast through the gathering it was as if the breeze had its own lips and whispered in every ear. Heads turned, some congratulated us quickly, others just nodded and raised their glasses in a silent ceremonial toast. When Daddy arrived, he was quickly surrounded by his friends and associates and congratulated as well.

Nelson's fiancée hugged me and wished me luck, too. She raved about my ring. Hers was a little larger, but I thought mine more elegant because of the baguettes. I was grateful to the jeweler who had given Samuel advice and eventually told him so. Except for a quick greeting and a smile and nod of congratulations from him, Nelson didn't spend much time talking to us. In all fairness, he was in demand at every turn and it was difficult for him to take too much time with any one couple.

Just before we all sat at the tables to begin the sumptuous feast, Daddy came to tell me he was making his subtle exit. He was too nervous about Mother to stay much longer, he said.

"She doesn't even know I left the house. She wasn't awake."

"She's been sleeping a lot now, Daddy."

"I know." His face was somber for a moment and then he smiled. "Everyone's raving about you, Olivia. I think you and Samuel stole some of the Childs' spotlight here."

"I doubt that, Daddy," I said. "This is quite an engagement party."

It was such an elaborate affair with caviar hors d'oeuvres, shrimp and lobster entrées, as well as prime cuts of beef and roast turkey, bowls filled with at least a dozen varieties of salads, a half dozen differently prepared dishes of potatoes, Portuguese breads and rolls and a Viennese dessert cart that actually drew applause. Nothing was spared to make this one of the most memorable occasions of the social season.

Those who took time to speak to me and to Samuel asked after Mother, but really didn't want to talk about her at all. It was as if any possible suggestion of anything unpleasant was absolutely forbidden this afternoon. "Just don't ask," I wanted to say, and leave it at that.

"What a wonderful surprise to give your mother at this difficult time in her life," Mrs. Roddentrout, one of Mother's friends told me before coffee was served. "Very thoughtful of you, dear," she added as if becoming engaged was something you went out and did to make others happy.

"I assure you, Mrs. Roddentrout, it wasn't preplanned to happen at any particular time," I replied and she looked at me in total confusion. I nearly laughed.

Samuel knew many of the business people at the party and found himself embroiled in conversation most of the afternoon. I watched Nelson and his fiancée and occasionally caught him gazing at me and throwing me a smile, or lifting his glass to toast me, too.

Dancing started and I was suddenly taken by surprise when Nelson asked me to dance immediately after he had danced with his fiancée.

"It's only proper that I dance with all the engaged women here today," he said. Samuel laughed. "Do I have your permission, Samuel?"

"Oh, absolutely," he said, "but you'd better ask Olivia. She's the one who has to agree," he wisely added.

"Miss Gordon?"

I rose from my seat and we went onto the dance floor. I felt every female eye on us as he took my hand and put his other hand on my waist.

"You look beautiful. I'm really happy for you, Olivia," he said. "I hope you'll be as happy as I will."

"I don't know how happy you'll be, Nelson, so I won't agree to that just yet," I said.

He laughed nervously.

"I can see that you and I will always have to be direct and truthful with each other," he realized.

"All right," I said, my eyes fixed on his. "Let's make that promise."

"Okay, let's play truth or dare, Olivia," he challenged.

"Let's."

He brought his cheek closer to mine and whispered.

"Are you in love, Olivia?"

"Are you?"

"I think so," he said.

"I expect to be," I said.

He pulled back slowly and I looked into his eyes. They were laughing and full of sparkling light. Butterflies panicked in my chest. I was afraid he would see how much I cared for him. I felt as though I would soon be standing naked in front of him, unable to hide a thought, a feeling, a dream.

"You and I are more alike than I would have first thought," he said, his eyes turning dark and serious for the moment. "I hope we will always be friends."

"So do I," I said.

When he drew me to him again, I was sure he could feel my heart pounding against his chest.

"Did you tell your sister to stay away today?" he asked. I stiffened.

"Absolutely not. She thought this would be a boring affair," I said and he laughed.

"That's what I like about her, too. She says just what she thinks and feels. It's refreshing when you spend most of your time surrounded by dishonesty."

"Refreshing?" I said thinking now about my mother's revelations. "Sometimes, keeping the truth to yourself makes for more happiness."

He shrugged.

"Who knows who will be the happiest of us all? I wish we had a crystal ball."

"It wouldn't stop some of us from making the same mistakes," I remarked.

He laughed again, but this time with a deeper, darker sound.

When the piece ended, he escorted me back to my table.

"I was getting jealous," Samuel said. "You two looked too good out there."

"Just let yourself go, Samuel. Relax more and you'll look good, too," Nelson advised him. He winked, thanked me for the dance and returned to his fiancée.

We had come to the party thinking we would steal the glitter and glamour, riding the wave of social acceptance, but at the moment, I felt as though I was sinking. A rush of sadness washed through my very being. The sky was still a soft blue with only scattered clouds, but the chill in my bones told me a storm was just beyond the horizon.

"I think I'd better go home, Samuel," I said. "I'm worried about Mother."

"Oh, certainly," he said. "This is about over anyway."

All the way home Samuel bragged about how his friends and acquaintances congratulated him on our engagement.

"Every one of them thought we were a perfect match, Olivia. We're going to do great things together."

He rambled on and on, but I didn't hear much. My mind was on Nelson and our intimate moments on the dance floor. What had he seen in my eyes? How had it affected him? Would we always be close friends?

"Well?" Samuel asked.

"What?"

"I just asked you when you thought I should come by tomorrow to take you to see the house and the property. I'll have the architect there if you like."

"Oh, I'm sorry. I was in deep thought about Mother. You should call me about ten and I'll let you know how things are," I said.

"Fine. I can't wait for you to see it, Olivia. Your father's seen it, you know. He thinks it's a spectacular piece of property."

"You took him to see the house and land already?"

"Well, not exactly to see *our* property. I took him to see the historic house when I was contemplating the purchase. I respect his business sense," Samuel quickly explained.

I was still suspicious of all this, but before I could say or ask anything else, we turned in to my driveway and I saw the ambulance parked in front of the house.

"Oh no!" I cried. "I knew something was wrong."

Samuel drove up quickly and parked. I jumped out of the car and hurried to the front door. I stopped in the entryway and looked up to see the paramedics carrying Mother on a stretcher down the stairs with Daddy trailing behind and the nurse behind him. Mother didn't look conscious.

"What happened?" I cried.

"I think she's fallen into a coma," the nurse said. "We're getting her to the hospital."

"Doctor Covington will meet us there," Daddy said.

"I can drive both of you," Samuel offered.

"No, no. I'm fine. You can do me a favor, however," Daddy told him.

"What?"

"Belinda. I called and told her we'd be by to pick her up, but she's in the opposite direction. Do you know where Thomas Hughes' house is?"

"I'll find it," Samuel said. "I'll go by and bring her over to the hospital. I'm sorry," he said watching them load Mother into the ambulance.

Daddy and I went directly to his car and Samuel drove off to get Belinda. They arrived before Doctor Covington had come out to the lobby to confer with us. Belinda always kept her eyes fixed forward on me or Daddy when she was in the hospital. She only glanced furtively at anything else around her as if she believed looking at nurses and doctors, patients and machines might make her sick, too.

"Samuel told me you two were the hit of the party," Belinda began. She didn't even ask about Mother.

"I'm hardly thinking about the party, Belinda. We just brought Mother here in an ambulance. Don't you ever think of anything but fluff?"

"I was just trying to say something nice," she wailed. "I'm scared, too."

She sat sulking between Samuel and Daddy. I paced by the window until Doctor Covington came out to see us. I could tell from the look in his face, despite his stoicism, that things were not good.

"She has indeed fallen into a coma. I'm afraid it might be for the best," he added. "Her cancer has spread."

"Can't you just have it cut out like the last time?" Belinda cried.

"I'm afraid not," he replied softly. "It's gone too far for any of that now."

Belinda began to sob. Samuel put his arm around her and she dropped her head to his shoulder and cried more freely.

"How long will this continue?" I asked the doctor. Daddy was just staring at him.

"Days, maybe a week. It's hard to say at this point, Olivia," he replied. "We'll do all we can to keep her from experiencing any pain," he promised. He turned to Daddy. "I'm sorry, Winston."

Daddy widened and brightened his eyes as if they were two small flashlights he had just turned on.

"Yes, thank you," he said and then looked to me.

"We'll look in on her and then go home," I decided. Daddy turned to Doctor Covington, his eyes questioning.

"Yes, that would be fine," the doctor said as if anything we did now had little consequence anyway.

Belinda couldn't stop crying so she remained in the lobby with Samuel. Daddy and I went into the room. The nurse stepped away from the bed as we approached. Her eyes were full of the prognosis; she had seen patients near death before, and there was no false hope in her face, only a slight smile of sympathy.

"I'll be right outside," she whispered and left us.

Daddy folded his hands into fists as we both looked at Mother. His body stiffened, the anger overtaking the sorrow in him for a few moments.

"She doesn't look like she's suffering, Daddy," I said. He nodded.

"No, she doesn't," he said relaxing. "In fact, she looks younger."

"If I know her, she's already dreaming of being someplace more pleasant," I said.

Daddy smiled through his teary eyes. He took Mother's hand in his and stood there, and for the first time in all my life, I realized that despite how I thought he viewed her all these years, despite what value I had imagined he had placed on her as a wife, he really loved her as much as a man could love a woman. Mother was right about that.

I wondered.

Would a man ever love me that much? Was Samuel capable of it?

More important, did I really want his love to be that strong?

Or was I like Mother, closing my eyes, and dreaming of a more pleasant place, a place where the man I really loved was with me?

Mother died four days later in the middle of the night. It had begun to rain softly only a few hours before we were called, the drops resembling the tick, tick, tick of a watch as they tapped against my window pane. They streaked and zigzagged like tears. Occasionally, there was a burst of lightning in the distance.

I heard the phone ring and not more than five minutes or so afterward, I heard a gentle knock on my bedroom door. My heart was throbbing in my chest. I felt a hot flush through my body. It was one thing to expect the bad news, but another to have it actually happen. I rose slowly, slipping on my robe, and went to the door to find Daddy in his pajamas, barefoot, his hair disheveled. He was chalk white. Even his lips had no color.

"It was the hospital," he said. "Your mother's gone." He turned like some mindless messenger of death and went to Belinda's room to knock on her door. It took her longer to answer. I stood in my own doorway and listened to him make the same report. Then I heard Belinda's wails.

"I have to go over there," Daddy said turning back to me. "There are papers to sign."

"I'll go with you," I said.

"No, no, just stay with your sister," he replied and returned to his bedroom, closing the door behind him.

For a few moments, I remained where I was just listening to Belinda's sobs and gasps. I had yet to shed a tear of my own. I went to her door and looked in on her. She was sitting on the floor beside her bed, her head on her arm against the bed, her body jerking in small spasms.

"Mommy," I heard her cry repeatedly. Finally, she caught her breath and turned to look up at me. "Olivia," she said, her mouth twisting, "what will we do?"

"Do? There's nothing we can do. I'll help Daddy with the funeral arrangements," I said. I didn't recognize the sound of my own voice. I felt as if I were speaking in a long, narrow tunnel, my words echoing in my ears and sounding mechanical, a recorded voice with little emotion, similar to the voices of trained telephone operators reading from prepared instructions.

"What should I do?"

"You must not do anything to cause him any more grief," I replied.

"What do I do? I don't cause him any grief!" she protested.

"I don't have the strength or the desire to go through the long list of troubling things you do, Belinda. Just don't do anything wrong for a few days, please," I concluded and returned to my own room.

I heard her crying again. Then I heard Daddy come

out and start down the stairway. I went to my door to call to him.

"Are you sure you don't want me to come along, Daddy?"

"What? Oh, no, Olivia. I won't be that long. Get some rest. Tell Belinda to get some rest, too. Everyone, just get rest," he said and disappeared down the stairway, his footsteps falling away like the drumbeats of a passing funeral parade. I heard the front door open and close and then all was silent. Belinda's crying began again, only louder.

I went back to bed and stared into the darkness, thinking about my mother's last bright smile, a smile I would see no more. Less than ten minutes later, Belinda came to me. She stood there at the foot of my bed, her arms folded across her bosom, her shoulders rising and falling with her deep breaths.

"She died before I had a chance to talk to her again," Belinda said.

"What would you have said?" I asked.

She was silent. She looked away and took another deep breath.

"I don't know. There were things to say, weren't there?"

"From you? Just I'm sorry," I said, "and she didn't want to hear it."

"I would have said more than just I'm sorry, Olivia. I would have told her how much I loved her, you know." In the glow of the hall light, her eyes glistened with her tears while her face turned red with fury. "How can you just lay there and be mean to me at this moment?"

"I'm not being mean," I said calmly.

"Yes, you are. You've been meaner than ever to me just because . . ."

"Because of what?" I asked. My heart stopped and

then started with a quickened beat. My ears were already ringing in anticipation.

"Because of what I did with Nelson Childs," she shot back at me. "I know you know."

"What? Why that's . . ."

"Nelson told me," she said. I just stared at her. "That's the reason you've been meaner to me, and you know it," she said.

How could Belinda have such insight? She couldn't. She was just taking wild stabs at me because she was in so much pain.

"I disapproved for other reasons, Belinda, but I never told anyone."

"You told him. That was enough," she said. "You've got Samuel now. You shouldn't hate me."

"I don't hate you. Don't be ridiculous. I told you not to do anything to cause anybody any more grief at the moment, didn't I? So don't."

"I'm not jealous of you. I've never been jealous of you, Olivia."

"And I'm not jealous of you, so stop it. Stop it!" I shouted.

She was silent.

"Well, maybe I am jealous of you," she admitted.

"Oh, and why would that be, Belinda? What do I have or what have I done that you could possibly covet?" I asked, amused more than curious.

"You spoke to Mommy last," she said. "You have that."

She stared at me in the darkness a moment and then she turned and went back to her room. Through the walls, I heard her sob herself back to sleep. I lay there finding myself feeling more sorry for her than I was for myself. I wondered if I always would.

* * *

Mother had a very large funeral. There were so many people in attendance that a large number of them had to stand outside the church door. We kept the coffin closed and strewn with her favorite flowers: jonquils. The minister eulogized her as a faithful loving wife, a woman who truly personified the Christian spirit, full of love and forgiveness, someone who brought light and joy into her home. At one point Belinda cried so loudly, I had to gaze at her with hard, cold eyes to get her to smother her sobs. Daddy looked stunned and stared ahead, shaking hands and thanking people mechanically after the service.

It wasn't until we were at the cemetery and we stood before the open grave, waiting to swallow Mother into the earth, that I finally faced the fact she was gone. I surprised myself with the intensity of my own grief. I would miss her very much. Ironically, she turned out to be the most honest person in my life. I could never be like her, but I recognized that I had needed her, that I still needed her, that I had never been more alone.

Samuel stood beside me. He gestured to embrace me, but I stood away, straight and firm. I would never depend on any man the way Mother depended on Daddy, I thought. No man would ever claim to be my rock and foundation.

Nelson and his family were at the church and at the cemetery. His fiancée was back in Boston. I heard some excuse for her absence, but didn't pay enough attention to remember it. They returned to the house with the other mourners to comfort us. Our house was full of people, their voices low and melancholy at first and then, as the day wore on, growing louder, stronger until there was actually the sound of laughter and what had begun as a gathering of mourners turned into a strange sort of party with people wearing their smiles and finding humor as a way to drive death itself out the door. For most, it worked. It worked for Belinda, of course.

Only an hour or so into the gathering, she was surrounded by her flock of bubble-gum friends and a number of young men. She soaked up their attention with her sponge smiles and her extra long hugs, turning her lips toward certain boys when they went to kiss her in comfort. I watched her become Scarlett O'Hara and then I fled from the scene and went to the rear of the house to just stand alone in the shadows. I could see the rain clouds in the distance turning toward us. It wouldn't be long before they dropped their tears into the wind funneling through the trees and over the knolls around our home. What could be more fitting than a night of rain, I thought and hugged myself against the chilled air.

"Cold out here?" I heard and turned to see Nelson standing behind me. He had a glass of bourbon in his hand and swirled it before he took another sip, his eyes on me.

"It's cold inside, too," I replied.

"Yes, I imagine it is for you," he said. "I always liked your mother. She was always very up and happy. She made you feel good when she was in your company or you were in hers. My parents were very fond of her."

I nodded.

"When are you and Samuel planning on getting married?"

"Samuel thought it would be nice if we timed it around the completion of our house. What about you?"

"A little less than a year. You might actually beat us to the altar if I know Samuel. He'll hock his eyeteeth to hire additional workers and speed up the construction."

"You met your fiancée rather quickly," I said, "or did you know her even when you came here?" I asked pointedly, my eyes on the boathouse. Nelson laughed.

"You don't have any subtlety to you, do you, Olivia? You go right for the jugular?"

"If you mean I go right for the truth, yes," I said.

"We knew each other. My decision to become engaged came shortly afterward," he replied.

"So you were just testing the waters to see if you were going to make the right decision?" I asked.

He shrugged.

"Something like that."

We stared at each other a moment.

"I wonder what it would be like being married to you," he said. "Does Samuel fully understand how strong you are, how assured and competent a woman you are? The other women he's known have all been like . . . like . . ."

"Belinda?"

Nelson's lips curled into a wry smile.

"Yes," he said.

I looked out at the sea.

"I haven't given him any other impression about myself than what I am," I said.

"Well then, either he's accepted that or he's deluding himself into believing he can change you," Nelson said. I smiled without turning back to him.

"You don't think I can change?"

"No. Actually, I'm not sure I'd want you to change," he said and held his eyes on me when I turned to him again.

I wanted to say I had thought he was coming back here to see me after he had come to dinner with his family that night to pursue me and not to have a dirty little assignation with Belinda in our boathouse. I wanted to say I thought he was a better man than that, but I didn't. I simply bit my lower lip and swallowed back my regrets and disappointments like so much stomach acid.

"Your father's lucky to have a daughter like you, especially now," he continued. "You're going to hold your family together. You're a strong person."

"Too strong for you?" I dared ask.

He smiled.

"No. I'm too frivolous a person for you. We would probably end up killing each other," he joked.

"Yes," I said, cloaking my disappointment in a smile. He took another sip of his bourbon.

"Can I get you anything?"

"No. I'm coming back in," I said. "I just had to get a breath of fresh air. All those people . . ."

"Yes," he said nodding as if he understood, as if he could ever understand. "Well, I'll be inside," he added, reached out to touch my hand and then turned and entered the house.

I stood there trying to swallow. I felt as if the air around me had turned to ice. A few hundred yards to my right, Belinda's dead fetus lay planted like some seed of deformity, a sin pressed down into the darkness in a vain attempt to keep it forgotten. Belinda was capable of forgetting. That was her strength. She could wipe away her yesterdays like she wiped the chalk board at school and start again.

I couldn't. Everything that happened and everything I did and thought was indelibly written on the surface of my heart. It was an organ covered with scratches and small tears already. The biggest tear came with the realization that Nelson Childs was never to be mine.

Desire was cruel. We should want only the things we can have, I thought; otherwise, longing becomes pain and pain turns us into creatures of dissatisfaction, sitting with arthritic, curled fingers, scowling at the horizon, furious at the sun for rising and bringing us another day of disappointment.

"There you are!" Samuel cried. "Nelson told me you were out here. My poor Olivia," he said sauntering over to embrace me. I smelled the odor of whiskey and onions on his breath and my stomach churned. "You shouldn't be alone at a time like this, Olivia."

"You can only be alone at a time like this," I replied.

"I'll make it up to you, Olivia. I'll work like a dog to make you happy again. I'll start tomorrow. I'll dig the first shovelful for our foundation first thing. I'll . . ."

"Let's go inside, Samuel," I said sharply. "It's getting colder."

"What? Oh, yes. Of course."

He kept his arm around me clumsily as we approached the door and then I stepped forward and his arm slipped away.

Just like Mother's hand, leaving me alone to face what was to come.

10

The Bride No One Would Have Believed

During the days that followed Mother's funeral, Daddy fell deeper and deeper into his own grave of despair. His eyes remained bleak, dark, haunted. I had never understood how much he loved and needed what I had thought was only her silly little jabber. However, without it, our home became an empty music hall, every sound echoing on the previous. I realized that Mother had created all the real melodies here. Her laughter, her symphonies of gossip filled with funny, inconsequential information about this one or that apparently had provided Daddy with a very necessary contrast and respite from the more serious, dour talk of business. She had been there to greet him with a kiss and a hug, to whirl around him in her newest dress or float her hand under his nostrils to give him a whiff of her latest cologne.

He could tolerate her illness because there was always the false hope that stems the flow of nightmares, the belief that something miraculous could still happen, that medicine and science would produce a cure just in time, what the Greeks called their *deus ex machina,* a last minute device to save the day and restore our world to its balance and health.

However, once death came calling, all that hope died with Mother's last breath. In the beginning, right after her funeral in fact, it was still difficult to believe she was gone. The heavy truth lingered like a persistent storm overhead, the truth seeping in more deeply each day. Mother was really gone. We were never going to see her again.

Even Belinda had trouble reviving herself. She moped about with large, teary eyes, took long naps, or just curled up like a baby in her bed and stared at the wall, her thumb against her lips. Her friends called, but her conversations were far shorter than usual and none of them came to visit. She discouraged them with her tears and moans of sorrow.

None of us had much of an appetite. Dinners were quiet and short. The nightmare continued to shadow our days until I announced I was returning to work. Up until now Daddy had visited the offices briefly and kept up with important business events over the phone. Our company was in a holding pattern. No decisions were being made. Everything was languishing.

"We've got to get back to full-time work, Daddy," I finally told him one night at dinner. "Mother wouldn't want us to mourn like this any longer. You know how much she hated gray faces and sadness," I said.

He nodded.

"Olivia's right," Belinda said. "I'm not going to turn down another invitation."

"That's not exactly what I meant," I snapped, but she didn't want to hear me.

The next day she was off with her friends, returning to the Bubble Gum Club and her unproductive activities. If

Daddy had difficulty seeing how wasteful she was before, he was incapable of seeing it now. It was almost as if he didn't notice her existence. She needed money? He scribbled out a check to keep his ears from ringing with her pleas. She wanted to stay overnight at some friend's house, go to an all night party, take a weekend in Boston? He nodded, waved his hand, not even comprehending what she was doing or what he was allowing her to do.

I was busy filling in for him at the office when he didn't appear or left early, moving things forward again, making decisions and signing agreements and checks. I reported it all to him, but he listened with half an ear and asked few questions.

Samuel visited daily. He tried to revive our lives by bringing the architect around to discuss how he would modernize the older portion of our home and how he would expand it. Daddy sat in on some of the meetings, but offered little comment or advice. It did provide a good distraction for me, especially when I faced the realization that this would be my own home, my own little world for a long, long time.

The work began almost immediately and with it came Samuel's frequent reports of progress. Once a week I would go to the site with him and inspect the construction. Nelson Childs had been right in his prediction about Samuel. Samuel had the foreman hire more laborers and the remodeling and the new additions to the house were being completed at twice the pace normally anticipated.

"It's wasteful," I told him, "to pay people time and a half just to get into the house a month or so earlier."

"Waste is directly related to what makes you happy and unhappy," Samuel replied in an uncharacteristic contradiction to what I had said. "I don't consider a nickel wasted if it brings me home to you one minute earlier, Olivia."

I raised my eyebrows and looked at him. How I wished I had the same intensity, the same desire and longing, and ironically I envied him for how much he seemed to love and want me. Usually, it was the woman who was impatient with the time it took to bring her to the altar. All the women I had known didn't have half the nervousness, the doubt, the insecurity as the men they were about to marry. Men, even though they did the proposing, behaved as if they were the ones who had been hooked and reeled in, not the women. It was as though marriage was the inevitable prison sentence awaiting them all.

Nelson behaved this way. Whenever I saw him and inquired as to his wedding plans, he would tell me nothing specific had been concluded yet. Why rush into what was inevitable? It wasn't going away, but, his impish smile told me, what was going away was his freedom. Soon enough he would have to behave appropriately. Why hurry it along?

Besides, he explained, the Branagans had insisted on using High Point House for the wedding reception and that had to be booked at minimum ten months to a year in advance. They were still discussing the actual date. The time in between was also necessary to get the families better acquainted. The Colonel and his wife were to be guests of the Branagans in Boston and the Branagans were to come more often to Provincetown.

They had already had a second engagement party for the Branagans' Boston friends. It was simply that there was much to do. He talked about it as if it were a campaign for the presidency of the United States, planning, planning, planning. For instance, there was the completion of the bride's trousseau, something Mrs. Branagan took quite seriously.

"Years ago, most mothers started making and embroidering linens for their daughter's trousseau almost from the day their daughters were born," Nelson explained. "Nowadays of course, women don't sew or embroider. They spend almost as much time, however, shopping, choosing, buying. Then there are the wedding plans. I swear, Olivia, cabinet meetings in the White House don't go on any longer or are treated with any more seriousness. Sometimes, our parents meet on neutral grounds!" he quipped. "Bridesmaids' dresses, my tuxedo and my groomsmens', the guest list, the menu, the design of the invitations, the decorations and the music, all of it has to be discussed and analyzed and concluded with almost the same ceremony as the treaty to end a war. Goodness knows there's lots of diplomacy at work to keep the respective mothers from scratching each other's eyes out. Dad says luckily he and my father-in-law have legal training. No," Nelson concluded, "ten more months is barely enough time as it is."

I didn't want to tell him I was doing all that myself.

"You're not anxious then?" I asked him.

"Admittedly, nowhere near as anxious as your fiancé," he told me when he joined us up at the house site one weekend a little more than a month and a half into construction. "You have possessed Samuel Logan. Look at him prodding and cheering those laborers to work harder, faster. If he could lash them with a whip, he would. You should never have agreed to a marriage date that was tied to the house completion. I hear the invitations are already at the printers. He told me he had you deliver the copy as soon as the electricians had started."

"You're not as possessed?" I felt like a lobster fisherman dropping traps to test the waters, but I was very curious about Nelson's feelings concerning his fiancée.

"I'm someone's possession," he quipped, "but I'm not yet possessed."

He smiled at me with those beautiful eyes and made my heart go into triple beats.

"How's your father doing these days?" he asked, perhaps wisely changing the subject.

"He's still not back to 100 percent. I'm afraid he might never be," I added in a matter-of-fact tone that took Nelson by surprise.

"I'm sorry," he said. "But maybe with time . . ."

"Time doesn't heal scars, as most people commonly think," I said. "It simply makes them firmer, stiffer. One must accept it and not hope to mend and return to what he or she once was."

"That's a hard and cold lesson, Olivia," he remarked.

"That's what the truth is, Nelson, hard and cold most of the time."

He stared at me and I did not shift my gaze.

"You're going to run this town one day," he predicted. "You're a natural born leader. You should have been born . . ."

"A man?" I finished for him. He shrugged.

"Sorry. I know that women are supposed to be treated with equal respect these days, but I'm still a bit old-fashioned when it comes to that, I suppose."

"You're just a typical chauvinistic male," I replied and he laughed.

He held up his hands.

"Guilty," he declared.

"Of what?" Samuel asked coming over to join us.

"Of stereotyping," Nelson explained.

Samuel looked from him to me and then shook his head and returned to pointing out the changes I had suggested be made in the historic sections of the house. It was a large two-story, side-gabled house. I had suggested capping the paneled front door with a decorative crown and then adding a row of rectangular panes of multicolored glass beneath the crown. I wanted the windows to have double-hung sashes and many small panes. Samuel complimented me on every suggestion I made. None of it came from imagination, however. I had researched the period and knew enough to make suggestions that the architect thought sensible.

Consequently, our wedding date was set with such speed it raised eyebrows. Some even had the audacity to suggest I might be pregnant. Belinda enjoyed the gossip. I did everything I could to end those rumors, but kept the date of our wedding. I was hoping it would help bring Daddy around again. Without Mother, he would have to represent my interests and I tried putting more decisions and questions on him, but his invariable response was, "Whatever you think best, Olivia. Don't worry about any expense, if that's a problem."

He even suggested I involve Belinda in some of the wedding planning, a suggestion I didn't take seriously, of course. Belinda had no taste, no real breeding, no sense of decorum. She would turn my wedding into a garish nightmare if she could. She tried to get me to invite some of the Bubble Gum Club, but I resisted.

"I'll have no one to talk to at the reception, no one to dance with. Please," she pleaded, "at least invite Kimberly and Bruce and maybe Arnold."

"It's not a party; it's a wedding," I told her.

"But I thought the reception was a party."

"Not the sort of party you attend," I said.

In the end I relented and agreed to invite Kimberly and Arnold.

"Kimberly and I will just have to share him," she

moaned. "I'm sure none of Samuel's friends or Daddy's business friends will ask me to dance. I won't have a good time," she threatened.

"It's supposed to be my day, Belinda, not yours. I think you could at least consider that," I lectured. "When you get married . . ."

"I'm going to have a real wedding. I'm going to get Daddy to rent a yacht that holds one hundred and fifty people and the wedding will be at sea, and there will be fireworks and the band will be on a boat beside the yacht, but playing so loud it won't matter."

"I can't wait," I said dryly.

"I can," she said with a laugh. "I'm not ready to be someone's wife just yet. I can't stand thinking about being with only one man forever and ever, just kissing the same old lips every night . . . ugh," she said shaking her shoulders as if she were shaking off a cold rain. "I don't think a woman should get married until she's at least forty."

"That's ridiculous, especially if you want to raise a family," I said.

"I don't expect to be a good mother anyway," she told me.

It always amazed me how Belinda could face her failings and weaknesses so easily and just as easily accept them. She was beyond feeling unhappy about herself. I despised and envied her for it simultaneously. It embarrassed me to think we had come from the same mother and yet she probably wouldn't ever develop a wrinkle from worry. She would go through life on those damnable bubbles, laughing and content.

She proved that in the way she recovered from Mother's death, returning to her philandering lifestyle with zest. Her wan, pale face of sorrow returned to that radiant visage that caused her to stand out like a vibrant, blossomed rose in a garden full of mediocre flowers. Even Samuel commented about it. The house reverberated with her giggles, her quick footsteps on the stairway, her telephone calls. At times Daddy looked shocked and surprised by her lack of sorrow. However, she was the only thing that brought a small smile back to those pressed tight lips and lifted the weight from his brooding forehead. I began to think she would replace Mother in his eyes. She would restore the music and the lightness and I was actually jealous.

For her part Belinda seemed no longer jealous of the attention my impending wedding to Samuel had continued to bring to our home. She was too happy again. I was filled with suspicions and trepidations. Surely, somehow, someway she would do something that would damage the family name just before my wedding, I thought. As always, I felt like someone staring up at the ceiling, waiting to hear the sound of the second shoe dropping.

Our wedding wasn't to be held on a yacht as Belinda dreamed hers would be, but Samuel surprised me one day with plans for our honeymoon.

"I've rented a yacht for us," he said. "We'll sail down to Hilton Head. What better place to be after our wedding than on the sea, don't you agree, Olivia?" he asked hopefully.

Samuel had come to my office, something he had begun to do more and more as our wedding date drew closer. I had actually been the one to work out a merger of his father's company with ours. It was more like a whale swallowing a minnow. Our appraisers fixed a value of just under a million dollars for the Logans' company, which was mostly tied up in their boats. I negotiated directly with Samuel's father and settled on three quarters of a million as the value and then made him take 90 percent of that in our company's stock.

"Oh well," he concluded, "it's all in the family now anyway."

Regardless of my marriage, I did not have documents written to that effect. Our financial interests remained separate and clear, but I did agree to give Samuel some managerial duties at our company and he was assigned an office. He complained that it wasn't side by side with mine, but he didn't complain very vigorously.

"One day the wall between us would come down anyway," he said. "I know it's what your father would like."

"We'll see," I said.

I knew it was always in Daddy's mind that someone would marry me and eventutally take the reins of our company. It was difficult for Daddy to envision a woman running his business, despite the amount of work I did and the decisions I made. He saw me as a temporary fix to be moved out and relegated to the house and child rearing.

It was during this dark period of his depression and despair that I worried about his capacity to make the right decisions concerning our company. Consequently, I had our lawyers draw up documents that in effect gave me the power of attorney and once I had that, I wrote bylaws that left me with control. No man, not even my own father, who I now knew to be my stepfather, would send me home to wipe the mouths of babies and change diapers. The sooner Samuel understood that, I thought, the better off he and I would be.

"That's fine with me," I said regarding the yacht, "as long as we have good weather."

"Oh, of course, of course," he replied beaming over my agreement. "I knew you'd like the idea. It's unique.

We're not just going off to some island hotel to languish in the sun. We'll sail and fish and explore together. I'm more excited about this than the actual wedding ceremony," he admitted.

I was too, but I didn't say so. Belinda was my maid of honor and some of our cousins participated as bridesmaids. The actual event did bring some life back to Daddy. His one big decision for me was to rent the Fisherman's Club for the reception.

The week of the wedding, the detailing of our new home was being completed. Since we would go directly there after our honeymoon, I began to have my things moved to the house. For the last few months, I had been ordering furniture. Most of it had already been delivered and set up. Everyone who visited claimed it would be a showplace. Nelson jokingly referred to it as "The Cape Cod Castle." He said he even envisioned me building a moat around it someday.

"To keep the riffraff away," he added.

"Too bad you won't be able to visit then," Samuel responded and they had a good laugh about it. I was beginning to wonder if Nelson had believed I thought too much of myself to ever consider him, not that Samuel was anyone more special, and not that he had ever really given me reason to believe there was even a shred of romantic interest. I was simply always looking for a reason why the man I could have loved as passionately as a woman should love a man never gave me a chance, even the chance he had given Belinda. Irony of ironies now: he was to be my future husband's best man and would be at the altar with me, but alas, only to hand Samuel Logan the ring I wished he himself would put on my finger.

We had a spectacular day for a wedding and the weather forecast for the upcoming week was excellent for sailing. For the first time in my life, it appeared everything was going to be picture perfect. Belinda revealed she was jealous of my good fortune.

"I hope I have a day as beautiful as this when I get married," she said, fluttering about the house, dressing herself, charging in and out of my room to make a suggestion about my hair, my makeup, and then rushing back to make some changes in her own hairdo. Anyone would have thought it was her wedding day and not mine. She was far more nervous and finally realized it, pausing as I calmly adjusted my wedding dress bodice.

"Aren't you excited?" she cried.

"Of course," I said calmly.

"You don't act it. You act like you're going to some business dinner. You're getting married today. Married!"

"People get married every day. There are probably fifty weddings going on right this moment," I said dryly.

"That's a silly thing to say. No one's getting married today but you. That's the way you should think. Who cares about anyone else? When I get married, the whole world's going to know it and stop to take notice."

"I bet it will," I said, but she didn't hear my sarcasm. Instead, she continued to flutter about me like a hummingbird until I finally had to tell her to go look after Daddy and stop worrying about me.

"I swear, Olivia," she said wagging her head, "you've got ice in your veins instead of blood."

She ran off to see about Daddy and I gazed at myself in the mirror. Did I have ice in my veins instead of blood? Was there something wrong with me because I wasn't giggling and taking deep breaths to calm my wild nerves? Even the thought of leaving this house didn't affect me as deeply as I had anticipated. I had grown up here, spent all my private hours in this room, dreamed and planned, had all my private little talks with Mother, and now, just like that, I was going to walk out that door, get into a limousine, be driven to a church and recite vows that would take me forever and ever away from these four walls. I should be shedding some tears, I thought. Where are my tears?

I leaned closer to the mirror and inspected my eyes. They were dry, bright and alert, hardly the eyes of someone struggling with emotion.

"Ready?" I heard and turned to see Daddy in his tuxedo standing in the doorway. "Today I give away my daughter. You look beautiful, Olivia. Your mother should have lived to see this."

"Thank you, Daddy. You look very handsome and distinguished."

"Only for you," he said with a sigh. "Well, then, I guess we're about ready. It's time."

I gazed at myself one last time and then started out, pausing in the doorway to look back at the bed and the furniture, the pictures and the curtains.

"It's going to be pretty empty around here with you gone, Olivia," Daddy remarked when he saw where my eyes lingered.

"I'll be here often, Daddy. You know that, and you'll be at my home often, too."

"Aye, but I'm not the sort who interferes in other people's lives, especially my daughter's," he said.

"You won't be interfering."

He nodded.

"Are we going?" we heard Belinda cry frantically. "I haven't done my makeup properly yet!"

"Do it in the limousine," I said. "You'll still be doing it as I walk down the aisle anyway."

Daddy laughed and Belinda moaned and complained, but followed us down the stairs and out the door.

Carmelita and Jerome stood by smiling and compli-
menting me on my appearance. They congratulated
Daddy and we got into the limousine.

As we drove off, I glanced back only once and focused
on the windows I knew were in Mother's bedroom. In
my imagination I saw the curtains part and her smiling
face as she threw me a kiss. There were tears of joy. I
sucked in my breath, swallowed a small moan and
looked out the side window at the passing scenery, my
mind on nothing at all. Finally, I realized what I was
doing. I was so in a daze, I hardly heard Belinda's
constant stream of babble, her complaints and worries
about how she would look in pictures. She badgered
Daddy, drawing compliments from him until she finally
appeared satisfied with herself.

"Look at all the people!" she cried as we approached
the church. "I'm as excited as I would be on my own
wedding day and I don't even have a steady boyfriend
these days!"

"Would you like to change places with me?" I challenged.

She raised her eyebrows, looked at Daddy, and
laughed.

"Hardly," she said. "I'm going to marry a movie star
or a musician, not some boring businessman."

"Your father's a businessman," I reminded her.

"That's different," she said gazing at me with that
sweet, flirtatious little smile. "He's my father."

She said it firmly, almost as if she somehow knew that
he wasn't mine.

As Daddy escorted me down the aisle, some of the
people who looked up at me from their pews still wore
faces of disbelief. Even the sight of me in my wedding
gown, the organ playing, the minister waiting at the altar

with Samuel and Nelson standing by, both looking handsome and distinguished, the mountain of flowers, the bridesmaids, none of it wiped the incredulous looks off their skeptical faces. I could see the questions and hear the gossip. How did Olivia Gordon win the heart of a man as handsome as Samuel Logan? Did her father buy her a husband? Green eyes of young unattached women still waiting for their dream lovers and perfect husbands glared at me. I gazed straight ahead, defiant and secure.

Nelson wore that impish grin on his lips as I stepped up to the altar. Samuel was beaming, his shoulders straight, his chest out. The guests fell into a hush as the minister began the ceremony, the recitation of words and the prayers and promises that would bind me forever to this man and this man to me.

As I recited my vows, I let my eyes shift so I could see Nelson standing there and I fantasized for a moment that it was he and not Samuel I was marrying. When he handed Samuel the wedding ring, he leaned over to give me a kiss on the cheek. It wasn't part of the rehearsal. I heard a few gasps behind me, and my heart jumped and fluttered as a hot blush stung my face. Samuel didn't appear to notice, or if he did, he thought it was he who had filled me with excitement.

The exchange of rings occurred and the words were spoken. When the minister pronounced us man and wife, the organ player began and there were cheers. Samuel kissed me and I kept my eyes closed so I could imagine they were Nelson's lips. Then we hurried up the aisle as children and some of the adults rained rice over us.

We got into the limousine quickly and were rushed away to prepare for the wedding reception. Samuel

looked so happy. His eyes were like two small bulbs, full
of brightness and joy.

"Well Mrs. Logan," he declared. "I bet all this feels
like a dream to you."

"Yes," I admitted. "That it does."

"Should I pinch you?"

"No, Samuel. That's quite all right. I'll pinch myself if
I feel the need," I said and he laughed and threw his arm
around me, drawing me closer to him. I closed my eyes
and for the first time wondered if I could really be a wife.

The reception was elegant and gay. I couldn't imagine
how the months and months of planning Nelson's and
his fiancée's parents were taking would have made it
much better. The caterers did a wonderful job. We
spared no expense and had prime rib, lobster, shrimp,
turkey, clams and pasta, beautiful plates of vegetables
and fruit, and the fanciest desserts. The decorators had
turned the room into a wonderland of flowers and glitter.
Our orchestra played well, and all the guests we wanted
and expected were there. It was at least as nice as
Nelson's engagement party. Whenever anyone complimented us on the reception, Samuel turned to me and
gave me all the credit.

"She's the one," he said, "who planned it all. I've been
too busy working on our home. There's not a more
competent woman in all of New England," he declared.

"You couldn't ask for a more loyal subject," Nelson
kidded me when he overheard Samuel commending me.

"I could ask for you," I shot back and he widened his
eyes and then laughed and performed an emphatic
European bow.

"No need to ask, Madam. I shall always be a loyal
subject," he declared and once again, asked me to dance
while his fiancée was occupied.

"However, I do now need to ask for Samuel's permission. You are his wife," he said and turned to Samuel.

"I'm his wife, but I'm still an individual," I interrupted. Nelson looked at Samuel who was already distracted by conversation, shrugged, and held out his arms into which I gladly went. In my mind we floated on that dance floor. However, when I opened my eyes and looked to the right, I saw Belinda staring at us and smiling. Instantly, I stiffened.

Later, before Samuel and I left for the yacht, Belinda came up to me to whisper in my ear.

"Maybe you got married too fast, Olivia. Maybe there was still a chance."

"Whatever are you talking about, Belinda? I'm sure it's something silly," I added quickly so she would say no more. "Just look after Daddy while I'm away. You have more responsibilities at the house now."

"What?" she snapped. "We still have Carmelita and Jerome."

"I'm not talking about the daily chores. I'm talking about looking after Daddy."

"Daddies have to look after their daughters, not daughters their daddies," she sang. "Have a fun time on your boat, Olivia, and tell me everything when you return."

She hugged me and then flew off to dance with Arnold.

"Ready?" Samuel asked.

"Yes. I just want to say good-bye to my father," I said gazing after Belinda. She was batting her eyes at Nelson now. I saw him hide a smile.

I pulled Daddy away from his conversation to tell him I was leaving.

"You looked absolutely beautiful in church today, Olivia. Your mother would have been proud," he said.

"Thank you, Daddy."

"Have a wonderful honeymoon and don't worry about a thing back here, okay? I'll be fine and the business will be fine."

"I hope so, Daddy," I said gazing at Belinda again. She was drinking too much champagne and I mentioned it to Daddy.

"It will be all right," Daddy assured me. "I'll keep my eye on her," he muttered.

We hugged and then I gave my hand to Samuel. We waved good-bye at everyone and left the reception. The limousine took us to the dock where our yacht and crew waited.

"This idea looks better and better to me, Olivia," Samuel said as we boarded and were directed to our cabin. "After something like that, it's good to go off on our own and have nothing but the sea, eh?"

"Yes, Samuel," I said. I did think it was a good idea.

"Let's change and go aft to watch the shoreline disappear," he suggested and started to take off his tuxedo. He was about to undress in front of me and he expected I would do the same, but I wasn't ready. I found what I wanted to wear and went into the bathroom to change.

"I like that," he said when I came out. "Modesty makes the promise of our intimacy that much more special," he declared. Then he smiled. "From now on, my dear Olivia, we will have nothing to hide from each other, least of all, our bodies."

I tried to smile, too, but my heart was pounding too hard and fast. Maybe Belinda was right; maybe she was better off preparing herself for this sort of day. Samuel took my hand and led me to the deck where we sat on lounge chairs, were waited upon by a crew member, and watched the shore slip behind us as we set out to sea and truly, for a new life.

We drank some wine and watched the sun go down.

"Tired?" he asked.

"Yes. It's been quite a day."

"An exciting day. I'm very, very happy, Olivia. I promise I'll be a good husband and father." He laughed. "I know if I stray an inch, you'll let me know, too."

"Whatever you do, you should do because you want to do it, Samuel, and not because I might get angry."

"Of course," he said. He leaned over and kissed me on the cheek. "Shall we go to bed, my darling Mrs. Logan?"

I took a deep breath, gazed up at the first visible star and nodded. We went below to our cabin. As soon as we entered, Samuel turned me to him and kissed me full on the lips, his arms around my waist. He held me so long, I had to protest that I couldn't breathe.

"Sorry," he said. "I'm just excited. I've waited a long time for this day."

"A long time? Hardly, a long time, Samuel. Look how long Nelson Childs is waiting to get married and go on a honeymoon."

"Oh," he said laughing, "Nelson's been on his honeymoon already, I assure you. You always wanted us to wait, and so, here we are after the waiting. Shall I help you?" he asked bringing his fingers to the buttons of my blouse.

"No, I can do it all myself," I said quickly. "Let's put out the light," I added. He laughed and turned off the lanterns before he pulled off his sweater. Even in the darkness, I turned my back and began to undress, my fingers trembling so much, I thought maybe I should have had him help me. Maybe that would make it easier. Yes, I concluded. I pulled the blanket back and lay down, still dressed. Samuel was in his underpants already.

"What are you doing?" he asked when he crawled in beside me and realized I still had on my clothes.

"Waiting. I've changed my mind," I said. "Undress me," I ordered as if he were my valet.

"Gladly," he said. I kept my eyes closed as he unzipped my skirt and slid it down my legs. I didn't open my eyes until I was naked and he pressed himself to me, his breathing heavy, his mouth nudging my breasts with his kisses. He moaned and nibbled gently at me and when he lowered his mouth to my stomach, I gasped. There was a rush of excitement in me that I had only imagined before.

"Olivia," he said. "My own Mrs. Logan."

He was between my legs, his firm, hardness tapping and then moving into me. I tried to swallow my cries. It actually was painful, but I was afraid to reveal it. I didn't have to. He knew.

"As I expected," he said, "a virgin. Thank you for saving yourself for me," he added as if I had known him all my mature life and had made some ridiculous love pledge. He laughed and moved harder, faster, shaking and rocking the bed so hard, the headboard banged against the wall.

"Samuel," I cried, "the crew."

"They don't have their ears to the walls. Don't worry. They've all been here before, I'm sure. They know what happens on a wedding night."

Men, I thought, could be so crass, even at this moment, even about something that was supposed to be one of the most special things in your life. The pain continued and overrode the pleasure for me, but I kept it all subdued, my eyes shut tight. My whole body was like a clenched fist.

"Relax, Mrs. Logan," Samuel chanted. "Relax and enjoy. I promise. It will get better and better," he said.

When he spent himself, he turned over and lay beside me, panting, his chest rising and falling.

"Good," he muttered. "Good."

I curled up and pulled the blanket closer to my face. Then I felt his hand on the small of my back.

"Are you all right, Mrs. Logan?"

"Yes. Just very tired," I said.

"Me too. Marriage," he declared with a laugh, "is more exhausting than I thought."

We were both silent for a while.

"Listen to the sound of the water against the hull," Samuel said. "Isn't that a sweet lullaby, Olivia?"

"Yes."

The boat sliced through the water, cutting away the old world I had known and exposing the new. What sort of a journey had I begun? I wondered. I fell asleep dreaming I had taken the rudder and I was guiding the ship through the purple night. There was no one else on board. I thought I heard Belinda's silly laughter coming from the darkness and then Mother's singing off in the distance. I steered in her direction, but there was no one there. It grew even darker. The boat tossed and fell against the waves. There was a small light ahead. As I approached, it grew larger, brighter and soon became Nelson Childs' smile. I sailed right through him as if he were a ghost and then turned back frantically as he dwindled behind me and disappeared.

Ahead, there was only more darkness.

11
&

The Honeymoon's Over

When I was very young, not even seven, I think, I believed that my parents had been together all their lives. I had seen pictures of them as children, of course, and seen pictures of them with their own parents, but none of that seemed real to me. I remember I thought that family albums and old photographs were like children's books, fairy tales and legends. How could my parents have had a life before the life I knew? They were always here, immortal, frozen in time, forever young. Daddy was always Daddy, firm, strong, smelling of cigars, his footsteps heavy, loud on the stairs, his laughter resonant, manly. Mother was always Mother, dainty, soft, full of smiles, redolent of perfume, her clothes colorful and her steps as light as her laughter, feminine.

Not until I was much older did I begin to wonder about Mother's first day of her new life, her life with Daddy. When she returned from her honeymoon, did she enter her own home full of excitement, eager to explore every moment of her new identity? Or was she terrified that she had made a disastrously wrong decision?

Daddy didn't carry her over the threshold, I know. She used to tease him for not having done that. Belinda and I often heard how he was too busy ordering his servants, supervising the unloading of luggage. I was sure she had entered the house first and stood there thinking, this is my new world for better or for worse. I am here. I wondered if she had an urge to turn and run out.

Samuel offered to carry me over the threshold, but I refused.

"It's a silly tradition. It makes no sense to me," I said pushing him away.

"Never say I didn't offer," he declared and stepped aside for me to enter our new home.

Actually, I could have used some assistance by that time. We had, as the weather report had predicted, good sailing weather for our honeymoon, and we did all the things Samuel had planned for us to do on the trip, including docking at ports and going to fine restaurants, but instead of returning refreshed and exuberant, I found myself feeling worn and frazzled. We had made love a number of times, and it did get more pleasurable for me, but he always seemed to enjoy it more than I did and that bothered me. The day before the end of our honeymoon, my period came. It wasn't supposed to, but I was never as regular as most women. When I told him, he immediately said I shouldn't feel bad. I didn't. I wasn't complaining. I actually felt relieved, but I let him be as solicitous as he wanted.

I had a great deal of input into what our house would look like, of course. Samuel didn't disagree with any suggestion I made, even when I insisted that we have separate bedrooms in our home. He was satisfied that we had an adjoining doorway.

"It will be like a romantic adventure every time I come to you, Olivia," he said when we first considered the architect's plans that included my revisions. "I'll knock softly and you can ask who's there? We'll pretend we're meeting secretly."

"I think we're both too old for games and pretending, Samuel."

"Oh, you're never too old when it comes to that sort of thing, Olivia. You can leave the lights off, as you like, and I'll make believe I'm some handsome stranger who on passing saw your lit window and then saw you gazing out," he said with a dashing smile.

"Ridiculous," I said, but I did feel my heart flutter with the images that crossed my mind, especially a fantasy that involved Nelson Childs. In my daydream Samuel had told him of our little games and he came to my house when Samuel was away. He knocked on that adjoining door and I turned off the light, not knowing until he was at my bedside that it was Nelson and not Samuel. I felt myself blush with the illusion. Samuel laughed, snapping me back to reality. "Are you teasing me, Samuel?"

"No. Well, maybe just a little, but that's what loving husbands do, Olivia."

"Not in this house and in this marriage," I announced. He laughed again, but he saw the firmness in my eyes and grew serious.

"Well, then, we'll behave as you wish . . . respectable to the core of our very beings. Even . . . when we make love," he said. He knew how that expression annoyed me. What a ridiculous way to put it . . . make love, as if love was something that was born out of lust.

I saw to it that there was a lock on the adjoining door and even though it was unspoken, it was understood that whenever that lock was in place, I would rather he didn't come to me. I had already decided that it would be in place quite often.

"You can rest assured that I will never lock the door from my side, Olivia," he quipped.

"And you can rest assured that I will never come into your room for any purpose other than to discuss something in private, Samuel. I'm not aggressive in that regard," I pointed out. He smiled.

"Unlike your sister," he replied.

"What do you know of Belinda?" I demanded.

"Only what your father has told me, confided in me," he said quickly. Then he smiled. "I can see why men are thankful when their wives give birth to sons."

"Belinda can drive anyone to thinking that way," I agreed.

As soon as we had settled in after our honeymoon, I decided to visit my father to see how he was getting along without me. In a way I hoped the whole house had fallen apart, that my supervision of the servants and the meals had been so necessary, nothing worked well without me there. My ego demanded it, but what I found did more to break my heart than prop it up.

Even though it was the middle of the afternoon, the house was dark, all the curtains were still drawn. I had kept my house key, so I simply entered. There was no light on in the entryway or in any of the rooms. It was so quiet, I thought no one was at home, not even Carmelita. I stood there for a moment listening, hoping to hear someone's voice, but I didn't even hear Belinda's idle chatter. I gazed up the dark stairway and then walked to Daddy's den.

At first I thought he wasn't there. It, too, was dark, the curtains closed, no lamps lit. I was about to turn away and go up the stairs to see if Belinda was in her room when I heard a small moan and stepped farther into the den. I saw Daddy asleep in the leather chair, slumped, his arms dangling over the sides, his head resting on his right shoulder. Beside the chair on the floor was an opened bottle of bourbon and a glass with at least two fingers of liquor in it.

I turned on the reading lamp above the desk and the light washed over Daddy, revealing he hadn't shaved for days. His white shirt was open at the collar and it was stained by food and bourbon. His hair looked like he had been running his fingers through it for hours. He grunted, licked his lips and then shifted in the chair.

"Daddy?" I said.

He grimaced as if the word brought him pain, but he didn't open his eyes.

"Daddy?" I shook his arm and his eyelids fluttered and then opened wide as he focused on me.

"What?" He started to sit up quickly, but stopped as if the movement brought him great pain. It was then that I saw the tear in the elbow of his left shirt sleeve and the dry blood on his skin. My eyes went to his pants and I saw the mud stains and what looked like a tear at the right knee.

He straightened up.

"Olivia? You're home? I mean, you've returned? What is today?" He scrubbed his cheeks with his dry palms vigorously and licked his lips.

"What happened to you, Daddy?" I asked softly. Had he been in a fight? I wondered.

"Happened?"

"Your clothes are torn and you've hurt yourself."

"Oh," he said as he blinked rapidly, his memory focusing. "I had a little accident out back. It's nothing. Looks worse than it is."

225

"What sort of an accident?"

"I tripped on a stump. It was dark."

"What were you doing out back in the dark? What's going on here? Where's Belinda?" I fired my questions at him so quickly he only heard one word.

"Belinda?" He ran his right hand over his hair. "Isn't she here?"

"I don't know. I just came in and I haven't checked upstairs. What were you doing outside in the dark, Daddy?" I repeated.

"Doing?" he said forcing a smile. It looked like his face had turned to glass and twisting his lips shattered his cheeks. All the tiny veins had come to the surface. "I was just . . . taking a walk, enjoying the night air. Your mother and I used to do that a lot. We'd sit out back and gaze at the ocean and the stars, but it was overcast and I wasn't watching where I was walking."

"You look like you took quite a fall, Daddy. You look like you were running, not walking," I said my eyes narrowing with suspicion.

He held his eyes on me.

"What really happened, Daddy?" I demanded. Lies between us were like fish out of water. They had a short, painful life.

"Can't fool you, can I, Olivia? Never could fool you," he said. His lips trembled; his whole face quaked and looked like it really would shatter like a piece of china.

"What happened, Daddy? What went on here? Has it something to do with Belinda?"

He shook his head and looked about frantically for a moment. His lips moved but no sounds emerged. Then he reached down to take hold of the neck of his bourbon bottle. He brought it to his lips and took a swig. It was as if the taste and the heat of the bourbon in his throat restored his ability to speak.

"I've been hearing his voice," he whispered. He leaned toward me, his eyes wide and wild. "I've been hearing him cry, Olivia."

"What?" I brought my hands to my throat and stepped back. "Whose voice?"

"Shh," he said looking back at the door. "She doesn't know anything."

"Who?"

"Carmelita, but she looks at me with those eyes of accusation sometimes, Olivia," he said shaking his head. "I think she hears him, too, and she wants to know what's it about. She told me yesterday she's thinking of leaving to go live with her sister in New Haven. Jerome's already given me notice. He's leaving next Tuesday. Going to Florida, he says. He claims it's the weather, but I know it's all because they know," Daddy added nodding. Then he took another swig of liquor and closed his eyes.

My heart was pounding. It felt like my ribs were knocking against each other. I took a deep breath. I knew what Daddy meant, but I had to hear him say it.

"Whose voice did you hear out there, Daddy? Who's crying?"

He opened his eyes, but stared up at the ceiling.

"Her little one, the unnamed. I planted him like so much seed. It always bothered your mother, Olivia. She used to stand by the window and look out back and think about him. She never said a word to you or Belinda, but sometimes at night, she would wake with a start and then she would sob softly. I didn't have to ask why. I heard the same cry and ignored it."

"You don't hear anything, Daddy. It's in your imagination, maybe because you're drinking too much," I said.

"No," he insisted.

227

"Okay, Daddy. Okay. You should go upstairs and get some sleep. I'll see if Belinda's at home. Have you been to the office while I was away?"

"I don't know," he said. "I think I was there one day. Time seems to have flown by. Your honeymoon's over already?"

"Yes, Daddy."

"Hmm. Where's Samuel?"

"He's at his father's house. I was hoping to take you to dinner tonight, Daddy, and Belinda, too."

"Oh, that's a nice thought. I'll just wash up and take a nap and then we'll meet you and Samuel," he said.

"You took a very bad fall, Daddy."

"What? Oh, yes, I think I tripped over a rock and fell down the hill a bit."

"Down the hill? You mean you almost fell down to the rocks?"

"Oh . . . no," he said. "It's nothing." He started to lift himself out of the chair. I could see that the bruise on his leg was more serious than he knew. It gave him great pain to put his full weight on the leg.

"Maybe the doctor should look at you, Daddy?"

"No," he said quickly. "I'll be fine. I'll just wash up and rest a bit."

"Did Belinda know you took a fall?" I asked.

"Belinda?" He stared, thinking. "Oh now I remember. I think she's been with one of her girlfriends. I think they went someplace."

"When?"

He scratched his head.

"It seems like she left right after your wedding."

"And she hasn't been back since?"

"I'm not sure," he said.

"Oh, Daddy. You know you have to keep better tabs on her. You promised you would."

I took hold of his right arm and guided him around the chair and toward the door. He looked like he was in pain when he walked on that leg.

"Are you sure you don't want to see the doctor today, Daddy?"

"I'm fine. I'll be all right," he said. "You don't have to hold onto me, Olivia."

"Okay. I'm going up to see if Belinda returned," I said and marched ahead of him.

The door to Belinda's bedroom was open and a quick perusal of her bed and the room revealed she hadn't been there for a while. I heard Daddy talking below and returned to the stairway. Carmelita had joined him at the foot of the stairway.

"Is that you, Miss Olivia?" she asked looking up at me. "I didn't know you had come home," she said.

"I just arrived. Do you know where my sister is?"

"I haven't seen her for days," Carmelita said.

Daddy struggled on the stairs, pulling himself up on the balustrade. I hurried down to help him because he wobbled. Carmelita was right behind him, too, keeping her right palm against his lower back to support and guide him. She looked at me and shook her head.

We got him up to his room and he went into the bathroom to undress and wash his bruises.

"How long has he been like that?" I asked her.

"He started the day after your wedding. Miss Belinda had left and he was alone. In the middle of the night, I heard him out back and sent Jerome to look after him. Your father had drunk too much. Jerome brought him in twice, babbling and crying something awful, but the third time, they had words. That's when Jerome gave him notice."

"And you're leaving too, I understand?"

"Yes," she said. "I can collect my Social Security now

and I'd like to enjoy my old age. My sister, who lost her husband last year, wants me to come live with her."

I stared at her and she shook her head.

"I'm sorry, Miss Olivia, but with your mother gone . . . well, this just isn't a happy, bright place anymore. I'm sure you'll find someone else fast, but I'll stay as long as I can," she added.

"Thank you. Where's Jerome?"

"Oh, he goes to town when he's finished working his hours now, Miss Olivia. That's where he is. Your father won't let him do any work on the grounds anyway. He doesn't want him to touch anything . . . flowers, bushes, no trimming, no digging. As you can see," she said nodding at Daddy, "your father's been in a bad way, drinking too much. I'm glad you're home," she said.

"I'll look after him," I told her. She nodded.

"If you need me, I'll be downstairs."

"Thank you, Carmelita."

"I'm sorry, Miss Olivia. Your mother was the heart and soul of this house. With her gone . . ."

"Thank you, Carmelita," I said sternly. She had made her point. I didn't have to hear it continually. She pressed her lips shut and left the room.

I knocked on the bathroom door.

"Are you all right, Daddy?"

"Yes," he said. "I'm fine. I'll just shower and take a rest and then you and Samuel can tell me all about your honeymoon."

"Are you sure, Daddy?"

"Yes," he said.

I thought I would go to the office and see how bad things were, especially what was left undone. Just as I started down the stairs, the front door opened. First her laughter entered and then Belinda followed, accompanied by some strange young man. He had his hand around her waist. She turned and they kissed in the entryway, the man's hands sliding down Belinda's back until he cupped her rear end and practically lifted her off the floor. She squealed with delight.

"Belinda!"

She broke away from him and gazed up at me, her hand going immediately to her lips, but her smile holding.

"Oops," she said and hiccupped.

The young man stepped back. He wore a yellow and white striped shirt and had long greasy hair. He wore a faded pair of dungarees and I was amazed to see that he was barefoot, too.

Belinda's light green blouse was open enough to reveal most of her braless bosom.

"Hello, Olivia. This is my sister Olivia," she declared. "Olivia, I want you to meet Bryan."

"Ryan," the young man corrected.

"Oh, right. Ryan. Ryan, this is my older sister, Olivia. She was just married. How was your honeymoon, Olivia? Was it bumpy out at sea?" she asked with a light, thin laugh.

I glared down at her. She wobbled, tried to hold her smile and then reached for the side of the doorjamb to steady herself. I turned to the young man.

"I think you had better be going," I said. He appeared to sober up instantly.

"Oh. Sure. I was just . . . I can't stay anyway," he explained. "I have to . . ."

"I'm not interested in why you think you can't stay. Please leave," I ordered.

He nodded.

"Now just a minute," Belinda began. "I invited Bryan to dinner tonight."

"It's Ryan," he corrected again and backed away.

"That's all right. I'm not hungry. Nice meeting you," he added glancing at me and quickly left.

"Hey?" Belinda called after him. She turned back to me, her eyes furious. "That's not very nice, Olivia. He gave me a lift home all the way from . . ." She hesitated. "From someplace far away and the least we could do . . ."

"You're drunk, Belinda, and you haven't been home since I left. Where have you been?"

"With friends," she declared, her hands on her hips. "You're married and living in your own house now, so don't come here bossing me around. And I'm not drunk." She hiccupped and stumbled toward the stairway.

"I have to get to the office," I said. "I'm not going to waste my time sobering you up and looking after you when you should have been here looking after Daddy. You're a selfish, inconsiderate person, Belinda, and one day you'll wake up and find yourself stranded on an island of insanity. I won't come to rescue you. I promise," I said and walked past her.

She tried to say something, but I slammed the door behind me before she could utter a word. My conscience told me she might fall down the stairs attempting to get to her room, but I didn't care. If she did, it would serve her right. As I got into my car and drove to our offices, my anger was so hot I was sure smoke came out of my ears.

What I found at the office confirmed my worse suspicions. Not only hadn't Daddy been there looking after our affairs, he hadn't returned phone calls made to the house and he had let some accounts drop us.

I went right to work, restoring as much semblance of order as I could manage in the few hours I was there. Samuel called looking for me.

"I had a feeling I would find you there when Carmelita told me you had left the house hours ago. I thought we weren't going back to work until tomorrow, Olivia," he complained when he heard what I was doing.

"I don't have that luxury. My father let too many things go, Samuel. I won't be home until much later."

"But . . . what about our dinner? I made reservations at the club. We have people to meet."

"I'm not very hungry. Go without me if you want," I said.

"This is ridiculous. Surely, it can all wait another day," he moaned.

"You might as well know right now that I don't procrastinate, Samuel. If something needs to be done, I do it," I told him in a tone of voice that would engrave the words in his brain.

"Of course," he muttered. "Maybe I should come there and help you," he added but without any enthusiasm.

"There's nothing you can do here. It would take longer to explain it to you first, Samuel. I'm very upset," I said and told him a little about Belinda's behavior while we were away.

"I see," he said.

"It's better I get to work and keep my mind off my anger."

"All right. I'll go to the club then and I'll wait for you there. Maybe you'll finish in time and . . ."

"Don't wait supper for me. If I can come, I will," I promised, but I knew it was an empty promise. Samuel accepted that offer quickly. He wasn't unlike so many other people I knew: satisfied as long as there was pretense, as long as they could fool themselves into believing something they knew wouldn't happen or wasn't true.

There was so much to do, I got lost in the work and didn't pay attention to time at all. When Samuel called again, he was already home from the club.

"I expected I would find you there," he said. "I can't believe you're still at it, Olivia."

Even I was surprised at the hour.

"I'll be home directly, Samuel," I said.

"Everyone at the club wanted to know where you were. When I told them you had gone right to the office, they were all impressed," Samuel said. I heard the way his voice dipped and I understood that "impressed" was not quite the way they really reacted.

"I'd better call and see about my father," I said realizing I had never even called him. "I'll see you soon."

When I called Daddy, the phone rang and rang until Carmelita finally picked up.

"Oh, Miss Olivia. Your father? I haven't seen him since we helped him upstairs. He fell asleep and didn't come down for any supper."

"What about Belinda?" I asked.

"I heard her in the kitchen a little while after you left. I came out to help her find something to eat and then she went upstairs, too. I thought she fell asleep as well, but an hour ago, I heard someone come to the door and she left."

"Okay, Carmelita. Call me if you need me for anything," I said and left her my home number.

Samuel was watching television in our den when I returned to our new home. He wanted to know all about the work I had done, but I told him I was too tired to repeat or describe it.

"Suffice it to say, it was considerable, Samuel, but there's a great deal left to do."

"Well," he said slapping his hands together and rubbing the palms, "starting tomorrow, I'll be there to help, Olivia. I'll take up the slack. That's a promise. We're going to build something here."

"We already have built something here, Samuel. We've got to hold onto it," I said dryly.

"Sure. Absolutely," he agreed.

I had some tea and toast and then decided to go right to bed. Samuel remained downstairs watching television. In the days to come, I had to interview and appoint our servants, as well as see if I could get Daddy back to work. I needed all my strength. I remember I was so exhausted, it didn't occur to me until I had my head on the pillow and the lights were out that tonight was the first night I was sleeping in my new home.

In the days and then weeks that followed, I became more and more concerned about Daddy. He returned to work, but I could see he was still drinking too much. Consequently, he wasn't taking good care of himself and occasionally looked as if he had slept in the clothes he wore to the office. I noticed that he often had problems with his concentration. It took him an hour to read and review something that would ordinarily take him minutes. He started to look so much older to me, too. His hair was grayer; the lines in his face grew deeper and his once powerful, straight posture degenerated until he walked with a slight bend in his torso as if his sadness had turned into lead weight on his shoulders.

It was pointless to ask him about Belinda. Now that I was gone from the house and Daddy was distracted, she was like a balloon someone had released in the wind. There was no way to get control over her. Her whims blew her randomly from one place to another. She avoided me as much as possible, was rarely home when I visited, and if she was, she was always getting ready to meet someone. Daddy was simply overwhelmed. I tried to get him to see what was happening.

"She was never very stable as it was, Daddy, and that was with my and your supervision. Now that I'm out of the house, you've got to take more interest in what she does, whom she sees and where she goes. Don't give her so much money. Get her to think about her future."

"I know," he would say. "I will," he would promise, but it was as if his mind was a magnet that had lost its powers. Everything that had stuck to it before, floated off, drifted away, fell out of his memory and his thoughts.

Samuel saw what was happening to him and to Samuel's credit, he did try to help. He visited Daddy almost as much as I did whenever Daddy didn't show up at the office or when I was too busy to get away myself. If he saw Belinda out at a bar or restaurant, he would try to take her home or get her to stop drinking so much. He knew how much it bothered me to hear about her exploits from other people, so he tried to soften the blow by telling me first.

Samuel was happy getting away from the office, despite his great oaths and proclamations to be at my side building our business. He quickly came to consider himself our public relations expert.

"We need to socialize with other business people, Olivia, and you're not fond of all this, what you call, fluff. I'll take care of it," he assured me and then proceeded to work up an expense account that quadrupled any we previously had, justifying it always by claiming it was a tax deduction or it brought in new business. It rarely did. In fact, some of the people he entertained had little or nothing to do with what we did and when I pointed that out, he would say, yes, but they are connected to people who are important to our business.

Daddy didn't disapprove of what Samuel did and at times, he even accompanied Samuel and seemed to enjoy himself. There weren't many occasions when he did these days, so I held back on my criticism. Samuel, on the other hand, seemed to realize and accept the limits of his own abilities, interests and concentration, and did not try to take on any of the responsibilities I had assumed.

"That's more Olivia's area of expertise," he would say. As it turned out, practically everything that involved real work was "Olivia's area of expertise."

However, in the beginning at least, I thought some of what Samuel was doing had value. We quickly became the darlings of the charity and social circuit, included on everyone's A-list for invitations to just about any and every high social affair. Samuel insisted I improve my wardrobe and buy some more expensive jewelry, much of which he chose for me and charged to our account. He never stinted on his own wardrobe either.

We began to host our own elegant dinner parties, and through Samuel's socializing, met more influential people such as politicians and government officials, many of whom did have some authority over our enterprises.

The social affair I looked forward to the most, of course, was Nelson Childs' wedding. It had been months since I had last seen him. He had finished his legal education, passed the bar, and joined his father's firm. His name had already been engraved on the sign outside his father's law offices, and every time I rode past and saw it, my heart would skip a beat. There were times I deliberately took a longer route just to ride past that sign. Later, I would chastise myself for it, telling myself I was behaving like a lovesick schoolgirl. He wasn't my beau; he was marrying someone else and I was married to someone else. What did I think I was doing?

Everyone who had been invited to Nelson's wedding knew how much preparation and thought had gone into designing the affair and reception. There was great expectation. Daddy and Belinda were invited of course, but Belinda told me she would not be going. I wasn't unhappy to hear that. It was one of the few times I had been able to find her at home recently. She was in her room packing a bag for a trip she was taking with some new friends.

"Who are these people?" I demanded.

"Just some people I met. You wouldn't like them," she added quickly.

"Why, because they drink and don't hold down jobs?" I fired back at her. She paused and put her hands on her hips.

"No, because they like to have fun more than they like to work."

"They don't have to work? What are they, spoiled rich kids like you or thieves?"

"I don't want to talk about them with you, Olivia," she said, tears in her eyes.

"So you won't be going to the wedding then?" I asked. She paused and smiled at me.

"No, Olivia. You can have him all to yourself."

I felt the heat rise up my neck and into my face.

"That's not funny anymore, Belinda. I wasn't the one in the boathouse. You were."

"Yes, but you wished you were," she countered.

I felt as if the air around us had grown too hot to breathe.

"Your husband knows how you feel about Nelson," she continued.

"Did you say something stupid to Samuel?"

"No, but he knows. I can tell." She started to pack again. "You and he aren't exactly sweethearts, sleeping in separate rooms in separate beds."

"That's none of your affair."

"No," she said laughing. "It's not and I'm glad, but maybe you're not giving Samuel enough of a chance to prove himself," she went on, defying my fury. "Maybe if you did, you wouldn't dream so much about Nelson Childs."

"Stop it!"

"All I'm saying is I think Samuel is . . . could be a good lover. Isn't he?"

"I won't continue this stupid conversation any longer, but I warn you, if you should say any of this rubbish to anyone and I hear about it . . ."

"You'll throw me out of the family. I know," she said. "Don't worry. I don't care enough to say anything. I'm too busy having fun."

"At our expense. Don't you ever want to make anything of your life?" I asked her.

"I think I am," she said. "I'm making a good time of it."

I left her and went to complain to Daddy who simply shook his head.

"She'll settle down soon, Olivia," he muttered. "You'll see."

"You're lying to yourself, Daddy. That's worse than lying to other people."

He just stared blankly at me. He had lost so much weight and was so pale and tired these days. I didn't have the heart to badger him about Belinda anymore. Let her destroy herself, I thought and put it out of mind.

Instead, I wanted to think of what I would wear and how I would look at Nelson Childs' wedding. Nothing I had in my closet looked good enough to me. I had to have something special. In the back of my mind, I hoped Nelson would glance at me and think that maybe he did miss his chance. He could have had someone attractive and intelligent. He could have had a perfect partner, someone who would have helped him become all that he was capable of becoming instead of just marrying some socialite.

I recalled the dressmaker Mother had gone to when she wanted something special for Belinda's graduation. She showed me some of the latest fashions and designed a gown for me. When I saw what she intended, I couldn't help thinking Belinda would cry green tears when she saw it. It was an emerald green chiffon with sequins down both sides of the V-neck that plunged into the valley of my bosom and sequins on the cuffs of my sleeves. I had a teardrop diamond necklace with matching earrings to complement it and I went shopping to find the perfect pair of matching shoes. Then, I had my hair styled and my nails done, something I had never before had done by a professional beautician.

"You're doing more preparation as a guest of a wedding than you did for your own," Samuel quipped. He smiled, but I wondered what was behind those laughing eyes. Many a truth was said in jest and who knew what Belinda had really said to him?

"You think you would be proud of me," I replied, looking away.

"Oh I am. Once again, we'll steal the limelight from Nelson and Louise. Why, that woman's going to come to hate you, Olivia."

"I hardly think so," I said, but in my secret place deep in my own heart, I hoped he was right, but not because I stole the limelight at her wedding, but because I stole the light in Nelson Childs' heart.

12
∞

The Wedding She Wanted

Nelson's wedding ceremony seemed far more elegant than mine had, perhaps because there wasn't the same expression of amazement and even disdain on the faces of many of the guests. There was a very different atmosphere, one that suited an affair in church. What's more, everyone treated this wedding as if it were the marriage of royalty, everyone except me that is. There were oohs and ahs over every aspect, from the red velvet carpet to the arrangement of multicolored roses in the form of an arch at the altar. When Nelson took his place with Samuel alongside him as his best man, all the women, young and old alike, gazed at him with such adulation, even a casual observer would think some Hollywood celebrity had stepped up to pronounce his wedding vows. There was a deep hush and then a nearly simultaneous sigh from the lips of his young, female admirers as he gazed out at the guests and beamed that handsome smile.

An electric shudder passed through the audience after the music began and Louise Branagan, on her father's

arm, started her march down the aisle. It was impossible
not to admit she looked beautiful. Not a strand of hair
was out of place and her wedding dress with its long train
looked as if it truly had been designed for a princess. The
train was held up by her older sister's twin seven-year-
old girls who resembled cherubs with their round, smiling faces and peach complexions. Louise moved with
grace and poise, a small, but beatific smile on her lips,
her eyes fixed on Nelson, whose eyes were locked on
hers. I could almost feel the excitement they had for each
other. Even the small children in the audience looked
like they were in awe. There was a deep hush with just
one muffled cough from the audience when Louise
reached the altar and her father stepped to the side.

The minister began.

That should have been Nelson and I up there, I
thought. If only I had been more forceful that night when
he and his parents had been invited to dinner, a dinner
Daddy had designed to develop a relationship between
Nelson and Belinda. If only I had been more forward
and seized his attention, first charming him with words
and ideas and then exciting him with my sexuality.
Weeks later it would have been Nelson and I in the
boathouse and not Nelson and Belinda. Instead of that
wasteful, wild assignation that amounted to nothing, we
would have begun an all consuming love affair that
would have lit a fire so strong in both our hearts, nothing
could quench it and calm our passions but the promise
of a life together.

But this was not to be. Some capricious and mean
spirit turned him away from me and dangled Belinda in
front of him, teasing and tempting him until he succumbed. I was not even an afterthought. Then, to put the
icing on the bitter cake I had to swallow, I had to be the

one to condemn him, the one to behave in the garb of some moral judge, the voice of conscience and decency, embarrassing and frightening him. He would always think of me as some ogre, I feared, some authority and power instead of someone soft and loving. Never before in my life did I hate who I was as much as I did that afternoon in the chapel watching Nelson Childs pronounce his vows of love and devotion to another woman. When she recited her words, I mouthed them to myself and when he spoke, I closed my eyes and dreamed.

The organ began again and everyone stood as Nelson and the now Mrs. Nelson Childs walked up the aisle, accepting congratulations, smiling at cameras, blinking at flashbulbs, waving and clinging to each other as they passed their loyal subjects, their doting guests.

"Wasn't that a magnificent wedding ceremony, Olivia?" Samuel asked with exhilaration when he returned to my side.

"Yes," I said quickly.

"She looked so beautiful, didn't she? What a fine looking couple they make, the darlings of Provincetown, eh?"

"I wouldn't go that far, Samuel," I muttered. "Don't get carried away with it."

He laughed and turned to Daddy.

"What do you think, Winston?"

"Fine wedding, beautiful, yes," Daddy muttered. I wondered if he regretted that that wasn't Belinda up there or even me. He looked distracted and was quickly pulled away by some of his business associates.

Nelson and Louise, along with their families, went off to pose for the photographer while the guests attended the reception. Because Samuel was the best man, we sat at the dais facing the dance floor. A full orchestra had been hired to play the big band sounds. There was a female vocalist as well. As the guests entered, the music began.

The Baers and Stevenses were at the dais as well because Ron Baer and Carl Stevens were junior partners in Nelson's father's law offices, a practice that was becoming one of the most successful in Provincetown, if not the whole North Cape area.

"I love what you did with your home," Janet Baer told us. She looked at Samuel as if he had done it all.

"What you see is mostly Olivia's creation," he replied quickly.

"Oh? You seem to be expert at everything, Olivia," she said with a saccharine smile, the sort of smile that could upset anyone's stomach, like too much candy.

"What is your sister doing with herself these days?" Tami Stevens asked. I saw the quick look she threw at Janet as soon as she asked. It was meant to be a jab in my side. I saw how she gloated after asking.

"She's waiting," I said dryly.

The two women gazed at me with cloudy, confused eyes.

"Waiting? Waiting for what?" Janet asked.

"To decide," I replied. Neither cracked a smile. Samuel laughed.

"Would you like to dance, Olivia?" he asked rising.

"Yes, I would," I said and stood up.

"Well," he said to the other husbands, "we're all here for a good time. Get off your legal briefs."

Never had I appreciated Samuel's humor more. I let him sweep me onto the dance floor, hiding my laughter by burying my face in his shoulder.

"Those two are so stuck on themselves, they're probably glued to the seats," Samuel quipped.

I laughed again. Afterward, I drank champagne, danced again, and then, when the orchestra stopped and the singer went to the microphone to announce the arrival of Mr. and Mrs. Nelson Childs, I, along with everyone else, stood and faced the doorway. Nelson and Louise made their grand entrance to thunderous applause and hurried to their places at the center of the dais.

"Cupid must have designed that marriage," Janet Baer shouted over the din. "They look perfect together."

"What do they say, a marriage made in heaven? There's one," Carl Stevens declared.

They took their places at the dais and Samuel rose immediately, tapping his glass with his fork.

"Ladies and gentlemen, I would like to propose a toast, the first toast of the evening."

Everyone stood up with their glasses of champagne and Samuel turned to Nelson and Louise.

"To Mr. and Mrs. Nelson Childs. May they be as happy as Olivia and I are."

I heard someone snicker behind me but there was a loud "Hear, hear," and everyone sipped their champagne. The music began again and so did the feast.

"Where are you going on your honeymoon?" Janet asked Nelson. He gazed at Samuel and me.

"Well, unlike the happily married Logans, we're not heading out to sea. We're going to the mountains, to Aspen. Louise is fond of hiking and she means to wear me out one way or the other."

He winked at me and then we all began to eat. Afterward, when Samuel had gotten up to speak to someone at the end of the dais, Nelson leaned over and whispered.

"Was he right, Olivia? Should I hope to be as happy as you two are?" he asked.

"I would hope you would always try to improve on things, Nelson," I said.

He chuckled silently and then turned to join some friends in a toast.

"Wait," he said reaching over to pour some more champagne in my glass. "Won't you join us?"

I did and then I drank another. In fact, I drank more at Nelson Childs' wedding than I had ever drunk anywhere, anytime, and I suddenly began to feel woozy. It got so I wasn't secure on my feet and stopped dancing. Samuel thought it was funny, but I hated the feeling that I could fall off the world.

"I think we'd better go soon," I told him in a whisper too loud. Nelson heard it, too.

"Not before you dance once with the groom, Mrs. Logan," he said. "It's customary for the best man's wife to do so, isn't it, Samuel?"

"Absolutely," he said.

"I don't think I can," I murmured, but Nelson was up and taking my hand. I felt the eyes of the other women at the dais as we walked down to the dance floor.

"I'm sorry if I cling to you too hard, Nelson, but if you let go, I'll probably fold up like someone's old umbrella."

"Hold on as tightly as you like," he said and held me snugly against him. I closed my eyes and let the side of my head rest on his shoulder.

"So now we're all happily married," Nelson said.

"Not all," I said thinking of Belinda.

"She'll settle down one of these days."

"It's where and on whom that worries me," I said. Nelson laughed. I felt so good in his arms and with my eyes closed, the music in my ears, the laughter and talk drifting back, it was really possible to think of this as my own wedding. What would Nelson's first honeymoon night be like with his new wife? I wondered. Samuel implied that they had already had it many times over.

I was disappointed when the music ended. Nearly tripping as we rounded the dais, I steadied myself on Carl Stevens' shoulder, which brought laughter.

"I really do think we should go home, Samuel," I said as I sat, embarrassment turning my face crimson.

He agreed and we rose and bid our good-byes to Nelson and Louise.

"I hope we'll all become such good friends," she told me as she hugged me.

"So do I," I said.

Daddy appeared to be having a fine time with the Colonel and his other friends. I was happy for him. It put me in a light mood on top of my dizzy spell and all the way home, I giggled. Samuel was very amused.

He helped me up the stairs.

"It's rare you're ever in need of anyone's help, Olivia. I should cherish this moment," he said.

I laughed at that. I laughed at everything: Samuel's surprised face, my room, the adjoining door, the image of myself in the mirror as I swayed. I struggled to reach back and undo the clip on my dress, but I couldn't maneuver my fingers very well and that seemed hysterically funny as well.

"Let me continue to be of assistance, Madam," Samuel said. I plopped down on my bed and let him undress me with the lights still on. All the while I kept my eyes closed and hummed the last melody I heard at the wedding, the melody Nelson and I had danced to. Samuel's laughter seemed distant.

"Aren't you something?" he declared. "I never dreamed I'd see Olivia Gordon Logan in this state."

When I was naked Samuel stood away from me for a moment and then he knelt down and leaned over to kiss my breasts and move his lips gently down my stomach. I remember thinking this could have been my and Nelson's wedding night, and if it had been, this was very much how I would feel.

Yes, I thought when Samuel touched me in my most private places and brought his lips to every sensitive and soft part of my body, take me as I've never been taken before. Let me throw all caution out the window and be as reckless and as wild as Belinda.

My submissive manner aroused Samuel as he had never been aroused with me up until this moment. That night I felt he ravished me. As he would say, we made love until we were both exhausted. For the first time since our marriage, Samuel fell asleep beside me in my bed and was there when I awoke in the morning.

I rose with a start when my eyes opened and found him snuggled beside me.

"What are you doing?" I cried and sat up.

"What?"

"Why didn't you go to sleep in your own bed?"

"What?"

"Stop saying what," I snapped. I ran my hand through my hair, trying to remember things. Had I made a fool of myself at the wedding? How much of our love-making last night was dreamed and how much actually happened? My head felt as if there were steel balls rolling around inside, clinking against each other, each knock like thunder. I moaned, hating myself for permitting this to happen.

Samuel rose, stretched and yawned.

"You were something last night, Olivia," he said.

"Stop it."

"Stop it? You were. I had to take you home, you know.

Don't worry. No one was angry about it. Nelson was amused, matter of fact."

"Oh was he? I'm glad everyone had a good laugh at my expense," I said.

I marched into the bathroom and took a shower as cold as I could stand it. When I emerged, Samuel had returned to his room and was already asleep in his own bed. I closed the adjoining door and sat at my vanity table, gazing at my unmade bed, the sheets rumpled, the blanket twisted from a night of frenzied passion.

I enjoyed it, I admitted to myself, but only because I had fantasized another man beside me.

It would always be this way, I thought, and felt the hot tears come into my eyes.

Love is cruel, I decided. The pain it brings outweighs the happiness. I'd rather be incapable of love. That way, I would be safe and no one, no man could ever hurt me.

In the days that followed, there was some talk about my behavior at the wedding, but nothing compared to the gossip that continued to build around Belinda's actions in and around Provincetown. Twice, I was called by the Provincetown police because she had drunk too much at an area pub and caused a scene when the proprietors refused to serve her and her friends any more beer. Once, I had to go to the police station and get her. She claimed it was always someone else's fault or else she was being picked on because her father was a wealthy man.

I tried to shield Daddy from some of it, but after a while, I thought it might be better if he knew more. It might make him take a firmer hand with her. We had the same conversation so often, I could have recorded it and simply played it back.

"If you don't send her to a school or find her something substantial to do, Daddy, she's just going to get into more and more trouble. Don't give her any allowance."

"I'll do something," he promised. "I'll make some calls, see if I can get her into a good school."

Maybe he did make one or two calls, but if he didn't succeed on the first or second try, he would put it aside, and if he did find something that might work, Belinda threw one of her tantrums and turned it down. She was always promising him she would improve or find something or someone. For a few months, she was going with the son of one of the more successful restaurant owners in Provincetown and it looked like they might get serious enough to plan marriage, but just like the other times, Belinda grew bored with him and betrayed him openly. He broke up with her and hopes for a stable relationship went with him.

I wanted to do something more, take firmer action myself, but Daddy's energy and interest in our business continued to dwindle. He did his own drinking every night to put himself to sleep and he continued to take less and less care of himself. I found myself taking on more responsibility and having less time to spend on myself and my family.

My handyman and driver Raymond found a friend to replace Jerome for Daddy, and I located another maid and cook to replace Carmelita, but that maid had words with Belinda and quit and I had to find another. I was going at so rapid a pace these days that I didn't stop to think about myself much until one morning I woke and almost immediately became nauseous and vomited. Samuel heard the commotion and knocked on my door.

"Are you all right, Olivia?"

I caught my breath and sat on the edge of the tub, thinking.

"Olivia?"

"Yes, yes," I said. "I'm fine, Samuel."

"Are you sure?"

"Yes," I said, but a cold fear came over me. I was always so irregular, I never thought about my not getting my period and I had been so busy lately, that I lost track of the days and weeks. This wasn't just irregularity, I thought. It had been too long even for that.

Without Samuel's knowledge, I made an appointment with Doctor Covington and had an examination. He gave me a test and called a few days later to confirm the diagnosis.

"Congratulations, Olivia. You are pregnant," he announced with fanfare in his voice.

The word hit me like a pail of ice water. Ever since that morning when I had opened the door to Belinda's room and saw the secret fetus curled on the floor, pregnancy and babies were dark and mysterious things to me. What would my birthing be like?

I didn't tell Samuel immediately. It was as if by keeping it a secret from him, I could keep it from being true. And then there was the strange dream I had the night the doctor had called to tell me the news. I dreamed the baby that was born looked so much like Nelson, Samuel believed Nelson and I had been together. I had fantasized so strongly when he and I had made love that my body put Nelson's features into the baby and not Samuel's. It was a silly dream, but it frightened me. Later, when my baby was born and he looked more like Samuel than he looked like me, those wild thoughts would seem even more ridiculous.

The morning after Doctor Covington had called, I finally announced the news to Samuel at breakfast.

"It seems the problems I've been having these last few mornings relate to my condition, Samuel," I began.

"Condition? What condition?"

"Doctor Covington tells me I'm pregnant."

"No? Pregnant? That's wonderful," he cried jumping to his feet. "How many months?"

"A little over three," I replied dryly.

He slapped his hands together.

"We'll have to tell my father, your father. We'll have to make plans for the nursery. Preparations! Preparations! We'll have to think about how you'll cut back on work and plan duties I should start to assume and . . ."

"We will not," I declared. "I will not be cutting back on my work."

"But . . . you're having a baby and I just assumed . . ."

"Don't assume anything. Having a baby isn't like having a deadly disease, is it? Well, is it?"

"No, but your father and I, we thought, we always expected that you would want to diminish your responsibilities and turn more of the day to day business over to me as soon as the prospect of a family loomed over us."

"That's not going to happen, Samuel," I said fixing my gaze on him so intently, he had to look away. "I've built this business alongside my father and since my mother's death, as you know, I've had to take on more and more of the responsibility, but I've improved our positions everywhere and I'm not about to see any of it lost just because I happen to be pregnant."

"I won't do anything to lose our business, Olivia," he said with pained indignity. "I've done my share of bringing us new clients. Why . . ."

"Just continue to do what you're doing then," I said charitably. "And I'll do the same. They'll be a short period when I'll reduce my workload, but we'll have a nanny and I'll keep up with everything. I won't have a family any other way," I insisted. He could see from my expression that there wasn't room for any sort of compromise when it came to this.

"Fine," he agreed, sitting again. He looked like a boat that had lost wind from its sails. "Whatever you think is best, of course." He fingered his coffee cup. "This is . . . wonderful news. My father will be pleased and so will yours. How are you feeling?" he suddenly thought to ask. "Does the doctor say everything is all right?"

"Everything is."

"Good, good. I wonder if we'll have a son, another fisherman, eh? Well," he added, the smile returning to his face like a dying spark that had been fanned back into a small flame. "I'll be walking about with my chest out today."

"Don't make too much of it, Samuel. I don't want a lot of nosy people sticking their faces in my business."

"Don't make too much of having a baby? You can't make too much of it. It's . . . why we're here, Olivia. You always tell me that, tell me it's something your father taught you . . . family, right?"

"Right, Samuel," I said. "I just don't want a great deal of commotion at work."

"I'll call my dad. You'll tell your father at work?"

"Yes," I said, only that day, Daddy didn't come to work. He called in to say he wasn't feeling well and he would stay home and rest. The first chance I got, I left the office and went to the house.

During the early morning hours, the fog had rolled over the landscape in great billowing waves, turning everything cold and eerie. This dreary sky was still overhead when I arrived at Daddy's house.

Effie Thornton, the newest maid, greeted me at the door. She was a short, round-faced stout woman of forty-seven with rolling-pin arms and thick-fingered hands. She looked more like a peasant farm worker than a maid, but she was a hard worker who took her responsibilities seriously. I knew she would find fault with Belinda quickly, but unlike the other maids and cooks, she wasn't a quitter. The skin covering her feelings was so thick even Belinda's nasty remarks and actions couldn't pierce it. Belinda was always complaining about her, asking Daddy or me to fire her, but the more dissatisfied Belinda was with someone, the more I liked that person.

"Oh, Mrs. Logan, I'm glad you're here today so you can see what I have to contend with," she said on greeting me.

"What now?" I asked.

"Just follow me," she said and led me to the living room. I stopped dead in the doorway. It was as if I had been slapped across the face. The room looked like it had been hit by a hurricane. There were glasses and beer bottles strewn about, along with plates, some overturned, some caked with food. I saw food stains on the sofa and chairs, Mother's prized furniture. A lamp had been knocked over, the Tiffany shade shattered.

"What happened?" I asked when my breath returned.

"Your sister threw a late night party. She had at least a dozen people here and they carried on into the wee hours."

"My father let this happen?" I asked.

She scowled.

"Your father was dead asleep in his office, a bottle of whiskey in his lap. I think you're going to have to have some professional carpet cleaners and furniture cleaners here with their machinery, Mrs. Logan. I'll do the best I can, but . . ."

"Of course, Effie. I'll call them myself in a little while."

"I'll get started on the room. I was waiting for either your father or you to see it first."

"Where's my sister?" I asked. "Is she home?"

"She is, but she's not alone," she added, her eyebrows lifting.

"And my father?"

"He went up to his bedroom early this morning without so much as glancing at the living room and has been there ever since. I tried to get him to eat some breakfast, but he had only a cup of coffee."

"Okay, thank you, Effie."

I turned, my heart racing, my limbs tightening like strung wire. I could feel my neck muscles harden. Anger built like a small tornado inside me, spinning up from my stomach to my chest and into my throat. When I reached Belinda's bedroom door, I took a deep breath and then I lunged at the door knob, surprised at my own strength. I shoved the door open so hard, it swung back and banged against the wall.

Belinda and her boyfriend, naked and entwined in her bed, opened their eyes with a jolt.

"Huh? Olivia?" she said sitting up slowly, the blanket falling away from her naked breasts. She wiped her eyes to clear her vision and perhaps hopefully clear away the image of me standing there.

"You're more disgusting than I could ever imagine," I said. The man beside her turned on his back and covered his eyes with his hands as if the light stung him. I just glanced at him and saw it wasn't anyone I knew.

"You should knock before coming into my room," she cried.

"I'm not talking about this. I'm talking about the disgusting mess you made in our house. How dare you bring those degenerates into this house? You might not have any respect for yourself, but you will have respect for this family," I charged.

She started to cry and stopped. Her boyfriend drew the blanket over himself and started to laugh.

"It isn't funny. I don't know who you are, but you better get out of here immediately," I said.

He lowered the blanket and smiled at me.

"Oh. Okay," he said and started to get out of the bed naked.

"Stop!"

"Fine," he said getting back under the covers.

"You can't do this," Belinda wailed. "You don't live here anymore. You have your own home."

"As long as Daddy is alive, this is still my home, too," I said. "Is there no limit to your depravity?"

Her boyfriend started to laugh.

"You should be locked up," I told her, "and I'm sure there'll come a day when you will be."

I slammed the door closed, my entire body shaking so badly, I had to pause before walking across the hallway to Daddy's bedroom. I caught my breath and knocked on his door. There was no answer so I knocked harder and then I opened the door and peered in. He wasn't in his bed, but there were no lights on and the curtains were still drawn. I listened for the sound of running water in the bathroom. I entered and saw that the bathroom door was opened.

Perhaps he rose and left while I was in Belinda's room, I thought. But how could he walk by without hearing the shouting? Confused, I stood there a moment and then I saw his feet around the corner of the bed. I approached slowly, my heart feeling as if some tiny sprite was pounding a nail through it. Daddy was sprawled on the floor, face down, his right arm under his body, his left out, the hand cupped into a claw. He was in his pajamas.

"Daddy!" I screamed and went to him. I knelt beside him and took his hand in mine. It was warm and when I looked at his face, I saw he had his eyes squinted shut as if trying to see some scene scorched on his brain.

"Daddy!" I cried again, shaking his hand.

His eyelids opened like two leaden doors on rusty hinges. He gazed at me, but his mouth, horribly twisted, uttered no words, just an incomprehensible grunt. His tongue looked swollen and extended.

Without further hesitation, I went to the phone and called for an ambulance. Then I ran down the hallway to the top of the stairway and shouted for Effie. She hurried out of the wrecked living room, a washcloth in hand.

"My father!" I cried. "He's collapsed on the floor. Come help me, please."

She started up the stairway and I turned as Belinda, a sheet wrapped around her naked body like a toga, opened her door and peered out.

"What's all the commotion now, Olivia?"

"Your father," I spit at her. "You've finally done it."

"Done what?"

I gazed at her with all the fury and anger I could muster.

"I have no time for you," I said and then returned to Daddy's side.

Effie and I managed to get him up. He seemed incapable of using his right leg and his right arm dangled limply at his side. By the time we had him on the bed resting comfortably, Belinda, now dressed, came to the bedroom.

"What's wrong with him?" she asked, her voice full of fear and remorse now.

I stared down at Daddy.

"I'm not a doctor," I said curtly, "but it looks like he's had a stroke."

Of course, that's what it was. The ambulance attendants came and took him to the hospital where Doctor Covington met us after he had examined him.

"It's too early to tell the actual extent of it," he explained to Belinda, Samuel and me in the lobby, "but for now he's lost the use of the right side of his body and his speech is impaired."

"How did this happen?" Belinda asked quickly.

"Well, your father has been suffering from hypertension for some time now."

"What's that?" Belinda asked with a grimace.

"High blood pressure. I've been after him to take better care of himself, cut back on his smoking, drinking, salty foods, but sometimes too much stress and worry does it too," he added.

I glared at her and she looked away.

"We believe he's had a blood vessel hemorrhage in the brain. Without blood, sections of brain tissue quickly deteriorate or die, resulting in paralysis of limbs controlled by the affected brain area. In this case, his speech has been affected, too."

"Won't he get better?" she whined.

"He'll improve with therapy, I believe, but he'll never be the same as he was," Doctor Covington told her in his brusquely honest style of diagnosis. He turned back to me. "I have a neurologist coming in to see him later today. Most of his progress will be made during the next six months. We'll have to take better care of him and he'll have to cooperate now," Doctor Covington continued with a small smile. "No more alcohol or cigars and we have to watch his diet."

Belinda looked dazed and sat.

"Let's see how much he recuperates over the next week or so, Olivia, and then we'll talk about the therapy," Doctor Covington concluded.

"I understand," I said. "How is he now? Can we see him?"

"You can see him, but don't let him see how upset you are. We have to encourage him, build up his hope," Doctor Covington lectured, looking more at Belinda than Samuel and me.

When we went up to see Daddy, Belinda remained in the background whimpering. I held his hand and he looked at me with his helpless eyes and tried to talk.

"Not now, Daddy," I said. "You've got to rest and get better."

He closed his eyes. I could almost hear him say, "The bottom line is I won't."

It wasn't until we left the hospital that the question occurred to me: what would I do now with Belinda? Daddy wasn't much of a brake on her wild ways before, but at least he was something. Without him home, what would she turn the place into and what would she be like? And yet, I wasn't excited about bringing her back to my house.

Samuel was the one to bring it up in the car.

"What about Belinda?" he asked as we drove away in a dead, sad silence.

"I'm afraid," she moaned.

"You should be," I said. "It was your behavior, your antics that aggravated him and caused this, Belinda. You heard the doctor talk about stress," I accused. She wailed louder.

"Olivia," Samuel said softly. "Don't . . . it won't do any good now, will it?" he asked quickly when he saw the fury in my eyes.

I felt myself calm down.

"No, You're right. It won't." I turned around and looked at my sister. "You'll come home with us for the time being," I said, "and let Effie get the house in order. It's better you're not there anyway."

"I'm sorry, Olivia," she said.

"It's too late for that. It's been too late for a long time," I said in a voice too low for either Samuel or Belinda to hear.

"What a bad time for this to happen," Samuel said. "I bet you didn't even have a chance to tell him, did you, Olivia?"

"No."

"Tell him what?" Belinda asked through her tears of self-pity.

"That she's pregnant. Your sister's pregnant and you're soon to be an aunt," Samuel told her.

"Oh, really?"

For a moment my mind raced years ahead and I envisioned Belinda having a bad influence on my child. One of the first things I would have to do as soon as he or she was old enough to understand would be to warn him or her about Belinda. She would always be a burden, I thought.

"I'll help," she volunteered. "I'll change, Olivia. I'll come to work again. I'll help you."

I had to laugh.

"And do what, Belinda? Misfile documents, tie up the phones, flirt with delivery boys?"

"I can change," she whined. I grunted. "I can!" she insisted.

I looked out at the sea. The waves were higher, the wind stronger.

"I'm tired," I said. "Just take me home and then take Belinda to get some of her things, Samuel."

"Aye," he said.

I glanced back at Belinda. She was gazing out the window, too. She looked like a little girl again, lost and bewildered. I tried to find a place in my heart for compassion, but all I could think of was that night in the boathouse and how she clung to Nelson Childs.

13
❧

Belinda's Last Chance

After Samuel had taken me home and left with Belinda to gather some of her clothing and bring her back, I phoned Effie to inform her of what had occurred and gave her instructions about cleaning the house. I could tell from her tone of voice that even though she was upset about Daddy, she was particularly happy Belinda wouldn't be in her way during the next few days. She took great pride in her work and was almost as upset about what Belinda had done as I was.

As soon as I finished the phone conversation, I asked my own newly appointed maid Loretta to make me a cup of tea. Loretta had come to me by way of a Boston agency and was, I thought, similar in character to Effie: serious, sincere and efficient. I sat by the window in my own den-office and gazed at the still very gray world. From this angle I had a small but clear view of the ocean behind the house and caught sight of a trawler making its way north.

The vessel revived memories I had as a child occasionally sitting in the gazebo at early evening with Daddy.

Belinda was always bored with just sitting, talking and looking at scenery and was usually in the house on the phone or entertaining some friends who had come over to visit with her.

"We're very lucky to be living by the sea," Daddy told me. "I can't imagine what life is like stuck in some city high-rise gazing out at more brick, concrete and steel. We can look out like this and see ships go by day and night and imagine ourselves traveling to some exotic ports or beautiful lands. Some day I suppose you'll do a great deal of traveling, Olivia. You're sure to see more of the world than I have."

"Why, Daddy? Why haven't you traveled more?"

"Oh, I guess I've been too involved in my businesses. Nailed myself to the floor of my office, I'm afraid. Don't be like me. Get out there. Do things. See things. Explore," he advised. "See the world. Take an ocean voyage whenever you can."

Ironically, I felt that was more of a fantasy for me now than it ever was for him. Our business was literally three or four times the size it was when he and I sat out back and gazed dreamily at passing ships. Along with the economic growth came three or four times the responsibility, and with a sister who was more a child than a woman, a husband who had limited business abilities, and now a father who was to be an invalid, my ship of adventure would remain moored to the dock for a long time to come, I thought.

Anyway, I was reminded of Ishmael telling Captain Pelig in *Moby Dick* that he wanted go whaling to see the world. Pelig told him to stand and look over the side of the ship and tell him what he saw. He saw nothing but water and considerable horizon. "Well then," Pelig said, "what does thou think of seeing the world?"

That was the view of the world from a ship for most of

the journey a sailor made. I could see the same world from my own shore. I was really no sailor and the sea, as beautiful as it could be, held no irresistible attraction for me. Maybe my real father was a sailor as my mother had revealed, but the sea quest that was in his blood did not seep into mine. I was content enjoying an occasional sail and living here in my own world where I could be secure and had some control over my destiny.

Sitting here now, I recalled one special time alone with Daddy. We had remained outside longer than usual. The first stars had long since appeared and the sun had dipped below an azure horizon turning the ocean into a deeper silvery gray. The lights of boats miles off shore appeared. We sat quietly, neither of us having the need to say anything. Finally he declared it was time to go in. Mother had already gone up to bed and Belinda was in her room jabbering on the phone and laughing that giddy laugh that drove me mad. Daddy went to his office and sent me up to my room. I heard him come up the stairs afterward and stop at my door. He peeked in at me.

"All in bed are you?" he asked.

"Yes," I said feeling snug and content.

Nevertheless, he approached and tucked me in a little tighter before leaning over to kiss me good night. It wasn't something he did that often and I remember thinking it was a very extraordinary moment.

"You and I have had some very grown-up talks, Olivia," he said. "I think you're going to become an adult much sooner than other girls your age. I'm happy and sad at the same time about that," he said. "You'll miss something of your childhood."

"Don't be sad, Daddy. I don't mind."

"Okay," he said smiling. "Good night, Little General."

"Good night, Daddy," I said.

There weren't all that many soft moments in my life to remember like that, but tonight, sitting here alone, thinking about Daddy half destroyed by a stroke and now incapacitated in the hospital, those memories, few and far between, returned, some only vague images, some vivid. I sat there thinking so long, I didn't realize how much time had passed. It obviously had taken Belinda quite a while to get her things together; she probably protested the whole time about having to make any choice at all.

The gray skies had turned leaden and the sea practically disappeared in the dusk before I heard Belinda and Samuel come into the house. Belinda was loud, complaining. I rose and went out to see what was wrong.

"Effie didn't offer to bend a pinky to help me, Olivia. She took one look at us and went off to do some cleaning or something," Belinda moaned. "What kind of a maid is that? I want you to fire her."

"She's the best one we've had since Carmelita," I said. "This is not the time for us to go firing help and having to look for new servants, Belinda. There are much more important matters at hand. Just go up to the guest room. Loretta will help you," I said as Loretta appeared. "We're having dinner soon and then we're all going to try to calm down and gather strength for the days to come."

"Oh great," she griped to Samuel. "It sounds like I'm going to become a prisoner in my sister's house now."

"Hardly," I said, "but you are going to behave yourself while Daddy is in that hospital and especially when he comes out and needs your help."

"Maybe I should plan a trip so I can get out of everyone's way," she suggested as a threat.

I nodded.

"Yes, maybe you should," I replied. It took her down a

peg. She started to stammer, but headed up to the guest room instead.

Belinda didn't take a trip until after Daddy had been released from the hospital and his therapy at home had begun. His neurologist felt Daddy might reach 60 percent of his previous motor capabilities during the first six months of therapy, and his speech would become understandable, but after that, improvement, if any, would be very slow and hard in coming. It meant he had to spend hours with a speech therapist and physical therapist Equipment was brought to the house and the master bedroom became a therapy center. We had to have a special duty nurse round the clock for a while. The activity and presence of all the medical personnel unnerved Belinda. Ironically, Belinda, who was his true blood daughter, couldn't stand the sight of him twisted and diminished in his wheelchair. She avoided him as much as she could during the months of therapy at home. She was at the office more than usual just to get away from it all, and finally decided to take a trip to visit some friends in Florida. I was in my last trimester of pregnancy and although I was feeling the best I had during the entire term, I was glad to get her out of my hair for a while.

Daddy felt horrible about being a burden and began every one of my visits bemoaning his condition and telling me to simply send everyone away and let him be. He cried a lot too, which Doctor Covington explained to be part of his condition.

I tried keeping his spirits up by making detailed business reports every afternoon, but most of the time, he was too exhausted to listen or understand, and he often fell asleep while I read off figures or discussed deals and negotiations. I would sit awhile longer to see if he would wake, and then I would leave him in the hands of his nurse.

Samuel was good about visiting with Daddy and went almost daily. He really didn't enjoy being trapped in an office anyway and looked forward to every excuse to go out and meet with people, even if it meant sitting and watching Daddy go through his therapy. He got permission to take Daddy for some rides and even worked out a short motor boat ride on a particularly beautiful weekend day.

Before Belinda returned from Florida, Nelson and Louise Childs visited Daddy. Samuel came to tell me that afternoon and I regretted not having been there, even though I thought I looked like a small blimp. I had seen Nelson only a few brief times since the wedding, but before I had become bloated and waddled instead of walked. He and Louise were busy sitting up their home and Nelson had begun to take on more legal chores at his father's firm. I heard he had done well in court and there was even some early talk about him running for a local judgeship. Six months after their wedding, Louise became pregnant, too.

"He's just trying to keep up with me," Samuel bragged.

"I hardly think fathering a child is much of an accomplishment, Samuel," I told him. "It's certainly not my test of manhood." He just laughed and shook his head at me the way he always did when I said something with which he didn't agree.

During the last month of my pregnancy, I spent less time at the office. Samuel brought home the important papers for me to peruse. One night I had some bleeding and I had to be taken to the hospital. It turned out to be nothing serious, but I was irritable and uncomfortable all through my final two weeks. Then, on a Sunday, right before dinner, my water broke and Samuel rushed me to the hospital where I delivered my first-born, a son, whom we named Jacob for my father's father.

I held my baby in my arms and looked up at Samuel's beaming face.

"He's the best piece of work we've done together, Olivia," he declared.

"We've done?"

"Well, I did have a little to do with it, didn't I?" he protested.

"Yes, you did, a little. That's what men contribute, a little. You didn't have back pains, vomit, struggle to get up from a chair and go through hell in a delivery room," I reminded him. He laughed.

"I guess not, but he looks like me, doesn't he?"

"Maybe he'll grow out of that," I said and Samuel laughed harder.

"I declare, Olivia, if I didn't know better I'd think if you could have been both mother and father, you would have, and liked it, too," he said.

Maybe he was right. In any case, I thought, looking at Jacob's tiny face and hands, I had begun my own family.

We hired a nanny immediately to help me with Jacob. Her name was Thelma Stuart. She had had five children of her own, all now grown and away living their own lives. Her husband had died two years before. She was looking for work to keep her occupied and had served as a nanny for a year and a half for a couple I knew, who had recently moved to California. She was a soft-spoken woman, and caring. I was lucky to have her, especially during the early days because Jacob was a colicky baby.

Nevertheless, Samuel was ecstatic that our first-born was a male and the sight of Jacob did appear to help brighten Daddy's spirits. He truly enjoyed our visits with Jacob and seemed more animated when the baby was present. He enjoyed holding him. By that time, he had regained use of his arm and he had enough strength to cradle the baby for a few minutes, as long as Thelma stood over him. I didn't have to ask her to do so. From the first day she came to work in our home, Thelma was as protective of Jacob as I would be.

Belinda had a strange reaction to the sight of her newborn nephew. She complimented him, of course, but she had no interest in holding him, feeding him, or being around him long for that matter. She told Thelma that babies made her nervous. When she looked at Jacob and then lifted her eyes to look at me, we both knew what put this tension in her face.

"Who'd have thought you would have ever become someone's mother?" she said with a laugh. She meant to tease me, but I glared at her.

"Why not?" I replied after a moment, "I've had to be yours for so long."

"Very funny, Olivia. You see, Thelma, she's always knocking me down. I could get a complex."

"Please, spare us," I cried.

Thelma laughed but I knew she was perceptive enough to see how much of a burden Belinda had been, and still was.

When Louise Childs gave birth, Samuel was again ecstatic. He came to the office to tell me with a wide, gloating smile on his face.

"Guess what?" he said stepping into my office. "Louise gave birth this morning, but it was a daughter."

"There's nothing wrong with having a daughter, Samuel. Are they both doing well?"

"Yes, but Nelson's not. He went into hiding," he said with a laugh.

"The only thing with less intelligence than a chauvinistic man is a clam," I declared and he roared.

"Nevertheless," he bragged, "I've got a boy."

The first year of Jacob's life passed so quickly, I couldn't believe we were celebrating his first birthday so soon. Daddy had improved to the point where he could carry on a short conversation and walk with a walker. His arm didn't quite regain half its strength and his hand was more like a claw. He had to eat very slowly and it was always very messy. Belinda got so she couldn't take a meal with him and avoided doing so.

"It turns my stomach to see the soup drool down his chin or the food on his lip, Olivia. Don't yell at me," she cried when I complained about her leaving Daddy to eat his dinner alone every single night. "I can't eat and that upsets him more!"

I didn't doubt she had trouble sitting there. She was never good at stomaching anything. Even a cut on her finger terrified her. The sight of blood turned her a shade whiter than milk. I never forgot how sickly pale and terrified she looked the night she gave birth to the premature fetus.

"Well, try not to make him feel like some sort of creature, Belinda. Imagine what he's going through and remember some of the unpleasantness he helped you through," I lectured.

"I'll try," she promised, but still she rarely ate with him.

Maybe Daddy was better off with her out of his sight. She was still doing little with her life. She tried to take an adult education secretarial course given at the high school in the evening, promising to master some skills and really do some worthwhile work at the office. Daddy actually had high hopes for her, and was very upset when he learned a few months later that she had stopped going to the class. She pretended she had been attending, but simply met her degenerate friends and either went bar hopping or, when the weather was good, to a party on the beach or on someone's yacht. It got so I couldn't keep track of whom she was with and when. There were just too many new boys in her life.

The stories about her flowed freely my way, of course. Our acquaintances, especially the wives of our business associates, loved leaking the tales to me or to Samuel. Finally, I decided to take some serious action and I went to see Daddy early one afternoon. I was determined to stop my sister from tearing down everything good and respectable about our family. Why should I be afraid to go to fine restaurants or social affairs, afraid that someone would mention her and ruin my evening?

I found Daddy dozing in the living room and woke him. I told him I had come to talk about Belinda. His eyes grew dark.

"We can't ignore her any longer," I began. "I've written to the Collier Business College in Boston, and I've gotten Belinda enrolled in their courses for a year. Yesterday, I spoke with Cousin Paula, and she agreed to rent her upstairs room to Belinda. It's walking distance from the school. You've got to insist she goes and you've got to threaten to cut off all funds from her if she doesn't go and succeed. If you don't take a strong stand with her now, Daddy, I don't know what will become of her. This is the very last time I'm going to try to help."

He stared at me with those big, watery eyes. His lower lip still looked unhinged in the right corner, just showing some of his teeth.

He nodded and promised, but I had to come to the house and be there when Belinda put up her usual opposition.

"I don't want to live with Cousin Paula," she whined.

"She's old and cranky. She'll make my life miserable. I'd rather have my own apartment," she concluded. "Or I won't go," she said stamping her foot like some petulant five-year-old.

"That's an enormous expense and frankly, Belinda, it would be a gamble in your case and Daddy and our family have lost enough money because of you. You don't need your own apartment. Cousin Paula lives alone. It will work out well for both of you."

"She never liked me, Daddy," she moaned, "and I never liked her. She's the one with hair on her chin. How can a woman look at herself in the mirror and let hairs grow on her chin?"

"She doesn't have to fall in love with you, Belinda, and you don't have to fall in love with her. Just obey her rules and go to school. This is your very last opportunity to do something with your life."

"Why? I'm going to get married anyway. I'll just make sure to marry someone with money."

"When?"

"Soon," she promised.

"Until then, develop some skills. You can return and work in our business if you have some skills," I added.

"Oh, won't that be wonderful," she moaned. She looked away and then at Daddy. "I can't go to Boston for a year. Daddy needs me here."

"You're not here much and when you are, you're of no help to him anyway," I snapped. "Now, Daddy and I have discussed this and you either go to school or get a job, a real job, not working for us. Frankly, you can't do anything for us, but maybe you can work as a waitress or something."

"A waitress? Never."

"Daddy is not going to give you any more money," I said sternly.

"Daddy," she pleaded, turning to him. I looked at him and he raised his heavy, sad eyes to me. I made a face, warning him to hold fast.

"Olivia's . . . right," he said. He struggled with his words, but he got them said. "I've been wrong not to make you do something before this."

"That's great. The both of you ganging up on me!" She folded her arms under her breasts and pouted for a moment, her conniving little brain twisting and turning in that spoiled head like some snake in a basket. Then her eyes brightened. "Am I getting an allowance for Boston, then?"

"You'll get what you need, what you reasonably need," I said.

"Daddy will decide how much I get," she fired back at me. "Then I'll go."

I looked at him and he closed his eyes, opened them and nodded at me.

"You're a spoiled brat, Belinda. You've only taken from your family and you haven't given back anything."

"I do the best I can," she cried. "Don't I, Daddy?"

He grimaced.

"Let's end this," I said. "Daddy can't take much more. I'll make arrangements for your transportation and call Cousin Paula tonight."

"You can't wait to get rid of me. I don't know why," she sang, her eyes bemused. "I'm not trying to take anyone away from you."

"There is no one you could take from me that I wouldn't give up if they went with you anyway, Belinda."

"Huh?"

"Forget it," I said. "I hope you really try to do something this time. I really do. Otherwise . . ."

"Otherwise, what?"

"I'll sell you to the highest bidder," I said and left to make the arrangements.

Despite her protestations, Belinda was happy to be leaving the house. She was always excited about going to Boston. She got Daddy to buy her a new wardrobe, over my objections, and I knew she was planning on moving out of Cousin Paula's house and getting her own apartment as soon as she could work it out. She would then invite her bubble-gum friends to Boston and the whole attempt to help her make something of herself would be another bust, I was sure. However, I had at least tried. I owed that to Mother and after this, I felt that my debt was well paid.

Little did I know I was just beginning to endure the true cost. I was actually fooled into thinking that I had finally made the right choice for Belinda. She enrolled and began her schooling without any more whining and crying. She even got along with Cousin Paula at the start, and after a few weeks, she sent us rather good reports from the school.

With her gone from Provincetown, the stories died and I was able to concentrate on business and my family. We expanded even more. Samuel told me Nelson thought we should consider offering stock in our company on the stock exchange.

"Let him come and discuss it with me himself," I told Samuel, but Nelson didn't come.

His father retired from the firm and Nelson became the senior partner. He won some significant cases in Boston and was written up in the local papers as well as the Boston ones. Nelson was then appointed to fill out the term of a judgeship. It was assumed he would run for political office in the near future.

I remember feeling that our lives had rounded some long and arduous turn and we were coasting along now, relatively secure and content. Jacob was running about and spending many of his afternoons with Daddy, who had begun to feel so good he started to violate the rules about smoking and diet. When I chastised him, he begged me to let him have the simple pleasures. That was all he had left, he claimed.

I was so involved in my own work that I paid little attention to Samuel and never noticed that he was unhappy. One night at dinner, he put down his silverware and put his elbows on the table.

"I think it's time you and I had a little talk, Olivia," he began firmly, his eyes so fixed on me they were like two welding torches.

It was quite uncharacteristic of Samuel to take this tone of voice with me, especially in the presence of our servants. I raised my eyebrows and then looked at Thelma who had just finished feeding Jacob.

"You can take him to his room now, Thelma," I instructed and she did so. "What is it, Samuel?" I asked as soon as she was gone. "What could possibly be bothering you so much that you would speak like that to me in front of Thelma?"

"You have no idea?" he said amazed.

"No, I don't. I'm sorry, but I've been quite busy these days. In any case I'm not in the mood to play some game of Twenty Questions. If something is bothering you, tell me what it is directly, without any unnecessary dramatics."

He shook his head and looked away a moment before turning back to me.

"Your door, Olivia, has been locked for months and months now. I've respected it and I haven't pushed myself on you, but it's not natural for a man and a woman to live like this when they're married," he said. Then he sat back. "Did you know that Louise Childs is pregnant again? There are no locked doors in that marriage."

"Oh, so that's it. You're afraid Nelson Childs will pull ahead of you in this baby-making contest," I accused.

"No, that's not it, Olivia. My God! I have needs, male needs, and I can't imagine why you don't have female needs. All these months . . . you were never once attracted, interested in me?"

He looked amazed, even hurt. I softened and sat back to sip my coffee.

"I've just been very occupied, Samuel. It has nothing to do with you."

"What do you mean it has nothing to do with me? How do you think I've felt all this time? You go to sleep at night. You put aside your work and worries for a little while, don't you?" He glared at me. "Well?"

"I'm sorry," I said. "I didn't have relations on my mind."

"On your mind?" He laughed and then leaned forward, his hands folded, his arms on the table. "I hope that door's not locked tonight," he said. It couldn't have sounded more like a threat. I felt the heat rise to my face and my heart began to thump.

"Don't take that tone with me, Samuel. I won't have it. I'm not anyone's plaything."

He snorted.

"Plaything? You're about as far away from being that as . . . as a nun."

"That's enough. Change the topic," I ordered. I turned away from him.

I felt him glaring at me a moment and then he rose and left the room. I sat there, trembling. How could he speak to me like that? What had given him the courage?

Miss Hot and Miss Cold . . . I could hear the children chanting it at us. Was it still true for me? Samuel was far from an ugly man and most of the women I knew flirted with him and probably fantasized about him. Why I should be so indifferent, I didn't know, but I couldn't help how I was, could I? Surely, I wouldn't have become like this if I had married Nelson, I thought. Or would I?

That night, I fingered the lock on the adjoining door, but in the end, I didn't unlock it. I went to bed with it remaining in place. After I had put out the lights, I heard Samuel try the door and then curse under his breath. Following dinner he had gone to the den and had sat for the remainder of the evening drinking brandy. He had his back to the door and didn't turn when I looked in on him before going up to sleep.

I started to drift off when I heard what sounded like a key go into the lock on my bedroom door. I opened my eyes and listened and then I saw the door open.

"Who's there?" I cried sitting up as the light spilled in from the hallway.

"Only your husband," Samuel said with a short, cold laugh. "Remember me?"

"You have a key to my room? What are you doing?"

He approached the bed, wearing a robe and then he undid the belt of the robe and let it fall to the floor. He was naked.

"Samuel, you stop this. You turn right around."

"I won't be denied my rights," he declared and crawled into the bed beside me. I tried to get out on the other side, but he seized me around the waist and held me tightly to him. I could smell the brandy on his breath. It nearly turned my stomach.

"Samuel!"

"You just forgot how good it could be, Olivia. I'm here to help revive your memory," he said and laughed.

I tried to push him away, but he was too strong and too determined.

"I swear if you don't cooperate, I'll tell everyone. I'll tell your father. I'll tell your sister. I will," he promised. "And you know what a big mouth she has. I'll even tell Nelson," he added, "so he won't tease me anymore."

My breath caught and my heart stopped and started.

There was nothing to do but stop resisting and lay back. Once I did that, he was at me like a sailor stranded in his boat for weeks who had run out of fresh water and finally been given a glass.

"There," he said after he had spent himself in me, "wasn't that good? Aren't you sorry you've not had more of it?"

I turned my back to him.

"You don't have to thank me," he muttered.

The next day I tried to be angry, but he behaved as if we were getting along just fine. He was full of laughter and jokes and jolly with everyone. When I returned home that night, I was shocked to discover that the lock on the adjoining door had been removed.

I started to complain and he put up his hand.

"Nelson Childs told me it's grounds for divorce," he said.

"What? You told Nelson? You had no right to tell anyone our private affairs. How dare you?"

"What difference does it make now, Olivia? That's over. We're really like husband and wife again. No more walls and locks between us. Right? Right," he said answering his own question.

He came to me twice more that month and quite often after that until I realized I was pregnant again. It seemed to be what he wanted the most.

"We're going to have another boy," he declared when he heard. "I just know it."

I used my pregnancy as an excuse to keep him out of my room and this time, he didn't protest when I had the lock returned. He didn't want to do anything to endanger the child.

A month later, Louise Childs gave birth to a boy they named Kenneth and Nelson and Samuel celebrated into the wee hours of the morning. I heard him come home and collapse in his bed. Slowly I rose and went to the adjoining door. Opening it, I looked in at him sprawled out, still in his clothes. He reeked of whiskey and cigars. I heard him groan.

"Where have you been?"

"What? Oh," he said smiling, "my wife has come to me? Tha's somethin' she said she'd never, never do. See, it worked. She does want me."

"Stop it. You're disgusting. I don't suppose Nelson got this drunk."

"Nelson?" He laughed. "They carried him home. Tha's how drunk your precious perfect Nelson Childs got."

"He's not my precious perfect Nelson Childs," I said stepping back. Samuel laughed.

"Come here," he said reaching up for me.

"Stop it!"

I turned, frightened. He struggled to stand and fell back on his bed.

"You get over here, Olivia Gordon Logan. Your husband wants you."

"My husband is a drunken fool," I snapped back at him.

"Huh?"

"Go to sleep and don't complain to me how you feel in the morning," I said, quickly retreating and locking the door behind me. I heard him laugh and then fall to the floor. A little while after that, he was pounding at the adjoining door.

"Samuel, you'll wake everyone. Stop," I cried. He

continued to pound on the door. I had to get up and unlock it. He stumbled, swayed and stepped into my room.

"I demand my conjugal rights," he said raising his right forefinger. He walked to my bed and fell across it on his face. I lifted his feet up, took off his shoes and threw his legs over the bed. Then I put on my robe and went down to our guest room, leaving him groaning there in his drunken stupor.

He was quite ashamed of himself and apologetic the next morning. I let him wallow in his remorse and gave him the silent treatment. Of all that he had done and said, his remark about "my precious perfect Nelson" frightened me the most. I had never done anything or said anything to give Samuel the impression I had strong feelings toward Nelson. From what well of knowledge did he draw that pail of truth, I wondered.

It wouldn't be long before I tracked it to Belinda, who in her innocent little way enjoyed planting the seeds of trouble in my world to see what crop of pain she could grow for me. Apparently, despite my anger, the harvest had only just begun.

14

❧

A Life and a Death

*M*y second pregnancy was much more difficult than my first, perhaps because I had really not intended for it to happen this soon and part of me resented having been forced to carry another child. It made me feel helpless, unable to control my own destiny. Whatever Samuel wanted he would get despite my opinion. This was beyond opinion. He had literally forced himself on me at times. It wasn't possible for a wife to say no to her husband when it came to sexual relations. He couldn't be accused of rape.

I think Samuel believed that another child would cause me to lessen my work responsibilities and give him the opportunity to become more important at our company. He expected that I would eventually relegate myself to running our home and rearing our children, much the way Louise Childs did. I knew that despite the façade he put on, it bothered him that I was doing so much more than he was. His friends, perhaps Nelson most of all, kidded him about being Mr. Gordon rather than me being Mrs. Logan, but I wasn't about to put any of our business interests in jeopardy just to satisfy the needs of Samuel's male ego.

After my third month, I suffered severe back pains and had more trouble with my digestion. I didn't gain weight so much as I became bloated and retained water. It got so I had to leave work earlier than I wanted day after day to go home and rest, and then in my sixth month, I had terrific abdominal pain and began to bleed so profusely, the inside of my shoes got soaked. I had pains that resembled contractions. It was even hard for me to breathe.

Samuel, who was at a luncheon with some clients, was called back to the office and then helped rush me to the hospital. I did not, as I suspected I would, abort. However, Doctor Covington put me on a very restrictive regimen.

"If you want this child, Olivia," he warned, his face as austere as a hell and damnation preacher's, "you'll have to spend more time on your back. Sitting for hours and hours behind a desk and traveling about is just out of the question at this point. Your pregnancy is in great jeopardy."

I found myself being treated like an invalid, rolled out in a wheelchair and helped along like someone who couldn't stand on her own two feet. Going up and down the stairs in the house was strictly forbidden. For the remaining term of my pregnancy, I was confined to my bedroom. That would be my little world.

Samuel seemed to enjoy my new-found helplessness. Now, instead of my going to the office every morning, he went and he took my calls and met with our clients. A number of times, I had to change or amend things he had done on his own. He wasn't happy about this and complained.

"No one treats me with respect, Olivia. They think everything I do, you'll change," he whined.

"I have to change what has to be changed, Samuel," I said firmly.

"Well, it makes everything so difficult. They don't know who's in charge," he continued.

"As long as I'm able to think, I'm in charge of what my father and I have created, Samuel," I said. "I didn't do so badly up until now, did I?"

He reluctantly admitted I was right, but I saw how unhappy it made him that even though I was on my back, I could still have a heavy hand in everything that we did and had to do. I never relinquished the need for my signature, for one thing, which meant nothing was official without it.

I regretted not being able to visit with Daddy as often as I wanted. Samuel actually brought him over once, but I had the feeling the two of them were in a conspiracy, hoping to force me to release my iron grip on our business affairs. When Daddy started to take Samuel's side, I threatened to get up and go to the office if either of them ever brought up the matter again.

"In fact," I said throwing my legs over the side of the bed and finding my slippers, "I think I'll just take a ride over there right now and see what else has to be done."

"No, you don't, Olivia," Daddy said. "You don't endanger my new grandchild. I'm hoping it will be a girl," he said. "I understand you and Samuel have already decided to name her after your mother."

When Daddy put it like that, I couldn't force the issue. I lay back, but I felt as though there were invisible chains around my ankles and neck. Doctor Covington came to examine me once a week, and even though I told him I was feeling a lot better, he still insisted I remain as inactive as possible.

"You're only feeling this way because you listened to me, Olivia," he said. "You don't have that much longer to go before you give birth. Don't make trouble for yourself and your baby at this late date," he admonished. Samuel stood behind him, gloating. I never realized just how much he resented my being stronger than he was.

When Belinda heard what was happening, she called to express her sisterly concern. Her voice dripped with syrupy false love.

"I should come home and help you," she declared. "I feel sorry for you."

"There's nothing you can do here except spend time with Daddy," I said. "Loretta takes care of all my needs. Thelma is looking after Jacob quite well. It's just Daddy who needs more tender loving care."

"Oh. Well, maybe I shouldn't just walk out on my schooling. I'm almost finished, but if you need me . . ."

"Don't worry. I'll call you," I said. "Is everything all right? There are no surprises waiting for Daddy and me, are there, Belinda?"

"Whatever do you mean, Olivia? You've seen my school reports and you've called Cousin Paula every week since I left, haven't you? Don't deny it," she added before I could respond. "I know you've been spying on me. For all I know, you've hired a private detective to keep an eye on me."

"That's not true, Belinda."

"Well, I'm glad to hear that," she said with a little giggle. There was definitely something in her voice that suggested she had done something of which she knew I would never approve. I regretted not doing what she had suspected: hiring a detective to watch over her. Now that she had mentioned it, it would have been a good idea.

However, I thought, in my condition and present state

of mind, it was no good for me to spend any time worrying about her. Whatever she's done, she's done, I thought, and let that be the end of it. Maybe she's run off and married someone. Wouldn't Daddy and I be fortunate.

On Tuesday of the second week of my eighth month, Loretta came upstairs to tell me I had a visitor. It was a little after eleven in the morning and I had just gotten off the phone with Samuel, reviewing some of the problems he had to deal with during the day. He hated my calls. I could easily envision him sitting there with a sharp grimace cut into his face, his forehead resting on his hand as if he had the world's worst migraine.

"I have a visitor?" I asked. I had no idea who it could be. Salesmen and the like were never permitted to come to the house. "Who?"

"Mr. Childs," she said. "I told him I would see if you could entertain anyone this morning. He's waiting downstairs," she added.

"Nelson?"

"I don't know his first name, ma'am."

"He's not an older man, is he?" I snapped at her impatiently. How could she live in Provincetown and not know who Nelson Childs was?

"No," she said.

"Very well, send him up," I said. "No, wait. Hand me that mirror there," I said pointing to the small silver-framed mirror on the vanity table. Because I was confined to home, I did little or nothing with my hair and wore no makeup. I knew my face was rounder, my lips looking like they were filled with air. I hadn't washed my hair for days. It resembled a mop with the strands hanging limply. I had Loretta get me a scarf to hide most of it, and then I put on some lipstick before I sent her out to send Nelson up to me.

What a surprise, I thought. Did Samuel know Nelson was coming? He didn't mention it on the phone. Why did Nelson come without his wife? I heard his footsteps on the stairway and straightened out my blanket as I sat up in anticipation. Nelson and I hadn't been alone together for some time. I couldn't stand how nervous I was. I was like some schoolgirl. My fingers were actually trembling.

Get hold of yourself, Olivia Logan, I ordered. He's only a man.

"Olivia," he cried coming through the doorway. He wore a dark blue, double-breasted pinstripe suit with a bright blue tie. His hair was styled and full and he looked tan, his eyes more hazel than ever. "I'm so sorry I haven't been to see you before this," he said approaching the bed. He leaned over to kiss my cheek.

"Hello, Nelson."

"I've been involved in a complicated case that took me to the Bahamas for weeks."

"I didn't know you were away," I said. "The Bahamas? No wonder you look so healthy."

He laughed.

"Well, all work and no play makes for a dull attorney." He stood back and shook his head, a big, fat smile on his face.

"What?"

"It seems so incongruous to see the iron lady of Cape Cod laid up," he declared. "I must say you look better than I had expected."

"I'm no iron lady, Nelson," I replied. "I'm made of flesh and blood and have feelings like most women you know."

"Don't be silly. You're not anything like most women I know, Olivia. Most don't have half your capabilities." He looked at the chair. "Mind if I sit awhile?"

"No, please," I said and he pulled the chair closer.

"How is Louise?" I asked.

"Oh, she's fine. She would have come along too, but she's busy with the children. One right after the other," he said with a shrug. "That's the way she wanted it."

"Really? Then it was all planned?" I asked, thinking about my own situation.

"Oh yes," he said, crossing his legs and sitting back.

"Well," I said after a pregnant pause, "I appreciate your stopping by, Nelson, but," I continued, studying him a little more intently, "why is it I have the feeling you've come for more than just to see how I am?"

He shook his head and laughed.

"You are amazing, Olivia. I am here to discuss something, but you're wrong, too. I was concerned about your health and the baby and I did want to stop in and see how you were. So wipe off that mask of suspicion and widen those narrow eyes." He laughed, nervously. "You make me feel like a teenager caught smoking in the boys' room or something."

"Well, go on, say your piece, ask your question, make your proposal, whatever," I ordered.

He straightened up.

"You know I handled the Bennington distribution deal for your company, something your father had begun with my father and something I finished."

"Yes, I'm aware of that," I said disappointed that I had been right about him coming for something other than a personal call.

"I stopped at the office this morning to say hello to Samuel and bring some papers over and he told me I might as well bring them here. You won't let him sign anything."

"I haven't given him that authority, no," I said. "Where are the papers?"

"Oh, it's really nothing that couldn't wait, Olivia. I'm not here on business. I'm here for personal reasons; I'm here as a friend. Remember, we pledged to always be friends?" he asked.

"Yes, I remember, Nelson," I said closing my eyes and then folding my lips into a small smile. "Go on, be my friend," I challenged.

"I swear . . . I'm here because I've become concerned about Samuel, Olivia," he blurted after a slight pause.

"Samuel? Why?"

"He . . . he's not his old self these days and I think it's because you have him on such a short leash."

"What?" I didn't know whether to laugh or scream. "Who came up with that? Short leash?"

"I did, myself. He needs to be given more authority, more responsibility. Some of our mutual friends call him your errand boy and it's bruising him. There's just so much a man's ego can suffer before his whole personality suffers."

I stared for a moment in silence.

"I hope you're not offended by my concern, but . . ."

"Did Samuel ask you to come here and plead for him this morning?" I demanded.

"Absolutely not," Nelson said with his hand raised as if he were being sworn in as a court witness. "I decided completely on my own to do this. I wanted to express to you how much confidence I have in Samuel and I thought it would be much better for your marriage if . . ."

"Nelson," I said slowly, "how would you like it if I went to see Louise and gave her some advice about how she treats you? How would Louise like it?" I asked.

"You and Louise don't have the relationship we have, Olivia," he said.

"What relationship?"

"Our friendship," he said. "The last thing I want to do here is upset you," he added quickly. He reached out to take my hand. "Please believe that."

I looked at my hand in his and felt my heart flutter.

"I'm not upset, Nelson. I'm . . . just surprised." I looked up at him. He looked so sincere, so concerned. Was he coming here pleading for Samuel only as a way to get closer to me?

"Maybe I shouldn't be so surprised. Maybe there is something more between you and me. Maybe we've always known that," I said very softly.

"Yes, there is. You're very bright and you've always been honest with me, even to the point of telling me off when you had to," he said smiling. "I thought it would be all right for me to tell you what I thought. I am very fond of Samuel and of you," he added. "I am, Olivia. You're probably the one woman, aside from my wife of course, whom I respect the most in this town. I've always been impressed with you."

My heart fluttered like a small bird gaining the courage to fly. Dared I say what was buried so long in the secret places in my soul?

"Too bad we didn't meet sooner somehow, someway, Nelson. We might have built a family like no other on the Cape. Just think what power we would have had together, what great things we could have done here. We'd have an empire by now," I said, my voice full of emotion.

"People shouldn't marry just to build a good business, Olivia. They have to have something more going on between them," he said in a condescending tone.

I pulled my hand out of his.

"Yes, you're right, of course," I said turning away from him. I felt so exposed, so naked for showing my emotions so clearly. "Well, I do thank you for bringing Samuel's problem to my attention. I'll do what I can, but

I won't do anything that's not sensible just to please some of your mutual friends, as you call them. I'm sure most of this is just men's club talk anyway," I concluded.

"I'm afraid I've upset you."

"No," I said and then turned to him, my eyes full of fire. "No, you haven't. You've simply reminded me what it's like for a woman to be in charge of a supposed man's role. Yes, I admit I run my company with an iron hand, Nelson, but I do that because I'm good at it and because I built it up to what it is today. There is no reason why I shouldn't continue to do so or not do so just because I happen to be a woman," I said. "Perhaps you should revisit your view of women, Nelson. You may not be as liberal and fair-minded as you believe you are."

He laughed.

"I only hope I'm never put in the position of having to negotiate with you, Olivia. Well, okay," he said, "I see you're fine. You're strong. I won't take up any more of your time. Please don't mention this to Samuel. He really doesn't know I'm here," he said standing.

"All right, I won't," I said holding my eyes on him. He stared at me a moment.

"I understand that Belinda is doing well in Boston," he said.

"Who told you that?"

"You know how people love to talk about each other in these small towns."

"I won't swear to anything Belinda does," I said. "I'll believe it when I see it. Why?"

"She . . ."

"What?"

"Asked me for a job when she graduates this business college next month," he revealed.

"What?" I started to laugh.

"She said she would rather not work for you."

"I'd rather not have her work for me."

"I thought I'd tell you," he said.

"What are you going to do?"

"I don't know. What should I do?" He looked like he was hoping I would give him permission.

"In light of the past, don't you think it might be an indelicate situation?" I asked.

"It might be indelicate to turn her down," he said gazing at the window.

My heart stopped and then started with a machine-gun rhythm that nearly took my breath away.

"You mean to say Belinda threatened you? Blackmailed you?"

"Not in so many words. Maybe she's changed," he said. "Maybe I should give her an opportunity."

"Do what you want," I said. "You men always do anyway," I added.

He started to laugh and then took on a very serious expression.

"We'll see," he said. "I'll call on you again and send those papers over tomorrow, if that's okay."

"Perfectly," I said turning away from him now. How could he even consider having Belinda around him? It made me furious.

"Have a good day," he said and left.

I felt like tearing up the room, raging like some wild animal. I wanted to swing my arms, pound the walls. This damn confinement drove me mad. I hated it; I hated being pregnant. It was as if Samuel had locked me up and thrown away the key.

"Loretta!" I screamed. "Loretta!"

She came charging up the stairs, rushing to my room. She stopped in the doorway, her hand on her chest, her shoulders heaving.

"Yes, ma'am. What's wrong?"

"Nothing's wrong. Help me get up and get dressed," I ordered.

"But . . ."

"This instant!" I cried. Had I lost my authority in the eyes of everyone, even my servants?

"Yes, ma'am," she said and went to the closet to fetch the clothing I selected.

Lying in bed so long had weakened me more than I had anticipated. Twice, I had a spell of dizziness while I dressed, but I fought it off. When I was ready, I sent for Raymond, who helped me leave the house and get into the car.

"Take me to the office," I directed.

When we arrived, he came around to help me walk, but I cast off his arm.

"I'm fine," I said. I wanted to enter my offices under my own steam so no one would doubt I was strong enough to take control of my affairs.

Our secretaries and sales people were shocked when I walked through the door holding my stomach and hiding my short breath. I had put on enough makeup to avoid looking pale. They were all overly solicitous, each offering to do something, but I shooed them off, telling them to return to their duties as I headed for my office. One look at it told me Samuel had taken it over. My desk was a sloppy mess, papers and files everywhere, a cup of coffee and a glass, still with some brandy in it on the desk as well. The room itself reeked of cigar smoke.

Samuel wasn't there.

"Open a window in here, Dolores," I ordered. My secretary rushed in quickly and opened every window. "Hasn't anyone attempted to clean this place while I was away?"

"Mr. Logan didn't want anyone in here," she explained.

"I'm not surprised. Where is he?"

"He met Mr. Brofman and Mr. Conde at the Whaler's Club for lunch," she said.

"For lunch? It's nearly three-thirty!"

"Mr. Logan never returns from lunch before four," she said and then bit down on her lower lip as if she had already revealed more than she should have.

"Never mind, Dolores," I said wiping off the desk chair and then sitting. "Let me look at some of this."

I began to wade through the documents, shocked at how many Samuel had never mentioned. There were things that should have been processed days ago and telephone messages from important clients that had obviously never been returned. I began slowly, signing as much as I could and calling whomever I could. One firm informed me they had had to go to someone else. All I could do was apologize.

By the time Samuel returned, I had gone through more than half of the backlog. When he entered the offices, I could see from the flush in his face that he had had too much to drink at lunch. His eyes looked like they were floating in his head. So oblivious and dazed was he that he didn't realize I was there until he literally entered the office and approached the desk. He stopped dead in his tracks, his jaw dropping.

"What . . . the . . . what are you doing here, Olivia?" he gasped.

"Working, Samuel, catching up on the mountain you let build on this desk, apologizing to client after client for your failure to return their calls, some of which were made in desperation. We already lost the Farmingdale account, and all I could do was apologize."

"I was getting to all that. There's been a lot more to do here than you know. I didn't want to tell you because I didn't want you worrying in your condition," he explained.

"You thought it would help my condition to let our business suffer?" I fired back.

"I wasn't letting it suffer. I've done a lot that you don't know about," he protested.

"That's what I'm afraid of," I said dryly.

"You shouldn't be here, Olivia. The doctor's going to be very angry with you and with me for letting you be here," he complained.

"You're not letting me do anything, Samuel. I'm doing what I want and have to do. Look at this mess. Look at how dirty this place is. What sort of an example are you setting for our employees? Didn't you think I would ever return to my office?"

"Sure. I was about to get this place straightened up. I had it down on my book to call in the cleaning service tomorrow or the next day," he said. "I'll show you."

He started to sift through the documents, searching for his plan book.

"Are you looking for this?" I said holding it up. "It was on the floor under the chair."

"Well, it must have just fallen off. Now look here, Olivia. Your coming in like this and bawling me out is not going to help me keep the respect of our employees."

"What do you mean keep, Samuel? Who says you have it?" I remarked. "Just go back to your office and leave me alone to fix as much of this as I can," I said.

"I must insist you go right home," he replied. I could see that the booze he had drunk had fortified him, given him courage. He stood there with his hands on his hips, his shoulders back. "You call Raymond. Go on."

"I swear, Samuel," I said. "If you don't get out of here this minute and let me work, I'll call the police and have you removed from the office," I fired back at him, my eyes so fixed on his face, he had to blink and look away.

"You're making a mistake, Olivia. I'm just concerned about you and our baby," he whined. I didn't move my head an inch nor did I shift my gaze. He fumbled about for a moment, sputtered like some old boat engine, and then turned and charged out of the office, nearly knocking Dolores out of his way as he crossed the room.

"Come in here, Dolores," I ordered, "and sit. You'll take notes on what I want done tomorrow," I said. She grabbed her pad and hurried into the office. "Close the door. I don't want to be disturbed," I said and we began.

Despite my enthusiasm and determination, my rage and the effort it had taken to get to the office took a severe toll on me. I ran out of steam less than an hour later and felt myself weaken. It came in a wave over my body, numbing my legs first and then making me feel as if all the weight of my entire body had been placed on my lower back muscles. The ache grew so intense, I had to take deep breaths.

"Clear off the settee," I told Dolores. Samuel had piled folders on the leather sofa. She did so quickly and I rose from the chair. Dolores could see my difficulty and nearly leaped to my side.

"Let me help you, Mrs. Logan," she said taking my left arm and putting her right arm around my waist.

"I just need to lie down a moment," I said.

"Of course. You haven't stopped for nearly an hour and a half."

I sat and then lay back. Dolores lifted my feet and placed my legs on the settee. She fluffed a pillow and placed it under my head.

"Get me some cold water, please, Dolores."

"Yes, Mrs. Logan."

By the time she had returned, the pain in my lower back had begun to travel around to my abdomen and felt like a thin wire being tightened and tightened, cutting into me. I drank the water and took some deep breaths.

"Are you all right?" Dolores asked.

"I need to rest," I moaned.

"Should I call Mr. Logan?"

"No," I said firmly. "I'll be all right."

I closed my eyes and actually fell asleep. When I opened my eyes again, Samuel was sitting in the matching leather chair beside the settee, his head back. He started to snore.

"Samuel!" I cried and he nearly leaped up.

"What? Oh," he said scrubbing his face with his palms quickly. Then he stopped and looked at me angrily. "Well, you've exhausted yourself. Satisfied now?"

"Yes," I said. "We'll go home. Call Raymond."

"I did. He's been waiting outside for about an hour. Everyone else has gone home. They wanted to stay, but I sent them off."

"Good."

"I'm glad I did one thing right in your opinion," he said. I sat up and he rose to help me stand. "Any pain?"

"No," I said. The sharp pain had gone. All I had was the continuous dull ache in my back. We started out of the office, but just as we reached the door, the phone rang.

"Just forget it," he said. "It's after hours."

"That's why it must be something important, Samuel. See who it is." He hesitated. "I'm not losing another client because of an unanswered or unreturned phone call. Answer it!"

He mumbled his complaints under his breath as he returned to the desk. I turned and waited.

"Hello," he said and just listened, his face losing color. "No, you did the right thing. We'll go directly to the hospital and meet them, Effie," he said and cradled the receiver.

"What?" I cried.

"Your father . . . he collapsed and fell out of his chair. Effie called the paramedics and they're rushing him over to the emergency room."

"Let's go," I said and started for the front entrance.

"Maybe you shouldn't go, Olivia. You've already done more than you should."

"There were many times in my past when I had to do more than I should and I'm sure there'll be many times in my future, Samuel. Let's not waste another second talking about it," I said.

He put his head down and took my arm. Fifteen minutes later we pulled up to the hospital emergency room entrance and Samuel helped me out. We found Daddy had already been taken to the Cardiac Care Unit. The emergency room doctor told us there was no question Daddy had suffered a heart attack.

"How is he?" I asked.

"Critical," he said. "I've called your family physician."

They permitted us to go into the CCU, but all we could do was stand near the bed and gaze at Daddy hooked up to the monitors, the oxygen flowing into him. Doctor Covington arrived a short time later and conferred with the specialist who had reviewed the tests and Daddy's vitals. We met in the small waiting room for CCU visitors.

"I'm afraid it's rather massive, Olivia," Doctor Covington said. "He may not even regain consciousness. You shouldn't be here. You might end up in the obstetrical unit yourself," he warned.

"This is nothing," Samuel couldn't wait to say. "She went to the office this afternoon and put in hours and hours of work. I couldn't stop her!"

"Is this true?" Doctor Covington shook his head. "I'm disappointed, Olivia."

"I'm all right," I said. I glared darts at Samuel who quickly turned to Doctor Covington.

"Stubborn," he muttered.

"Go home, Olivia," the doctor said.

"I'll stay awhile," I said, "in case he does regain consciousness. I'd like to be here if he does," I said.

"Well . . ."

"I couldn't be in a better place, Doctor Covington, if something did happen," I pointed out.

He laughed.

"I suppose not. All right, but try to rest," he said. "I'll stay in touch with the CCU nurse. Right now, I'll go back and let them know you're waiting here."

I thanked him and he left us.

"I'll call Thelma and tell her where we are. Jacob's probably looking for us by now," Samuel said.

"You'd better put in a call to Belinda, too," I told him. "She's been looking for some excuse to leave the school. Now she has it," I added.

"Don't you think you're being a little too hard on her, Olivia?" he asked. I looked up with surprise. "I mean, that's her father in there, too, isn't it?"

I almost laughed.

"Yes, Samuel. That's her father, that's the man she has been unable to sit across the dinner table from. That's the man she's been unable to talk to, to be near, to help.

That's the man she's aggravated all her life. Yes, Samuel, that's her father in there dying."

"I just meant . . . in times like this, you can't harbor bad feelings," he said.

"I don't harbor anything. I just do what has to be done and say what has to be said. Don't worry, I won't make any scenes with her. Just call her. When you come back, bring me something cold to drink."

"Okay," he said and left me.

I sat there alone in the waiting room, staring out the door and thinking about Daddy. He wasn't my daddy really, but I had done more to make him proud than his real daughter, hadn't I? He loved me more. He had to. I was the one who wanted to be here if and when he regained consciousness. It would be me he saw last.

Samuel returned ten minutes later with a cold soda.

"Belinda wasn't in. I left a message," he said. "Are you hungry?"

"No, but you can go to the hospital cafeteria and get something for yourself," I said.

"You're just going to sit here and wait?"

"Yes."

"It could be hours. It could be days. You've got to think of our baby, too, Olivia," he said softly.

"I'll wait as long as I can and then we'll go home." He stood there looking at me. "I promise," I added.

"Okay. I'll just run down and get a sandwich. Should I bring you anything?"

"No," I said. "Thank you."

He left and I sat there sipping my drink. I was too tired to feel tired. It was more like being numb. I closed my eyes and lay back. I began to daydream and saw myself as a little girl wandering in our backyard, studying plants and watching the birds, especially the terns as they swooped down to pluck clams. I never heard Daddy come up beside me.

"There's a lot to learn from the sea," he had said. "Sometimes, when you're caught in a current, it's best not to fight it. It's best to go along with it and to maintain your self-respect and sense of control, maybe go faster than the current. Do you understand, Olivia?"

I thought about it a moment and nodded.

"Yes, Daddy. It happened to me once when I was swimming. A wave washed over me and I felt myself being drawn out, but I didn't resist. I went with it and popped up frightened, but I was able to get back to shore."

"That's it. Learn from every experience and you'll always grow, Olivia."

He patted me on the head and left me.

"Excuse me, Mrs. Logan," a nurse said, popping the bubble of my memories.

I sat up quickly.

"Yes?"

"Your father seems to be moving in and out of consciousness. I thought you might . . ."

"Yes," I said, "thank you." I rose and followed her back into the CCU.

When I approached the bed, Daddy's eyes were still closed. I took his hand and waited and a moment later, his eyes opened and he looked up at me. He started to move his lips. I leaned down to get my ear close.

"Yes, Daddy, I'm here."

"Olivia . . . please . . ."

"What, Daddy? What do you want me to do?"

"Take . . . care of . . . Belinda," he said. "Will you?"

I felt my throat tighten, but I managed to get out the word.

"Yes."

"Promise . . . me," he said, his voice so low, I barely heard it now.

"I promise, Daddy," I said.

His face took on a gentle glow for a moment and then he closed his eyes.

I waited for him to wake up again, but he didn't. A half hour later, he died. I was just sitting there when the monitor sounded its alarm and the nurses came rushing to his bedside to do what they could. They asked me to wait outside. Samuel was there in the waiting room. He looked up when I appeared.

"Something's happening," I said. "They're working on him."

"Oh?" He looked terrified, which made him appear younger, smaller, like a little boy.

The nurse came out ten minutes later. From the expression she wore, I knew what she had come to say.

"I'm sorry, Mrs. Logan," she said. She took my hand. Samuel rose and put his arm around me.

"Thank you," I said. "Did you call Doctor Covington?"

"Yes," she said. "Can I do anything for you?"

"No, thank you."

"The doctor wanted me to plead with you to go home now," she added.

"You don't have to plead. I'm going," I said.

We started to leave. When we reached the elevator, I thought my legs had fallen away. I felt myself sinking. Samuel realized it and tightened his grip.

"We need a wheelchair here!" he cried and the nurse ran for one.

They took me to the car in the wheelchair and Samuel practically lifted me into the seat.

"Maybe we should stay here," he wondered aloud.

"No, let's just go home, Samuel. I'll be all right once I'm in bed."

"All right," he said and we started away. "How are you doing?" he asked after a moment.

"Better," I said.

"When you were in there before, did he ever regain consciousness? Were you able to speak to him?" he asked.

I thought a moment.

Daddy had set his eyes on me last. I was there for him, but who was in his thoughts at the end? Not me. It was Belinda. It was always Belinda.

"Olivia?"

"No," I said. "I never got to say good-bye."

15
∾

Moving On

*B*elinda never returned the phone call Samuel had made. He tried again as soon as we were home from the hospital and then came to my bedroom to tell me she was still not there. He left a message for her to call immediately, but she didn't call us until late the next morning, claiming she had gotten home too late. I didn't speak to her. Samuel told me she was on the phone, but I instructed him to tell her to just come home. There was nothing to say on the phone anyway.

I realized from the way Belinda reacted that day and the days that followed that for her Daddy had died a long time ago. She refused to remember him or think of him as anything but strong and vibrant. The man who had become a prisoner in his own body because of his stroke was not the same man she had known as her father. The stroke had turned him into a stranger and she couldn't mourn a stranger the way she would have mourned her father. Perhaps in her own way she mourned him after his stroke, I thought. That was the most generous I could be toward her.

Of course, she put on a good act for everyone, moaning and crying about not being there at Daddy's side and not speaking to him before he died. She had never called him on the phone because she couldn't stand his stuttering, so she had really not spoken with him since returning to Boston. She relied on me and Samuel to give her the details of his final days and hours.

Jacob was still too young to understand all that had happened to his grandfather. Thelma did a good job with him, explaining that Grandpa had been called to heaven where he would live with the angels and watch over him from above. I heard her tell him this and answer his questions in his room. Jacob was a very inquisitive child and never shy about asking questions. I decided not to bring him to the funeral.

Daddy's funeral was even bigger than Mother's because we had developed so many more business associations since Mother's death and practically everyone sent a representative. Someone told me the police declared it the biggest funeral procession in the North Cape.

Because of my condition, we decided not to have people over after the funeral. People offered their condolences at the church and at the cemetery and then left. Belinda, of course, returned to my house and I, under Doctor Covington's supervision, was sent directly to bed. After I rested and had some dinner, I told Samuel that he and I and Belinda had to have a family meeting immediately.

"Can't it wait until morning, Olivia? Everything is still so fresh," he complained.

"That's why it's best to do it now. Besides, time won't make any difference in regards to what has to be done, Samuel. It only keeps other people on pins and needles. Go get Belinda," I said and his face revealed the real reason he had wanted to postpone our family gathering.

I could read it like the front page of a newspaper. The headlines were in his eyes and on his brow. "She's gone, isn't she? Where did she go?" I followed before he could even attempt to deny it.

"Out with some old friends," he confessed.

"Tonight? She buried her father this afternoon and she went out to party with some of her friends tonight? Why did you let her go?" I demanded.

He shook his head.

"I don't think I could have stopped her, Olivia. She doesn't listen to me," he explained.

"Well, why didn't you come up to tell me she was planning on leaving?"

"I didn't want you disturbed any more than you are," he said. "You're only ten days from your due date."

"She has no respect for her own family. She doesn't have the smallest concern about what people here will think of us."

"Maybe she'll just have a quiet dinner and come home early," Samuel suggested. I stared at him and the optimism leaked out of his face, turning his hopeful smile to a grimace of despair. "Do you want me to try to find her?"

"Of course not. How would that look and besides, she wouldn't come back with you." I thought a moment. "This confirms what I was thinking I should do," I muttered.

"What?"

"Never mind now." I swung my feet over the bed.

"What are you doing? Where are you going?"

"I'm going to go through some documents, family documents," I said. "I have everything in the den."

"Just tell me what you want and I'll go get it and bring it up to you, Olivia."

"You don't know where it is and it would take too long

to explain. I'll be all right," I snapped. "Hand me my robe. Please do as I ask, Samuel," I said when he hesitated. "I won't sleep if I don't do this now."

Reluctantly, he got me my robe and slippers and escorted me down to the den. I sat at my desk and opened the top drawer, taking out the key to my wall safe. He stood by watching my every move.

"You can leave me now, Samuel. I don't need anyone hovering over me. I'm fine."

"I could help you."

"There's nothing for you to do. Watch television, read, relax," I said. It came out more like an order. He stared a moment.

"All right," he said, flashing me a tired look and a weak smile. "As long as you're fine," he added and then left.

Soon after Daddy had had his stroke, I had gone to his files and removed his personal documents. I took his will and his titles and deeds, all of his estate materials home and put them in my own safe. I had planned to read it all with Belinda present, but now I thought it would be better if I looked at everything first and decided on my own what would and would not be done.

Daddy had left half of his estate to her and half to me, but he had placed a great deal in trust to be kept for our children. It was a considerable estate. Belinda would have more than she needed and too much to waste. The only stipulation that gave me any promise and hope was the clause providing that in the event either she or I became mentally or physically incapacitated, the other would become the sole executor of the entire estate. Daddy had some foresight there, I thought.

Belinda had no idea where any of the trust funds were kept, nor did she have the slightest inkling as to how much we had. Money and property details were always boring to her. She simply wanted to have whatever she wanted when she wanted it. That was all that concerned her. I sorted everything out and planned out what actions I would take during the next few days.

Belinda didn't return until very early in the morning. I had gone back to bed and fallen asleep, which was a blessing, for if I had been awake to hear her stumble around in her drunken state, I would have gone into a rage. She didn't get up until late in the morning. I had brought everything up to my room and had it organized. I told Samuel to bring her to me as soon as she had had some breakfast. She wanted only black coffee and came upstairs in her nightgown, groaning, her hair wild, her eyes drooping.

"You look like a shipwreck, Belinda. Where did you go?"

"Just out with some friends who were feeling sorry for me," she replied. "I guess I had too much to drink, but I couldn't help it. I was feeling so miserable and everyone kept buying me a drink." She paused and looked at me as if just remembering I, too, had lost a father. "How are you?"

"Fine," I said sharply. "Sit."

"What do you want so early? I just want to rest today," she moaned, her eyes suddenly full of panic. "I don't want to be bawled out or hear any lectures."

"Just take a seat, Belinda," I said firmly and glared at her until she took the seat to my left. Samuel stood with his hands behind his back, rocking on his heels.

"She's just like Daddy with his family meetings," Belinda muttered to Samuel. He glanced at me and then stopped his smile.

I ignored her and opened the folders.

"These documents pertain to Daddy's estate," I said. "There's property we'll liquidate now, moving the funds into investment devices. I am designated as the executor so I will handle the work," I said. Actually, I wasn't the sole executor, but I knew she wouldn't challenge it and it would be easy to do everything I had planned by just adding her signature wherever it was needed or getting her to sign a paper. She would never read it first.

"Good," she said, obviously relieved it was only business, and started to stand.

"There's more," I snapped and she sat again. "Don't you care?"

"I never knew much about business affairs, Olivia. You're the expert. I'm sure you'll do everything right," she said.

"Thank you for your vote of confidence," I said dryly. "I plan to sell the house."

She looked up sharply.

"The house?" She looked from Samuel to me. "Sell Daddy's house?"

"Of course. What do we want with so big a home now? Why should we incur the cost of all those servants to keep it up? The proceeds will go into the estate and be better invested. Daddy made provisions for our children as well. There are things that have to be done correctly to avoid losing too much to estate taxes: shifting funds, activating the living trust . . ."

She shook her head and then clapped her palm to her forehead.

"I have such a splitting headache, Olivia. I'm sure you'll do the right things," she said. "Only . . ." She lowered her hand, finally a serious thought meandering through the maze of bubbles to reach her sleeping brain.

"Only what, Belinda?"

"If we sell the house, where will I live?" She looked to Samuel for the answer, but he had his lips pressed so tightly closed, the corners of his mouth were white.

"You can live here for a while until you find something sensible or . . ."

"Get married?" She laughed and bounced on her seat. "Why is it you and Daddy were always trying to get me married?"

"I don't know Daddy's reasons, but mine were purely revenge on the male sex," I said. Samuel finally cracked a smile. It flashed like car headlights in her eyes.

"You're not very funny," Belinda lamented. "You're all set. You have a husband, a nice little boy, another child coming, but I . . . I have no one."

"Whose fault is that?" I shot back at her almost as quickly as her words touched my ears.

She stared and then grimaced in pain again, squeezing her temples between her fingers and her thumb.

"I have a horrible headache. I have to go back to bed. I don't care where I live," she said rising, "but if you sell the house and I move here, I don't want you treating me like a little girl," she warned.

"Don't act like one and I won't," I replied. "What about your schooling?" I asked as she reached the door.

"Oh, I told them I wouldn't be back now. Besides, you just told me I don't need to work anymore. I'm an heiress." She laughed and left.

Samuel turned to me and lifted and dropped his shoulders with a big sigh.

"Okay, that's done," he said.

"I want to go to my father's house," I told him. "Right now."

"Now? Olivia, you are flying in the face of caution, doing everything against Doctor Covington's wishes," he lectured.

"You can come along or not," I said putting the folders aside. Then I looked up at him, my eyes firm and burning. "When something has to be done, I do it."

He shook his head slowly.

"I know," he said. "I know." His voice was full of resignation. "All right, I'll go along with you. Should we take Jacob along?"

"No, he'll only wonder where my father is and I don't have time for that," I said. What I really meant was it would be too emotionally difficult for me, even with Thelma's assistance.

In fact, the entire visit was emotionally draining. The house had become dark and foreboding to me ever since Mother's death and then Daddy's stroke. It was a shell of what it had been. It was hard to enter it now and envision the grand dinner parties, the laughter and music, even Belinda's music. Not that it wasn't clean and neat. Effie had done a great job of that, and that was why I wanted to meet with her as soon as possible to explain what I wanted her to do.

"I'd like you to remain awhile and keep the house up so it shows well when the real estate agents bring prospective buyers around, Effie. I will give you six months salary when you are terminated here, and of course, I'll do my best to find you another position in the area, if you like. I've always been quite pleased with your work."

"Thank you, Mrs. Logan. That will be fine," she said. I made the same arrangements with the groundskeeper.

I wasn't physically able to go through the whole house and look at everything, planning on what I wanted to bring back to our home and what I wanted to donate or sell, but I did wander through the first floor and spent some time in Daddy's den while Samuel checked on the upstairs and the boathouse. Sitting there, I couldn't help but recall my many private talks with Daddy. He always treated me like an adult and I know he had a high regard for my abilities. I wondered how often he had looked at me and wished I really was his daughter, born of his blood. How important family meant to him, so important that he would swallow what would have certainly choked most men.

There was something so masculine about Daddy's den, from its dark woods, to his cigar humidor and his pictures of seafaring men battling the elements. He had his old guns in their glass cases and his prize knives alongside them. There was a leather chess board with medieval figures on the corner table. He was proud of his room, proud of his home and proud of what he had accomplished. I would miss him, I thought.

I rose and walked to the rear of the house. Samuel was standing on the dock looking at the sea. Off to the right by the trees was the unmarked grave. No one but me knew what was buried there. It put a chill in me for a moment when I recalled Daddy's look of terror as he placed the wrapped fetus and afterbirth in that box and then disappeared into the night to bury Belinda's sins, which were sins visited on all our heads.

"Samuel!" I cried. He turned. "Take me home. I'm feeling faint," I said.

He hurried back. I paused to gaze once more at the dark place under the tree and thought, soon, soon I'll sell all this and never return.

Less than a week later, I went into terrible contractions and was rushed to the hospital where I gave birth to our second child, a boy whom we named Chester for Samuel's grandfather. I knew he was disappointed. He had wanted a girl and so had Daddy.

I remained in the hospital for three days after Chester's birth. Belinda came the second day to see the baby and visit me. She wore a very bright autumn gold blouse and a dark blue skirt. With her hair tied back neatly, Belinda looked young and vibrant. Lying in the hospital bed after just having given birth, I didn't feel very pretty. Never did the contrast between us seem more vivid.

"Don't worry about Samuel," she told me, "I'm looking after him. Jacob's very excited about his new brother, too. I took him for a walk yesterday," she said.

"You mean you're acting like an aunt?"

"Yes," she said laughing, "but a young aunt. He's so curious about everything and so serious. I'm afraid he takes after you, Olivia. Whenever he laughs, he looks guilty immediately afterward."

"That's ridiculous," I said, but I knew she wasn't wrong about Jacob. He was a thoughtful, pensive little boy and very bright, too.

"Nelson Childs told me you asked him for a job," I said suddenly, locking my gaze on her. Her eyebrows rose.

"He said I asked him?"

"Yes, why?"

"It's the other way around, Olivia. When he heard I was in business school, he asked me and I told him I wasn't going to work for anyone but my father," she claimed.

"Where did you see him, Belinda?" I questioned skeptically.

"In Boston. He stopped by to see me when he returned from the Bahamas," she replied so matter-of-factly, I couldn't doubt her.

"Why did he do that?"

"You'll have to ask him," she said. "I was just as surprised as you are." She opened her purse and plucked out her makeup mirror to check her face and then looked at me. "I'm telling you the truth, Olivia. Stop looking at me as if I am making up some lies."

"Fine," I said. Inside my stomach, hot coals turned. Was she telling the truth and Nelson lying? Was he just covering for himself in case she had told me? Was there any man I could trust? I wondered.

"You look so deep in thought," Belinda said.

"I think, Belinda. There's no shame in thinking. There's shame in not thinking."

"Chester is a very sweet looking baby," she went on, skipping from topic to topic like she was in a hopscotch game. "I think he's going to look more like Samuel. Samuel thinks so, too," she said, adding that because she thought it would bother me.

"Oh? Well, I'm not troubled by that. Samuel is a good-looking man."

"Yes, he is. Maybe not as handsome as Nelson Childs, but good-looking," she teased. I gave her my best scowl and she laughed. How she could vex me when she tried, I thought.

The next morning Nelson came to the hospital with Samuel to see Chester.

"He's a fine-looking baby," Nelson said. "Your father would have been very proud."

"Daddy was hoping for a granddaughter to spoil," I replied and then added, "like he spoiled my sister. Everyone is always spoiling her."

I watched Nelson's eyes. They shifted guiltily away and he quickly changed the topic.

Sometimes the world around me seemed like it was filled with small pools of deception, lies that like quick-sand would pull me down into confusion if I wasn't careful about where I stepped.

"I'm sure we'll have a daughter someday," Samuel declared with his chest out.

"Not someday soon," I said and the two men whose only pain in the birth of their children was the pain in the pocketbooks, laughed heartily.

Thelma said she would have no difficulty looking after Chester as well as Jacob. She truly enjoyed children and wanted to be more occupied. I considered her my best discovery and I was truly grateful I had her. It meant that as soon as I was on my feet, I could return to my work and feel confident that someone reliable was looking after our children.

Events in our lives took on a quick pace when I returned from the hospital. Less than a month after I had put Daddy's house on the market, we had a viable offer. I closed the sale satisfactorily and then went about selling, donating and bringing home the family possessions I wanted. I told Belinda to go to the house to see if there was anything she cherished, but she never went back once she had gotten her own things. Nothing apparently held any sentimental value for her. It didn't surprise me. She had spent most of her youth finding ways to leave the house. In my mind she used it like a hotel and all the rest of us, even our parents, as servants.

Belinda didn't settle down after Daddy's death. I learned that she had done passingly well at the business school and might even have graduated if she had wanted, but real work was not something she sought with any enthusiasm. Somehow, she was able to occupy her time with her frivolous activities, traveling with friends occasionally and always talking about doing something dramatic.

"Maybe I should become an actress. I might try out for a part in a play at the Provincetown Playhouse," she declared at dinner one night. "I met a young director who thinks I might be just right for a character in a play he's doing. I'm seeing him this weekend. For a private audition," she added, batting her eyelashes at Samuel. Amusement with her made his eyes brighten as if they had fireflies dancing in them.

"Acting might be just the right thing for you, Belinda," I said. "It comes naturally."

She took it as a compliment.

"That's what I think. I'll see. I'm really not too excited about having to memorize lines and be at the same place every day for weeks and weeks," she said.

Becoming an actress was just another thing she tinkered with, never really intending to do anything serious about it. To Belinda there was nothing worse than being bored. She had the attention span of a hummingbird, hovering over some sweet possibility for a moment and then jerking herself away to explore another and another. Even when she talked to someone at a party, her eyes wandered about to see if there was someone else to whom she should be speaking. The only way she would ever get married was if she were placed in a straitjacket and brought to the altar, I thought.

When it became clear that Belinda was now someone with some money, she attracted an entirely new clique of male acquaintances, dangling the promise of a serious relationship like fish bait. There seemed always to be someone calling on her. She played with them, amused herself with them and then dropped them as if they had contracted the plague. Still, they came around, called and begged for an opportunity to win her affections. I never stopped being amazed at how gullible most men were.

It went on and on like this for nearly a year, and then suddenly, a week went by and no one came. She remained at home watching television or reading magazines, having only an occasional phone call from one of her girlfriends. She stopped in at the offices more often and showed some interest in what we were doing. Samuel took her to lunch and answered her questions, ostensibly to keep her out of my way and amuse her.

Soon after that she started to go places again, but as far as I could see, she was always by herself. She had her own car, of course, and took herself wherever she wanted. Her comings and goings became more unpredictable and when I asked her what she was doing now, she was cryptic, and did not brag about the men she was stringing along, the places they were taking her and the money they were spending on her.

One day at the office, I went to Samuel and asked him about it. He seemed to know more about Belinda these days than I did. He thought a moment, sat back and nodded.

"I think she has someone," he said, "someone a little more serious than her usual male fare."

"Who? Is it someone who will disgrace us? Is that why she's being secretive?"

"I don't know," he said. "I'm just guessing. I really don't know. Why don't you ask her?"

"I have been asking her and she's avoided answering me."

"Have her followed," he suggested with a smile. I recalled her once accusing me of doing just that.

"Maybe I will," I said. He widened his eyes.

"I was just joking. You wouldn't, would you?"

"We have a great deal at stake in this community, Samuel, not the least of which is our family reputation. Congressmen, judges, major businessmen and their families have all been invited to our home. You are judged by the company you keep," I said, recalling one of my father's adages.

"Of course," he said. "If you think it might be necessary . . ."

"I don't want any more dramatic surprises," I affirmed.

He shook his head in despair, but didn't disagree. I let another week pass before deciding I would take some action. There were nights Belinda never came home. She claimed she had visited a friend down the Cape or had gone on someone's boat, and she got angry at me for even asking.

"I'm not a little girl anymore, Olivia. I agreed to the sale of Daddy's home and my living here as long as I wasn't going to be treated like a little girl. I don't ask you where you go every time you leave the house, do I?"

"That's quite different. Where do I go but places with my husband or places for business reasons?"

"Still," she said petulantly, "I don't give you the third degree, do I? Live and let live."

"You're spending money like it's going out of style," I said. "I have a pile of bills on my desk that would choke an accountant."

"What I spend, I need to spend," she claimed. "Isn't it mine to spend, too?"

"At this rate you'll deplete your inheritance in a few years," I told her. She shrugged.

"There will be someone to take care of me, I'm sure," she said with an arrogant confidence that made my blood almost hot enough to boil.

Frustration like arthritis crept into my very joints. Why I should even bother with her, I didn't know. I vowed to put her out of my mind, but I couldn't help worrying about what she would do to us in the community. Samuel's and my reputations had been growing dramatically. We were on everyone's A-list for parties again. People didn't necessarily like me, but they definitely respected me. I wasn't going to see all that jeopardized by an empty-headed self-centered sister.

Finally, I picked up the phone and called someone a business acquaintance had recommended. He was not a private detective so much as he was an insurance investigator. His name was Nicholas Koson. I didn't meet him at my office because I didn't want Samuel to know I was hiring him. I went to him and told him what I wanted.

"I don't have to emphasize how important it will be for you to be discreet," I said.

"Of course. That's what I do best," he claimed and I gave him his retainer, along with pictures of Belinda.

I could have waited and saved money. Less than ten days later, Belinda came to me on her own and revealed everything. The dark shadow that had been lingering behind my heart moved over it like a conquering army, full of joy and pleasure in its victory. I had been right; I had always been right.

Sometimes, when evenings were warm, after the children had been fed and were put to bed, I would go out and sit in my gazebo. Samuel liked to read his papers or watch some sporting event on television. More and more lately, he would go down to the wharf and talk with fishermen. I didn't mind the solitude. I welcomed it. My days were hectic and full of interaction with people. It was good to have these quiet moments during which I could reflect on how things were going and what I hoped to do in the future for the family. I was already thinking about Jacob's and Chester's prospects, what kind of men they would be, wives they would have. I hoped I would be a bigger influence on them than Samuel.

Tonight, the moon was big and bright with an occasional cloud streaking its face, making it seem sinister for a moment and then happy again. It was the way I felt.

"There you are," I heard and turned to see Belinda come out of the house and walk toward me. She was wearing a sleeveless light blue cotton dress and her arms gleamed in the moonlight. Despite her cavalier lifestyle, her drinking and late hours, she still maintained an attractive figure and a remarkably soft, rich complexion. Why she should be so blessed, I did not know. What I did know was she took it all for granted, never thanking her lucky stars.

There was a warm, steady breeze tonight. It made some of the strands of her hair dance wildly about her forehead. She paused at the steps of the gazebo.

"Honoring us with your presence at home tonight?" I asked. "Or am I invading your privacy by asking?"

She looked toward the sea.

"You're going to hate me," she said. My heart stopped and started.

"I thought you believed I already did," I replied. She turned.

"Don't joke with me, Olivia. I'm in trouble."

I took a deep breath. The fear in her voice, the smallness and little girl sound softened my hardened heart. I heard Daddy's death-bed whisper, urging me to promise to watch over Belinda.

"What have you done now?" I finally asked.

"I don't know how it happened. I have always been very careful ever since . . . ever since that time," she said. She sat on the steps with her back to me. I didn't move.

Against the horizon, a luxury liner with its glittering lights appeared. Although it was too far from shore, I imagined I heard the music and the laughter of people who had left all their cares and worries behind. They were floating on a ship of happiness where no one talked of sickness or failure or defeat. All their family problems had been left on shore. How I wished I could fly over the water and be dropped on its deck.

"So you're pregnant again?"

"Yes."

"Are you certain?"

"Yes," she said. "I went to a doctor. Don't worry," she quickly added, "he's not a doctor here. He's a doctor in Boston. He called me today to tell me I was pregnant."

"And like last time, you have no idea who the father is because there were so many in so short a period, right?" I said in a voice dripping with exhaustion and disgust. It was like déjà vu.

She turned. Even in the darkness, I could see her eyes burn.

"No. I know who the father is. He's the only one I've been with this last month or so," she said.

"Really? Well, that's some relief. Do you intend to marry?" I asked.

"No, we can't marry."

"Why not?"

"He's already married," she said.

I held my breath. Ice seemed to enter my lungs and shrivel them with constricting pain. It couldn't be. No, it couldn't be.

"Who is it?" I finally found the courage and strength to ask. She looked at the sea again.

"Don't be mad at me," she said.

Was she going to name Samuel? My own husband had betrayed me. Was that why he was always defending her, why he didn't want me to hire a detective? I had left them alone together too many times. I should have known. What a fool I've been. What could be more embarrassing?

I didn't reveal my fears.

"Why should I be mad at you? It's not like I didn't expect you'd come to tell me this one day, not with the life you lead, Belinda."

"Promise?" she asked.

"Oh, stop these childish games. Out with it and that's that."

She turned.

"Nelson," she said, "Nelson Childs."

How many times can you die in one life? How many times can your heart sink, can everything that kept you buoyant and energetic be swiped away from you? Did I ever go to sleep without some fantasy involving Nelson? Could I ever stop my heart from pounding when he approached or touched me or when we danced at affairs? His laughter lingered in my ears, his breath on my cheek. How I enjoyed the way he always drank me in with his eyes, those laughing eyes, full of sparkling lights. When it came to Nelson Childs, I was the cockeyed optimist. It was practically the only time I was.

"You're lying," I said.

"I'm not. I wish I was," she moaned.

"When could you . . . did you . . . and he, I mean . . ."

"We met in Boston whenever he had to be there for a trial or to do some legal business. I couldn't help it!" she cried.

"Why would he bother with you? He's happily married," I said desperately trying to find reasons, ways to disprove her confession and accusations.

"His wife's always pregnant. She's pregnant now. I don't know why. He likes me. He's always liked me, but not enough to marry me," she wailed.

"Then why didn't you stay away from him? How could you let this happen?"

"I don't know. I was bored and Nelson's always been lots of fun."

I sat there, fuming. I didn't know who I was angry at more, Nelson or Belinda? After I had confronted him with what I had seen him and Belinda doing in the boathouse, he had assured me nothing like that would ever happen again. Men should never be permitted to make promises, I thought. Their tongues should shrivel as soon as they begin to say the words "I promise."

"I guess I have to go get an abortion," she said through her tears.

I thought for a long moment.

"No," I declared.

"What?"

"No, you're not getting an abortion, Belinda. You're not letting him just get away with this, not this time. I forbid it," I said.

"Well what will I do then? I can't have a baby. What am I going to do with a baby?" she wailed.

"It's not just your baby, is it? It's Nelson's child, too," I said.

She whimpered and sobbed and stared up at me.

"What do you mean, Olivia? You're going to make him keep the baby? His wife won't like that, will she?"

"I'm not thinking about his wife right now. Did he think about his wife when he met with you in Boston? Did he?" I snapped at her. She shook her head.

"I don't want to have another baby," she cried. "I'm frightened."

"That's stupid, Belinda. I've had two, haven't I? The reason you had that horror show the first time is you kept it a secret and didn't do the right things. It will be different this time. Yes," I said with a strong sense of determination turning my spine to steel. "It will be quite different. This time you have me."

"I'm still afraid," she said. "It gives me chills just thinking about it," she said shaking herself as if she were shaking off ice water. "And I have nightmares every night. I can't fall asleep unless I drink myself to sleep. Olivia, do you hear me?"

I snapped out of my deep thought and glared down at her.

"I said I'll be with you, didn't I? You won't have to be afraid of anything," I told her. "Now, does he know yet? Well?" I demanded when she hesitated.

"No. I thought I'd do what had to be done. I wasn't going to tell him. I'm afraid to tell him. I was afraid he would just blame me or he would deny it and make me look foolish. He's a very important man now. Do I have to tell him?"

"No," I said softly, "you don't have to tell him. I'll tell him," I said.

"You will?" she asked, drying her eyes and sniffling.

"Yes," I said turning back to the sea. The luxury liner was gone. There were no lights except the reflections of cold stars above. "Yes, I will."

16

❦

Forced Confessions

If I had had any doubts that Belinda was telling the truth, and I wish I had, they would have been snuffed out the following afternoon when I received a phone call from Nicholas Koson.

"Is it all right for me to talk?" he asked in a loud whisper, which I thought was overly dramatic. He sounded like someone with a hoarse throat.

"Pardon?"

"Is this a secured line, Mrs. Logan?" he explained. I nearly laughed aloud at his cloak and dagger style, but that was what these people were paid to produce, I supposed.

"Of course it is," I said. "You think my telephones have been tapped?"

"No, no, not at all. I've completed a report and following your instructions for hard facts as soon as possible, I thought I would give you the highlights verbally. During the past week, your sister was in Boston twice. She checked into the Admiral's Inn, which is just north of the city, and signed her real name."

324

"Belinda is not a spy," I reminded him. "She's my sister."

"Yes, of course, but when people conduct clandestine affairs, they usually take some basic precautions."

"Not my sister," I muttered. That was painfully true now, I thought.

"Yes, I see. Continuing," he went on in a rather nasal tone, "she was soon visited by a prominent Provincetown attorney." He paused. "Are you sure it's all right to give you this over the phone?"

"Please finish this," I snapped. "I have a desk covered with business that cries for my immediate attention."

"Yes, I'm sorry. You surely know the gentleman to whom I refer, Nelson Childs. I think he was recently appointed to a judgeship. He remained at the location with your sister for nearly three hours the first time and a little more than four the second," he added.

What could possibly keep Nelson there that long? I wondered. It surely couldn't have been Belinda's conversation. Were men really that easily amused? Making love for three or four hours didn't seem a possibility to me either. Even with Samuel's groping and wet, sloppy kisses, we never had sex more than ten or fifteen minutes at the most. What could Nelson possibly do with Belinda for three or four hours?

"These meetings between the two are somehow confirmed?" I followed.

"I took some pictures of him entering and leaving."

"You took his picture?"

"From some distance, of course," he quickly explained. "I wasn't seen, I'm sure. It's what I do for a living, Mrs. Logan."

"I'd like those pictures today," I said quickly.

"Very well. I did some discreet questioning, Mrs. Logan. These . . . meetings . . . were not the first.

They've met at this location a number of times before these two occasions. I have certain indisputable evidence and . . ."

"All right. There is no need to go into any more detail over the phone. However, I don't want you coming to the office," I told him and gave him directions for our rendezvous in two hours. When we met he handed me a packet that contained detailed information and the pictures and I gave him his check.

"Thank you," I said. "I have no more need for your services."

He nodded, gazed at me for a moment with a little curiosity and then left. I felt dirty using him. Despite his polite ways and businesslike manner, his profession and purpose seemed as sleazy as a peeping Tom who had turned his depravity into his life's work. I shuddered at what I had him do, but then I sat in my car and went through the documents.

Mr. Koson was meticulous with his details, going so far as to describe the weather conditions at the time of the assignations. Somehow he had gotten copies of the room receipts as well. He had more than a dozen in the envelope, covering a period of four months. It took my breath away. What a good liar Belinda had been, and what a better liar Nelson Childs was.

Having the confirmation in black and white as well as pictures didn't make me feel any better, any stronger, or any more complete. It left me with a stomach that resembled a washing machine, tossing and turning its contents. There was a deep emptiness in my chest as if my heart had shrunken and left a cavern echoing with the heavy thump, thump, thumps. I took deep breaths to bring in cool air and turn down the furnace under my breast. It had been one thing for Belinda to make her confession, but another to gaze at a clear color photo of

Nelson lumbering along toward the entrance of the Inn, his face bright with expectation, eager. When he left, the pictures revealed he wore the look of a satisfied, confident man, his shoulders back, his head high, pride rippling across his lips.

I returned to my office and worked as hard as I could for the remainder for the day, trying to chase back those images. Toward the end of the afternoon, Samuel stopped by to remind me that tonight was his weekly card game with his fishermen cronies down at the Wharf Ale House.

"Unless you have something else in mind for us," he added. He always added that and I always said, "No, nothing."

"I'm too tired to do anything tonight anyway," I said.

"You do look down, Olivia. Aren't you feeling well?"

"I'm just tired, Samuel. I had a lot to do today. If you were here more, you would notice."

"I wish you would let me do more here, Olivia. I really do," he said in that whiny, pleading tone of voice I had come to despise.

"We'll see," I said.

He nodded again, skepticism filling his face.

As soon as he left the office, I sat back and thought about what I would do next regarding Belinda's situation. There was no sense in putting it off, I decided. I got up to close my office door and then called Nelson's office.

"Just one moment, Mrs. Logan," his secretary said, "I'll see if he's available."

Oh, he's available, I thought and waited, my heart puttering like an outboard motor.

"Olivia!" Nelson cried. "What a nice surprise. Business or pleasure?"

"Neither," I said. "You and I have to see each other tonight, Nelson."

"Pardon me?"

"I've been sitting here thinking of an appropriate location and I've decided my yacht. We'll have the required privacy for certain. Be there at eight," I said sharply. He was silent for a long moment before replying.

"What's this all about, Olivia?"

"It's better that we discuss it at eight, Nelson," I told him.

"This is rather short notice. I promised Louise I would take her to a movie and . . ."

"I wouldn't be calling and making these plans with such short notice if it wasn't important to both of us, Nelson."

"Maybe we can meet tomorrow night," he began to suggest. "I have something I can easily cancel and . . ."

"The Admiral's Inn, Boston," I said.

"What?"

"I don't really have to repeat that, do I, Nelson? Eight o'clock you will find me on my yacht," I said and hung up, my heart now beating more like a gong in a grandfather's clock.

Concentrating on my work was impossible for me after that call. Every time I began something, I found my eyes slipping off the page and my thoughts meandering back to Nelson's voice on the phone. Would he have the nerve not to show up? Finally, I decided to give up and leave the office for home a little earlier than usual.

Samuel noticed a difference in me at supper and kept questioning me about my health. Belinda, who sat like a beaten puppy at the other end of the table, her eyes low, her words few and far between, glanced at me each time he inquired.

"I told you I was just tired, Samuel. Leave it be," I finally ordered.

"Just trying to be a good husband," he quipped and looked to Belinda for some support, but unlike any other time Samuel smiled at her, she dropped her eyes quickly.

Needless to say, he was eager to leave and get to his card game and happier surroundings. As soon as he left, Belinda turned to me.

"Did you . . . do anything yet, Olivia?"

"No, but I'm about to," I told her.

"What should I do?"

"There's nothing for you to do. You've done it all," I growled. She started to whimper.

"You're wasting your tears, Belinda. Daddy's gone."

She pulled up her head and glared at me.

"You're going to really hate me now, aren't you? You're going to make my life miserable," she predicted.

"No, you've done that yourself," I said calmly. "I'm going to rescue as much of your life as I can, as much of all our lives as I can. That appears to be my role in this family."

"You enjoy it," she accused, her eyes smaller now. She followed that with a mad, light laugh. "You always did. You should have been a schoolteacher or a minister. Or better yet, a prison matron."

"I am what I have to be," I said firmly. "I don't have time to enjoy it, believe me. I don't expect your thanks, but I do expect your respect, Belinda, and especially your appreciation."

She held her smoldering look of resentment for a moment longer and then her face folded as she shrank into a tight ball, wrapping her arms around herself and looking down.

"I'm going to meet with him tonight," I revealed and she looked up, her eyes wide.

"Tonight? Where?"

"It doesn't matter where. I don't want you there," I said.

"How are you . . . I mean, what will you say?"

"I'll come to see you before you go to sleep," I promised, "and tell you everything."

She nodded, looking more grateful than defiant now. I knew what she was about to say.

"Don't say it, Belinda. I'm tired of hearing how sorry you are. Please, just . . . go to your room, watch television, talk to your empty-headed friends, fix your hair, be yourself and wait for my instructions."

She shook her head, her eyes filling with tears. Even she knew now that in the end, excuses were like the fabled straws everyone tried to grasp to keep from falling. The only thing that could keep her from sinking any farther in this life was the actions I would take on her behalf. That realization was written in her eyes.

She rose and left the dining room with her head lowered like a flag of defeat, but I harbored no pity for her. She was the one who was carrying Nelson Childs' baby, not I.

I spent some time with the boys before I left the house. Thelma had done wonders with Jacob, actually teaching him how to read a little and teaching him his additions and subtractions. He loved to show off for me. Chester was a far more physical child, walking months before Jacob had and thus becoming a constant problem because he could reach for things and had interest in touching everything in sight. Twice already, he had gotten into Samuel's fishing tackle and tangled himself up so badly that he had to wail for help. Samuel thought it was amusing, but I warned him if he left his gear out again, I would dump it all in the garbage.

"Jacob has more sense than you," I told him. Jacob

was so much more serious when it came to watching his younger brother and keeping him from doing mischief. I began to wonder how two boys from the same parents could be so different in nature.

Our yacht was moored at the dock behind the house. It was a 62-foot sailing cruiser, driven solely by sails and included living facilities. Normally all the deck chairs were put away, but Samuel had used the yacht just the day before to take some prospective clients out to enjoy a half day's sail. This particular evening was murky with fog. I could barely see twenty yards or so out to sea, but I could hear a foghorn off in the distance and occasionally caught the blink of a light through the steamy air. It was humid however, the air heavy enough that I thought it might rain. I boarded the yacht a little before eight and waited, listening and watching the grounds. Just a minute or so after eight, I saw Nelson emerge from out of the swirling mist, looking like a figure rising from the darkest underworld. He strode along firmly, his posture revealing his anger and annoyance as he swung his arms and approached.

"Well," he said boarding the yacht and standing in front of me, his hands on his hips, "I'm here as you commanded." He wore a light jacket and a pair of dungarees. I stared at him a moment and then looked at the fog.

"Why don't you sit, Nelson. This will take a while," I said calmly.

He hesitated and then plopped into a deck chair across from me.

"So?"

"You've been seeing my sister for months and months," I began. "As recently as last week," I added.

"She told you that?"

"No, she didn't tell me half of it," I said. "There's no

point in your denying anything either," I said. I reached down to turn on a lantern and then I handed it to him along with the folder Nicholas Koson had given me. He twisted his lips into a crooked smile and shook his head.

"What is this, I wonder?"

He read and I waited as he turned the pages. When he found his pictures, he blew a soft whistle.

"You had us followed?" he asked incredulously.

"I did on a suspicion that quickly turned into a dreadful reality," I said.

"I can't believe it," he muttered closing the packet.

"Imagine how I feel, Nelson. I think I feel more betrayed than Louise will feel," I said. With the light glow of the lantern on his face, he looked as pale as a ghost, his dark eyes strangely haunted.

"You intend to tell her?" he finally asked.

"No," I replied and took a deep breath. "I'll leave that aspect of your life to you."

"Olivia, I have no defense except to say my life has been so complicated lately, I needed some distraction. I happened to meet Belinda in Boston one night and she . . . well, she can be so beguiling. I shouldn't have succumbed to temptation again, I know, but I had been drinking and she's so full of lightness, it . . ."

"I don't really want to hear all that, Nelson. You did quite a job on me, put on some act, especially that fiction about her asking you for work. I should have realized Belinda is too simple to deceive and connive."

He nodded and leaned forward, his hands clasped.

"I want to promise you, to swear to you on my children that from this night on, . . ."

"It's too late for that," I said with a heavy voice, the voice of a judge pronouncing the most severe sentence, a voice he himself knew so well.

"What do you mean?" he gasped. "What are you going

to do?" He waited through my silence a moment. "Surely you realize this wouldn't do either of us any good, Olivia. This town feeds on nasty gossip. There are real sharks in these waters, Olivia," he continued, his voice rising with warning. "Don't underestimate any of it. Please consider both our families and . . ."

"Belinda is pregnant, Nelson, pregnant with your child," I blurted.

Even in the dim light, I could see his face turn blood red. He seemed unable to speak, unable to move. Finally, he released a small gasp and then took a deep breath. He shook his head.

"No, she can't be. She told me she was on the Pill. She even showed me the packet. She can't be pregnant. She's lying."

"It's been confirmed by a doctor, Nelson. Belinda might have taken one or two or even a dozen pills, but I'm sure she missed days and neglected them, leaving what what we would euphemistically call a window of opportunity, and since she's been only with you these past few months, repeatedly with you as evidenced here," I continued, indicating the packet of papers and pictures and driving nail after nail into his weakened manly armor, "there is no doubt you are the father of Belinda's illegitimate child."

"Oh no," he cried covering his face with his hands. "This can't be true." His shoulders shuddered. "What was I thinking? How could I be so weak."

I couldn't permit myself to feel sorry for him, but a small warm feeling managed to penetrate my fortress of anger. I had hoped to sit and enjoy his turmoil and squeeze his remorse dry, but the affection for him I carried in the secret places in my heart sounded a note of mercy.

"There's no point in dwelling on what happened. It's happened and it's done," I said softly.

"What are you going to do about it?" he asked, dropping his hands from his face, still handsome but dark and grave. "If she's having an abortion, I'll pay for it, of course, and do anything . . ."

"She's not having an abortion," I said. "It's too late."

"It can't be that late, Olivia."

"I don't mean physically or medically too late, Nelson."

"What do you mean then?" he asked, almost in a whisper.

"Belinda has made this sort of mistake before," I began. "We've always cleaned up her messes and limited her suffering to a minor inconvenience."

"Yes, but using this as a means of teaching her a lesson . . . I mean . . ."

"I'm not just teaching her a lesson, Nelson," I said sharply. My eyes held his for a long moment.

"What do you want to do?" he asked, practically pleading.

"She's having the baby and the baby will live here, with me," I said. "No one will know the identity of its father."

He sighed with some relief. Then his thoughts turned charitably to Belinda.

"You know of course that this will destroy her in this community, Olivia."

"I really haven't held up any hope for her in this community or any community for that matter for some time now, Nelson. Belinda is never going to amount to anything," I pronounced with the certainty of a Biblical prophet.

"Do you really think you should decide all that for her, Olivia?"

"The decisions were made long ago, Nelson," I replied. "I'm just carrying them out, trying to cope."

He shook his head.

"Well, if you're determined to do this, I suppose there's nothing I can do to stop it."

I laughed.

"No, hardly," I said. He looked at me sharply.

"What do you want from me? Money?"

"I'll call on you from time to time to help in little ways, always discreetly of course," I said nodding. "As long as I can depend on your cooperation, that is."

"That sounds almost threatening, Olivia."

"It's not meant to sound that way," I granted. "However, you should never underestimate my determination."

"No," he said with that soft, charming smile returning, "I can see that." He sat back. The fog thickened. Drops of mist made our clothing damp. "Does Samuel know?"

"No, not yet. I'll deal with him later," I said.

"So he doesn't know what you intend to do about the child? Don't you think he should have a voice in this? I mean, you're going to ask him to be a father."

I felt myself coil tightly like a spring.

"You'll always be the child's father, Nelson. You and I will always know that to be so," I reminded him curtly.

"Why are you doing this, Olivia? There's more to it. I know there is. Why do you want to bring up my child in your home?"

"It's my sister's child, too."

"Yes, but . . . there's more to it, Olivia."

"It should have been my child," I said, disbelieving my own voice, my own utterance. How did such a truthful feeling escape the prison in my heart? Nelson nodded. He seemed to understand.

"Don't do this, Olivia. It won't be what you expect it to be," he said, now sounding prophetic too.

"I'm doing it," I said. "We're doing it," I corrected.

He blew air between his closed lips and looked away. The first drops of rain began to fall.

"We're going to get caught in something here," he said.

"Let's go inside the yacht," I said and rose. He followed, but with reluctance. I snapped on a small lantern in the lounge and sat on the sofa. He stood in the doorway, leaning against the wall. The rain began to grow harder.

"There's a small storm sweeping through. It won't last," he said.

His damp hair fell over his forehead. How young and handsome he looked and how much he reminded me of that night when he and I and Belinda had gone walking on the beach, the night he went swimming with her, the night it all began.

He stared at me.

"Olivia, you don't know what you're doing here. You can't play with people like you play with pieces on a chess board. Chess pieces aren't made of flesh and blood and haven't feelings and emotions."

"You should be more grateful that I can play with people, Nelson. I'm solving your problem and saving your reputation, your career, your life."

He smiled.

"How do you want me to show my gratitude, Olivia?"

"You found it so easy to show Belinda how grateful you could be," I said. His smile faded.

"You really don't want me to . . . want us to . . ."

The rain that tapped on the roof of the yacht seemed to tap on my very soul as well.

"Am I so distasteful to you?"

"Of course not, but this is different. It's . . ."

OLIVIA

"What?"

"Samuel is a good friend of mine and . . ."

"Oh please," I said. "Don't start quoting that fiction about males who've bonded and don't betray each other. You're all cut from the same cloth when it comes to this."

He shook his head.

"I'm sorry you're so bitter."

"Are you?" Tears came to my eyes. "What do you know about being bitter? You've always gotten what you wanted, haven't you? You don't know what frustration is, what longing can be, how lonely it's possible to be."

He fixed his gaze on me as if he were looking at me for the first time. I had to turn away and while I did, he drew closer. I felt his hand on my hair and then on my shoulder, but I didn't turn to him. He sat beside me and then I felt his lips on my neck. I closed my eyes. How I had dreamed of this, I thought. His lips moved to my cheek and his hand turned my face to him so he could kiss my lips. Then he brought his hand to my breast and he pressed his lips harder against mine.

The scent of his damp hair, the taste of his mouth on mine, the feel of his hand on my waist, moving under my jacket and my blouse to find my breast all drummed a rhythm through me that turned the heat up in my body and made my breath hot. I moaned and moved so he could lift my legs and run his other hand under my skirt. When he touched me, my breath caught and for a moment, I thought I might faint with excitement.

"Is this really what you want, Olivia?" he whispered.

"Yes," I said, my eyes full of determination. "Yes. It's what should have been."

He said nothing. Instead, he began to undress me and then to undress himself. Above and around us, the storm ensued, the sheets of rain now slapping against the yacht,

337

the ocean rising and falling to create a frenzied rhythm that I wanted to capture and hold between Nelson and myself.

He made love to me with his eyes closed. Despite the fact that he was really there, really holding me and making me part of him in the most intimate way a man and a woman could become one, I didn't feel as satisfied as I had anticipated. Wild, refusing to be disappointed, I rushed into an orgasm and felt him shudder inside me, both of us gasping like two sprinters on the beach who had fallen into each other's arms.

The rain continued to fall. Neither of us spoke.

"You hated every minute of that, didn't you?" I accused.

"I didn't hate it, Olivia, but what you expect is not something you can command to happen. You're so used to giving orders and having your way, you think you can just apply the same techniques to everything. You can't."

I turned away from him.

"I'm sorry," he said. "These circumstances . . . it's just not conducive to . . . it's just not . . ."

"Romantic?"

"No, it isn't," he said.

"And meeting Belinda at some hotel is?" I asked with a sharp, cold laugh.

"It was a fling, something to distract me, just as I told you," he said. "I'm not in love with Belinda. I'm in love with my wife," he concluded. It put a lump of lead into my throat.

I sat up and began to dress and so did he. Suddenly, I was feeling very cheap and foolish. I hated it more than I hated not having him love me the way I had dreamed he would. It was better to live in my fantasy than to have this as reality, I thought.

The rain hadn't let up.

"We'll have to run for it," he said contemplating leaving the yacht. I found an umbrella and handed it to him. "What about you?"

"I don't have as far to go," I said.

"Olivia . . . this is . . ."

"I don't want to discuss it any more tonight," I said. "I'll keep you informed and you'll do what you have to do when that time comes."

He stared at me, not with anger, but with genuine curiosity as if I were some sort of alien creature.

"Very well. If this is what you really want," he finally said. "I'm sorry."

"Those two words ought to be eliminated from our language. They are sorely abused," I remarked. He nearly smiled, nodded, opened the door and the umbrella, and then, with one look back, charged into the night and the rain. I watched him disappear into the darkness like some apparition, a ghost I had conceived out of my illusions and dreams.

For a few moments I stood there crying. I couldn't remember when in my life I had cried like this before. I hadn't even cried as much or as hard when Mother died. The tears felt like drops of steam on my cheeks. I finally caught my breath, wiped them away, sucked back my final sobs, buried my self-pity forever, and walked out into the cold rain, not feeling any of it and not even knowing I was soaked to the skin until I had opened the door to Belinda's room and she gasped when she set eyes on me.

"Where have you been? What happened to you?" she asked. "You're drenched."

"It's all over," I said in a voice resembling the voice of someone who was devoid of all feeling. "He knows what's happened and he knows what we're going to do. He also realizes his obligations after you give birth."

"You mean he didn't try to get us to . . . not have the baby?"

"It's not for him to decide, to even suggest," I said. "He has no rights except the right to be guilty."

"But Olivia . . . I'm really frightened," she moaned.

"That's nonsense. I won't permit it," I told her.

"I can't help it!" she cried, grimacing.

I walked into the room and seized her by the shoulders.

"You will help it. You will do exactly what I want you to do. For once, you will bear some responsibility for your actions, Belinda. Do you hear me?" I shook her hard and she just started to cry. "Do you!"

"Yes," she said, nodding.

"Good," I muttered. I released her. "Good. Get some sleep. You're going to live an exemplary life for the next few months and you're going to give birth to a healthy child."

I paused in the doorway. She looked at me with terror in her eyes.

"This you will do," I said slowly. "This you will definitely do."

Early one evening three weeks later, the doorbell rang. We had just finished dinner. Belinda was upstairs and Samuel was down at the dock working on the yacht. I had gone to the den and had begun to look at some papers I had brought home when Effie came to my door.

"There's someone here to see you, Mrs. Logan."

"Who?"

"Mrs. Childs," she said.

It was as if my heart fell to my stomach. I hadn't seen Louise for some time and we had never really been close. She had certainly never visited me by herself.

Louise Childs was one of those women who just seem

to grow more beautiful, more elegant and statuesque with time. Having children hadn't taken away from her svelte figure. She still looked like she had just come to life off a magazine cover.

"Hello, Olivia," she said. "I hope I'm not intruding by making this unannounced visit."

"No, not at all," I said. "Please come in, Louise."

She entered the den, gazed around and then sat on the leather settee. I had taken many of Daddy's things from his den right after the house sale and moved them into my own home office.

"Is Samuel fond of guns?" she asked looking at the collection displayed in the case.

"No, those were my father's antiques," I said.

"Oh."

I sat in the leather chair across from her.

"Can I get you something to drink, Louise?"

"No, I'm fine," she said. She fumbled with the snap on her purse for a few moments. "I suppose you know why I've come to see you, Olivia."

"No," I said. "I'm afraid this is a total surprise."

"It's about . . . Nelson and what he has done," she said, holding her gaze on me. I stared at her without changing expression. "He told me everything," she continued.

"I see," I said, feeling as if my body had deflated like a balloon and no longer had enough air in my lungs to utter any sound, much less sentences. I seized control of myself as quickly as I could and sat with my back steel firm. "What exactly did he tell you?"

Surely, he hadn't confessed to our sexual episode on the yacht as well, I thought.

"He told me about . . . the baby," she said, "and about Belinda and what you want to do about it," she replied, her eyes steady, her voice strong. I waited. That was apparently all he had confessed. Even so, I was amazed she had come. I had certainly underestimated her backbone, I thought.

"He did, did he?"

"Yes. I'm not here to make any excuses for him," she added quickly.

"Then why are you here, Louise?" I demanded. I couldn't help feeling another sort of betrayal. It had never occurred to me that Nelson would be so close to Louise that he would share even his sins, and it certainly never occurred to me that if he had, she would tolerate or forgive him.

"I'm here because I think you're making a mistake. I think you should consider finding another home for the child. Nelson and I have discussed it and we are willing to bear all the costs. There are many couples who would love . . ."

"You discussed it? You? It's my sister he has impregnated, Louise."

"I realize that," she said quickly. "I don't come here to assign any blame on anyone, especially Belinda. I . . ."

I laughed.

"It might interest you to know that I don't excuse her. She's certainly at fault, too, but as far as giving the child away, pretending it never happened, burying the facts . . . no," I said shaking my head. "I won't let that happen."

"But Belinda's future . . ."

"Is my worry, not yours," I said. I sat back, pressing my fingers together and smiling as a realization gave birth in my mind. "I understand now. You're worried that it will come out someday and you will be devastatingly embarrassed."

"No, not at all. It's . . ."

"Please," I said holding up my hand. "Let's not add deceit upon deceit. I have assured Nelson that his fatherhood or should I say sirehood, will not be revealed. You can rest as easy, as easily as you are able to rest knowing what you do know," I said pointedly.

"Well, have you really thought this out, Olivia? Are you sure this is what you want to do?" she asked.

"Yes, Louise, it is."

She saw my determination and she sat back, her lips trembling.

"It took every bit of strength I could muster to come over to speak with you, Olivia. Nelson told me your mind was made up, but I think he believed I might be able to change it, that once you knew he had confessed all to me, you might reconsider."

"Why should he think that?"

"I don't know," she said.

"Then perhaps you don't know everything, Louise."

She took out a handkerchief and blew her nose. Then she sucked in her breath and stood.

"This is such bad business, such a terrible turn of events," she complained. "Our lives were so perfect up until now."

"Life isn't meant to be perfect," I said. "That's an illusion and if you let yourself think it is, you only suffer when disappointments come."

She looked at me with admiration and shook her head.

"How I envy you for your strength. You've always been so powerful." She smiled. "Somehow I think you'll work all this out," she concluded.

"And you'll all be safe," I said.

She bit her lower lip, glanced at me and then turned to go.

"Louise," I said when she reached the doorway. She paused, turning.

"Yes?"

"If you want to be stronger, never let your husband get you to do his dirty work again."

"I didn't come here for him. You were right, Olivia. I came here for myself. Or maybe for my children, too," she added. "You once said something I never forgot."

"What was that?"

"Family, family should be the most important thing of all," she replied. "If there is every anything I can do, please don't hesitate to ask me."

I watched her leave, hating her for being strong enough to come.

17
❧

Penance

I didn't believe Samuel was capable of the rage he demonstrated in front of me the following afternoon. His eyes were so filled with it that they looked bloodshot. His normally tan cheeks had eggshell white spots and the skin on his temple was so taut, it could have been used over a drum. He nearly took my office door off its hinges when he entered and he slammed it so hard, the walls shook. I was about to protest when he extended his arm, his long right forefinger jabbed at my surprised face.

"Don't," he commanded. "Don't say a word until I'm finished speaking."

After saying that, he fumed a few more moments, pacing in front of me. Then he paused, took a deep breath and put his hands palms down on my desk as he leaned toward me. I could feel the heat radiating from his eyes of fire. I half-expected he would burn his palm prints into the wood.

"Your sister came to you and told you she was pregnant with Nelson Childs' baby and you met with

Nelson and told him you and I were going to keep the child as our own? Does that sum it all up in a nutshell?"

"Hardly," I said, "but for now, yes."

"But for now yes? When exactly were you going to tell me any of this? When exactly was I going to learn what would happen in my own home? When . . ."

"Please, Samuel. Stop it!" I cried.

He glared. His lips firm. He was shooting so many daggers across the desk at me that I had trouble looking at him.

"Stop it? Stop it, you say? I know I'm not the businessman your father was. I know you do a great many things better than I do here, but I know I'm still your husband, the father of your children. All I ask, Olivia, is you treat me with this much respect," he said holding up his forefinger and thumb as if he were showing a pinch of salt.

He paused, waiting for my response.

"You're right," I said after a moment. "You're absolutely right." His eyes widened with surprise. He had been expecting my characteristic fortitude. "I should have involved you sooner in all this. I was wrong, but I was just so upset over Belinda and what had happened, I saw red and took matters into my own hands."

"Which is what you always do," he said nodding.

"I am who I am. I'm not perfect, Samuel."

"Well." He stepped back. "I must say it's a novelty to hear you say that, Olivia." He gazed at me a moment and then sat in front of the desk, sinking into the seat. "What do you expect to accomplish here? Why are you permitting Belinda to have the baby and keep the baby at our home?"

"It's her child, our niece or nephew, isn't it? We don't give away children like so much extra fish," I said.

"But for an unmarried woman to have a child fathered

by a married man and for us to keep the child, bring him or her up alongside Jacob and Chester . . . it will simply complicate matters so much more, Olivia. You haven't thought this through and considered all the aspects," he concluded, shaking his head.

"Did he send you here to tell me all this, to plead with me, to have me give the child to some agency so that his conscience is clear and he has no worries? Well? Did he?"

"He asked me to reason with you, yes," Samuel admitted.

"I thought so."

"He's quite distraught about it."

"Oh please," I said turning my chair. "He's quite distraught. Why is it men can only see the suffering they endure?" I thought a moment and then looked at Samuel again. "Is this what you would do, Samuel, if it were all reversed? Would you have gone to him and asked him to go to his wife and plead your case, asking for the same things?"

"That's a ridiculous question. I don't have affairs."

"Of course you don't. You're better than that, Samuel. I realize that. Haven't you told me time after time that you believe in family, as I do? Didn't you tell me my father was right in building that belief in us all?"

"Yes, but . . . well, what does Belinda want?"

"Belinda?" I laughed. "She wants everything unpleasant to disappear. She always has. She's a lot like my mother in that way, but this time it won't work."

"You mean you won't let it."

"I mean we'll bear the burden of our responsibilities. What she has done affects us. Surely, you won't want me to turn the child out of our home, Samuel. You're not that sort of a man and that's why I wanted to marry you in the first place," I said. "You credit me with intelligence; credit me with the perception to see your good qualities, too, Samuel."

He gazed at me and I kept my eyes so fixed on him and so full of sincerity, he swallowed down my words and felt good about it. I could see his ego inflate like a life raft.

"Well, if you put it that way, I suppose we could manage it fine. It's not a question of money or anything and as you say, the child carries your family blood. Is it what you really think we should do, Olivia?"

"I wouldn't do it otherwise, Samuel. I'm sorry I didn't come right to you with the problem, but I was sorting it out in my own mind first. I was going to tell you everything today."

He nodded.

"All right then," he said. "I do feel sorry for Belinda though," he said in a wistful tone. "She's made some mess for herself."

"With someone else's help," I reminded him. He raised his eyebrows.

"Yes. Well," he said slapping the arms of the chair as he stood, "every family has its skeletons in closets. Ours won't be the first, huh?"

"Hardly," I said.

"Is there anything I should do?" he asked.

"Tell Nelson Childs to stop sending emissaries and accept his responsibility. Tell him to be half the man you are, Samuel," I said.

He smiled.

"I don't think he'd like to hear that, Olivia." He started for the door and stopped. "How are we going to handle Belinda? I mean . . ."

"Leave it all to me, Samuel. It's mostly all female problems anyway from here on until she gives birth," I said.

"Yes. Yes, I suppose you're right." He thought a moment. "Sorry I came bursting in on you like that."

"It's all right, Samuel. I understand and once again, I'm sorry I didn't speak to you sooner."

He smiled.

"Would you like me to take you to lunch today, Olivia? We haven't done that in a while."

I thought a moment.

"Yes, Samuel," I said. "Yes, I would."

His smile broadened and then he left. I sat there quietly in my office listening to the tick-tock of the miniature grandfather clock on the shelf. Was I a monster for handling Samuel that way? The only one left for Nelson to petition was Belinda and that would be the most futile effort of all. She would do exactly as I told her to do and he wouldn't understand why. He wouldn't understand that I had really been more of a mother to her than our own mother.

The next evening that was exactly what he tried. He pleaded with her on the phone and offered to take care of everything if she would just do what he wanted. She came down to the living room where I was reading and listening to music to tell me. She was very excited. In her mind it solved the problem.

"He knows a place where I can go to have the baby and he'll make sure the baby has a good family. He's right, isn't he, Olivia? I can't raise a baby and I can't put that on you and Samuel. You have your own children to raise."

"He's not right. We've had this conversation. I don't want to hear another word on it."

"But I don't want to have a baby, Olivia. I don't want to . . ."

I rose from my seat with such fury, she cowered before me.

"You don't want to have a baby? You don't want . . ."

"Olivia, please."

"Shall I remind you of a night not so long ago, a night filled with screams, a night that aged your father years in seconds? Shall I take you for a ride tomorrow and march you out to the back of our old house? Should I show you where he's buried?"

"Stop it!" She put her hands over her ears.

I drew closer, relentless.

"Did I ever tell you how it drove Daddy mad? How he heard a baby crying in the night? Did I ever tell you how he cried like a baby?"

"Stop it! Please," she begged.

"You will have this baby, Olivia, and it will be brought up in this home. We will bury no more children, not in the ground and not in someone else's family," I said through clenched teeth. "Don't you ever speak to him again. Do you understand? If he calls you, hang up the phone or tell him to talk to me. Are you listening?"

"Yes, Olivia. Yes."

"Go upstairs. You need your rest."

"I'm starting to show, Olivia. I have to wear something to hide it. I can't go out and meet people without their knowing eventually," she moaned.

"Don't worry about it. Soon, you'll stop going out and meeting people anyway," I said.

"What?"

"We're going to tell people that you're away and you're going to stay confined to the house and grounds until you give birth, Belinda. Don't worry about it."

"Confined?" She looked about, dazed.

"Just go upstairs. Do as I say," I told her firmly.

"But . . ."

"How many women would be willing to take on the burden of their sister's illegitimate child, Belinda? How many? He or she will grow up with my boys and have the benefits they enjoy. When are you going to show me some gratitude and at least be cooperative enough to help me help you? When?" I screamed.

"Okay, Olivia. Okay," she said in a small voice. "What should I do?"

"Just . . . go upstairs," I said. She nodded, lowered her head and left the room.

The days turned to weeks and the arrangements I had described for Belinda came to pass. To ensure she didn't disobey, I had her phone disconnected. When her bubble gum friends called after that, I had them told she was visiting relatives for a few months. In time, the calls stopped and our lives settled down for a while.

Samuel did his best to amuse her during this period. He brought her presents, newspapers and magazines, records and tapes to occupy her time. By the middle of the ninth month, Belinda took to remaining in bed most of the day and never getting dressed. She let her hair go and she ate constantly, satisfying every craving, driving Effie mad with requests for this and that.

"It's not good for her, Mrs. Logan," Effie complained to me. "She's getting too fat. Thelma agrees."

"When I want opinions on diet, I'll ask. For now just give her anything she wants," I ordered.

However, I had to admit that when I looked in on her now, she reminded me of one of her stuffed animals, her face bloated, her stomach lifting the blanket into a small hill. Her arms resembled balloons. This pregnancy was a tumor eating away her beauty and good looks. She seemed to have lost all concern about herself anyway. Without her doting friends and her stream of boyfriends, she stopped using makeup. Even her hygiene began to suffer and if I didn't insist she take baths, she wouldn't wash her face and her hands for days. She got so she didn't get off the bed to urinate, but used a bedpan and left it for hours beside the bed until either I or Effie came by to empty it.

Eventually, I instructed Thelma to keep the children away from Belinda's room.

"She'll give them nightmares," I said.

Thelma was very worried about Belinda and how we were handling the pregnancy. She wasn't the type to interfere, but she stopped by my den-office one night to express her concern.

"I appreciate that, Thelma," I told her, "but for now it has to be this way."

"Why, Mrs. Logan?" she pursued.

I put aside what I was doing and sat back.

"It's really none of your business, but you've become part of our family so I'll tell you," I said and then went on to describe the disgrace. Without mentioning a name, I explained that Belinda was carrying an influential person's baby and we were trying to protect the child as well as Belinda. I asked her to just cooperate and understand and it satisfied her.

"I'll need you to spend more time with the children. I have to give more to Belinda right now," I said.

"Oh, of course, Mrs. Logan. Please call on me for anything," she said and I thanked her.

For Belinda every day seemed harder than the one before it now. She knew she was drawing closer and closer.

"When's the doctor coming, Olivia?" she asked me one evening. "He's never been to see me."

"We're not having a doctor, Belinda. I told you. I have made arrangements with a midwife. It's more discreet."

"Why does it have to be discreet?"

"People don't know about the pregnancy. Let's try to

352

keep it that way as long as we can. I'm only trying to protect your reputation," I said.

"My reputation? My reputation?" She laughed and looked at the wall as if someone was standing there, as if the room were crowded with male admirers the way it once was. "Did you hear that? She's worried about my reputation." She laughed again, each roll of laughter coming like a cough and then continuing like uncontrollable hiccups.

"Stop it, Belinda."

"My reputation." She shrieked and laughed madly.

I stepped up to the bed and hovered over her, my hands in fists.

"Stop this nonsense this instant!" I commanded.

Her laughter wound down until it became a subdued sob and then she closed her eyes and sighed as if she had passed away. I stood there, waiting. Her eyes opened and she smiled up at me as if nothing in the world was wrong.

"Please tell Effie I'd like some ice cream—strawberry. No, butternut crunch with chocolate syrup and some marshmallow sauce."

"Fine," I said.

"I had a pain today, Olivia. It hurt a lot," she said.

"It's no wonder you have pains lying there like some pig in mud, but you know what labor pains are. That's when we've got to become concerned."

"It was a labor pain. It's starting," she said with a nod. "I should see a doctor. I don't care about my reputation."

"I'll call the midwife and she'll examine you tomorrow," I told her and gave Effie her request for ice cream.

The midwife was a Brava who ministered mainly to poor people, but had on occasion handled situations for the well-to-do that had to be kept as secret as possible.

Her name was Isabella and she looked like she was nearly seventy, although I knew she wasn't much more than fifty-four, fifty-five. She wore her smoke-gray hair long and stringy to her shoulders. Her face was leathery with wrinkles even in her chin. Belinda gasped the first time she set eyes on her. Later, she told me she thought she was a witch.

"She's put a curse on me!" she said.

"Don't be ridiculous," I told her, but she looked even more maddened after the examination.

Isabella predicted that it wouldn't be much longer before Belinda delivered, maybe a week. As it turned out, she had underestimated, for the very next day, Belinda went into such terrific labor, Effie had to call me home from work. I sent for Isabella immediately, but she was delivering another woman's baby just north of Hyannis. All afternoon, Belinda shrieked and squirmed in her bed. Effie and I did all that we could to make her comfortable, but nothing seemed to help.

"She oughta go to a hospital, Mrs. Logan," Effie finally said.

"The midwife will be here soon," I told her. Samuel, who had come home, too, stood outside the door looking very somber.

"We're making a mistake trying to do it this way, Olivia. Let's just bring her to the hospital."

"She'll be all right, Samuel. Many women have had their children at home. In fact, most have."

"Not these days, Olivia."

"Just go see what you can find out about the midwife. Maybe she's back from Hyannis, Samuel."

He lingered as Belinda screamed again and again, squeezing my hand, pleading with me to do something.

"There's nothing to do, Belinda. The baby's getting ready to be born."

"It wasn't like this before!" She grabbed my wrist and pulled me down with such strength, I was astonished. Then she whispered, "I'm being punished for what I've done. That witch cursed me. Help me!"

"Stop it," I told her. "Be a grown-up for a change." I tore her grip from my wrist, but she clung to my dress. I had to pry her fingers away.

"Stop acting like an idiot. I'll get you some water and some cold towels for your face."

"Don't leave me! I don't want to be alone like I was the last time. I'm afraid."

"You're being absolutely ridiculous," I said and left the room, closing the door to shut off her cries of agony.

For a moment I stood there in the hallway trying to decide what I wanted more, Nelson's baby to be born healthy and well, or Nelson's baby to die just like Belinda's first child had.

I covered my face in my hands and shook my head. Daddy's dying words echoed. "Look after Belinda, take care of Belinda."

"Belinda, Belinda, Belinda!" I screamed in the dark confines of my own mind. "What about me, Daddy? What about what I feel, what I suffer?"

I took a deep breath, gathered my wits and went downstairs to find Samuel rushing out of the house.

"Isabella's back. I'm going to get her," he said.

"Good."

I took my time returning to Belinda's room. The fact is I left her screaming and squirming in agony by herself for nearly a half hour. I heard her throw something against the wall. I heard a thump and then I returned to her room.

When I opened the door, she was giving birth, her eyes so wide I thought her head would tear apart.

"Why did you leave me? Help me!"

For the first time in my life, I felt nailed to the floor, unable to do anything, mesmerized, rendered paralyzed by the sight before me. I could see the child's head! Belinda screamed and reached down like some wild animal trying to ease the fetus from its womb.

I heard the sound of footsteps on the stairway and turned to see Thelma hurrying up, Effie right behind her.

"What's happening, Mrs. Logan?"

I just nodded at Belinda.

"Oh dear, she's having it!" Thelma cried and rushed to the bed.

In the end it was Thelma and not the midwife who delivered Belinda's child.

A girl.

Ironically, although she wasn't mine, she was the daughter Samuel had wanted.

Belinda had no interest in her own baby after the birth. She didn't offer a single suggestion for a name. In the end it was Samuel who had always wanted a girl to name after his mother, Haille, who named Belinda's child.

The night Haille was born, I sat in my den and called Nelson at home. His maid answered the phone and then he came on, his voice subdued.

"She had a girl," I said. "We're calling her Haille after Samuel's mother."

"The baby is all right?"

"As far as we can see, yes," I said.

"And Belinda?"

"She's not all right. She'll never be all right," I reminded him.

"Do you need anything?" he asked, his voice testy, reluctant.

"Not at the moment. If you want to see the child, come by tomorrow night after ten," I said.

"You're making a mistake, Olivia," he said in a tired, defeated voice.

"I don't think you have the moral right nor the insight to make that conclusion, Nelson."

"Okay," he said. "I'll be there after ten."

He was. He would do whatever I asked him to do from now on, I thought. Haille was like a whip in my hand. As long as she was in my home, Nelson would be at my beck and call. It gave me a sense of power. It wasn't love, but for the moment, it seemed to satisfy me.

I quickly realized that something dreadful had happened in the dark corridors of Belinda's mind after she gave birth. She became very withdrawn, almost catatonic. Whenever she saw the baby that night, she looked at it as if she were surprised to see it. It was as though she had lost her memory of her pregnancy and especially the delivery. Even days later when she rose from her bed and moved about the room, she was like someone who had emerged from a coma. She wore a strange, blank look on her face, smiled and laughed at the silliest things, behaving as if she were not much older than Jacob. In fact, she wandered into his playroom often and sat amusing herself with his toys until I would come home and demand she shower and dress. I had Effie put her on something of a diet, but she cheated, sneaking around the house, nibbling on crackers and cookies and even stealing the children's desserts.

She avoided Haille, sometimes acting so terrified of her own child that she would tremble and cry. It was as if she thought the baby might return to her womb and she would have to give birth again.

Sometimes, right in the middle of my talking to her,

Belinda would burst into tears. When I would ask her why she was crying, she would just shake her head and moan, "I don't know. I can't help it."

Frustrated, I would leave the room. The truth was I was frightened by her behavior, frightened at my inability to change it or stop it.

Nelson didn't see her the first time he came to see Haille. Belinda's door was shut and she was asleep. I greeted him at the front door myself and led him up the stairs to the nursery. Samuel, who was reading in our bedroom, came out to see Nelson. They shook hands, but said little to each other. I brought him to the nursery and he entered slowly. Thelma wasn't there, so it was just Nelson, myself and Samuel.

"Pretty, isn't she?" Samuel said when Nelson peered into the bassinet.

"Yes."

"I bet she's going to be a beauty, huh, Olivia?" Samuel said.

"We'll see," I said.

"She does look healthy," Nelson said, his voice thick with surprise.

"Babies born out of wedlock can be healthy, too," I remarked. He grimaced.

Then he straightened up and looked at both Samuel and me.

"Can I talk you people out of this? Can I offer to have her placed in a good home?"

"No," I said sharply. I looked at Haille. "She's a Gordon now. Maybe she'll never know who her father really is, but she'll always know this part of her heritage," I said.

"When Olivia's determined about something, Nelson, she's unmovable," Samuel said, smiling.

Nelson glanced at me.

"I know," he said. He looked at the baby again. "Do you want any money now?"

"When I need something from you," I said. "You'll be told."

He turned away from me quickly.

"How about a drink, Nelson?" Samuel offered him. He put his arm around Nelson's shoulder.

"Sure," Nelson said. He glanced at me furtively once more before leaving with Samuel.

I gazed down at the sleeping infant. She was pretty. I didn't want to admit it to Nelson, but I had expected her to be uglier, even possibly deformed because she was Belinda's child. My emotions were frazzled. Part of me had hoped she was going to be that way, and yet a part of me was happy she was a perfect little girl. She would dazzle people right before Nelson's eyes and he would look at me with an aching heart. It still seemed like delicious revenge.

In the months that followed, Belinda finally got so she took some interest in herself again and did her hair and her makeup, but now, she overdid her makeup and she looked foolish, even clownish. It didn't matter what I told her. She would look at me and smile, agree and then keep doing what she was doing. I grew disgusted and talked to Samuel about sending her away for a while.

"Perhaps a holiday would get her back to normal, not that I ever approved of what she called being normal," I said.

Samuel agreed and we looked into a trip for her, perhaps visiting some of our relatives in Charleston. She had been there years and years ago.

Work became demanding again. Our business went into a dramatic upswing and I had less and less time to

V. C. ANDREWS

spend at home and worry about Belinda anyway. Then, one afternoon, Effie called to tell me Belinda had left the house.

"Did someone come for her?"

"No, Mrs. Logan."

"Well, did she say where she was going?" I chastised myself for not hiding her car keys.

"Yes," she replied with some hesitation.

"Well?"

"She said she was going home, Mrs. Logan."

"Home? Did you see her drive away?" I asked quickly.

"She didn't take the car, Mrs. Logan. She just started walking."

"Walking? All right, thank you, Effie," I said and went to tell Samuel.

When we found her less than an hour later, she was strolling on the main highway. Cars were whizzing by, sometimes dangerously close, but she didn't seem to notice or care. Samuel pulled up in front of her and I got out quickly.

"Belinda, where are you going? What are you doing?"

"Oh, hi Olivia. I was just . . ." She looked about as if first realizing where she was. "I was just going somewhere." She laughed. "I forgot exactly where," she said. "Silly, I know, but it's such a beautiful day it seemed a crime to stay inside."

"Get in the car, Belinda," I ordered and opened the door. "Come on, get in," I said.

"Are we all going somewhere?" she asked and got into the car.

"Yes," I said. "We're all going crazy."

She thought that was funny. We brought her home and I saw that she went up to her room.

"She's in no condition to go on a holiday yet, Olivia,"

360

Samuel said. "Let's just do what we can to get her healthy."

"I just don't have the time for this now, Samuel," I told him. "She's got to snap out of it herself and she's got to do it immediately."

He shook his head as if I were talking gibberish. After dinner that night however, I went up to Belinda's room. She was sitting at her vanity table, mindlessly running a brush through her hair and smiling dreamily at her image in the mirror as if she saw a much younger, thinner face again.

"Belinda, I want to talk to you and I want you to look at me and listen," I told her. She turned slowly.

"I always listen to you, Olivia," she said.

"Yes, but do you hear me?"

She giggled.

"If I listen, I have to hear you, don't I?"

"You've got to get a hold of yourself now. I want you to stop behaving like a . . . a crazy woman. I want you to eat right, dress right, be judicious about your makeup and start thinking about what you want to do with the rest of your life. We can't have you continue as a burden on everyone. Do you understand?"

"Yes," she said.

"Good."

She turned back to the mirror and continued to brush her hair.

"Actually, I've very upset. No one's called me today, Olivia."

"Your phone was disconnected, Belinda, remember?"

"Oh. Was it? Well, can you connect it again? I'm expecting calls."

I stared at her and she brushed her hair and then started to put on her lipstick far too thickly.

"This is ridiculous," I said. "It's coming to an end right now."

I marched out of her room and went to my bedroom to call Nelson.

"I have something I want you to do," I said when he was called to the phone.

"What?"

"Come to my office tomorrow at eleven."

"I have appointments too, Olivia. I can't just drop clients like that," he pleaded.

"All right," I said softening. "When can you come?"

"I'm free between two and three."

"Good," I said.

I hung up and thought for a moment. I wasn't breaking my promise to Daddy, I concluded. I was keeping it. My conscience was clear. As I left the room, I paused at the nursery. Thelma had Haille in her arms and was rocking her to sleep.

"She's a beautiful child, Mrs. Logan," she said.

"I know."

"Belinda will be all right," she added. "I'm sure. Once she realizes what a wonderful little girl she has, she'll be fine."

"We'll see," I said and went downstairs to tell Samuel what I thought had to be done. He was upset and tried to talk me out of it, but I was confident.

The next day Nelson arrived at my office at two-thirty. Samuel was not yet back from a lunch meeting so Nelson and I were alone. He came in, closed the door and sat on the sofa across from my desk.

"Is this the way it will be forever now, Olivia? You summon me and I come?" he asked, his eyes glaring like two orbs of glass with candles behind them.

"I called you to meet with me because I need your help

now, Nelson," I said and the disgusted smirk left his face to be replaced with an expression of deep concern.

"I see. What is it?"

"It's Belinda," I said. "She's not getting much better. We both underestimated the traumatic experience she has undergone," I continued, rising from my chair to come around the desk and lean against it. He followed me with his eyes.

"I don't understand," he said.

"You remember I told you she was having emotional problems after giving birth?"

"Yes, but I know that not to be uncommon . . ."

"I don't need a lecture about maternal problems. This is a more serious mental illness, Nelson. She's become . . . a burden on top of everything else."

"I warned you, Olivia. I told you keeping the baby was . . ."

"I'm not talking about the baby, Nelson. I'm talking about my work, my business, my social obligations. The baby is not a problem. Belinda is a problem."

"Do you want me to recommend a good doctor?"

"I want you to do more," I said. "You're a judge now. I want you to sign a commitment order. She needs to be institutionalized."

"What? You're joking. Institutionalized?"

"She needs serious mental treatment. She always has. This is just the last straw. My parents never wanted to admit it to themselves, but Belinda has always been unstable. Now she's practically a lunatic."

"But you haven't even had her properly diagnosed, Olivia," he protested.

"I don't expect any other conclusion anyway, Nelson. I want you to help me with this, make it smooth. There's a clinic nearby. She'll be comfortable there; only there's a waiting list a mile long. I need you to use your political influence to get her in next week."

"Next week!"

"Do what has to be done and call me with results," I said.

"I won't do it," he said defiantly.

I smiled at him.

"Won't you? You're going to shirk your responsibility?"

"I'm not shirking anything, but . . ."

"You know why she's this way, who did it to her. You didn't just impregnate my sister and produce an illegitimate child; you've caused a terrible mental problem. I should just give up and let everyone know everything," I declared. "I'm sick of covering for everyone's weaknesses."

I returned to my desk chair and stared down at the desk.

"Olivia, are you sure about this?" he asked softly.

"It's the best thing for her and for us right now," I said. "It's not easy to do the right thing, Nelson, but I've always been able to do it anyway."

"Always?"

"Yes," I said meeting his gaze. "Are you going to take care of it for me?"

"It might damage her even more severely, Olivia."

"You mean more than she has been damaged, Nelson?" I asked pointedly. He tried to hold my gaze and then he lowered his eyes and nodded.

"All right," he said softly. "I'll take care of it."

"It's better for everyone, even her," I said. "You'll see."

He stood and held a small smile on his lips as he gazed at me.

"Why are you smiling?"

"I was just thinking, what was it they called you in school, Miss Cold?"

"Yes, and Belinda was Miss Hot. Which one of us was better off?" I challenged.

"That's something you'll have to answer for yourself," he said and left to do what I wanted.

Epilogue

Confused, I paused outside of Belinda's bedroom door. She was laughing and talking with great animation, but I knew she had no visitor and I also knew I had not had her phone reconnected. She laughed again. I opened the door slowly and gazed at her seated at her table, the phone receiver pinched between her shoulder and her head as she polished her fingernails.

"Belinda?" I said and she turned, swinging her eyes up at me.

"Oh, sorry, Arnold, my sister just walked in. I have to hang up. Call me tomorrow," she said. "I'll be waiting," she sang and cradled the receiver.

"What are you doing?" I asked, my heart pounding.

"Just talking to some friends," she said. "I know, I know. I spend too much time on the phone. Don't go running to Daddy," she said. "Don't you like this color, Olivia?" She showed me her fingernails. Her right hand had a dark red and her left had more of a pink. "I'm going to do my toenails in it, too. Quin thinks it's hysterical. Why do girls do their toenails? he asks.

Hardly anyone ever gets to see them, he says. But that's not true. Lots of times I walk barefoot or I wear sandals or . . . oh dear," she suddenly said. "I'm sorry."

"What?"

She picked up the phone again.

"Hello. I can't talk now, Louise. Can you call me in an hour? Thanks." She hung up. "So," she said turning back to me, "what's up?"

"I hope you didn't forget that you were leaving today, Belinda."

She blinked rapidly and then smiled.

"Oh no, I didn't forget, but I haven't had a chance to do much packing, Olivia. Don't start chastising me. It wasn't my fault. This phone hasn't stopped ringing since everyone heard I was going on holiday. They're actually all jealous."

"The car is here, Belinda. Don't worry about your things. I'll have them sent," I said.

"Oh, will you? Thank you, thank you. I really do appreciate how efficient and reliable you are, Olivia. Most people would kill for a sister like you looking after them all the time. Well," she said looking around. She stood up. "I guess I'd better put on my jacket then. I decided to wear the light blue coat. It's good for traveling, comfortable and easy to keep," she said and went to the closet.

I watched her put on her jacket and then look at herself in the mirror to fluff her hair. I must have seen her do that a thousand times, I thought. She smiled, content with her appearance.

"I guess we can't keep my driver waiting any longer. I'm ready," she said.

I stepped out of the room and she followed.

"I didn't get to everyone, Olivia, so a lot of my friends

will still be calling. I know it's a bore, but you'll tell them where I am, won't you?"

"Yes, don't worry about it," I said.

"Good."

She went down the stairs with a light bounce in her step and paused at the door to wait for me to catch up.

"You look so sad today, Olivia. You wish you were coming along, don't you? Why don't you? You can stop working for a while," she said. "We could have fun together, be real sisters for a change, just doing silly things."

"I'll follow later, Belinda," I said.

"Will you? Good," she replied and we walked out.

The nurse was waiting at the car. She opened the door and looked at me in anticipation.

"Everything's fine," I said. She nodded and turned to Belinda.

"Hello, Belinda," she said. "My name is Clara."

"I love your hair. Is that your natural color?" Belinda asked her. She smiled at me.

"Yes, it is."

"I've been thinking about changing my color." Belinda got into the rear of the limousine.

Clara turned to me.

"Everything's all set, Mrs. Logan," she said. "We'll be fine."

"Thank you. I'll come by tomorrow," I said. "If there are any problems . . ."

"There won't be," she assured me. Then she got into the limousine.

"Oh, Olivia?"

I lowered my head and looked in at Belinda.

"Yes?"

"I almost forgot. There's a letter on my desk to be

mailed out. I wrote to Adam Franklin. Finally. He keeps writing and writing and sending me presents. Would you see that it's mailed?"

"Yes, Belinda."

"Thanks." She looked at Clara. "If you want something done, you ask Olivia," she said.

"I'll see you soon, Belinda."

She smiled and I closed the door. The limousine started away. I stood there watching it disappear down the drive and then I went into the house.

Thelma was feeding Haille, and Chester was running through the house behind Jacob. They were pretending to be a railroad train.

"I'm the caboose and Jacob's the engine, Mommy," Chester cried as they passed me.

"Be careful, Jacob."

He gazed back at me with that serious face, his eyes telling me how unnecessary it was to give any admonition. They disappeared down the corridor.

I went upstairs and looked in Belinda's room. There was no letter on the desk. She had written one, I was sure, but she had written it three or four years ago. For a while I just stood there gazing at her things. I suddenly felt very tired. I was happy I had decided to take the whole day off. The last few days had been trying, going up to the clinic, making the arrangements, doing what had to be done.

I wouldn't make any changes in the room. I was sure Belinda would go in and out of that clinic for some time. I closed the door behind me and went downstairs, deciding to go out back and sit for a while, and do something I hadn't done for some time: relax.

It was a crystal clear, beautiful day with the air just crisp and cool enough because of the light sea breeze. Across the sky long clouds looked stretched and wispy. A pair of herons circled above and then dove beyond the hill. Just on the horizon, an oil tanker headed northeast and off left, I saw a yacht much like ours approaching the Cape. The whitecaps glistened in the afternoon sunshine. The water was a dark, silvery blue.

I sat for some time just looking out at the sea. I was so deep in thought I didn't hear Samuel come home and come out to find me.

"Well?" he asked standing at the foot of the gazebo.

"Well what?"

"How did it go?"

"It went well," I said. "As I expected it would."

"Did you call to see how she's doing?"

"No, not yet. They need time and they don't need us annoying them."

"When do you intend on visiting?" he asked.

"Samuel, she's just gone today. I think we need to give them time to work with her, don't you?"

"It's just . . . I feel sorry for her," he said.

"You've got to control your emotions if you want to do what's best for people you love," I said.

He looked at me with sudden interest.

"Funny," he said, "I never think of you as loving Belinda."

"Of course I love her. She's my sister, isn't she?" I said.

He nodded and gazed at the sea, too.

"Nelson called. He wanted to know how it was going."

"Generous of him," I said.

"He really is filled with remorse, Olivia."

"You're breaking my heart," I said grimacing. Samuel laughed.

"Nelson calls you the Iron Lady of the Cape now."

"I'm not interested in what he calls me," I said. Samuel smiled at me. "I'm not."

"Okay," he said. "I'm going in to take a shower and get ready for dinner."

"I'll be in soon," I said.

"That Haille . . . I swear she's smiling already when she looks up at me. She's going to be a charmer," he remarked.

"I have no doubt," I said.

He went into the house and the breeze became a little stronger. I thought I could hear the boys shouting and laughing. In the days and years to come, they would all be playing on this lawn, I thought, the three of them growing up as one family.

"I'm right. I know I'm right," I muttered to myself. I thought if Daddy were here, he would agree. Even Mother would agree, although she wouldn't want to talk about it.

Someday, I thought, Nelson would realize all that I had done for him and he would be more grateful. He might even come to love me for who I was and not resent me. I felt confident of that.

Why did I feel so sad though? If I was right, why wasn't I feeling more satisfied?

I was a very successful and powerful businesswoman. I had my sons and I had Nelson's daughter. Wouldn't everything be just what I wanted it to be?

If I could only see the future, just get one glimpse and be absolutely sure, wouldn't it be wonderful? However, that was impossible. That was like believing in magic, I thought.

I remembered once when I was a little girl I had picked up a seashell, put it to my ear as Daddy instructed, and heard the roar of the ocean.

"How could the ocean be in a seashell, Daddy?" I asked.

"It's not in there. The seashell is like ears that hold the ocean's roar," he told me. "Then, at night, the roar escapes and returns to the sea."

I laughed.

"That's silly, Daddy."

"No, Olivia, it's true. The roar you hear is the roar that sounded a hundred years ago. It's the ocean's voice, captured. If you listen really hard, you might even hear a sea gull's cry."

Skeptical, I listened again and I thought I had. My eyes widened with surprise.

"Believe in something magical, Olivia. We all need to believe in something magical," he advised.

He took my hand and we continued down the beach. I held on to the seashell and then I dropped it in the darkness.

All my life, I thought, I would be searching for it.

The Phenomenal
V.C. ANDREWS®